~THE RISING TRILOGY~

Book Two

Relinquish

Also by Amy Miles

THE AROTAS TRILOGY

Forbidden

Reckoning

Redemption

LOVE & LUST

Captivate

The Rising Trilogy

Defiance Rising

~THE RISING TRILOGY~

Book Two

Relinquish

AMY MILES

This book is a work of fiction. Any references to historical events, real people, or real locales are used fictitiously. Other names, characters, places, and incidents are products of the author's imagination, and any resemblance to actual events or locales or persons, living or dead, is entirely coincidental.

Copyright ©2013 by Amy Miles Books, LLC.

All rights reserved, including the right of reproduction in whole or in part in any form.

Also available in eBook format.

First paperback edition 2014

ISBN 9781494945824

Acknowledgements

To Rick and Landon~
My amazing reasons to always return from my fantasy worlds.

To Danielle Bannister~
You have been a constant over the past two years of my writing life. I am
deeply grateful for all of your help, advice, and sound wisdom when you know I'm reaching for an unreachable deadline.
You are always there for me.

One

Nearly one year later…

The inky black sky above is littered with feathered clouds, lighted by vivid bursts of red and green, which mirror the battle below. A near constant rumble rises from the ground as I press my palms into the cold, moist earth. The spider drones are on the move.

The hairs along my arms rise in warning a split second before a red laser zings past my cheek, charring the raven hairs that fall about my face. Mud splatters against my forehead when I raise a hand to shield my eyes as the ground erupts less than ten feet ahead. The scent of burnt swamp muck stings my nose as a rain of slimy mud pelts down upon us.

"I'd say we're getting close," I whisper over my shoulder to my second-in-command. The young man beside me turns and silently passes on the message to the rest of our squadron.

He inches closer and breathes his questions into my ear. "Where to now?"

Wiping my hands free of the frigid and dank-smelling mud, I dip my head once more to trace my finger along the weathered paper map. A thin black line marks our entry path and continues on toward our target. One of Commander Drakon's bases lies just in front of us.

We will have to belly crawl through half a foot of putrid slush and God knows what else to reach the wall, but I've been through worse.

"We're heading just north of the fighting." I point toward the southern gate where all the laser fireworks have converged. Even as I speak, green and red lasers connect in midair and explode back to Earth in a shower of fragmented color. "We need to veer off now. Send your men to the wall. We'll go around and meet up on the other side."

With a cutting hand motion, Carleon signals his men to move off. I notice much of his hair has been plastered to his head, the mud only a few shades lighter than his own short-cropped hair. His eyes are wide and alert as the squelching sounds of boots fade and another volley bursts overhead. "Our enemy is getting antsy."

I tuck the map into the front of my jacket before zipping it up to my chin with fingers stiff from the cold. It will be a miracle if the map manages to survive the trek through the marshlands that surround the base like a moat.

I don't like swamps or the creepy crawly things that live in them. Wolves, bears, and mountain lions I can handle, but I don't do snakes. I'm just praying with winter well on its way, the snakes will have gone to ground. "Drakon's men know they are surrounded. What would you do?"

"Probably head to the canteen and down as many sodas as I could." My eyebrow rises with amusement. Carleon shrugs out of his pack. He won't need it once we're through the wall. "What? I've grown to like the stuff."

I laugh softly and shake my head. Leave it to him to think with his stomach at a time like this. "Should I leave you behind to have a snack, then?"

"And miss all of the good stuff? Nah. I'll stick with you." He raises two laser pistols and checks the power gauge. Full charge. "Besides, I want to see the look on Drakon's face when he surrenders to you."

That is what I look forward to most.

When we first received notification that Drakon was back on Earth, Kyan was concerned with how the news would affect my training. To be honest, I think things couldn't have gotten any worse.

I'm struggling… again.

My boyfriend Eamon thinks that's why I'm here, leading this mission, but that's only a half-truth. I need to be here, need to feel the thrill of making a difference. Ever since the City fell to our command over a year ago, I have been trapped within its confines. What I need is space.

No. I need a good fight.

"Eamon's soldiers did a good job breaching the front gate. It's almost as if he wants to make this easy on us." I smile tightly at the men around me. Seven have placed their lives in my hands. I know three of them well, but the others only by name.

I remove a pair of binoculars from my pants pocket and train them on the wall. It's hard to get a clear line of sight with the web of lasers flashing brightly in my scope. I tuck them back into my pocket and hope Eamon is in position. "The base is cut off and our men should be in place. Let's move out."

"You ready for this?" Carleon asks, grinning from ear to ear. His breath hangs in thick clouds before his mouth. The temperatures are dropping rapidly now that the sun has set.

Great. That's going to make this trip through the mud that much more pleasant, I grumble silently to myself.

Since the first time I met Carleon, on the day we infiltrated and brought the City to its knees, he has always been the first to leap into battle. His walnut eyes grow wide with excitement and he bounces on his toes, ready for anything. His enthusiasm during a fight never ceases to amaze me, even after fighting at his side through countless skirmishes.

He anticipates my thoughts better than anyone I know, making him an excellent second-in-command. "Ready when you are."

Tucking his pistols into the holsters at his hips, he throws himself onto his belly and begins wiggling forward through the mud, using powerful arms to pull himself through the high, sharp-edged weeds that have yet to die off from the frost.

I hate the mud, but not as much as I hate snow and ice. Winter battles are the worst. We stand to lose many lives this year on the plains to blizzards and dagger-tipped ice storms. Why couldn't Drakon set up camp somewhere warm instead of hole up in this smelly swamp?

Under Kyan's leadership, we've campaigned deep into new sectors of the land. We traveled from the mountains and swept down into the plains, where vicious winds can tear at a person with merciless rage. Long frigid hours spent camping in snowy wastelands is not my idea of a good time.

I miss the mountains. Miss the trees. I miss our home.

I haven't been back to the caves. Eamon sided with Kyan against me, worried it would dredge up too many sensitive memories. I suppose a part of me agrees with them, but still I long to go back.

I follow only a few inches back from Carleon's boots, trying my best to stay just far enough back to avoid the mud splatters. My stomach clenches at the smell of moist, decaying vegetation. It clings to my skin, a foul taste upon my tongue. I force myself not to think of what might live in the murky depths of the standing water all around me.

I can hear the men moving behind me and wonder how many of them will give their lives for our cause tonight.

I have to be on top of my game. This siege is a big one.

Word arrived through the rebel spy channels that Drakon was holed up somewhere in the Midwestern quadrant. Our entire camp braced, sure an attack was imminent, but nothing happened.

Confused by Drakon's lack of initiative, Kyan sent out scouting troops. Several failed to return, probably never will, but one came back with the intel we have been waiting for: Drakon is here and he is looking for me.

Eamon wanted to send me back to the City to be placed under a squadron of our best warriors. Thankfully, Kyan saw this as an opportunity and now here I lie, wallowing in the marsh, as I move inch by agonizing inch toward my enemy.

A year has hardly been enough time to heal the wounds Drakon left behind. He unleashed something inside me that I didn't know was possible. My powers have been volatile since our encounter atop the Shard. I anger swiftly and cry with annoying ease. I'm a bundle of emotions, none of which I welcome.

Carleon holds up his hand and I refocus, watching as clumps of brown sludge drip from his hand and elbows. A chain fence surrounds the fort, towering nearly ten feet above us. Its links have begun to rust; no doubt the frequent ice storms are increasing the speed of corruption. Spirals of jagged wire roll across the fence top, convincing me that I do not want to attempt a climb. Less than five feet beyond that stands a block wall twice the height of the fence and thick enough to repel a blast from a spider drone's cannon.

I'm sure Drakon's guards think their perimeter to be nearly impregnable. They might have been right if I were not leading this mission.

I can tell by watching the bursts of laser light against the wispy layers of cloud that the battle at the main gate is growing with intensity. Eamon is there fighting alongside my mentor Kyan and childhood friend Toren. They are the bait. While all eyes are focused forward, my job is to sneak in with a handful of men and bang on the back door.

Carleon listens to the muffled chatter in his earpiece and gives me the thumbs-up. My soldiers are in position. They will create a diversion, attacking the snipers along the top of the wall from the cover of the tree line below while Carleon and I slip by unnoticed.

I have only one mission: Find and torture Drakon. Well, perhaps I'm supposed to capture him first, but that's just a technicality. My fun will come later.

"Are you ready?" he asks.

I blink, realizing that while lost to my thoughts, Carleon has cut a small hole through the fence with his laser gun and doubled back. I can see he is worried about me. He usually is. No doubt, Eamon has added extra pressure on his young shoulders to make sure I come out of this alive. My boyfriend can be quite the force to be reckoned with when he wants to be.

"I'm fine." I offer my friend a smile that I'm sure in the full light of day would have betrayed my momentary doubt, but if he sees any hesitation, he doesn't say so.

I raise my hands and concentrate, trying to ignore the way they begin to ache from the chilled water that soaks through. I remove the soggy gloves and toss them aside, waiting for the ripples of electricity to come.

The hairs along my arms rise and I brace myself, rising up onto my knees to create a solid foundation. An invisible blast erupts from the palms of my hands. Wisps of hair flying about my face are blown back as the wall before me shudders and then implodes from within with a terrible splintering of stone. Carleon doubles over to protect his neck and head with his hands as a rain of fist-sized rubble assails us from above. A few seconds pass before he raises his head, blinking with confusion.

"You didn't really think I was going to let all of that hit us, did you?" I smirk and lower my hands. A cloud of thick, gray dust hangs in the air before us, making it difficult to see how big the hole is that I carved from the wall. The ground all around us is littered with varying sizes of stone fragments, sharp enough to slice open our hands if we aren't careful as we move forward.

"You could've at least warned me," he grumbles as he rubs out the blush rising along his neck.

"And miss the look on your face? Not a chance." I swat damp muck from my pants and then crawl forward, shoving aside thick reeds growing along the perimeter. A low fog hovers over the ground, concealing our final approach. The night air is cold against my skin, but the water squishing up between my fingers still clings to trace amounts of warmth from the day's sun.

I crouch and duck my head to sneak through the crudely cut hole in the fence and then drop to my stomach to wiggle my way through the thick concrete wall. My ribs protest as I drag myself through the uneven hole and then emerge on the other side, powdered with gray dust.

Once free of the hole, I call back to Carleon to follow. Above his loud grunts, I hear the scraping of his laser gun across the stone. I bend low and reach in as far as I can to grasp it. A series of muttered curses floats my way as I hear fabric tear. "You okay in there?"

I glance back over my shoulder, worried we are running out of time. Someone will surely come soon to check the perimeter. "I'm stuck."

"Seriously?"

"No, I'm just overly fond of tight spaces." His voice echoes from within the dark tunnel. "Of course I'm serious!"

"Well, you don't have to get snippy about it." I set his gun to the side and raise my hands in front of me, trying to concentrate despite the sound of his grunting and the explosions to the south. "Just hold on. I'll get you out."

"Hey, Illyria?"

"Yeah?" I hesitate, feeling the energy swirl in the palms of my hands.

"Just remember I'm in here. No bringing the whole wall down on top of me, okay?"

I grit my teeth and close my eyes, slowly turning my hands around in a circle to carve out the edges of the hole to accommodate Carleon's broad shoulders. I hear him breathe a sigh of relief and jerk my hands back a bit too fast. The exit of the tunnel collapses in a pile of rock.

"Dang it," I grumble as I shake out my hands and grab for the first rock, chucking it aside. By the time I have the space cleared, Carleon is ready to emerge. His hair is dusted gray and his face ashen. "Are you okay?"

"I'm pretty sure I wet myself back there," he mutters as he pulls his feet free at last and rolls onto his back, gulping great breaths of fresh air.

I stay low beside him, searching the shadows for movement, but see none. "You good to move out? We don't want to be around when those soldiers arrive."

Carleon nods and rises, grasping my hand tightly as he darts away from the tunnel. We keep our heads ducked low as we cling to the wall, melding seamlessly with the shadows as we search for a place to hide out until we get a lay of the land.

The compound is larger than I had originally thought, dotted with single-story hut-like buildings. Sparse grass sprouts up from the ground, evidence of training drills in the yard where the earth has been packed down. One long row building across the yard peeks out from being a towering, and slightly off kilter, three-story block building. I can see at least three doors running along its length and assume there are probably more.

I point it out to Carleon. "I think that may be the armory. Let's head that way."

With a silent nod, he leads me, weaving confidently through the staggered buildings that dot the landscape. Many of the windows are broken, chips of jagged glass rising from empty frames. I try to peer in as we pass, but it is too dark to see anything.

This entire section of the base seems eerily vacant. "Where is everyone?" I whisper in a hushed tone and Carleon holds up a hand to signal a stop. He pokes his head out, peering toward our destination.

"They're probably all at the front gate fighting."

Even though I know this could be a possibility, something just doesn't feel right. Where are all of the footprints leading away from the huts? It rained earlier in the day, a wintry mix that flitted back and forth between true drops and icy pellets. The prints should still be fresh, but I can't make out a single one.

"I don't like this. I think we need to find some cover." I rise onto my toes to see over his shoulder and point to a slanted roofed building less than thirty feet from the armory.

"Over there." I shout loudly to be heard over a great explosion from the south. I don't take time to worry about Eamon's safety or that of my friends as I run. If I do, I will lose any chance of getting my hands on Drakon and all of this effort will be for nothing.

Carleon yanks me to a stop just before I slam into the dilapidated wooden side of the squat building that appears to be abandoned like all the rest. He rises up just enough to peer through the broken window and nods. I catch a glimpse of an oil tanker just on the other side of the wall but don't have time to think about it as Carleon pulls me along behind him.

I follow right on his heels and dive through the door into complete darkness. It takes a moment for my eyes to adjust. As they do, I begin to see the interior walls have been stacked with interlocking concrete blocks, just like those used on the outer walls, but the roof above is held up with only a few wooden rafters and poorly nailed down shingles. The floor isn't even a true floor. It is nothing more than packed dirt with a ratty rug tossed over it.

It is crudely formed, like so many of the buildings that Drakon's men have constructed in this area—temporary shelters, nothing more. I've mentioned my concerns to Kyan about this very thing, but each time he brushes me off.

I saw firsthand the skill and precision with which Drakon employed to clear away the City and begin to rebuild. Why be so lax now? It doesn't make sense.

A sense of dark foreboding begins to sink into the pit of my stomach as I shove the door closed with my boot and breathe heavily. The air within is stale and laden with newly unsettled motes of dust. Two overturned tables line the far wall. Several chairs have been tossed haphazardly about the room with great carelessness. Four steel-framed beds, with covers torn and frayed draping off the sweat-stained, inch-thick mattresses. Papers litter the ground, trampled underfoot as if someone left in a great hurry.

Carleon glances out of the window, his back rigid as he cranes to see in both directions. "I don't think anyone saw us."

"That's because no one is looking for us." He glances back at me. "Doesn't that seem a bit odd to you?"

"Well…" He frowns, scratching at the drying flecks of mud on his cheek. "Maybe we are just that sneaky."

I point in the direction we just came. "I blew a hole in their wall. They had to have heard it, so why has no one come to check it out? Something just isn't right about this."

He looks thoughtful for a moment and then glances back at the empty yard once more. "So what do you want to do? Turn back?"

"No. Bring your gun over here." I call him over from

his post at the window. He thumbs the switch of his laser gun and warm green light spills over the dust-slick floor. I try not to breathe too deeply for fear of what might be growing on that rug.

I remove the map from within my jacket and spread it out below me, tracing my finger over the dampened paper. The edges have been rubbed clean, smeared in long, streaking black swatches. I search for any sign of this hut on the map but can find none. "I think we are getting close. The bunker should be about a hundred feet north of here. Can you see anything?"

Twisting his neck, Carleon peers through the opposite window. He sinks back down and shakes his head. "It's too dark to tell. The clouds have covered the moon again. I can't see any laser light either."

I have a bad feeling about this. After that last big explosion, the fighting has mostly died out. That means either our soldiers have penetrated the front gates and are slowly moving toward us or they have lost, and… I force myself not to continue with that line of thinking. *Eamon is fine. Nothing will happen to him.*

But even I know our chances of winning this battle are slim. I can only pray that Kyan saw an opportunity present itself and he took it.

"What do you think is happening out there?" Carleon asks. My friend's face is almost completely cloaked in shadow as he powers down his laser and I stuff the map safely back inside my jacket.

"I don't know." I crawl on my hands and knees to the nearest window. Broken shards of glass are scattered across the floor before me, creating a tangle of razor-sharp debris. I get as near to the window as I can and peer up into the sky. The clouds hang low and heavy but remain a dull gray. "Whatever has happened can't be good. We need to move."

No sooner do the words cross my lips than the ground begins to tremble beneath my palms. The glass rattles, tinkling against itself as the trembling rises, then fades. I retreat quickly to Carleon's side. I can see the whites of his eyes, wide with fear as he grips his laser. "Spider drones?"

"No," I whisper, raising a hand to silence him. The tremor comes again, harder and faster this time. Its rhythm is unsteady, unusual, yet something tickles the back of my mind, as if a memory is struggling to surface. "I think this is something else."

Carleon kneels beside me, waiting. He is used to my freaky abilities and has learned to trust my instincts. If I say it's not a machine, he believes me without fault. I only hope I am right. We don't have time to face off with a spider drone.

My abilities seem to be changing with each day, morphing into new hybrids of powers that even Kyan struggles to keep up with, though my focus is horrendous and my control is pathetic at best. Toren and Eamon have been forced on more than one occasion to put out my fires.

"You feel something?" he asks in a voice hardly above a whisper.

I nod and close my eyes so I can concentrate. "There is someone out there. Someone powerful."

"Drakon?"

I know the time Carleon spent as one of Drakon's soldiers has given him a deep respect for the commander's gifts, and his affinity for using them to torture innocent people, but even I'm surprised by the slight tremor in my friend's voice. Shaking my head, I motion for him to fall silent. I need to focus.

It is difficult to still my mind with all of the fears and doubts flitting through like a runaway subway car. I worry about my friends' safety, of being too late to capture Drakon, and of making a mistake that could cost men their lives. The weight upon my shoulders in nearly unbearable, but I know Kyan trusts me, so I must as well.

The soldiers fighting within these walls are not my enemy. They are simply doing the bidding of an evil man. If we win this battle today, they will be given the chance to throw down their arms and join us, or return to Kyan's home world, Calisted, with the other prisoners. Most will stay. Those that don't will not be harmed.

The thrumming of the ground and the sounds of

Carleon's breathing fade away as I search the unseen spaces on the other side of the base. I have felt strong minds before, but this one is different. It is not a mental ability that I sense, but a physical one.

"Do you know of a man who could create such tremblings…?" I trail off as my eyes widen with recognition. "Vikesh."

Carleon cries out as the rafter directly overhead creaks loudly, splintering down the center. He raises his hand to shield himself as it tumbles down upon him. I grunt as I throw out my hands, catching the heavy beam only inches from crushing his head. I grit my teeth and toss the beam aside. The walls rattle and shake as the beam slams into the wall, splintering the concrete blocks along their mortar lines. I grasp Carleon's hand and tug him to his feet. He coughs, beating his chest as he expels the cloud of dust he inhaled. "We have to stay out in the open. It's the only way!"

My friend stumbles behind me as I yank open the door and surge from the hut. A tremor ripples through the ground and I cry out as a wave of dirt sends me flailing to my knees.

"Someone you know?" Carleon cries out as he fights to remain upright.

"Yes." I scream and yank him out of the way as the building in front of me falters on its foundation. The roof groans loudly as the entire wooden slant slides from the top of the building and spills down on top of us.

I throw out my hands and focus with all of my might on creating a protective shield around us as three stories of stone and wood crumble down around us. I wince as each large chunk slams into the shield, draining on my strength.

"You can do it," Carleon says with a shaky voice as he watches the debris connect with the invisible armor mere inches above his head. Instead of the oppressive weight, I try to focus on the terror in his eyes and the way the color has drained from his face. When I glimpse the slight tremor in his lips, I growl and toss away the biggest section of the wall. My arms ache as I lower them to my sides.

If my blasting a hole in their wall didn't get their attention, tossing that building aside sure will!

It is hard to breathe around the cloud of dust trapped within my shield. I cover my mouth, coughing wildly as I wave off the dome. Carleon follows right on my heels as I stumble forward, our footing unstable on the debris beneath our feet.

"Who is this Vikesh guy?" He coughs, wafting his hand before him to clear the air. Dust clings to his hair and cheeks, matted with the sweat that beads along his forehead.

"Do you remember the battle in Sector 14 last summer?" My voice sounds raspy. When I clear my throat, it feels raw and chafed.

I pause as I realize Carleon is no longer following me. I look back over my shoulder and see the droop in his shoulders and his open stare. "There weren't many survivors left from that battle, were there?"

I don't want to scare him, but he needs to know what is coming our way. If I know Vikesh, he will already suspect I am here and will be looking forward to our reunion. He is no average, run-of-the-mill Caldonian. "I managed to save twenty-three that day. We arrived with over three hundred men."

His gulp is audible in the eerie silence that has fallen over the base. The night seems darker and the shadows deeper than before. A shiver works its way up my spine. "We're in trouble, aren't we?" he asks.

"Yes." I dart a quick glance around, wondering from which direction the alien will approach. "Vikesh is a Rumbler. He uses vibrations to attack. It can be something as simple as an explosion, a tree falling upon the ground, a bird chirping, or even a footstep that unsettles the earth. Any sound, any move you make can be turned against you."

"Then what does he do?"

I shake my head, swallowing roughly. "You don't want to know."

Sometimes at night I can still hear the men screaming,

pleading for death as the ground opened up around them and swallowed them alive. Others were pummeled by falling stone, cut in half and left to slowly bleed out. Still others were caught in the fires that spread through the forest, searing their flesh as they spasmed against the ground with no end in sight. Vikesh seemed to take the most delight in making her men suffer as he sought her out, using their own rhythmic pulses of their hearts against them as the fist-sized organs imploded in their chests.

Only the men within my protective shield had survived, but I was drained from the battle and too weary to do anything more than defend those few that stood nearest me. I still blame myself for not saving more. Eamon knows of my nightmares, but we never speak of them. To do so would be to admit my fear and my inadequacy.

I thought I could handle the alien on my own. I learned a hard, terrible lesson that day, but that was half a year ago. Am I strong enough now to save Carleon and my friends?

Vikesh is the only Caldonian that I have ever feared, apart from Drakon. And now he happens to show up at this particulate base? That can mean only one thing. The intel was correct... Drakon is here.

As the ground begins to roll beneath our feet again, screams pierce the night air. My comm unit goes crazy. "Illyria? Where are you?" Eamon screams. I wince as I pull the earpiece from the inner drum of my ear, alleviating some of the blaring pain. "Are you all right?"

I fight back against my panic as a second wave ripples through the ground, faster and harder than the first. *Am I all right? I don't really know,* I think silently, lost in a torrent of doubts.

"Illyria, answer me!" Eamon roars.

My annoyance with my boyfriend for breaking protocol helps me to see through my fear. "I am here and on target. Now stop shouting my name so everyone can hear! You are endangering my mission and our men," I yell back and let the earpiece dangle beside my cheek.

Carleon takes a deep breath and waits for my order. I can see how white his fingers are against his grip on his laser gun. For the first time I see him truly terrified and rightfully so. "Let's go."

He follows behind me at a near crouch, moving with extreme caution and as little noise as possible. We leave tracks in the softened ground, but there is no time to hide them, and with Vikesh tracking us, there's no point either. I watch as Carleon's gaze darts toward every shadow, no doubt convinced the alien is sneaking up on us, but that is not his way. He doesn't need to hide.

"So you think you can take this guy?"

My shrug does little to ease either of our fears as we pause against the side of the building I thought to be the armory. I rise up and look over my shoulder into the window and am struck by a mixture of disappointment and relief. Long rows of bench tables span the length of the room. This is the mess hall, not a storage locker of weapons. *At least he won't be able to blow us up with it!*

"That's the bunker over there." I point to a single door that rises from the ground. An entrance rises in an arch that stands barely eight foot tall, plated with sheets of hammered metal. The roof of the structure disappears into the earth, as if the tunnel has been swallowed whole. "Drakon should be through that door."

There is no telling just how many exits there are to this bunker, or how many soldiers lie in wait beyond that door. I can feel my heart thumping wildly in my chest as I peer out into the dark. *Where has all of the laser fire gone?*

The clearing between us and the bunker appears to be vacant, but looks can be deceiving. I take a calming breath and attempt to lower my heart rate. The last thing I need is Vikesh to use it against me.

But he wouldn't want to do that. It's not in his nature to end a foe so easily. No, he will want to make a public show of defeating me and he will want my friends to have a front row seat.

"Let's go." Silently, we dart across the clearing. Wailing cries suddenly rise from the other end of the base, tearing through the calm like a chainsaw gone rogue. I can feel Carleon hesitate beside me so I grab him by the arm and force him to keep moving.

"We can't help them." I know Eamon is alive, for the moment, but what about Toren or Kyan? I haven't heard anything from them since the battle began.

An explosion from behind slams us to the ground. A scream lodges in my throat as I cover my head with my hands, feeling the fibers of my jacket begin to melt against the thin layer of my shirt. The intensity of the heat filters slowly away and I look up through a mess of tangled hair.

The forest all around the base has erupted into blue fire. The abnormal flames lick at the bark, scorching the barren branches. Like a hundred tiny flamethrowers, streams of fire shoot out from miniature cannons that have risen along the rooftops. Rebel and alien soldiers alike run amuck as they fling themselves into the mud to extinguish the flames that eat away at their uniforms.

"They're killing their own men!" Carleon looks green as he watches the charred figures flail about in the distance.

"It's war," I say simply as I tug him on, knowing there is nothing we can do to help them. Carleon raises his hand to shield himself from the heat and I'm stuck again by how young he looks. Even though he physically appears a year or two younger than I am, he has already lived more years on Calisted than I have here on Earth. Time passes differently there. The beauty of youth is not stolen away quite so swiftly. "Drakon is our mission. If we go to help those men, then he might slip away in all of the chaos and their deaths will be for nothing."

I can see how hard it is for Carleon to turn away, but he does so without a single protest. We all knew the risk in coming here. Death was inevitable, but I would have liked to have kept it to a minimum. Apparently Drakon isn't playing by the same rules with his own men.

Movement from across the clearing catches the corner of my eye almost a second too late. "Watch out!" I shove Carleon back to the ground as the large oil tank explodes in front of us. The fumes burn my eyes and the blistering heat singes the hairs on the back of my arms. I choke on the thick smoke rolling through the clearing.

My lungs burn on the acrid scent that boils around us. Everywhere I look, orange and blue dances with deadly intent. I close my eyes and press my hand out to the side, using a gust of wind to expel the flames nearest us. My nostrils flare as I halt the movement of my lungs until the worst of the fumes passes by. I notice the black soot that clings to my hand as I pat Carleon on the back. "You good?"

"No," he grunts as he rolls to his side, clutching his chest. His face is a coated with a similar tarlike substance. His eyes gleam whiter than usual in the dark. "I think I landed on my spleen."

"At least you're alive."

"What happened?" he asks, rolling up to his knees. He clutches his side, his chest rising and falling in a rapid tempo.

"Vikesh," I whisper.

"How can you tell?" He turns and freezes when he follows my gaze. I can see the shadowy outline of a man approaching from the south, his form unclear, rippling with translucidity. His gait is slow, unconcerned. He knows I will not run. If I do, everyone will die.

"Illyria." His taunting voice carries on the breeze, deep and filled with mockery. I brush sweat from my brow and clench my fists at my side. I breathe a tiny sigh of relief as the blissfully chilled night air begins to seep back into the yard, combatting the blistering heat all around.

I can see Carleon from the corner of my eye. He looks paler than before, although I hadn't thought it possible. His Adam's apple bobs as he widens his stance beside me. I motion for him to be silent. He nods and shifts his weight to the side, unsettling the thin crust of newly heated dirt about his boot.

"Don't—" My cry cuts off as a terrible rumbling rises from the earth. The ground writhes like an angry snake and a deep crevice appears before us.

"Jump!" I toss myself to the side as the ground under my feet disappears into a sinkhole. I land on the edge, teetering precariously.

Carleon cries out as his chest slams into the crumbling edge. He frantically digs his fingers into the shifting dirt, but there is nothing to cling to. "I can't get a hold!"

His legs flail about as he begins to slip. I harness my energy, closing my eyes for a split second to focus, and fling him out of the sinkhole with my mind. He flops once as he lands hard on his stomach, his arm bent awkwardly beneath him. I'm just about to escape the hole myself when I hear a voice behind me, much nearer than before. "You seem to be struggling, Illyria. Are you sure you are up to the challenge?" Vikesh taunts.

I dig my fingers deep into the ground and feel something solid, a tree root that wound its way under the wall and into the depths of the yard. I grab hold of it and pull myself hand over hand from the hole.

"Why didn't you just fling yourself out?" Carleon asks as he comes to help me the final couple of feet. My stomach feels bruised and my hands raw from gripping the branch so tightly. My palms sting as I shake them out at my sides.

I'm breathing heavily by the time I'm fully on solid ground again, but I know I have no time to rest. "Because I'm going to need all the strength I have left. Now I want you to run. I don't care which direction as long as you don't head south. Get as far away from here as you can. When you are at the extraction point, wait for Eamon and his men to fall back. I don't want any more men to die tonight."

"No way." He shakes his head and he helps me to a sitting position. I wince, realizing my right side is far more sensitive than I had originally thought. It hurts to breathe. "I'm not leaving you here with him."

I grab the front of his uniform and pull him close. "If you don't, I will lose because I will be trying to save both of us. You need to leave. That's an order."

Static hisses in the comm that dangles from my cheek. I snatch it up. "Find Drakon and get out. Carleon will meet you at the rendezvous point. I'll take care of Vikesh myself."

I yank the comm from my ear and crush it underfoot. The last thing I need is Vikesh using the static against me.

Don't you dare take him on alone, a voice bursts loudly in my mind. I wince and Carleon turns to watch me. I offer him a weak smile but keep my eyes focused on Vikesh's approach. He seems to be waiting for something... or someone.

You don't have to yell, Kyan. I can hear you just fine.

Good. Then I forbid you to go through with this. Eamon is beside himself. You know he will come for you.

No! Knock him out and drag him back to the woods. He can't help me. No one can.

"Go, Carleon," I hiss as I shove at his arm. He hesitates but rises slowly.

We're coming for you.

I grit my teeth, knowing I have to finish with Vikesh quickly. As much as I adore my friends, their stubborn streak really gets on my nerves at times.

Vikesh's tall form appears to shimmer in the firelight as he allows himself to fully materialize. His uniform is scarlet from neck to overly polished black boots. I can see a mirrored image of the flames on the ground, contorting on their glossed surface as he passes. Huge silver spikes protrude from his ears, spanning nearly from cheek to scalp. A thick metal bar is shoved through his nose. The skin of his forehead and cheeks has been tattooed with black scrawling symbols. He stares down at me with scarlet eyes filled with barely concealed elation.

You won't make it in time, I say back to Kyan and sever the connection.

I am on my own now.

Two

I stare down the giant before me, unnerved by the difference in our size. Vikesh towers over me like a mighty oak tree, as broad and round as one too. His skin glows bronze in the light of the fire. His bald head shiny and slicked with sweat.

At least I'm not the only one who is showing some weakness, I think idly as I plant my feet and release my hold on my wounded side. "I had hoped you'd be dead by now."

Vikesh's laughter rumbles deep in his chest. Dark hairs escape out from the collar of his uniform, curling over the lip of his rounded neckline. "I had the same hopes for you, my dear, but alas… here we are."

He steps to the edge of the crevice that separates us and balls up his fists against his hips. "Although, I have to admit I am pleased to see you. I was so hoping we could tango one more time. You weren't exactly fair competition when we last met."

When his tongue snakes out between his lips, I see he has added a few more studs to his collection. Each one lining the center of his tongue is spiked and slick with moisture. How he manages to swallow around those things I will never know.

I don't let my disgust show as my gaze drifts over him. The sleeves of his uniform have been torn off at the top of his shoulders, revealing a patchwork of burns, scars, and glowing blue tattoos. There is hardly any bronze flesh left barren.

His eyes glint crimson in the flickering flames, but I know this is not their true appearance. No, his eyes are void of color, like the blackest pit where sunlight never reaches.

The scarlet uniform melds with the muscles that

protrude obscenely from his large frame. I can actually see the rise of his veins through the glove-like material. His calf muscles are larger than my thigh, his arms brawny enough to snap my neck like a twig if I were ever foolish enough to get that close.

I fight to stifle my snort of disgust as his eyes roam freely over my body, pausing to take in the curves that are amplified by my mud-slicked black uniform. Eamon would do something insanely reckless if he were here to see Vikesh's leer.

"You haven't changed one bit," he says, raising his gaze from my chest.

"Wish I could say the same for you," I growl back. My fingers clench into fists at my side. Vikesh loves to taunt, to draw out his playtime, but I have no intention of letting him have that satisfaction.

I flicker my gaze just to the side of him and nearly grin as he falls for my ruse. I am already halfway across the crevice before he realizes my intent. My hair whips against my cheek as I twist to connect my boot with his jaw.

The outline of his body ripples a split second before he dematerializes, stumbling backward. I plummet to the ground, landing hard enough on my hip to suck the breath from my lungs.

"A nice strike," his ghostly voice calls from somewhere to my left. "I did not think you had it in you."

I spring back onto my feet, turning slowly as I search for any hint of a disturbance in the air that will betray his location. The smoke is thicker now, rolling in giant, stifling waves from the forest. The night sky overhead gleams burnt orange as the fires spread from tree to tree, never crossing into the base. *The swamp muck is good for something at least*, I think as I grit my teeth against the pain, stuffing it down deep so I can focus.

A near constant buzzing rises in my ears as I feel ripples of energy coursing down my arms. I wonder if Vikesh can hear it or sense its presence. Can my own energy be used against me? I'd rather not find out.

I step away from the crumbling rim of the crevice and

pause beside a rock. With hardly a thought, I toss it through the air to my left, but it slams into a section of the wall that still remains intact and falls uselessly to the ground.

"Tsk. Tsk. You are starting to disappoint me." His voice comes from my right. I turn to see him lounging against the wall of the bunker, one leg crossed over the other as if he doesn't have a care in the world.

I grin as I throw out my hands. An invisible blast of energy spirals across the clearing and shoves him back into the steel wall, the weakened metal crumpling in around him. His growl of fury is cut off as I latch onto him again, seizing the front of his uniform with my mind, and hurl him past me, slamming him into the concrete wall. The top row of blocks rock from their mortar bed and tumble down upon him. His cry of outrage rises as he crawls to his feet and I turn to face off with him.

I brace as he draws his arms out to either side of his body and swings them in rapidly as his fists connect. I throw up a protective shield only seconds before the explosion hits. My hair whips behind my back as I plant my feet, leaning into the blast. Rocks, beams of splintered wood, and brick pelt at me, grazing harmlessly off my shield, grinding into a fine sandy texture that piles about my feet.

"Impressive." Vikesh mockingly claps as he stands to his full height. I can see blood dripping from his shattered knuckles, but he seems oblivious to the pain. "How about this?"

He whirls his hands in a circular motion in front of him, sucking the flames from the oil tanker into a vacuum before him. It swirls into a ball, the bright orange and blue flames entwining as he throws out his hands and hurls it toward me.

In my mind, I burrow deep into the ground, searching. I grin as Vikesh's eyes widen in shock as the ground before me erupts into a geyser of water from a spring hidden many feet below us. Steam places a veil between us as the water and fire collide.

"Equally impressive." He doesn't sound quite as

haughty as he did a moment ago. I ache to release the tension wound painfully between my shoulder blades, but I know I can't show any sign of weakness or he will exploit it.

"Is that all you've got?" I goad, stepping to the side of the geyser so I can keep my gaze focused on him. My hair falls in dripping strands over my eyes, clinging to my cheeks. The water is cold, making the skin beneath my uniform pimple with sensitivity, but I ignore my discomfort. I am running out of time. If Eamon arrives before Vikesh is dead, he will attempt to help me and that will put all our lives at risk.

I order you to wait for us. My mentor Kyan's voice breaks into my thoughts.

I grit my teeth. *I'm trying to concentrate.*

You can't win this battle, Illyria. He is far too strong.

I swipe the clumps of hair from my face, blinking back the streams of water that pour down my face, and glare at Vikesh as he shifts, crouching low as if he might pounce at me any second. *I can do this.*

You are not ready. You overestimate your abilities.

Anger and resentment swirl through my chest, making the energy rippling along the length of my body visibly spark. *And you underestimate how ticked off I am!*

I sever the connection and shove Kyan firmly from my mind, making sure he takes the hint. I don't need him. This time the fight is between Vikesh and me. Only one of us is walking away and I have no intention of losing a second time.

"I like you, despite your puny size and offensive tongue. You are a strong woman, foolish and bullheaded, but strong. We could make a great pair."

"Sorry." I crouch low, never leaving his gaze. "I'm already taken."

"A pity." His grin is truly gruesome when his lips peel back to reveal teeth the color of honey with pockmarked black stains between. "I could have had a lot of fun with you, but then again, perhaps your goodies have already been plucked by that boy…" He mockingly taps his finger against his chin. "Bastien, was it?"

"Don't flatter yourself." I can feel the vibrations begin in my chest the instant I hear Bastien's name and I try to regain my composure.

Vikesh grins, closing his eyes for a moment. "I can feel that I have struck a nerve. Good. I've been aching for a decent fight."

The winds begin to whip about me, tugging at my water-drenched clothes. A chill settles over me as my teeth begin to chatter from the cold. The veil of grey dotting out the stars overhead begins to shift, mounting upon themselves into thunderous storm clouds. Vivid white lightning forks across the sky.

Vikesh opens his eyes and cranes his neck back. "Is he here? The boy who turned you down?"

The energy rippling through my fingers increases into such a frantic rhythm that it makes my bones ache from trembling.

"No, of course not." Vikesh leers at me. "I hear he's forgotten all about you now."

"Enough," I growl, lifting my hands overhead.

"Illyria!" The cry fights to pierce through the rising winds. I turn and look back over my shoulder to see Kyan and Eamon arrive at the far end of the barren yard. Eamon's brow has been cut open and blood pours from the wound. A bandage has been wrapped around his thigh but has already begun to seep through. He leans heavily upon Kyan, who looks only slightly less damaged. I can't see Toren anywhere.

"Stay out of this," I shout and wave one hand back toward them to push them into the shadows, but it is too late. Vikesh's attention has shifted toward my friends.

"This is between you and me, Vikesh!"

"Is it? Oh, you would like that, wouldn't you?" His eyes appear to glow from within as he turns his head. "Can you hear it? The music of their heartbeats?"

Sheer terror grips me as Eamon limps forward, shrugging off Kyan's grasp. I dive without thinking, waiting for the splintering pain that will seize my shoulder when I slam into Vikesh's midsection, but it never comes. Vikesh dematerializes and I collapse to the ground in a bruised heap.

"Illyria!"

I press my palms into the soil and push myself up to my feet. I don't have to look to know what I will find, but when I do, my stomach gives way.

"He seems awful taken with you. Is this the other one? The one you settled for when Bastien cast you aside?" Vikesh holds Eamon by the neck several feet off the ground. He stands on the opposite side of the sinkhole, nearly thirty feet from where Eamon was only a moment ago. *How did he move so quickly?*

Eamon flails, kicking out at Vikesh, but the giant hardly pays him any attention. Static electricity ripples in the air around me, lifting wisps of hair from my shoulders as hatred pools in my belly. *I will kill him for this,* I silently vow.

"Eamon, don't move." His eyes widen with fright as a fork of lightning spears down from the clouds. Vikesh's mouth gapes open in horror as he tosses Eamon aside and throws out his hands, grappling for control of the bolt.

Get him out of here! I scream at Kyan as I step forward, pressing with all my might against Vikesh's strong hold. I can feel him attempting to disintegrate the lightning by rearranging the currents. Already, sparks of fire ricochet off the bolt and sizzle as they sear the metal of the bunker.

I don't have time to see if Kyan is following my order as I take another step, biting down on my lower lip until my teeth pierce my flesh and blood pools along my gums. I jerk my head to the side as Vikesh sends a spark my way. A narrow miss.

I struggle to refocus, but I can feel a quivering beginning in my arms. Facing off with Vikesh is sapping my energy too quickly. I won't be able to hold this much longer.

Vikesh's mounting fear is nearly palpable as whirlwinds of dust rise in attempt to distract me. I swipe them away easily as I take another step. A mere dirt trick won't be enough to sway me as a new idea forms in my mind.

I focus the main part of power on my struggle against Vikesh but streamline the remainder back up into the clouds. A single, spear-like bolt of pink lightning lances toward his heart. His eyes widen with horror a second before the electricity strikes. He dematerializes with a horrific scream.

Flaming particles drift on the air as his shriek rises to ear-splitting heights.

"Get down!" Someone slams me from behind as the released lightning bolt careens into the bunker. Sparks explode in a shower of color. The explosion is deafening, echoing deep into the forest.

Molten debris rains down from above. A distressed cry in my ear sends me into action and I close my eyes, shoving the person laid across my back out of harm's way as the chunks of heated metal rain down upon me. I cry out as it connects, melting the fibers of my jacket to my skin. The scent of burnt flesh makes my stomach lurch as I weakly throw up my arm, creating a partial protection.

White-hot metal glows on the ground around me, but I barely give it any notice as my shield sputters and dies. One shriek rips from my lips as something lances through my side. Darkness encroaches on my vision as my arms and legs give out, spilling me to the ground. I'm only vaguely aware of someone screaming as my eyes flutter closed and I am trapped within my pain.

Everything hurts.

"Illyria!" I blink, struggling to focus on the man kneeling beside me, cradling my head in his hands.

"Carleon?"

"Oh, god." His voice trembles as he lifts his hand. I can see in the flickering of firelight that it is slick with blood. Fresh blood. My blood.

I grind my teeth as he attempts to roll me over. "Don't!"

Nausea washes over me when something large shifts in

my abdomen. "Don't look, okay?" he whispers as he wipes his hands against the breast of his uniform.

I try to nod but clench my eyes shut as bile rises swiftly into my throat, tainting my mouth with its acidic taste. I stare up at the stars, amazed at how beautiful the cloudless sky is. I blink, fighting to remain conscious as I wonder what happened to all of the clouds.

"Is he gone?" I croak, coughing up blood. It bubbles from my lips, coating my tongue. I gag, trying to swallow it back down.

"I think so." Carleon darts a cautious glance around the charred courtyard. There is little left that hasn't been singed. "I don't see him."

"Eamon?"

"Kyan is taking care of him. A broken leg and a nasty bump on his head, but it could have been a lot worse."

I dig my nails into the dirt, fighting to still the wild spinning of my head. "Then you're going to have to do it."

"What? Oh no, no way!" Carleon looks between me and the two-foot metal spike protruding up from my stomach. His face takes on a decidedly green tint. "I do minor healings, like headaches and ingrown toenails. You know I'm not good at big repairs."

I close my eyes and fight to breathe around the pain. "You have to. I'm too weak to heal myself and Kyan is busy. Besides…" I lift up and a hiss of pain passes my lips as the metal slices deeper into my flesh. "You owe me."

"How do you figure that?" I can see his pupils are dilated with fear as he leans over me, brushing hair out of my eyes.

"You didn't run." I blink rapidly to clear my vision. It does little to help.

"You knew I wouldn't."

I start to speak, but a scream bursts from my throat as the spike shifts enough to cut deeper into my flesh. The pain is overwhelming.

"Please, Carleon," I beg as I grip my friend's arm. "There's no time."

Carleon's hand shakes visibly as he moves to grasp the

metal. He winces at the heat radiating off of it but doesn't let go.

"You can do this," I whisper as my eyes flutter closed. I can feel the pool of blood growing around me as it seeps beneath my fingers, moistening the earth.

"I should get Kyan," he says, almost as an afterthought.

"No need," a new voice calls, emerging from the shadows. "I'll help her."

My vision is dim as I struggle to see the approaching figure. I know by his voice that he is a man. It sounds strangely familiar, but I struggle to place it.

He drops down beside me and I flinch as he takes my hand in his. Startling sapphire eyes stare down at me with such intensity that my breath catches. "Bastien?"

His eyes look the same. Even the rugged stubble that has grown upon his chin is recognizable. The minty scent that clings to his breath is deliciously familiar, but it isn't until he smiles that I begin to trust my eyes. "Are you really here?" I whisper.

His deep, throaty laugh nearly makes the pain worth bearing... nearly.

It has been nearly a year since I last saw him in the alley down from the Shard. An eternity since he turned his back on our love and gave me up for the sake of a destiny I did not ask for, nor was able to deny. It took months for the sound of his name not to feel like a knife serrating my heart, and several more months for the numbness to come and steal away the ice he left behind. I have tried to tell myself I no longer care for him, that I have moved on. It was a lie, oh such a terrible, foolish lie.

"Yeah," he whispers as he places a hand to the side of my wound. I flinch, but his touch is firm, demanding. "Don't move."

"I can't believe you are actually here. Kyan never said—" My words cut off with a groan as Bastien presses around the edge of my wound.

"Maybe you two can reminisce after Illyria is done hemorrhaging." Carleon grunts with disapproval.

I bury my teeth in my lower lip as Bastien lifts my side to blindly examine the exit wound.

"This is a pretty nasty deal you got yourself into," Bastien mutters, rubbing his jaw with bloody fingers as he sinks back onto his heels. "I think the only option is to just pull it straight out."

He turns to Carleon. "You need to find a stick, something large enough that she won't bite through. Then I'm going to need you to hold her down."

I offer my friend a brief nod of approval as he rushes away and watch as Bastien eyes him up. "He's a friend," I say, surprised to find he still cares enough to be jealous.

"A very protective friend," he mutters.

He looks tired. I can see it in the lines drawn heavily around his eyes. A laser gun has been set down beside him, forgotten. Why didn't I know he would be helping with this attack? "He's just worried about me."

Bastien's gaze hardens as he turns to look back down at me. "Does he do that often?"

I look away, afraid if I meet his gaze I will betray myself. "I can take care of myself."

Bastien's chuckle sends ripples of warmth along my body, stealing away the creeping cold that has gripped the lower half of my body. I feel stiff, wrong. "Not really proving that point too well right now. What were you thinking to take on that man by yourself?"

I wince. "I had no choice. Vikesh tried to kill Eamon..." I cut off the instant I speak his name, but the damage is already done.

An emotion crosses Bastien's face, fleeting but pained nonetheless. A veil falls over his eyes as I turn to look at him. All emotion is wiped clean by the time Carleon returns with a branch in his hand. "I got it."

The branch is hardly more than a stick. One end is badly charred, as if Carleon snatched it out of the fire and beat the flames away. "Good," Bastien says. "Now I need you to hold her shoulders. She will buck when the pain starts."

"No, I won't."

Bastien's gaze flickers toward me for a split second before looking away. He rises onto his knees, getting into position. His biceps flex as he grips the metal, showing no hint that the heat still clinging to it bothers him. He looks down at me one more time. "Yes. You will."

With a tug that feels as if Bastien has removed all of my intestines, I feel pain as I have never known before. I hear a distant shriek of agony and then darkness floods in as a wave of pain sucks me under.

Three

I reach for the hand resting beside me. It is warm and strong, gripping back tightly as my eyelids slowly flutter open. "Bastien?"

The texture of the hand feels wrong against my fingers, the palm soft instead of roughened by callouses. "Sorry to disappoint. It's just me."

I jerk upright and the room tilts on its axis. "Easy," Eamon whispers, firmly pushing against my shoulders until I am lying prone on the bed once more. I don't put up much of a fight.

"Where am I?" I draw my hand away from my forehead and squint against the brilliant fluorescent light overhead. I never have liked false lighting. After we took control of the City, Kyan moved our entire camp into the heart of the brick-and-mortar prison. Some people were thrilled by the change, but I was not.

It held too many new things: electricity, toilets that gushed water that wove through pipes in the walls, vents in the ceilings that pumped out heat that dried my skin into a flaky mess. I miss the cool damp of the cave, the flickering of flames as we sang around the campfire. I miss the waterfall and the delicious privacy that I could always be sure to find in one of the blacked-out tunnels.

I can't be alone here. Thousands of people live within the city perimeter now. Entire streets are lit up like blinding stars. Sometimes I go to the rooftop and sit alone, staring beyond the borders of the City to the dark and familiar heights of the mountains.

Repairs are still underway in the far reaches of town, but even now, with my hands pressed against the soft mattress, I can barely make out the rumbling of the subway cars passing beneath the surface.

A name was voted on for this place not long after we began to settle in: Thalar. It means peace in Caldonian. An ill-fitting name in my opinion since we have seen little peace since we began our rebellion.

If only Bastien were here to see the changes. He would love to see the subway in action, I think, remembering how he had spent months living within the lifeless hull of a subway car, in the dark and alone.

"We're home?" I ask, suppressing those memories.

I should have known from the first instant I caught the scent of smoke that seeps in through the open window beside my bed. It puffs in black clouds from the spider drones' exhaust as they roam the streets, ever alert for attack. They make it nearly impossible to keep a window clean.

"Yes. Kyan thought it best for us to return after—"

"How?" I cut him off, rolling my head to the side to stare at the inky black of night on the other side of the window. I have never liked the medical wing. It is too white, too clean. Not to mention it is in the heart of the Shard and I don't exactly have fond memories of the last time I was here. "How did we travel so quickly?"

Eamon clears his throat, fiddling with his fingers in his lap as I turn to stare at him, demanding an honest answer. "You were out for nearly a week."

"A week?" I whisper, aghast at the amount of time that has been stolen from me.

"Why?" Heat stains the tips of his ears and I know the answer without him answering. "Because Kyan knew I would refuse to leave on my own."

"It was for your own good," he insists, but we both know it's a weak excuse and one that I've heard countless times before. I've lost count how many times in the past year they have done "the right thing" for me instead of letting me make my own choices.

"I hate it when he messes with my mind," I grumble and tuck my hand under my head. Kyan's ability goes beyond just reading minds and healing wounds. He has become rather practiced at inducing comas when they suit him, too.

The thick blanket that covers my lower half feels

stifling compared to the chill that clung to my body the night I passed out in Drakon's base. Suffocating heat pumps steadily from a vent above my bed, staving off the frost that clings to the bottom of my window. My other hand hovers over the bandage that has been wrapped tightly over my abdomen. I grimace as I feel pain swell as I attempt to twist. "Why do I still hurt?"

Eamon's hand tightens around mine, squeezing my fingers so hard my bones begin to grind together. "Carleon did his best to repair your wound after Bastien removed the shrapnel, but he could only do so much."

"What about Kyan?"

His jaw clenches and heat rises from the collar of his black uniform. I can't help but notice the stark difference between Bastien and him, how Eamon's tousled mane of blond hair glows rich amber in the false lights. Bastien would be dark and coolly indifferent but admittedly handsome in his formfitting uniform. "He has been preoccupied…"

I don't like the way Eamon trails off. "Were there many losses?"

He scrubs his hands over his face, his mouth downturned when he draws his hands away. A single nod brings tears to my eyes. "Many were lost to the fires. Others when we first infiltrated the base. No one could have known Vikesh would be there."

"We should have." I protest, clenching my eyes tightly against the surge of guilt. *How many of those lives could have been spared if we'd had better intel? If Kyan had let me scout it out on my own first instead of insisting I remain behind? Darn his pride!*

"And Bastien?" I ask, pinning my arms down by my sides. "He's gone, isn't he?"

"He returned to his base after the fighting was over," he replies. His gaze looks flat, his expression hardened. "He had injured men to attend to as well."

I knew this was bound to happen. Leave it to Bastien to swoop in at my time of dire need only to sneak back out again before things got too personal. I blow out a breath and roll my head to the side so Eamon can't see the pain that needles at me, drawing fresh tears into my eyes.

"He saved you, Illyria. For that I am grateful."

I bark out a bitter laugh and roll back to stare up at him. His jawline is firm and his eyes veiled by shaggy curls that he makes no move to push aside. He is hiding. "I know you better than that. Why not just say it?"

"What?" The muscles along his neck quiver as he swallows. His nostrils flare. "Say that I'm ticked that he was the one who rescued you instead of me? That if I hadn't been a fool and interfered with Vikesh, you wouldn't have almost died?"

His pain is visible and utterly raw, as haggard as the lines carving into his face. I place a hand gently on his arm and wait for him to look over at me. His lips pinch tightly as he glances at me. "You came because you cared."

"He wouldn't have," Eamon says. "He would have trusted you, believed you capable of finishing what you started."

I purse my lips, unsure if I should draw back my hand or if the action would cause further pain. We both know how troubled our relationship has been this past year. In all fairness, I did try to give us a fair shot. I pushed aside my pain and inner torment to try to make him happy, but it was never enough.

No amount of caring and declarations of love were enough to make him believe me. After a while, he simply stopped coming to visit after work and would walk the long way back to his barracks just to avoid seeing me on the street. Losing Bastien is the hardest thing I have ever experienced. Losing Eamon too has nearly crippled me.

The only thing I live for now is the hunt. It used to be bears and wolves that I stalked in the night. Now it is Drakon, only ever him.

"You are not him, Eamon," I say softly.

He snorts and pulls away from my grasp. I feel cold, awash with a tingly numbness, at his withdrawal. "I don't need *you* to remind me of that."

His words hit me like a slap across the cheek. "Hey!" I

grasp onto his arm and yank him around to face me, gritting my teeth as I stuff down the pain flaring in my stomach. "That's not fair. You're the one who closed the door on us."

"Really?" The dull monotone quality in his voice makes me cringe. His hands hang limp in his lap. "You're going to say that when you never even entered the same room as me?"

"I…" I release his arm as if his touch has seared my fingers and cross my arms over my chest, wishing I could roll away from him, could stare at the wall until the smudged lines of glue that used to hold up a hideous motif of floral wallpaper would blur into a dreamless sleep.

Eamon sighs and plunges his hands in his hair. His shoulders slump as he curls his back and rests his elbows against his knees, a broken man before me. I close my eyes, praying for this nightmare to end. Why do we keep doing this to each other? Maybe because we are home, where everything is a reminder of the pain we have both endured over the past year.

Clasping my side, I fight to sit up. For a moment I have to pause and will the room to stand still before the lightheadedness seems to pass and I'm able to rise. Eamon turns and mechanically holds a pillow behind my back, as if the action is expected of him.

"Thanks," I mutter sourly. I push back the snarl of hair framing my face and wince. Memories of shivering in the dark, drenched from the geyser, and the slashing pain that staked me to the ground swell up within my mind. I remember watching the flames dance along Bastien's outline as he leaned over me, feeling his hands upon me, cold yet steady. New memories to plague me in the long stretches of night when I am alone. I release a long, slow breath, forcing Bastien from my mind. "Did you at least capture Drakon?"

"No," Eamon begrudgingly admits. He shifts in his chair and the metal legs squeal against the tile floor. "He was long gone by the time we arrived. Vikesh proved to be an adequate distraction."

My lip curls with disgust, thinking of the countless lives we tossed away for nothing. "Kyan should have gone after him instead of me." I bunch my fingers into the pillow beside me and hurl it across the room. It hits the far wall with a dissatisfying puff of air and then tumbles to the ground. I want to break something. No. I want to break someone.

"Easy, Illyria." He presses back on my shoulders. "I know that look and you're in no shape to be following through with that."

"He was within our grasp and we just let him walk again," I growl, digging my nails into the mattress. I can feel my anger mingled with an equally disturbing feeling: panic. "What if he is gone for good? What if he buries so deep we never find him again? What if this was our last shot?"

"It won't matter," he says, turning away from me. His hands drop back into his lap. "We found something."

"Something?" I press, sure I'm going to scream if he doesn't give me more details.

Eamon's shoulders rise and fall several times before he turns to look at me. I can see him weighing his words, no doubt wondering what I will do with the information once I have it. He sighs and splays his hands atop his thighs, clenching tightly. "We found Drakon's diary buried in the remains of the bunker. We think Vikesh was meant to burn it all when he was finished with you, but obviously that didn't happen."

"I want to see it."

"I thought you might," he responds in a flat tone. Reaching inside his jacket pocket, he pulls out a small, rectangular book. It is the color of marble, its leather cover worn with use. If I look close enough, I can see the indents on the back cover where he pressed his writing utensil as he scripted the final page.

I snatch it from Eamon's hand and rapidly flip through. Each page is filled with sketches, symbols, letters that hardly make any sense to me. "Is this written in code?"

"Yes and no. It is written in a Caldonian dialect that

even Kyan struggles to translate. He says it originates from Trilar, one of the nearby planets where Drakon spent time. Kyan's a bit rusty, but he thinks with time he can decipher it."

"Time?" My voice rises an octave as I clench the book against my chest. Eamon makes a move to steal it away, but I'm not willing to just hand it back over so quickly, not when we've fought so hard for this tiny scrap of insight. "We don't have time. Drakon is on the run and we need to flush him out."

"*We* don't need to do anything," Eamon snaps, adopting a defensive tone. "*You* are on mandatory bed rest until further notice."

"No!" I cry, lurching forward, but instantly gasp as pain lances through my abdomen. I swear under my breath as Eamon easily plucks the book from my grasp, and I sink back into the pillows, blowing out short breaths until the pain eases.

I glare at him, sure he was in on this plan. "That's why Kyan hasn't healed me. It's not because he's been too busy. It's because he doesn't want me to lead this mission."

Eamon rises slowly, the book held firmly in his grasp. "We thought you might react like this."

I scowl, clasping my hand against my side. I can feel warm blood oozing through my bandages and a wave of lightheadedness washes over me. "I thought you were my best friend. That you would always have my back."

His eyes widen for a second and then narrow, his gaze rimmed with ice as he pauses in the doorway. "Some things never change… but some things do."

I turn my back on him as he turns out the light and closes the door, leaving me alone to fume in the dark.

Four

I lay on the flat of my back, eyes clamped shut. My breathing is steady and deep, almost trancelike. Images flash rapidly behind my eyelids, pictures of people and places I have yet to encounter. My destiny approaches with bone-chilling speed, a destiny that I neither asked for nor would have chosen if given the chance, but fate never stopped to ask my opinion.

My eyes open and my pupils dilate, adjusting to the sunlight that streams in through my window. It is a welcome change from the dreary wintry skies we have seen recently. I can see moisture clinging to the window frame where the morning frost has begun to evaporate.

Although the pain in my abdomen healed several days ago, the pain of being removed from action continues to fester. Two weeks have passed since the battle at Drakon's base. The first I spent in a near comatose state in the medical wing of the Shard, the second as a prisoner within my own home. Guards stand on either side of the door to my apartment at Kyan's orders. We both know I could take them out with a single thought, but I won't. They are innocent.

I look at the open doorway that leads into the bathroom attached to my quarters. Although I may be opposed to most of the modern conveniences I have been forced to endure since moving into Thalar, there is one I embrace as often as possible: a bath.

Despite the fact that it isn't as refreshing as the waterfall back in the caves, I do enjoy a long soak in the slightly rusty yet beautiful claw-foot tub. It was once white and flawless. Now it has taken on a slightly dingy hue and boasts a few chips, revealing black metal beneath.

My room is simple, no frills like some of the homes

I've been in. Candles line the wooden dresser on the opposite wall, their wicks charred and burnt to the halfway point. A wooden staff and a crossbow and leather quiver rest against the closed cupboard, reminders of my former life. Four knives of varying lengths are spread across my table, glistening beautifully in the warm sunlight. I love these most of all.

I'm not allowed to use the weapons to hunt in Thalar. Kyan says there is no need with active supply lines up and running smoothly. I have more food than I've ever wanted, yet I am unhappy, for many reasons, but mostly because I feel unneeded.

Eamon and I used to be the hunters of our group. We would spend our days in the forest in search of meat. It was freeing, rewarding. We ate what he killed and nothing more. Now I feel confined and lazy, trapped within a new prison.

A pile of books collects dust on my bedside table. A gift from Aminah not long after I was moved into these quarters. She was worried I would feel lonely. I cast a contemptuous glance at the pile, knowing nothing within those pages could ease the hollowness I feel.

Bastien would have loved those books, diving through them to discover their untold treasures. Maybe that is why I've never opened their covers.

Kyan has gone to great lengths over the past few months, teaching me about Earth, the way it was before. My vocabulary has swelled. I can now walk through Thalar and know what dumpsters and hairdryers are, read the faded billboards that perch on rooftops, and decipher a cookbook, although it is a waste of time. No one would want to eat anything I make.

I look beyond the books to the walls. They are a light yellow, the paint a bit worn and faded, but still hold a hint of false cheer. I suppose I could have picked a room with a more drab color scheme to fit my mood, but I liked the southern light in the morning.

My walls are free of decorations, barren. I like it that way. It reminds me of the dismal grays of my cave.

I sit up, rolling my neck from side to side to release some of the stiffness that settled in during my jaunt into the future. Kyan would be proud of my accomplishment if not for the fact that I was directly disobeying his orders and blocking him completely out of my mind at the same time. He knows I am angry. Let him stew over it for a bit. Maybe it will do him some good.

Aminah came to see me last night with a basket filled with freshly baked bread and Zahra in tow. I know she only came at Kyan's bidding. Despite the friction Zahra and I used to share over her affections for Eamon, our relationship has begun to improve, slowly. That doesn't mean I trust her any further than I can throw her, which is a pretty good distance. I'm pretty sure I could get a good mile out of her.

Eamon has remained absent from my quarters, although I don't find that surprising at all considering how we ended our conversation the week prior. I knew he was hurt, but so was I. He can't always treat me like a child that needs to be protected. As much as I love his concern, I also find it to be irritatingly suffocating.

From my window last night I saw the tip of Shard lit up until well after midnight. Kyan must have called together his advisors, no doubt to discuss the next plan of attack. I wonder if he discovered anything within the pages of Drakon's diary. Surely if he had, I would be the last person to know about it.

A knock at my door draws my attention away from my thoughts. "I'm not allowed visitors. Head pain-in-my-butt's orders," I call out.

"It's me."

I sigh, unsure if I'm ready to go head to head for round two with Eamon. I wrap my arms about my waist, preparing for the worst. "It's unlocked."

As the wooden door begins to swing open, I can't help but wonder if he has already seen how this conversation will go? His ability to look into the future, to manipulate it and bend it to his will, has grown exponentially over the past year. Kyan has been a wonderful teacher, always patient and understanding.

But it was Eamon's obsession with the future that first drove a wedge between us. He always had a plan of attack when we argued. He would stunt my anger before I even had a chance to get wound up. This I could have lived with if it hadn't been for his obsession with one future in particular: mine.

A cloud hung over us from the first day he began digging into my future. He became withdrawn, sullen. He lost weight despite my best attempts at cooking something moderately edible. Eamon turned inward, trapped within his own powers.

It annoyed me how desperate he was to know about my destiny when I wanted no part of it. Didn't he know I could look myself if I so desired?

Those moments when he would drift away during a conversation, I knew where he had gone. What little time we had to spend together was eaten away by his driving need to know. Having me in front of him was no longer good enough.

I tried to make things work between us, but the chasm was too great for either of us to repair on our own. Bastien left behind a gaping hole in my heart, as if he tore off a chunk and took it with him when he left, but with Eamon it was different. His rejection was the slow poison of death that rotted out my heart from the inside, making me bitter. And that bitterness was left to smolder for far too long.

I snatch a robe off the end of my bed and wind the tie around my waist as Eamon enters. He clears his throat and shifts away his gaze, as if I were immodestly dressed. I can remember a time when he would have jumped at the chance to see me like this. "I'm decent. You don't have to be such a prude."

Heat stains his cheeks as he clears his throat. He clasps his hands behind his back and stands rigid, the door open wide to the hall beyond. I release my grip on my stomach and rub my forehead, already feeling the seeds of a headache beginning to take root. "Can you at least close the door so the guards have to strain to hear our conversation?"

Eamon takes a step forward and turns to close the arched wooden door. It squeals on its hinges as the lock falls into place. His movements are inflexible. His discomfort painfully obvious. A deep sadness falls over me. *How far we have fallen,* I muse as I slip to the edge of my bed, lacing my fingers together as I wait for him to announce why he has come.

It is hard to recognize the man I grew up with in the strong, hard planes of his face. His cheekbones are more prominent with his weight loss, his eyes slightly more sunken, giving him a severe look that contrasts sharply with the laughing boy I once knew.

His gaze sweeps over my face, slowly at first and then a second time with far more scrutiny. "I'm fine. Thanks for asking," I say.

"I was assured by Aminah that you were."

I bite my tongue against the sharp retort that is begging to escape from my mouth. "It was good of her to come and see me. I'm surprised she got past your guards. Did they pat her down in search for weapons too?"

He grimaces and shifts his weight. His hands hang awkwardly at his sides, as if he's unsure what to do with them. "Don't be like this. It's for your own good."

"My own good?" Anger simmers in my chest as I rise swiftly to my feet and face off with him. "You are not my father, Eamon. You have no right to scold me or send me to my room when you think I've been bad."

"I have every right!" His face reddens as he shouts. His stance widens as he juts out his chin. "I wouldn't have to do something this rash if you would just do as you are told."

I step back, feeling the color drain from my face at the impact of his words. "What is that supposed to mean?"

"Nothing," he mutters and lowers his intense gaze.

"No, not nothing." I move toward him, attempting to restrain the urge to throttle him. I tuck my elbows in close to my body to keep from doing just that. "I want to know."

For a moment, I think Eamon is going to lash back at me. I can see the desire in his eyes, darkening their lovely ice-blue color to something resembling a washed-out and dingy gray of a winter sky. And then he cracks.

The tight line of his mouth sags, his shoulders wither, and he slumps back into a chair that sits in the corner across from my bed. He looks utterly broken.

His eyes look over-bright, his face flushed as he looks up at me. "I can't do this anymore, Illyria. I can't keep fighting you, trying to keep you safe, when all you want to do is run headfirst into mortal danger."

His head droops low as he buries his face in his hands. I watch in disbelief as his shoulders begin to quake. At the first sight of a tear hitting the floor I rush forward and fall to my knees at his feet.

"Talk to me," I whisper, heartbroken by his wretchedness. My chest tightens and my throat feels dry, sore.

When he looks up at me, I can see the streaks of red in his eyes that betray sleepless nights. Dark circles ring his eyes. His cheeks are gaunt, his face drawn. It is as if he is wasting away in front of me. "I…" His voice trembles so fiercely that he pauses to clear his throat. "I'm going to lose you and I can't bear it."

"Is that what this is about?" I twine my fingers with his and hold firm. I can feel how badly he's shaking. "You can't lose me when I am sitting right here."

"For now." Haunted eyes shift to meet mine. "But it won't always be. You will be taken from me."

I attempt a smile but know it pales in comparison to a genuine expression so I let it falter completely. I settle for drawing his hand up to my mouth and pressing my lips against his knuckles. They feel cold against my lips, as if he has stood outside for far too long. I close my eyes and feel the tears that begin to build in the corners.

"I'm not going anywhere." I pause, knowing I need to continue but dreading the effect it will have on him. "But you have pushed me so far out of your life I don't know how to stay."

I don't have much time; we both know that. My destiny hangs in the room like an invisible stalker that can't take a hint. I take in a calming breath and then release it slowly through the tiny gap between my front teeth before I speak again. "I want to be with you Eamon, but you won't let me."

His face crumples completely. The trembling of his lips makes me ill with regret, but this conversation, this truth, is long overdue. "I don't know how to. Every moment I spend with you feels as if it will be my last. I keep waiting for you to be captured… or taken to *him.*"

"Drakon still has to find me before he can present me to Aloysius."

Eamon shakes his head, looking down at me with tear tracks on his cheeks, shiny in the sunlight filtering in through the window. "I wasn't talking about Drakon."

I feel this low blow straight in my gut. It takes me a moment compose myself because I speak and when I do, I can hear the shakiness in my voice. "Bastien is gone."

"Yeah, but he came back once. He can do it again."

The raw pain in his voice tears me away from the whirlwind of volatile emotions that always come with hearing Bastien's name. "He left… twice. I don't think he came back for me the other night."

"You didn't see the look on his face after you passed out." His chin lowers to rest upon his chest. He stares blankly at his feet.

The sudden need to know more nearly yanks the question from my lips, but I clench my teeth shut at the sight of his hunched shoulders. I frantically struggle to lock Bastien and his piercing gaze back into the hole that I shoved him in months ago to preserve what little life I had left. *He made his choice… and so have I.*

"He is where he belongs." I clench my fingers into my palm so tightly that I can feel my skin begin to protest. I speak quickly so I don't have time to dwell on my words. "I am meant to be here, with you."

"But you still think about him…" He presses, his eyes wide with a fervent pleading for me to deny it, but I can't. He would know it's a lie, yet he still longs to be comforted by it. To wrap up inside my lie and hide just for a while longer.

"I think of him," I admit softly, letting my hand fall away into my lap. I unclench my fist and find red crescents punctured into my palm. "More so now that you have dumped me."

Eamon splutters. "I think dumped is a bit of an exaggeration."

He pales at my livid glare. "Do you want me to remind you of how much time you have spent with me off the battlefield in the last month? The last half of the year? I won't need more than one hand to do it!"

I can feel I'm close to crying and I struggle to rein my anger back in. Why do I have to be so emotional all of the time now? Why can't I go back to the way I was before all of this mess landed in my lap? When life was simple and a solid spear and hunting sack slung over my back was enough to clear my head.

I never asked to be drawn in the middle between Eamon and Bastien. In fact, I would rather both of them left me alone in the first place. Then Kyan had to spout off about my stupid destiny and the whole world went into a full tilt, and I was left grappling for something to hold on to.

Bastien thought by leaving me, my life would get easier, but he couldn't have been more wrong. I used to lie awake at night, trying to hate him for walking away, but I knew why he did it. It wasn't because he was weak. No, it was because he was selfish.

He knew what I wanted from him, what I needed, and he wanted the same thing. If he had stayed, I would've freely given up everything for him. I know a part of him would've embraced our love, but he would have known it was wrong.

Fate is a cruel bastard.

I rise slowly and head toward the far wall, sinking down onto the wide seat that perches just below the window. I like to sit here in the early morning, before Thalar wakes and the noise drowns out the call of the birds or the splashing of water in the fountain square. It is the only time I can almost trick myself into thinking I am in the forest again.

Eamon rises, shuffling his feet as he comes to stand behind me. He reaches down and clasps my shoulder as he settles onto the bench, speaking so softly I struggle to capture the words. "I'm sorry."

I close my eyes, wishing more than anything he had said this before. "Sorry isn't good enough anymore."

I lean forward and press my forehead against the windowpane. A small circle of fog puffs to life near my mouth. Two smaller ones appear and fade with each breath that passes through my nose.

"I've been hard to live with. I'll admit that." His hand shifts to brush thick strands of hair off my shoulder. My skin tingles under his touch. It has been far too long since he touched me like this. "I guess I didn't really know how to deal with all of this."

"And you think I did?" I turn to face him, realizing just how close he's sitting to me. My shoulder presses against his chest as I shift around. Our knees brush against one another. "I've been so lonely without you."

He offers me a rueful smile as his hand falls upon my arm. "I guess I haven't been the best boyfriend, huh?"

"Or a good friend."

He winces at that jab. "You're right and I'm sorry."

"You already said that."

"And I mean it." He stares at me, his gaze sweeping over my face as if memorizing my features for the first time. He hasn't looked at me with such unveiled longing in nearly a year. My stomach clenches as he pauses over my lips.

"This changes nothing," I whisper, wondering if I really believe those words. If it were true, why do I have a yearning beginning to grow within me? I want to be touched, to be reminded that the world is not crowded only with sorrow and disappointment. The past year has been filled with nothing but darkness. I long for a hint of light, even if only for a moment.

"You have to stop saying good-bye to me before I've

even left. I've been here, waiting. You just needed to wake up and realize that."

"And Bastien?"

I growl and shove his hand away. "He has nothing to do with this. He's not in my life anymore."

His gaze darts away. "Do you hate me?"

"Hate you?" I gasp, taken aback. "How could I ever do that?

He leans his head back against the wall, staring blankly up at the ceiling. "I always wondered if you wish you'd chosen Bastien instead of me. If you felt trapped by your decision."

So that was the root of all of this. I should have known he couldn't let his own insecurity go. It wasn't losing me to my destiny that he feared most, but that he'd never had me in the first place.

I cup his face with my hand, forcing myself not to notice the difference between the softness of his cheeks compared to the rugged stubble of Bastien's. "If I still wanted Bastien, I wouldn't be here now, fighting for us. I love you, Eamon, despite your bull-headed, annoying, overbearing tendencies."

"I know," he murmurs as a single tear slips from the corner of his eye. I watch as it trails down his cheek and falls onto my wrist. I can't remember the last time I saw him cry.

"I don't think you do." I shift closer, tucking my leg in so I'm mere inches from him. I stare into his anguished eyes, seeing the guilt and poisonous doubts he has clung to for far too long. I trace my hand along the contours of his face, searching for the boy within that I know would sacrifice anything to make me happy. "I love you."

His nostrils flare and his heartbeat pulsates against his throat. He reaches out his hand, tentatively cupping my neck as he lowers his lips, softly brushing against the corner of my mouth. I lean into him, encouraging him not to pull back as he has done more times in the past few months than I care to remember.

His touch is feather soft as he trails his lips over my

check, nuzzling my ear. His fingers flex against my neck and I know he's trying to resist drawing me closer. I rise, lifting one leg over him before I sink down into his lap.

His eyes are wide and searching as I lean in and press my lips against his, burying my hands into the curls that sweep over his ears. My grip is firm, insistent. His hands fall about my waist, gripping my sides to match my intensity.

His hands feel warm against the bare skin exposed along my lower spine, the sash about my waist loosened to reveal my tank top and shorts beneath. His hands slowly work their way up my back to immerse in my glossy raven strands, tugging gently.

I still miss my golden hair, the way the sun would glint off the brighter highlights in the summer, but I've accepted this change as readily as I've accepted my expanding powers. One look in the mirror reveals how far I've come and how little I still know about myself.

My head lolls to the side as Eamon's lips drift toward my ear. His breath gives birth to a thousand goose bumps as he whispers into my neck, "I've missed you."

Warmth creeps back into my heart, slowly radiating out. Eamon's touch is gentle, exploring, yet hesitant as he waits for me to give him permission. His lips trail to the hollow of my neck and I hear him sigh. "I've missed you too."

I enjoy the rapid beat of his heart under my palms as I press my hand to his neck, letting his lips explore the line of my jaw. He flinches as my other hand dips under the hem of his black uniform and traces the fine contours of his chest. A breathy groan escapes as he crushes his lips against mine.

My fingers trail north to explore the cut of his chest, marveling over how much he has changed. A year ago, he was still a boy coming to know a new body. Now he owns it. Too bad it's hidden beneath his Caldonian uniform.

As I run my finger in a straight line down his breastbone, Eamon snatches my hand just before I reach his belly button and pulls away. "What's wrong?" I try not to let the pain of his rejection show.

Eamon's chest rises and falls rapidly as he withdraws my hand from under his shirt and clasps both against his abdomen. "I'm trying really hard to control myself right now and here you sit like a temptress, taunting me mercilessly."

"Is that so wrong?"

"No," he groans but gently pushes back on me until I surrender and rise to my feet. "I just feel like I'm taking advantage of you. Five minutes ago you were ready to lop my head off, and for good reason, but this just feels… wrong."

I scrunch up my nose, wishing more than anything the just and fair side of Eamon had remained locked away for a little longer. I needed to feel wanted again. Not in a hormone-induced haze, but as he used to love me, pure and true. "I guess you are right."

Even though he was the one who pushed away first, I can see that my agreement hits him hard. "I should probably get back."

"Sure," I nod, clasping my arms around myself and desperately trying not to think about how the cold has begun to seep back into my heart. "Kyan needs you."

Eamon steps toward me, his hand outstretched, but it falls away, as if he thinks better of risking another touch. "He needs you too. He's just worried. We all are."

"I know." I sigh and sink down onto the edge of my bed as he offers me a halfhearted smile and closes the door behind him. "That's the story of my life," I whisper to the empty room.

Five

By the time Kyan finally calls for me, I'm beyond ticked, and he knows it. That's why he sends Zahra to fetch me instead. She arrives at my door with her silky blond hair draped over one shoulder in a braid, a stark contrast to the high collar of her black uniform. There is a shimmer of color just over her eyes, a mixture of silver, gold, and bronze. Her full lips are glossed, with a hint of rose added to them. I don't have to lean in to smell the floral scent that wafts from the hollow of her neck and wrists.

No doubt a gift from Kyan. He does so love to spoil her. Not that Zahra ever complains. She lives to be treated like a princess.

A year ago, Zahra and I were cordially cool with each other… some of the time. At others, it was sheer open hostility, but things change. I lean against the doorframe of my quarters with a rueful grin on my face. "I knew he'd send you to do his dirty work."

Zahra's slender shoulders rise and fall with an indifferent shrug that is almost believable. "He thought a pretty face might help soothe the savage beast."

My lip curls into a smirk. "And he sent you?" I shake my head, tsking. I half anticipate a sharp retort from her, but instead, I'm amazed to see a smile spread along her lips. I arch an eyebrow in surprise and she laughs.

"Oh, come on. I'm not *that* bad." I snort loudly as she bumps her hip against mine, laughing. "Okay, maybe I used to be, but I'm not the same girl anymore."

"So I see." I look her over and realize how obvious the change really has become. When she first met Kyan, there was a sense of dumbstruck awe in her eyes. Now that has been replaced with the same deep contentment I see each day when Aminah is near Toren. That look of rightness, of finally having found their other half.

I lower my gaze and try to stomp down my jealousy, but it's hard. I'm happy for my friends, truly I am, but it is difficult to be torn so completely in half when they're all whole.

Zahra's hand falls upon my arm. I look up, surprised. "I wanted to say I'm sorry."

"For what?" I'm pretty sure I've never heard her use those exact words before. Certainly never with me.

She shifts her weight and bites on her lower lip, as if unsure if she should say anything. "We all know how hard this past year has been for you, and even though you don't think it, I do kinda like you."

"Huh." I purse my lips and tilt my head to the side, confused.

She laughs and swats at my arm. "I'm trying to be serious here."

"I know. That's what's freaking me out."

Zahra shakes her head and removes her hand from my arm. Although her touch isn't bad, per se, it is odd. What has gotten into her?

"Look, I just want to say that I know how hard it's been since Bastien left. And then with everything going on with Eamon…"

I flinch. "How do you know about that?"

Zahra rolls her eyes as if it's the most obvious answer on the planet. "Everyone knows, Illyria. He's the easiest guy in the world to read and you're… moodier than normal."

"Gee. Thanks." I step back and lean against the wall. "If this is meant to be a pep talk, it's really starting to take a dive in the wrong direction."

"I'm just saying you aren't alone, okay." I find Zahra's mounting discomposure to be oddly comforting.

I swat at a fly buzzing through the room, wishing more than once today that I had something other than a shoe to swat at it. I nearly grabbed one of Aminah's dusty books but thought better of it. She'd probably be hurt if she ever turned it over to find insect guts plastered to the cover.

"Thanks… I think." If someone had told me this morning that I'd be having this heart-to-heart moment with Zahra, I would've told them where to shove their lies, but here it is, and I honestly don't have any clue how to react.

Zahra clears her throat and winds her arm through mine, drawing me out into the hallway. I can't help but notice how the two guards, who hardly look old enough to be shaving, straighten as she smiles at them. *Oh, please!*

Her heels clack against the polished floor as we pass by closed doors on either side of us. The rooms are vacant, per Kyan's orders, and not just during my two-week imprisonment. Permanently. Aminah's boyfriend Toren went to great lengths to remind Kyan of what I'm capable of when I'm high on emotions. I guess he thought giving Eamon and me some space to explore would be a good thing. That, of course, never happened.

The entire three-story building is all mine. When I first moved in, I would wander the empty halls at night. Aminah was worried about the effect this would have on me, but I was too lost to my own Bastien-induced fog that I found the stillness of the building comforting. Once I came out of that comma, I began to realize just how painfully alone I really was.

Kyan and Zahra took up residence in the Shard, one level below the command center, so Kyan could be found at a moment's notice. Zahra was thrilled to literally be the focal point of the entire city. Aminah and Toren took up more humble accommodations in a newly renovated two-story brownstone several streets over. There has been talk of a wedding, but I don't think anyone really needs an official announcement to declare their bond.

Eamon's quarters are farther away, situated in the eastern quadrant of the city. He has been crucial in overseeing much of the repair work in that area and felt the need to be close by. What that translated into was that he needed space away from me.

"So what's up?" I ask as we pass the tenth locked door. "I've been rotting away in that room for nearly two weeks now and Kyan suddenly decides I'm no longer grounded?"

Zahra's eyes twinkle with mischief as she releases my arm and pushes open the steel door at the end of the long hallway. This building used to contain many one and two-bedroom apartments. Families lived here. Children no doubt took full use of the rusted heap of metal in the yard behind the building that once housed a swing set. The grass is overgrown now, nearly shielding the playground from sight. This empty lot isn't exactly on the top of the repair list, but someday I hope it will be restored to its former glory.

As I raise my hand to shield my eyes from the brilliant sunlight, I can't help but wonder if children will ever play here again. The kids we took care of in the caves have all been placed with couples around Thalar, adopted into loving families who weren't able to start ones of their own because of the war. I see some of them from time to time, but not nearly as much as I would like to.

I never was very good with kids, but sometimes, in the darkest hours of the night, I miss hearing their whispers when they thought everyone else was asleep. There was something so wonderful about their innocence.

"Earth to Illyria." Zahra breaks through my trance.

"Sorry." I jog to catch up with her. She waits for me on the corner of my street, stray wisps of hair unsettled in the breeze.

It's getting colder. Already I can feel the sun's warmth radiating up from the concrete beneath my boots. I know that snow is on the air. Soon winter will unleash on us.

I'm suddenly gripped with a need to return to the forest and watch as the animals scurry about the trees in last-minute winter preparations. To see the flowers begin to wither and fade into the cracks between the rocks that dot the rugged landscape. Watch the geese take flight as they begin their migration south.

I sigh, knowing I'll never be allowed to go back. Not on my own at least. Eamon and Kyan are far too protective to allow that.

"Man, you really are out of it today."

I blink, realizing I've done it again. "Sorry.

Involuntary solitude messed with my mind, I guess."

Zahra laughs. "Well, I thought you were taking all of this rather calmly."

"Taking all of what calmly?" I frown, grabbing her arm to pull her back.

She obliges and raises her free hand to point to the towering building before us. It rises like a spear of reflective glass from the center of town, casting rainbows of color along the sidewalk. The Shard never fails to take away my breath. I can only imagine what it must have looked like in its prime before the Caldonians arrived.

"About your mission of course," she says. My grip on her arm tightens as I step forward. Her smile widens as she leans in to whisper, "They found Drakon's main base."

Elevators make me nervous. I prefer taking the stairs, but Zahra flat refused, pointing to the three-inch heels she has stuffed her feet into. I begrudgingly agree to enter the "box of death" but only because I'm anxious to hear what my mission is.

Did Eamon know? If so, how could he have kept this from me? Even as the thought trickles through my mind, a sense of unease falls over me. I know why. He has probably spent the past week trying to talk Kyan out of it.

I grip the walls as the elevator rattles, rising far higher off the ground than I'm comfortable thinking about. I watch the floor numbers light up, silently pleading with it to hurry. A sheen of sweat appears on my brow and I wipe it away with the back of my hand. Zahra gives me a knowing glance but resumes her humming.

I've been told that music used to play in elevators, that it was soothing to the ear. I doubt that very much. How on earth could music be heard over the twanging of cables and rattling of gears?

With a high-pitched ding, the elevator shudders to a halt and the doors disappear into the walls, revealing a finely decorated waiting room. I blow out an uneasy breath as I step off the elevator and into the past. I've avoided coming to this floor for one very crucial reason: I'm not ready to face my memories.

Why did Kyan have to choose this location as command central?

The decor is much the same as I remember. The worn white carpet remains, but the bloody footprints I tracked through the last time I was here are gone. The cracked leather couches that once formed a semicircle have been replaced with plush fabric high-back chairs that line the exterior walls.

The framed pictures along the walls have been replaced by paintings with skillful brush strokes. Some are large and rectangular, spanning the length of an entire wall, while others are small and clustered together.

I pause beside one to admire its unusual beauty. This particular image is of a beach, its sandy shore the purest white I've ever seen. Waves travel high into the dunes of the cove. I lean in closer, squinting in attempt to decipher if the waves really are lavender or if the twilight that has fallen over the beach scene gives the water that rich color. I'm startled to realize that in the mists that rise from the lapping waves, I can see shapes in the star-strewn sky—rounded distant planets.

"It's Calisted."

I turn at the sound of a deeper voice and instantly feel my ire rising. "Kyan." I dip my head with a stiff sign of respect.

He wraps his arm around Zahra's waist, pressing a kiss against the crown of her head, but his eyes never leave mine. He pats her side gently and she smiles, casting one last look over her shoulder toward me, and then reenters the elevator.

Kyan waits until the double doors slide shut before he approaches. "Every one of these images depicts my favorite places to visit on Calisted. This one is a beach not far from the cliffs that lead to Calahorra, the City of the King."

"Where Aloysius lives?" *My future husband*, I think but can't bring myself to say.

"Yes." I turn to look at him. He has aged since the attack on Drakon's hideout. I can see it in in the pinched skin at the corners of his eyes and the frown lines that trace along his brow. The warm tone of his skin has begun to face. There is a distinct bagginess around his stomach where his uniform used to fit snuggly.

"You look awful."

Kyan laughs, nodding wearily. "I've felt better."

I open my mouth to say the same thing, but something in his eye holds back my anger. There is a hollowness about him that I've never seen before.

"You found him?" is all I say. We both know exactly whom it is I'm speaking of.

"Yes." He turns and motions for me to follow him into the command center.

It hardly resembles the pompous decor that Commander Drakon had used for his office. Gone is the enormous mahogany desk, replaced with table upon table of maps, each one dotted with the location of our troops. The circular room feels smaller now that it is filled with rows of bulky furniture and black-clad men stooped over stacks of paperwork.

The windows have been replaced since I shattered them all the last time I was here. The bookcases have been swept clean of Drakon's trinkets and filled to overflowing with books that Kyan no doubt feels are vital to our mission.

There is a buzz in the room as I enter, a charge that instantly grips me as Kyan closes the door behind us. Excitement. Apprehension. Elation.

I'm easily swept away by it as I approach the center of the room. Kyan grasps my arm just above my elbow and steers me toward a table with a wide map spread along its surface, the corners curling slightly from use. Two other men converse in low tones as I reach the table.

Toren looks up first and stiffens. His smile is genuine but plagued with tension as Eamon raises his gaze to meet mine. I instantly know I was right about my earlier assessment. He did try to stop this from happening. A jolt of bitterness seals away any welcome that I might've considered as I turn to face Kyan with only a nod in Toren's direction. "What is my mission?"

He casts an uneasy glance toward my friends before pointing to a location on the map. It's circled in black, a larger circle than I'm used to seeing. *How big is that place?*

"This is the location of Drakon's base. It was previously unknown to us, but our scouts in the field have confirmed that it's not only an operational base, but it's also the central command for all of Drakon's operatives in the Midwest quadrant."

I place my hands on the edge of the table and lean over the map. The base is ideally located among dense woodland. "I suspect that even if we could fly one of our Hover Wings over it, the intel would be spotty at best, correct?"

Color flees from Eamon's hands as he suddenly grips the table. I glance over at him, confused. "Our *Sky Ships*," Toren says, placing emphasis on the name, "have not been able to infiltrate that area successfully."

It takes me a moment to catch on to my slip, but the instant I do, the contents of my stomach turn to a churning ball of acid. Bastien used to say Hover Wings. I never did. *Dang it. Smooth, Illyria. Real smooth.*

I choose to plod on ahead and ignore Eamon's anger. "Why not?"

"Because none of them ever make it back to base," Kyan speaks up.

I turn to look at him, startled by the tension in his voice. "None of them?"

He shakes his head, his mouth set in a grim line. "We lost four ships already. I refuse to send any more."

I push off the table and cross my arms over my chest. It doesn't make sense. What sort of place can have such extensive amounts of firepower? None that we have encountered so far have even come close to being that well stocked. "What does this place run?"

"Everything," Eamon replies.

I stare at him with a mixture of horror and annoyance and then finally turn away, shaking my head as I try to gather my thoughts as they tumble through my mind at accelerating speeds. "How could we not have known about this, Kyan? This is huge!"

"We know," he responds. I can hear the clipped tone in his voice and feel slightly mollified. He was just as much in the dark as the rest of us. At least I can be thankful for that. "But now that we know of its location, it won't be long before they strip it down and move everything again."

"So then what's the plan?" I plant my hands upon my hips and take in a calming breath. If I stop to think of how close we came to Drakon and let him slip through my fingers, I'll begin ranting, and it's not fair to any of the men in the room. They all fought alongside me; their friends shed blood just as mine did. No one in this room is at fault, yet I feel as if the weight of this revelation falls heavily upon my shoulders.

I'm the one everyone looks to for leadership and I failed them. I should've known, should've seen it somehow. Maybe if I hadn't been so weak in dealing with my personal life I would have.

"We're going to take it," Toren says in a tight-laced, no-nonsense kind of voice.

I glance over at him and see a hint of the boy I grew up with. Toren was always a natural-born leader. We all saw it and respected him for it. He did his best to guide us as we lived in the caves after the last of the parents did, but when the Caldonians fell into our laps, he knew he was out of his league. Since the day we entered Kyan's camp, Toren began relinquishing that leadership to him.

I'm sure it wasn't easy for him in the beginning. No trueborn leader likes to step aside and take orders, but Kyan has proven himself to be someone worthy of our trust. Looking at Toren now, I see no hint of wounded pride or desire to reclaim power. I see a man filled with blind belief in a cause. Our cause.

I smile at him. I've seen very little of him over the past few months. We seem to always be going in opposite directions—him to fight with the southern regions and me with the plains. It is good to see him again. "How many men am I taking?"

"This isn't your mission to lead." Eamon protests

loudly enough to capture the attention of several soldiers nearby. He doesn't seem to notice the disruption, but Kyan does.

He motions for us to all follow him back outside. Once the doors are closed firmly behind him, he turns on Eamon. "Your reservations on this mission have been noted countless times this past week, Eamon, but I will remind you that this is my command and I will not accept disobedience in front of my men." I blink, shocked at the stern, lashing tone in Kyan's voice. Apparently I'm not the only one frustrated at the moment.

Eamon's neck reddens as he looks from Kyan and then back to me. A vein pulses down the center of his forehead, peeking out through his mass of curls. Was it really only a week ago that we put aside our differences for a few precious moments to embrace? There is no part of him now that I recognize, beyond the pain and fear that sharpens his features into a grimace. "This will end badly and you both know it."

"Illyria is capable of handling herself," Kyan says with no small amount of restraint. His hands clasp at his sides, tightly enough to whiten his knuckles. "She has proven that time and time again."

"She nearly died!" His shout echoes around the deserted room.

I open my mouth to protest, but Toren holds up a hand to stop me. "This will get us nowhere. Time is short and we must focus on the task at hand." He turns his back on Eamon and faces me after getting a nod of agreement from Kyan. "The plan is simple. You will be part of a small team that will infiltrate the base. We have planted some of our people within their ranks who will make sure you are able to get in and out without any trouble. As Eamon so eloquently pointed out, this is not technically your mission. However, your role is vital."

"Bag Drakon and bring him back. Got it." I nod.

"No." Toren shakes his head. Waves of walnut hair fall over his forehead and he sweeps them to the side. He has let his hair grow out. I pause only a second to wonder if he's trying to grow into his adulthood or if Aminah secretly prefers longer hair. "You're not going for Drakon. By now he is probably long gone. We want you to retrieve a ship."

"A ship?" I repeat out loud, just to be sure I heard him correctly. When he doesn't deny the claim, I laugh. "Oh sure, no problem. Do you want me to just back up a truck and haul it all the way home?"

"No," Kyan says, stepping forward. "We're sending someone with you to pilot it back."

My hands drop to my sides as I shake my head. "There's no way we can get past their perimeter without being seen. We'll be shot on sight."

"That is why you'll be invisible when you leave." Kyan smiles.

Six

I can hear him calling my name as I round the corner of my street, but I don't turn back. Whatever Eamon has to say to me will only make me angry, and right now I'm too stunned to think of anything else.

Kyan wants me to waltz into the largest enemy base that we've come across, steal a ship, and magically make it disappear. Poof. *He is insane!*

"Illyria, stop!"

"What?" I growl, rounding on him. His eyes widen with surprise as he slams into me, knocking me backward onto the ground. My teeth pierce my lower lip as my tailbone slams to the concrete.

"I didn't think you would actually stop," he says as he holds out a hand to assist me.

I grip it with enough force to crimp a couple bones, muttering a long string of curses as I release his hand and brush myself off. My backside throbs painfully as I shift my weight, trying to hide my discomfort. "What do you want?"

"We need to talk." I roll my eyes and turn to walk away. He follows close on my heels. "I'm serious. This isn't going to end well."

"Why?" I jerk to a halt and turn on him. He nearly bowls me over a second time, but I shove out my hand and push him back. He teeters on his toes before rocking back onto his heels. "Because you wasted time looking into the future again? What can't you just leave it alone?"

"Because I can't," he spits back. Anger disfigures his handsome face, drawing his eyebrows into a deep V. "I can't stop looking because I need to protect you!"

I step back, shocked at the vehemence in his tone. His chest puffs with anger as he turns and slams his fist into the brick wall. To his credit, he hardly makes a sound as his knuckles shatter. Blood trickles down toward his palm.

I sigh and pull his hand into my own. A ripple of warmth floods down my arm and a golden glow spirals over his hand. A moment later, I step back, all hint of injury vanished. "Was that really necessary?"

"No," he mutters, clutching his hand to his stomach, "but it felt like the only thing I could control."

I lower my gaze and breathe out a weighted breath. "I really don't want to do this again with you, Eamon. I'm tired of hurting, of being alone, of feeling like you're always looking too far beyond me to even see me standing right here in front of you."

He steps forward and grips my upper arms. His grasp isn't painful, but it is firm, demanding. "I know where this leads, Illyria. If you go, you won't be coming back."

"You don't know that," I whisper.

"I do."

"How?" I look up into his ice-blue eyes for some hint of the man I love. Only deep, profound sadness looks back at me. "You told me my future is veiled from you."

His grip tightens as he draws me close enough for me to feel his heart pounding in his chest. "I don't need to see the future to know. I can feel it in my gut."

"Well, your gut isn't my commanding officer, Eamon." I push back from him, nearly losing my resolve as he crumples before me, as if a great weight presses down upon him. "I'm sorry, but I have to go pack. Carleon will be by to get me soon."

I glance at him one last time and turn my back. I keep my head held high as I walk away, each step resonating loudly in my ears. He doesn't call out for me, but I can feel him watching, silently begging. I can't listen. Not when there is no point staying.

I swat at a swarm of mosquitoes that seem to have a rather large appetite for my blood. They've hovered about my head for the past couple of hours, dive-bombing the instant I stop swatting to give my weary arm a break.

Shouldn't these things be dead by now?

When I first heard about this assignment, I was thrilled most about being back in the woods. Kyan told me to pack light but to prep for a hike. That means trees, fresh air, and a campfire. Pure bliss. At least it would have been if Kyan had been a bit more forthcoming as to whom my companions would be on this little trek.

I march at the back of the group, fuming in silence. *How could Kyan not tell me that Eamon was leading this group?*

I should've known there was a catch. It was probably the only way Eamon even considered agreeing to let me go. One thing continues to nag at me as we wind our way down the side of the mountain, keeping to a steady pace.

Eamon hasn't been trained to fly a Sky Ship. Nor have any of the other men in our group. Quickening my pace, I whistle softly and Carleon hangs back. "What's up?"

"You want to tell me what I don't know?"

Carleon attempts to keep a straight face as he shakes his head. He shoves a branch out of his face, nearly letting it swing back to smack me up the side of my head, but he catches it at the last second. "Why do you always try to get me in trouble?" he hisses as he rises onto his toes to see Eamon storming through the woods at a clipped pace.

Everyone is struggling to keep up with his grueling speed, but no one complains. Not loud enough for him to hear, at least. It is thick in here. The brambles sprout angry-looking thorns the size of my thumb and errant tree roots appear out of nowhere to trip you when you least expect it, rising from the newly fallen snow.

"Just spill it. You know I won't tell anyone who told me." I adjust the straps of my pack against my back. Its weight is draining on me, rubbing my shirt against my stomach. It rises a few inches over my head and straps about my waist, brown to match the barren trees. I have everything I need to survive for at least a week on my own. A tent to pitch for inclement weather, three changes of clothes, a sack of food and pots to cook with, a few hunting knives that I'd sorely like to use on Drakon as target practice, and a comm unit to signal for help. Everything else the forest can provide.

"Oh, come on, they all know how close we are. It wouldn't take a genius to figure out who told you."

I grin over at him and reach out to ruffle his hair. "I wonder if Anwen knows that sometimes you suck your thumb at night while you sleep."

His ears flame on cue, and I chuckle, deeply pleased to be able to throw out that tidbit of blackmail at the perfect moment. I've been holding on to it for a while. "That's below the belt, using my girl against me."

"All is fair in love and secrets." I grin.

Carleon motions for us to slow just a bit to add more distance between us and the rest of the group. I don't really know the other men in our team, only by name and reputation. "Eamon is escorting you to a pick-up point. That's all I know, I swear."

"And the others? You?"

"We're just your hot bodyguards." He beams and ducks to miss my wild swing. He prances away, grinning from ear to ear. I shake my head, laughing at his antics.

Anwen is a lucky girl, I muse as I grip the edges of my pack and plod forward in silence.

Not long after the last glint of the Shard is concealed from sight by the dense timberland, night begins to fall. Weariness from disuse settles into my muscles, and I begin to fuel myself with the anger I've held on to for the past three weeks. Before my injury, I was in peak form. Now I find my breathing labored and my back screaming in protest of the long hike.

As the stars begin to dot the partially clouded sky overhead, I realize what the other men must have already known. We aren't stopping to rest.

There are no lanterns to light our path as we weave through the brush, our pants snagging on unseen bramble patches. Only the dim green glow of laser guns, pointed to the ground, reveal the location of my team up ahead.

The walk is treacherous as we begin our descent into the foothills. The ground is moist and easily unsettled with a wrong step. I take a knee several times before releasing the first of many curses for the night. The full moon hangs high, swollen in the sky, but the dappled light that manages to peek through the canopy is hardly helpful.

Carleon hangs back from the group, halfway between me and the rest. My pace is slowing; I can feel it with each shaking step that I take. *I knew I should've eaten something before we left*, I silently berate.

But it isn't completely my fault. Eamon made the decision not to stop either. Surely I'm not the only one among us that's starting to feel drained.

We march long into the night, attempting to cover as much ground on the first day as possible. I wish I knew exactly where the extraction point was meant to be. The only thing I can tell by the flight of the moon is that we're heading steadily due south.

Eamon pushes us hard, stopping only long enough to fill our canteens from a gushing spring before pressing on once more. No one speaks. The only sound that rises above the rustling of the forest is the breath that expels from our abused lungs.

He leads with unfaltering steps, as if there were a line carved through the woods that only he can see. None of us question him. We just follow and attempt to keep up.

By the time the moon begins to sink toward the horizon, my legs are on fire and my back hunched painfully. It'll be a miracle if I'm able to walk straight tomorrow.

As the first drops of color begin to spread along the eastern sky, Eamon raises his hand for us to halt. "We'll set up camp here. I need three men to collect firewood. The rest of you start setting up tents. I want dinner done before dawn."

I sink ungracefully to the ground, feeling as if every muscle in my body has mutinied. Blisters along my heels have long since popped, leaving my socks plastered to my feet. I groan as I slip out of my pack and lean back, breathing heavily.

A shadow rises over me and I open my eyes. "I know.

I'll grab wood," I groan as I begin to rise, but Eamon kneels beside me and pushes me back.

"Rest. The men can take care of it."

Resentment instantly flares to life. "I'm capable of doing my part."

"I'm well aware of that," he says curtly, drawing his hand back from my shoulder. "But I can't have you worn out. This mission will only succeed if you're in top form."

I want to protest, to stand upon my given rights as a soldier to do my part, but even as the words try to form, I feel drowsiness beginning to tug me down. "Fine," I mumble as the first yawn takes me by surprise. "But I'm helping tear down."

I don't actually know how I ended up inside my tent. I suspect Carleon had something to do with it, judging by the care with which I was tucked into my blanket. He even gave me his pillow.

I really am lucky to have a guy like him in my life, I muse as I pull back the flaps of the canvas tent. Ever since I first met him on the rooftop during the siege, and entrusted him with protecting Bastien while I went off to save Kyan, we've been close friends. He's almost like the brother I never had. We bicker, spat, and make up all within a heartbeat.

If not for his friendship, I'm not sure I would've made it through the past year.

Eamon has always watched our banter with open jealously, but I've never apologized for it. There will never be anything between Carleon and me, but he did help replace the hole that Eamon left behind when he leaped out of the friendship realm and into the turbulent waters of dating. If he were honest, I'm sure Eamon is jealous because of that reason mostly.

Things used to be effortless between us. We knew each other's thoughts without having to voice them. We would spend hours lying together on a hill to count the stars. Usually one of us would fall asleep and wake the next morning layered in snow or dew.

It has been far too long since Eamon and I had that sort of a relationship.

As I emerge from the tent, I realize Carleon has posted himself just outside, his mouth gaped wide in an almighty snore. I smile ruefully down at him as I nudge him with my shoe. "Wakey, wakey, princess."

"Go away." Gripping the edge of his blanket, he rolls over and finds himself face down in snow. He coughs and splutters, then slowly rises, swiping flakes from his face. "I was having a good dream, thank you very much."

"I can tell by the drool trailing down your chin."

"What?" His eyes widen in surprise as he wipes at his chin.

He glares up at me as I laugh. "Why is it always so easy to get you, Carleon?"

He scowls and runs his hands through his unruly locks. I love the way the fading light dims the auburn highlights in his usually black hair. His eyes are dark, like a pool of water on a moonless night, but there's always life dancing in them.

"See if I give you my pillow tomorrow," he grumbles and snatches his blanket off the ground, shaking it before he begins to roll it into a tight bundle.

"Thanks for that, by the way. I think I slept like the dead." I attempt to comb my fingers through my hair but instantly give up, deciding to wind my tangled mess into a ponytail at the back of my head instead. I've learned to bring a lot string with me for this reason. It's a mystery how I used to live in the woods and managed to avoid tangles for the most part. Maybe city living has softened me more than I thought.

"Glad you did. I couldn't sleep a wink with Bodhi sawing logs all day." He scratches at his chin and I can hear the beginnings of a new day's growth under his nails.

It's still weird to me that Carleon can shave. He has changed so much in the past year. When I first met him, he looked like a boy, although his eyes betrayed wisdom that only comes with age. I liked him instantly, reminding him that war doesn't care how old you are. But now, looking at him as he rummages through his pack, I realize he isn't the only one who has changed.

We all have. I guess that comes naturally with age, but I can't remember there ever being a harder fought year. My childhood was spent hunting and scavenging for food to feed our people. There was never enough and most nights I went to bed with a hole still in my stomach, but even then, life had been easy in comparison.

I turn and drop to a knee as I begin tearing down my tent, lost in thought. I do that a lot these days, reminisce. Aminah tells me it's my way of avoiding the present, but I think it's actually just the opposite. I'm trying to make sure I remember the past so when my future arrives, I won't forget everything.

Kyan and I have spoken in length about my destiny. It isn't pretty.

Someday soon, I'll be brought before King Aloysius. It's unclear if this will be by choice or not, but I'm sorta leaning toward the latter because I'm not exactly keen on the idea of just turning myself over. Aloysius is a man of great power. He controls minds, bending people's wills to his own. Drakon possesses similar abilities, but not quite on the same level of grandeur.

When I first heard of Aloysius's desire to claim me as his own, I felt numb first and angered later. That anger hasn't helped convince me that submitting myself to the king's mind games is the best plan. Kyan says it is my destiny. Marry Aloysius, assume the throne, and then overthrow his rule. The only kicker is that he doesn't have an accurate timeline on when all of that is supposed to happen.

As I reach for the final peg holding my tent down, I shudder at the thought of that vile man touching me. I'll no longer be in control of my actions, a mere puppet to be played with at will. How can anyone accept such a fate?

"You all right?"

I look up to see Carleon hovering anxiously over me. His pack is made and I'm shocked to see that he has a plate of steaming venison held out to me. "You've been zoned out for a while. Everyone is almost ready to go and you're still messing with your tent."

Normally I would laugh at his chiding tone, but I'm still in a bit of a daze. How did I lose so much time?

"Here, I'll finish up while you eat." He glances back over his shoulder at Eamon deep in conversation with two men. One of them is Arlo, a dark-skinned, rigid man with eyes the color of a fierce sunset. The other is Kohen. Although his is a bit stouter than Arlo, he is no less fearsome. A vine of crosses rest across the back of his hand, weaving up into the sleeve of his shirt. He collects one for every enemy he kills. As morbid as this may be, I have to admire the man's death count. He's the sort of guy you want on your side in battle.

"What are they talking about?" Carleon's shoulders rise in a shrug. After a pointed glance my way, I sink my teeth into the meat, closing my eyes to savor the robust flavor. My stomach growls obnoxiously. "You slept through dinner so I gave you the biggest piece. I thought Nixon was going to lop off my hand when I reached for it, but Eamon insisted."

"Of course he did," I mutter as the venison turns bland in my mouth. I gnaw on the bite but vow not to touch the rest. I don't want to give the men the satisfaction of thinking me weaker than them. "Do you know where we're heading?"

"South."

"I know that." I chuck my plate at him and he ducks as it whizzes past and clatters against a tree. Eamon looks up, frowning with disapproval at our laughter.

"What's got him all fired up today?" Carleon asks, yanking the ropes tightly over my disassembled tent. If there is one thing my friend excels at it's getting a job done with speed and efficiency. I've often wondered if that was a trait ingrained in him growing up as an only child.

He never really talks about his family and I don't push. All of us that survived the invasion were left as orphans. It wasn't until we met Kyan that we discovered that each of us had parents waiting for us on Calisted. I wonder if anyone waits for Carleon. "Me, I think. He doesn't want me here."

His brow knits with confusion. "But aren't you the key to all of this?"

"Yep." I grunt as I shove my arms through my pack and stand up. I bite back my groan as the familiar weight settles onto my abused muscles. Despite the full day of sleep, my body is no less weary than the night before. "He doesn't see it that way."

I lift my shirt and gingerly run my fingers over my abdomen. A black smear of bruises and raw skin line my waist where the straps rubbed the night before. I've never been forced to rough it quite like this. Usually we move in large groups, camping within only a few miles of our next target. As I lower my shirt, hoping no one saw the damage, I can't help but wonder just how far this march will take us. "Well, he should."

I clip myself into my pack, biting my lip to still the cry of pain that rises in my throat. "Nice to know someone has faith in me."

"Always."

Seven

I welcome the frigid air as our nighttime hike brings us down into the foothills where the ground feels oddly flat. The burning in my ankles from the uneven terrain lessens as we pause for a brief rest. I sink onto a rock, my head drooping low as I suck in great gulps of air.

"How much longer are you going to ignore it?" a voice calls.

I look up, squinting to see a form emerging from the shadows. Most of the men went off in search of a tree to relieve themselves on. I hadn't realized anyone had returned.

"Ignore what, Kohen?"

I don't like this man. His beak-like nose and sharp piercing eyes unnerve me. He has the hands of a hunter, steady and calloused from years spent killing. He moves with the grace and ease of a mountain lion. "You are wounded. I can tell by the way you walk."

"You don't deny it," he says as he perches himself on a partially rotten log that looks like it was felled after a lightning strike.

"Nope. Not really in the mood to talk about it either," I say pointedly as more shadows emerge from the woods.

"Talk about what?" Eamon asks.

I clench my eyes shut, silently damning Kohen for opening his mouth. "He has a rash. Probably didn't want you guys to know about it.

Kohen scowls at me and thrusts up to his feet. I almost think he's going to pass Eamon by in a huff, but he stops and turns back. "She's wounded."

I toss my canteen at him, but it falls short. "Typical," I mutter as I lean my head back against the tree behind me. Its bark is surprisingly smooth against the bare skin of my neck.

"Is this true?" Eamon asks. I can hear twigs snapping underfoot as he approaches.

"So what if it is? You going to play nurse?" I open my eyes to glare up at him but instantly regret it when I see softness has washed away the hard lines of his face. "Sorry."

He nods and kneels down before me, his gaze searching. "Where does it hurt?"

I debate whether or not to show him. A part of me wants to tell him to shove off, that I can easily tough it out, but another wants to believe that Eamon's concern runs deeper than just the impact this might have on the mission. I reach down and slowly lift my shirt, pausing with it just above my bellybutton. Eamon hisses as he stares at the angry redness that now sweeps across my entire waist and around the back. "You should've told me."

"I'm fine."

His gaze hardens and the ice begins to reform in his glance. "Clearly you are not."

Carleon and Arlo emerge from the tree line. Their conversation instantly stalls as they spy Eamon and me. I drop my shirt. "What's going on?"

"Did you know about this, Carleon?"

"Know about what?" He steps forward into the moonlight and I can see his concern pinching the corners of his lips. He looks to me and I shake my head. Eamon sighs heavily and reaches down to yank my shirt up, exposing my abdomen to both of them. A hiss passes Carleon's teeth while Arlo whistles a long, mournful sound. "Looks nasty, boss. What are we going to do with her?"

I bristle. "I'm not an animal that you can just put down."

"Wasn't implying that you were." As he turns to walk away, I can tell that none of us really believe that.

Eamon releases my shirt and rises. "Can you manage her pack, Carleon?"

His furious glare cuts off my protest as my friend nods. "'Course I can. It's not so heavy."

"All the same, I think we need to take it in shifts. An hour each should do it." Eamon lifts his face to the sky. "We only have a few more hours of night left. We need to pick up the pace."

He leaves without a backward glance. As I watch him go, I feel torn by confusion. A huge part of me would love to take the roll of bandages Carleon hands me and stuff it up Eamon's nose, and the other can't stop thinking of the tenderness he'd let slip though for the briefest of moments. I know Eamon still loves me, but sometimes I wonder if it is enough.

I wake to screams, high in pitch and filled with terror. At first I think it's a dream, but shouts begin to rise from around camp and I know I'm awake. Drawing back the flaps of my tent, the biting chill hits me. Eamon, Nixon, and Bodhi are already on the move, lasers charged and in position as they disappear into the woods.

The scream doesn't come again. Carleon comes to stand at my side, his shoulder against mine as I lean into him. "Who was it?"

"Arlo, I think. I didn't see him leave." My lips press into a thin line. Arlo may have been a pain, but he was a good soldier. He didn't deserve this. "What do you think got him? Wolves? Mountain lion?"

We've seen fresh tracks, heard the howls in the distance. From time to time, we see scat piles as we walk with our guns trained on the forest floor, but so far none have come close to camp. They prefer to hunt at night when we are most active.

I glance to the sky and see the sun has already begun to slip beyond the horizon. Night will fall soon. My stomach growls. Carleon glances over at me, but I shake my head. I won't be able to eat until they find Arlo.

We wait together, perched upon a small log just outside the fire ring to keep warm. The winds have begun to pick up again, bringing a chill that sinks deep into my bones. The clouds overhead are thick and hanging low. It won't surprise me if we hike through snow tonight.

Nearly an hour after dark falls, I see movement in the woods. I rise, finger over the trigger of my gun as Eamon emerges. His face is expressionless, but his eyes tell me all that I need to know. "How'd it happen?" I ask.

Eamon stands before the fire, warming his hands. "Slipped on a ridge. Looks like he decided to do some hunting and lost his footing."

Carleon blows out a breath and I look over at him. "What?"

"At least it wasn't a wolf. I hate those things."

Eamon's jaw clenches as he stares at the flames dancing before him within the circle of rocks. "They'll still come. They're drawn to the scent of death."

Carleon looks to me and I nod. "He's right. Once they catch the scent, they'll head this way."

"So we just need to pack up and move on before they get here, right?"

I pat him on the arm. "Trouble is we don't know which direction they're coming from. We might walk right into them."

A clanging of pans captures my attention. I turn to see Bodhi shoving the cooking pots back into his bag. "We don't have time to eat?" Carleon questions, absently rubbing his empty stomach.

I know he must be hungry. He's been sneaking me extra portions along the way, knowing our rations are slim.

Eamon steps back from the fire and meets my gaze head on. "There's no food left. Arlo had it in his pack when he fell. The climb is too steep and treacherous for us to make with the ice clinging to the rocks."

"So what, we're just going to starve?" Carleon snaps.

Eamon starts to speak, but I cut him off, knowing how much he would love to use this accident as a reason to turn right around and head back to Thalar. "No. I have a little bit of meat left in my pack."

"And I have a few root vegetables in mine," Eamon says. "We can make do for a couple of days."

"But will we reach our destination before we run out of food?" Carleon protests. I can feel the concern in his gaze as he looks toward me.

"No," Eamon says.

I step forward and place a hand on Eamon's arm. He flinches but doesn't pull back. "Then we hunt, just like we used to."

I press my fingers against my coat, grimacing at the hunger pangs gnawing through my stomach. I haven't eaten anything in two days. None of us have. Arlo's death has left us with few supplies. Eamon considered turning back several times, most likely would have if I hadn't been able to remind him that this is who we are.

Winter in the mountains brings snow and along with it wolves. These beasts used to be just as much of a threat to our existence as the Caldonians. One took over our planet; the other stole our food source. Starvation, disease, infection—those were our daily enemies before we moved to Thalar.

"Illyria." Eamon's whisper pulls me from my thoughts. His chin juts toward a clump of bushes less than ten feet away. A dirt-encrusted finger hovers over his lips, silencing me. I nod and wait, ignoring the needle pricks spreading along my calves.

I pull a tattered scarf over my mouth to hide the puff of moisture as the temperature continues to plummet. The day's melted snow has already begun to freeze over. Our trek back to the camp will be a treacherous one.

Movement catches my eye. A swatch of brown shifts behind the brambles. A hoof paws nervously at the frozen earth. The young doe senses our presence. *Come on. Just a little farther,* I plead silently.

Eamon raises his hand-whittled spear, no bigger than the length of his arm, a remnant from our past. It was always his favorite, probably because I made it for him. I hadn't realized he still had it.

A piece of glass, bound by fraying bits of twine, juts from the end. Flecks of dried blood remain from a previous kill. He rocks up onto the balls of his feet, biceps coiling as he prepares.

The doe skitters forward, nose to the ground in search of frozen blackberries among the densely arched stems. Its hide stretches taut over its emaciated frame. Tufts of hair have fallen away, giving it a mangy look. There is barely enough meat on it to feed our group, but it'll have to do.

My stomach growls. I bite down on my lip to still its trembling.

I watch Eamon, stunned by his patience. His gaze is steady, riveted on his target. I blink and nearly miss his attack. The spear careens through the air, impaling an inch from the deer's heart. It screams, legs buckling under. A dark stain spreads out into the snow around it. Eamon rises fluidly, without any hint of the agony that assaults my limbs. His lip curls with disgust as he yanks the spear free before landing the lethal blow.

"Well done." I toss him a lopsided grin before staggering to my feet. I wasn't really sure if he still remembered how to do this. City life has softened all of us in ways that I'm not entirely sure are to our benefit. "I'm impressed."

With a scowl that distorts his handsome features, Eamon wrenches the lance from the fallen doe's chest. "It suffered."

My smile fades at the sight of his remorse. I reach out and pull his face away from the cooling carcass. It feels weird to touch him, even as innocently as this, but he doesn't seem to notice. "You can't always be perfect."

"If I'm not, we don't eat," he grinds out. The struggles of the past year have drawn away the mischievous glint that used to reside in his eyes. His smile is a rarity now, like far too many of us. With each day that passes, I watch the weight of Eamon's burdens press upon his shoulders, and I know if I were able, I would still try to take it from him.

He pulls away from me as I hand him my knife and stoops low to remove the organs so the meat doesn't spoil. Blood clings to his hands as he tosses them aside, shiny in the moonlight. Maybe that will keep the wolves off our trail for a while. Already I can hear their howls in the distance. It won't take long before they catch our scent.

Eamon hoists the young deer onto his shoulders, indifferent to the blood that streaks his jacket. Without another word, he stomps away.

Guess we are back to the not speaking to each other phase. Snatching up the forgotten spear and wiping the blood clean from my knife, I fall into step behind him, weaving through the trees. Our path is marked by nature, carved from the earth long before the Caldonians arrived.

One of the first things I learned while living in the wilderness was to use landmarks to plot my way. Today we used a frozen stream we discovered running through a deep crevice. I try not to think of the one we found Arlo lying in the bottom of, neck snapped and legs twisted so far around they were touching his head.

Eamon had tried to shield me from it, but I stared down at his lifeless body and felt numb. His death was senseless and careless. He wasn't meant to be in the woods any more than I belong in a city.

I am a hunter. It runs in my veins. This is my domain, not streets of concrete and glass. "Wait up," I call as Eamon attacks a snowy ridge, leaving me to flounder on my own. It's not like him to be so callous. Distant, yes, but not like this. Something is bothering him. Something more than me.

The soles of his boots punch through a thin layer of ice. The muscles of his back contract as he shifts the weight of his kill. Eamon has always been lean and strong, his body adapted to a rugged life, but now there is a confidence about him that he lacked before. Toren has evolved much like Eamon.

Although I have never been overweight, lack of food making that a near impossibility, I can feel that I've lost some of my muscle mass and added a few extra pounds since moving from the caves. Aminah and Zahra have fared similarly, although they don't keep to rigid training schedules, so it won't be long before the ample amounts of food will start to take its toll.

Sometimes I struggle to recognize us anymore. I can walk right past a friend on the street and not even realize they were there, looking so out of place on city streets. Homesickness strikes me most when I'm out here. That's probably the biggest reason Kyan has kept me from being alone in the woods for long.

Eamon halts at the top of the hill to wait for me. His chest rises and falls with exertion. The grim set of his features betrays the anger simmering just under the surface. I can see it in his eyes, the way his pupils dilate in the moonlight and his lips press into flat lines.

"Are you going to do this the whole way back?" I hold the stitch in my side.

"Do what?" he grunts. His shoulder dips, neck rolling to adjust the weight.

"This pouting thing. I'm used to your cold shoulders, but this is different. What's eating at you?"

Eamon opens his mouth to speak, but a howl cuts him off. My head whips around in the direction of the call. It is close, much too close. "They're tracking us."

He nods and grabs my hand, yanking me behind a thick patch of bush. I strain to hear, listening for rustling of branches or the cracking of ice. It is hard to hear anything over the winds.

The curved dome of latticework branches overhead makes it difficult to see. Small thorns dig into the palms of my hands as I shove the branches open wide enough to pass through. I glance back to see Eamon's indecision in the dim light. "You have to leave the deer."

He shakes his head. "The wolves will get it."

My stomach wars with my mind. Yes, I'm hungry, but it's not worth our lives. With only a hunting knife and spear, we can't hope to fight off an entire wolf pack.

"I shouldn't have let you talk me into leaving the laser guns behind." His jaw clenches, his back teeth grinding as he drops the deer. He presses it up against the base of the tree and works to cover it with leaves. His bare fingers tremble as he claws into the ice, fighting to free large chunks of snow.

A breeze unsettles my hair, whipping it around my cheek. It carries the scent of dog, wet and unclean. "Eamon, now!"

I grab his forearm and yank him toward me. The scent of pine invades my senses as I emerge from the small space. A single howl rises from the valley below. Goosebumps rise along my arms as a resounding chorus quickly joins the hunting cry.

"How far?" I whisper, peering into the night.

"They're close."

As I run, I stare at the dark stain across Eamon's back. Even if they will leave the deer behind, one or all of them will most likely track Eamon too. "Toss away your jacket."

"What?" He calls back over his shoulder. Winds whips at his hair, unsettling his curls into his eyes.

"You've got blood on you. They will smell it." He wiggles out of his jacket, wadding it up as he tosses it to the side. I trample over it, stomping it into the snow before racing behind him.

Evergreens hem us in on both sides as we flee north over the rough terrain. I can barely make out the path before us in the light of the moon. The frozen river must be around here somewhere. How did we get so far off course?

The sound of wolves crashing through the forest chases after us, nipping at our heels. I cling to Eamon's spear, so small and insignificant against the pack. There is little chance we will make it back to camp.

"Can you do something about this?" I hear him shout as my steps falter. My bare hands plunge into the snow as I stop my fall. The cold damp seeps in through my pants.

I try to summon my powers, but it's too hard to concentrate. I toss out my hand behind me and a tree trembles but remains rooted in place. "Apparently not. Where's your radio?"

I push back to my feet and scramble up the hill after him. His breath hangs before him as he pants, holding his side. "It was in my coat."

I peer down from the ridge and can just make out the glint of the stream nearly thirty feet below. If we stick to the ridge, we would run into camp within a half hour, but we don't have that much time. "I have an idea," he says, yanking my arm in the opposite direction.

"But this is heading away from camp." I protest, gasping for breath. The air up here is thinner than I'm used to.

"I know." His feet pound the ground as he attacks a small incline. At the top, I realize the brilliance of his plan. We skirt along a narrow ridge, no wider than Eamon's shoulders. The wolves will be forced into a single file line and might give us a small advantage on the open ground beyond.

Calloused hands reach down to encircle my wrist and Eamon tugs me forward as he hits a clearing. My legs weaken as I struggle to keep up. I'm burning through what little energy I had left after our arduous hike earlier. My lungs constrict, wrenching every drop of oxygen from them.

"I can't do this," I cry out. The pain growing in my side is like a serrated blade jabbing between my ribs.

"You have to. We can't stop now." He shoves me ahead of him, positioning himself between the beasts and me.

The wild howls ricochet off the trees and rocky cliffs behind us. How close are they? I imagine I can feel their breath on the back of my neck and it spurns me on.

The frosty night air lassos around my legs. New blisters along my feet threaten to burst as I slide around in my boots. My coat flaps in the wind, barely offering any resistance against the falling temperatures.

"I see them," Eamon shouts.

My head jerks around to see a large gray wolf emerging from the far tree line at a sprint. Five more wolves, each with varying shades of earthen-toned fur coats, quickly flank it. They'll be on the narrow land bridge in only three bounds. "What do we do?"

"Just run. Don't look back." Eamon's hand presses against my back.

My hair whips around my face as I force my legs to work. The moon shines brightly overhead, illuminating our path. "Almost there," Eamon shouts as the braying intensifies. The wolves have crossed the land bridge. We are running out of time.

I swerve down the steep hill, praying my feet keep up with my momentum. I try to jump when I reach the bottom, but gravity pulls me down.

"Not that way!" Eamon's cry comes too late. The soles of my boots make contact with a large patch of ice and I sprawl to the ground. My arms and legs flail against the ice as I spiral out of reach. The spear disappears into the shadows. My stomach lurches as the world hurtles around me.

I know what is coming even before my feet slide over the edge of the cliff. A waterfall of snow cascades past me, falling to the depths of the ravine. My hands bury into the snow and grasp the exposed roots of a tree growing up from the cliff face.

Pain spikes through my shoulder as I slam to a halt. My legs smash into the dirt wall; debris rains down onto my face. I clamp my eyes shut and will my frozen fingers to hold fast.

"Hang on. I'm coming for you," Eamon shouts. I can hear a loud thump followed by raucous growls.

"Eamon!" My scream spirals down through the canyon.

"I'm fine." He grunts, appearing overhead. He wraps his hands firmly around my wrist and tugs. The muscles along his neck pull taut. His jaw sets firmly as he pushes back against the tree trunk. My feet scramble for traction against the wall, but the dirt crumbles. The tree quakes, rattling my teeth as the roots shift from their foundation. "Eamon!"

"I know!" He yanks on my wrist so hard it feels like he's going to crush my bones. My shoulder screams in agony as I twist, flailing for something to hold on to.

I can feel a wave of energy sputtering across my body, sparking as it fizzles out in the wake of my terror as a throaty growl rises from behind Eamon. His eyes widen in fright at the sound of its approach, but fierce determination quickly replaces it. "Don't look at it. Look at me. I'm not going to let you go."

"I know." And I do. I glance down into the darkness, unable to see anything beyond my feet. The drop must be at least fifty feet. *Maybe something will break my fall on the way down.*

"Don't even think about it." Eamon's fingers tighten. My gaze rises to meet his as a hulking shadow appears over his shoulder.

"You have to let me go," I cry, prying against his hold. "I'll be fine."

Eamon's nostrils flare. His arms have already begun to quiver under my weight. With or without the wolf's presence, he won't be able to hold me much longer. "You're insane. You can't survive that."

I tighten my grip around the roots, testing my weight. The tree shifts and I look back up at him. "Do it."

My heart freezes when his fingers tighten their grip. The coppery scent of blood seeps from the pack leader's fangs as he appears next to Eamon's ear. A feral snarl rises from its throat.

"Let go!" I scream. The wolf's hackles rise as it crouches low, ready to attack. Eamon doesn't look to the side. "Please," I beg.

"No!" I toss out my hand as the wolf attacks. A pained yelp echoes in my ears as it hurtles backward and out of sight. I hear crunching of bone followed by a chorus of howls.

"Illyria?"

I'm shaking, consumed with protective anger. My fingers curl inward as I feel myself slip and my terror rushes back in.

"Don't let go!" Eamon latches onto me as the final inches of the roots slip through my fingertips. The tree groans as it plummets over the edge. A rain of dirt and snow follow.

I swing wildly, screaming as my stomach rushes to beat the tree to the ground below. Vertigo immobilizes me as Eamon struggles to pull me over the edge, using both of his hands just to keep me from tumbling into the ravine.

"Help me," he rasps. I reach up and clasp his forearm. "See if you can get your leg up here."

My fingers dig into his flesh as I throw my torso to the left and jerk back right. All I manage to do is get a mouthful of earth. "Again, Illyria."

His command spurns me on. I spit to clear my mouth as I rock. The tip of my shoe just misses the ledge. I swing back again, stretching my foot out, and my ankle hits snow.

My hold on the cliff is precarious at best, but with Eamon's help, I manage to hoist myself up. I lie in the snow, sucking deep gulps of night air into my lungs. My pulse hammers wildly in my ears. I smile as the howling grows faint as the wolves retreat.

Eamon collapses beside me. I can hear his labored breathing over my own. "Next time we're bringing the guns."

Eight

The next two days are just as maddeningly strenuous as the first we endured after entering the woods. Eamon keeps a solid lead ahead of the pack while I amble at the back, ever on alert in case the wolves return. We've heard their braying in the distance, but they haven't ventured close to us since I killed their leader. All of us carry our guns at the ready, just in case.

The alpha wolf provided us with the meat that we needed to continue on. The gamey flesh made me sad as I slowly ate it, reminding me of the times Eamon would bring me bits of roasted meat while in the caves, knowing I would turn my nose up at it. Now, he hardly showed a reaction as he skinned and gutted the fallen animal.

None of us talk much. Losing Arlo has been a grim reminder of the reality of our situation. Caldonians may not patrol these woods anymore, but the dangers are still present. Even Carleon has taken the hint and has fallen into a sullen silence.

Despite Eamon's threats that if I didn't heal myself he would send me straight back to Kyan, we continue to trek through the wilderness. From time to time, we spy a campfire off in the distance, but we stay clear, sometimes going miles out of our way to do so. We avoid towns, abandoned roads, and farms that we come across, sticking with the rugged wilderness for safety.

My feet are a mess of blisters. I tried to tough it out for the first few days, but when my limp became prominent, Carleon insisted on healing me. I tried to wave off his concerns, but as his healing warmth flowed over my pockmarked feet, I couldn't deny how good it felt to be whole again.

The sore flesh around my waist has scabbed over nicely now that I'm no longer wearing my pack. After a rather irate tantrum on my part, which I'll admit to not being entirely proud of, Eamon allowed me to carry one of the lighter sling packs that hangs below my waist so it doesn't hurt.

I could have healed myself, but I chose not to. Not just to spite Eamon, but to prove to myself that I'm tough enough to endure this trip. If I can't handle a four-day hike, how can I even think I can handle the full scope of my mission?

As the sun begins to rise, Eamon calls us to a halt. "We'll stop here."

That's all he says. I frown, confused as to why none of the men begin to search for firewood or unpack their bags. Something is different about this camp.

"What's going on?" I whisper to Carleon, but he just shrugs.

"I don't think Eamon trusts me anymore," he mutters and plops down on his pack. I follow suit, groaning under my breath as I work the kinks out of my calves. Already I can feel the frosty night air beginning to change. Soon, the sun will rise and with it the temperature. Up ahead, I can hear the clanging of pots and my stomach growls in appreciation. At least we will eat before we push on.

"We need to talk."

I turn around to see Eamon standing beside a tree, his hands shoved deep into his pockets. Carleon shoots me a quizzical look before he mutters an excuse and hurries off. Eamon comes around the side of the tree and shoves my pack out of the way. I watch and wait, but he neither moves to sit nor offers to help me stand.

"I'm all ears, although if I start snoring, just kick me." I yawn, stretching my arms high over my head.

Eamon tucks away the flyaway strands around his eyes and then immediately shoves his hands back in his pockets. Sighing, I push up to my feet, ignoring the stern protests of my legs. "I assume you want to do this outside of earshot?"

He nods and turns without saying a word. I shake my head, tired of all of the mind games, and follow him. We walk for several minutes before he slows. I wait for him to turn and look at me, but he doesn't. He continues to peer out into the rapidly brightening woods. Light greens, pale yellows, vivid oranges and reds bursts to life as the sun's rays beam down onto the forest. Any other time I would have stopped to marvel, to notice every detail, but not today.

"Please tell me you aren't going to make me guess what all of this is about." I shift my weight, wincing at the needles that have begun to prick my calves. "My wounds are fine. Nothing to worry about there. I'm pretty sure Kohen has forgiven me for that rash joke, and Nixon is just as weird as usual. Bodhi… well, everyone has been complaining about his snoring so I don't think you can really blame me for—"

"It's time," he whispers, cutting me off.

"Time?" I rub my hands down my sleeves, wondering for the hundredth time why Caldonians never made white uniforms. They would've blended so much better in snow and been cooler in the summer.

Eamon turns slowly, his arms hanging uselessly at his sides. "This is the extraction point and the end of my mission."

"Oh." I wrap my arms about my waist, only vaguely aware that I hardly feel any pain from doing so. "When… when will they come for me?"

"Soon." His gaze is riveted on the ground, as if the intricate tree root system weaving around our feet is the most fascinating thing he's ever seen.

"Why do I get the feeling you're saying good-bye?" This feels wrong and completely awkward. Why can't he just give me a hug, a peck on the cheek, and say, "See you soon," like most boyfriends would? Why does everything with him have to be such gloom and doom?

When he doesn't respond, I take a step toward him, weighing his reaction. When there is none, I step again and again until I am only a couple feet from him. "I'll be back in a few days. A week tops if I have to walk all that way again." Inwardly, I'm praying to the God of Earth and whoever lives on Calisted that's not the case.

I stretch out my hand and wait. Eamon's sandy-blond

curls shift as he lifts his head and stares at my hand. I begin to fidget when he doesn't move, doesn't react. *Is he really going to make this harder than it should be?*

His hand surges forward, clasping around my wrist and yanking me toward him. I stumble forward, slamming my chin into his chest. He winces but quickly steadies me as I regain my footing. I can see the softness in his eyes encroaching back in, stealing away the firm set of his lips and the hard line of his jaw.

I blink rapidly as I begin to see a year of bitterness and sorrow melt away from his face. The hand that rises to cup my cheek is gentle, his thumb lightly brushing over my skin as he searches my eyes. I can feel a yearning within him, making his fingers tremble as they press against my cheek.

His other hand slides around my waist, pressing against my spine, drawing me closer to him. I step forward and into his embrace. He feels warm and firm, but not with the rigidity I've come to know over the past few months.

I close my eyes and lean my forehead against his chest. He doesn't speak. He simply holds me. A thousand unspoken apologies pass between us as I wind my arms around his back, clinging to him.

I'm terrified of what lies ahead and regretful of what is behind. So much of this year has been wasted with indifference, cold shoulders, and bitterness.

All I ever wanted was my friend and now he is here. Not the Eamon who professed his love for me with awkward pleading or the Eamon who eagerly accepted Kyan's assurance that we were meant to be together, but the Eamon who used to hold me in the long hours of the night simply to be close.

No expectations. No drama or heartache. Just us. The way we were always meant to be.

"This is nice," I whisper as I lean up onto my toes and press my cheek into his neck.

He nods and wraps his arms around me, sealing me into his embrace. I close my eyes as the first tears form and I hide them in his shoulder. There are some things I still can't show him. "I've missed you," he murmurs against my hair.

I dig my fingers into his back, praying that this moment will not end, but as with all things, there is almost a finality to it. Before I'm ready, Eamon unwraps my arms from around his neck, clasping them against his chest.

I can't remember the last time we stood like this. Was it beneath the shadow of the Shard after Bastien left me? No, I don't think even then it was this pure. It must have been before that.

"I'm afraid," I whisper as I lay my hands against his chest, feeling the steady pulse of his heart beating just beneath the surface.

"Me too."

"Not just of this mission. Of everything. I have been for a long time. I just…" I trail off as I see the flash of hurt cross his face. It is fleeting but present all the same.

He releases his hold on my hands and steps back. "Isn't it ironic how we wish for so many things at the end, when we thought we had all the time in the world to mend the hurts?"

I nod, knowing exactly what he means. Things should've been different between us. Instead of lashing out at each other, we should've bonded together, stood strong side by side to face what would come. Instead, we broke.

"I don't blame you," I whisper. "I mean, it hurt, but I know you didn't back away to cause me pain."

"Never." His lower lip trembles as he shoves his hands back into his pockets. "There has never been anyone but you, Illyria. That's why I need you to stay with me. Don't go on this mission."

I close my eyes to his pleading, knowing if he'd said these words sooner, I might have been swayed. "It's too late now, Eamon."

"I know." He slumps back against a tree and hangs his head. "A guy can still hope, right?"

"Always." My voice cracks and I can feel my control starting to fragment. I rush forward and throw myself into his arms, burrowing into his chest one last time. The warmth of his tears patter against my face. I clench my eyes shut, praying he isn't right, that we will see each other again soon.

A whimper rises in my throat and I thrust back, needing to flee. I turn to run and stop short, shocked into utter silence. *Bastien!*

I can't breathe. My lungs literally refuse to expand as I stare across the small clearing at Bastien. An odd, croaking sound rises from my throat as I step hesitantly forward. "What...?" I swallow, feeling as if my throat is suddenly parched. "What are you doing here?"

Bastien looks beyond me, his expression darkening. "I assumed you would know I was coming."

His brow pinches with disapproval as Eamon stands up beside me. When Eamon reaches for my hand, I wrench away from him, stepping back. "You knew? Why didn't you tell me?"

"I wanted to. I tried to but..." He glances away, appearing to struggle to swallow. "It doesn't matter. He's here now."

"Doesn't matter?" The pitch of my voice rises to glass-splintering heights. "How can you say this doesn't matter? Didn't I have a right to know? You can't just drop this... him on me and expect me to be okay with this!"

I begin to pace, wringing my hands before my stomach. All hope of playing this off cool went out the window after the first unattractive croak. Now all bets are off.

"Should I come back?" Bastien asks, clearly uncomfortable, yet I realize also infuriatingly amused by the scene he's stepped into.

"No!" Eamon and I both shout at the same time. I double over and grasp the back of my knees, fighting for a calm that I know is currently residing about a hundred miles from here. "I just... I need a moment."

I can feel my panic rising. *I can't handle this. Why does fate have it in for me? One gut-wrenching good-bye wasn't enough? Now they have to throw an imploding heart into the mix as well?*

I'm acutely aware of Bastien crossing the clearing, his steps strong and confident. I used to love that about him, but right now it's driving me mad. I hold out my hand and he stops less than ten feet away. "Please. I can't…"

From upside down, I see him raise his hands in surrender. I suck in another breath and count to ten. It doesn't help so I hold out for a full twenty count before I release my breath.

"Does she always do this?" Bastien asks.

"Never seen this before," Eamon responds.

I rise back up, my ponytail whipping past my vision as I take my time to glare at both of them. "I'm standing right here."

Bastien's eyes narrow, but he says nothing. Eamon starts to protest but cuts off when I shoot him a withering glare. "I want answers and I want them right now." I plant my hands on my hips, widening my stance in attempt to keep my knees from quaking. My control of my powers is tremulous right now. Ripples of energy vine down my arms in waves, sparking over my clothes.

"Illyria…" Bastien reaches out his hand toward me but draws it back.

"Start talking, Eamon." My fists clench tightly against my hips, my nails carving deep ruts into my palms. I can feel the warmth of the blood that spills around my nails, seeping between my fingers, but I don't release my grip. I can't. Not until I have myself under control.

Eamon clears his throat and I try to focus on his face. He is paler than usual, making the ruddy tint to his cheeks all the more prominent. "Kyan hinted that someone from Bastien's base would be coming to collect you. I swear I didn't know he would come himself."

"Of course you did," Bastien growls. I can feel the pent-up anger writhing beneath his calm exterior. *Perhaps he isn't as amused as I first thought.* "Do you really think I would entrust her safety to anyone else?"

Eamon kicks at the ground, obviously less than thrilled to be put on the spot. "I didn't think—"

"Exactly," I roar, leaping into the middle of their

conversation. "You didn't think."

A strong gust whips my hair against my neck. A second sends a flurry of icicles lancing toward the ground. "Illyria?" Bastien shifts.

"I'm on it." I grit my teeth and take another round of calming breaths. It helps, minimally, but I'm still ticked at Eamon's deception. Bastien is right. He should've known.

I try to focus on things other than the frustrations simmering within. Like the fact that Bastien's hair has been cut short and spiked up at the front. *Why didn't I notice that when he saved me back at Drakon's hideout? I liked him better with longer hair.*

Another stark change is his eyes, deep sapphire and filled with emotion. The dull, lifelessness of them has haunted my dreams for months. The day I chose Eamon over him, the glow was drawn from his gaze. It hurts now knowing I'm not the reason for bringing that life back to him.

A new scar runs down the hollow of his cheek, still bearing the reddened signs of new flesh. Another faded scar appears over his right eye, a few shades lighter than the warm tone of his skin. He is bathed in a bronze glow that speaks of hours spent in the sun.

Gone is the boy who swept me off my feet not so long ago, showering me with kisses that could've melted the ice caps. Standing before me now, I see a battle hardened man who seems a bit too adept at keeping his thoughts in check.

As the winds die back down, Bastien releases a breath I hadn't known he was holding. His hand shifts away from his side and I realize with a start that he had been reaching for a stun gun.

"You would have shot her?" Eamon rages, surging past me to face off with Bastien, whose gaze never leaves mine.

"I remember what happened the last time she lost control." Finally, he shifts to look at Eamon. "Have you forgotten?"

"Of course not. I seem to remember you were the exact reason she nearly wiped Thalar off the map."

"Exactly," Bastien growls, rising to his full height.

"Which is exactly why you should have warned her ahead of time."

Ice and fire go toe to toe yet again. I hold my breath, silently pleading for an end. *I can't do this again. I just can't!*

"Enough!" Both men turn to look at me, then shift their gaze beyond me. I look to my left and groan, realizing when I threw out my arms, I also tore the trees on either side of me up from the ground by their roots. "Oh, for goodness sake," I grumble and chuck the maple trees aside as if they were mere sticks instead of hundred-year-old timbers.

"You two bickering like the old days isn't going to solve this. Bastien is here to take me back to his base and I'm ready to leave."

"But—" Eamon grabs my hand and yanks me toward him. I stumble on my footing and slam into his chest, crying out as my nose connects with his breastbone, and then slump to the ground.

Bastien is instantly at my side. I cry out as Bastien slams his foot into Eamon's abdomen and sends him sprawling. "Touch her again and I promise you'll regret it," he threatens ominously as he stands between us, shielding me.

"Just let it go, Bastien," I mutter as I rub the end of my nose to make sure nothing is broken.

He whirls around, staring at me with sheer disbelief. "You're just going to take that from him?"

"It's not… He'd didn't mean to hurt me. He was just upset…" I trail off, knowing my lame explanation isn't helping Eamon's case.

"She's not yours to protect anymore," Eamon grunts as he rises, clutching his ribs. No doubt Carleon will have to do some repair work on him when we get back to camp. "She's mine."

He just had to go one step further, didn't he? I close my eyes, pinching the bridge of my nose as a pounding begins to grow.

I don't have time to react before he is atop Eamon,

rolling side to side as he land blows hard enough to bruise bone.

"Well, this is going well," a voice calls from behind me.

I turn to see Carleon walking toward me. "How did you find us?"

"It wasn't too hard, what with the tree tossing and all the shouting." He stares past me, shaking his head. "Was this what it was like before Bastien left?"

"Yeah," I mutter. "Something like this."

"Looks like Bastien hasn't forgotten you after all." He glances at me from the corner of my eye.

My lips thin into lines of annoyance. "Either you stop them or I will."

Carleon watches as Bastien rears back and slams his fist into Eamon's nose. Blood splatters fly at the sound of cracking bone. "You might want to take this one. I don't fancy getting in the middle of that."

"Fine." I heave a sigh and mentally wrench to the guys apart, pinning them on trees lining opposite ends of the clearing. "Cool off," I command.

"Let me down," Eamon growls, fighting against my hold.

"Not when you're about to do something you'll regret."

Eamon locks a crazed glare onto Bastien, his lips peeled back into a full snarl. "I'd never regret it."

"I'd like to see you try," Bastien goads. His right eye looks a bit worse for wear, but it's no surprise to see he's in far better shape than Eamon. He always was a great fighter.

"Enough!" I slowly lower both of them to the ground, ready to yank them apart again if necessary. Thankfully, it isn't.

The sound of a laser charging surprises me. I turn to find Carleon with his gun leveled on Eamon. "Don't do anything stupid."

Eamon's eyes narrow. "You would threaten your commanding officer?"

"Nope. I'm threatening my friend."

Under normal circumstances, I would have found the unusually serious edge to Carleon's tone amusing. Despite his brash and rather reckless sense of duty to protect me, I am proud of him. "It's okay." I place a hand over his arm, urging him to power down. "I can handle this."

"I know, but I've got your back, just in case."

Bastien appraises Carleon. "I think this guy's starting to grow on me."

"That's because he's on your side," Eamon snaps. He slumps back against the tree, looking winded and forlorn. He shakes his head back and forth, eyes clamped shut as if what he's feeling is a physical pain. Judging by the beating he took from Bastien, he probably is.

I lower my gaze, unable to see him like this. "I have to leave, Eamon. Please don't make this any harder than it already is."

I wait for him to say something, but he doesn't even look at me. I bite on my lower lip and turn away. I clap Carleon on the arm as I pass. "Take care of him for me."

"Of course." He smiles and pats my hand as I let it slip away. "Let's talk over here."

I let him pull me aside, feeling as if I'm about to unravel at the seams. My fingers quake as he takes me into his arms. "Are you okay? That got pretty intense back there."

"Yeah, I'll be fine."

"And what about Bastien?" Carleon casts a pointed glance in his direction.

Even now, looking at him feels like a punch to the gut—wonderful, amazingly painful. *Why does he have to look so irresistible even when he's angry?* "He's just a guy, right?"

Carleon laughs. "Sure." He continues to stare at Bastien, so I elbow him in the ribs. "Sorry. It's just…" He leans in closer to whisper in my ear. "I think I sort of have a man crush on him."

A giggle bursts past my lips. I bury it in his shoulder as I feel some of the earlier tension lift momentarily. Leave it to him to make me laugh when I need it most. "I'm serious.

Have you seen that guy?"

I sober instantly. "Yes, every night in my dreams."

Carleon grimaces. "Sorry. Guess that wasn't the best thing to say."

"Don't worry about it. I think Bastien has that effect on most people." I pat him on the back and pull away from his embrace. "Thank you, for everything."

Bastien casts a darkened glance at Eamon but says nothing as he turns to follow me. The walk back to camp is silent and unsettling. It feels weird for him to be here beside me, but even more so that he didn't hesitate a second to leap to my defense.

I know Eamon didn't intend to hurt me. He was upset and didn't realize how hard he pulled me forward, but Bastien doesn't know him like I do.

The pounding in my head mounts as I spy a spiral of smoke rising from the center of camp. Tents have been set up and appear to be occupied. Bodhi's droning snores escape from the canvas near the rear of camp. I grab my pack and sling it over my shoulder.

No farewell. No wishes for a successful mission. "Are you ready?" Bastien asks.

I glance one last time around my camp and feel a surprising, yet profound sense of homesickness. "Yes. I'm ready."

Nine

The winds whistle through the trees, whipping my hair against my face and tangling with my downturned lashes, but I hardly notice. I feel completely out of sorts, not just over having left Eamon in such a terrible way, but also because of who it is that walks before me

Bastien.

Seeing him twice in one month is almost more than I can fathom. I used to dream about what it would be like to see him again. Would he still be the haunted man I'd grown to hate or the smug boy who could irritate me with whip-like speed? What I find before me is neither of those yet both at the same time. He is a walking contradiction that shouldn't even be here to start with.

I don't like how distracted I feel, how my gaze keeps rising enough to notice the way his uniform fits his muscular form to perfection. He has put on some weight since I last saw him, but it is housed in thick ropes of muscles. I can see it in the definition of his calves as he leaps over small trickling streams and weaves around downed trees.

Strong, powerful arms propel him over rocks large enough to provide a challenge. He moves with the ease and grace of a man who grew up in the forest, yet I know he didn't.

The sunlight overhead is dappled, ever shifting with the waving evergreen branches. The scent of pine is strong as we begin our final descent, emerging from the mountains into smaller foothills. More of the large hill variety, really.

I pause atop a boulder, partially sunken into the dark, fertile soil, to stare out at the landscape before me. Once-beautiful oak and maple trees now stand barren, squeezed out by a thick overgrowth of pine and spruce. Needle boughs dance in the winds, carrying their scent for miles.

The sky is clear today. No hint of cloud for as far as I can see. The rich blue is breathtaking, the fresh air filling my lungs invigorating, burning in my throat.

I can hear Bastien's feet crunching a noisy path along the snowy forest floor ahead. Last year's leaves have been trampled underfoot by wildlife, beginning the stages of decomposition that will feed the earth for another year. Pinecones poke up from the snow amid a blanket of browned needles.

Bastien pauses and glances back over his shoulder at me. I try not to acknowledge that my gaze automatically searches his eyes. What is it that I am looking for? I don't really know the answer to that. Maybe a sign that he missed me as much as I missed him.

Keep your head down and move. One foot in front of the other. That's all that matters right now, I silently scold as I leap to the ground and hurry to catch up.

I keep pace with Bastien as the sun climbs the sky, chasing away the shadows from the land, but I remain back several feet. His questioning gaze unsettles me. Bastien has always seen too much, known and understood far more than he should about me. It was one of the things that annoyed me in the beginning but then endeared me to him in the end.

He never asked me to be anything but what I was. He believed in me when all others feared me. He alone loved me for exactly who I am.

There have been several backward glances and troubled looks as we wind through an unseen path, ever moving south. Although he plows ahead with the same confidence that Eamon showed, there is something disturbingly different about Bastien. It is almost as if this land is well known to him.

Has he been here before? Been within only a few days of our city? An even darker thought makes my pace slow. *Has he come into Thalar without my knowing?*

My stomach begins to pinch uncomfortably as I try to tell myself that it doesn't matter, but deep down, I know it does. How can it not?

He told me he would come back. I knew even as he spoke the words that he didn't mean them, but what if something else had forced him to return, just like back at Drakon's hideout? What if *someone* commanded it?

I grit my teeth as I duck low to avoid a low-hanging branch jutting across my path. It's feathery needles brush along my head as I pass under. As I straighten, I realize there is a slight stickiness left on the back of my neck.

The longer we walk, the more I realize it bothers me that Bastien doesn't talk. *Shouldn't he say something to me? Maybe an explanation for why he showed up just in time to save my life and then disappeared before I awoke.* But with that question comes another that makes my throat clench. *Shouldn't I be thanking him for saving my life?*

It bothers me that I know nothing about him now. Kyan had been very strict about not allowing me to know of his whereabouts. I'm not sure if he did this at Bastien's request or for my own good. Either way, for over a year, Bastien just dropped off the face of the planet.

I have a sneaking suspicion that Aminah kept tabs on him through Toren. It would make sense for her to do that, not just for herself, but for me as well. She knew all too well what his leaving did to me. She, being the motherly figure of our small band of friends, always felt responsible for each of us. Although Bastien may not have been part of our group for long, he became family, and families don't give up on each other, no matter how far apart they are.

Watching as he adjusts my pack on his back, I wonder for the hundredth time what his base looks like. I've heard tales from soldiers who move from squadron to squadron. They all seem to be in agreement that Bastien is not only a good leader, but a strict one at that. Funny that the boy who used to love to break all of the rules is now the one enforcing them.

Who are his friends? The people he confides in before heading into battle? Has he regressed back into his old habits? When I first found Bastien, he was alone in the Thalar, amidst thousands of enemy soldiers. He was a renegade, a hermit with a purpose.

A part of me thinks he liked having no one to order him about. He liked his freedom, to what little extent he could be free trapped within the confines of enemy territory. He had no one to care about. It was the way he wanted it… until he met me.

I blow out a shaky breath. *Why am I doing this to myself?*

Using my sleeve, I wipe my brow clean of the sweat that clings just below my hairline. Stray beads curve along my forehead, curling down into the corners of my eyes where it burns, blurring my vision. Despite the freezing winds, I feel warm.

I pause to lean against a tree, its light-colored bark smooth to the touch. It rises high over my head, so high that I have to crane my neck to see the handful of branches that spider out from the top ten feet. We don't have trees like this where I'm from. Their unusual beauty isn't lost on me as I unscrew the cap from my canteen and greedily suck down several gulps.

The water splashes out around my lips, pouring from my chin and onto my shirt. "Are you all right?" Bastien asks, coming back for me.

I'm sure he is taking note of the color that stains my neck and cheeks. "Yeah. I'm good."

He gives me a knowing look and slings my pack off his shoulder, dropping into a crouch beside it on the ground before he reaches into his own bag. "I have some food to hold us over until we reach camp."

He pulls a small cloth bundle from the pack and holds it out to me. "I didn't realize we were so close to your base."

"We're not." He resumes rummaging through the pack for a cup. "I meant our camp. In the woods. We are still a three-day's hike from my base."

The dried venison that I just bit into goes down with great difficulty as I swallow it whole. Anything is better than wolf meat. "Three days?" I choke, pounding on my chest.

I snatch my canteen and take another long drink, easing the burning in my throat. It settles heavily on my stomach. When I finally look over at Bastien, I can see his frustration. "Did they tell you nothing about this?"

"If you mean Kyan, then no, he told me nothing apart from what I'm supposed to be stealing."

Bastien grinds his back teeth as he thrusts up to his feet and plants his hands on his hips, the silver cup dangling from one of his curled fingers. "Why would he do this? It doesn't make any sense."

"Really?" I chuckle and hand him the canteen. He accepts it without looking at me. "You haven't figured it out yet?"

"What do you mean?" I hear water sloshing in his cup and then a single gulp as he downs his share of the water in one go. I sink to the ground, weary and exhausted but suddenly unwilling to even consider sleep.

"Kyan knew Eamon would never agree to this if he knew you were my guide and I…" I trail off, suddenly unsure of what my reaction would've been.

I wrap the venison back into its ball of cotton and toss it at Bastien, uninterested in eating anymore. As he digs out a chunk of meat, I draw my knees up into my chest and hug my legs close. "Why did you agree to this?"

As I wait for his answer, I become aware of the thick tree root I've sat upon. My gaze follows the intricate root system and I realize I'm completely surrounded. The only free space is beside Bastien. I decide to stay put, at least until my tailbone cracks or I tumble off.

"It was a mission of great importance. We both know that."

"Yes." I nod in agreement. There has never been a sighting this big. What if we could take out an entire enemy base? To actually steal one of their ships and be able to infiltrate their armada as they return soldiers back to Calisted?

I've often dreamed of what Kyan's planet looks like. In my visions, it is bathed in delicate, shifting pastel colors. Flowers grow there, the likes of which I've never seen.

Colors so vivid they seem fake, unnatural. Almost as if trapped within a dream world.

"But why did you accept it? Personally, I mean." I glance over at him and see that he too has set aside the food.

The sunlight trickling from the canopy overhead highlights his dark hair. I realize with a start that our hair color is nearly identical now.

His face is lean, not in the same way that Kyan's face has become drawn under the pressure of leading the rebellion on so many fronts, but almost as if he has finally grown into adulthood. His shoulders have broadened, as has his chest. He has filled out, grown another inch or so while he was gone.

His fingers are thin, but I know they hold great strength. Cords of muscle rise from his wrists, twining around his forearms and biceps. I lower my gaze to his chest and stop myself, remembering all too well what lies beneath the thin layer of his uniform.

"What I told Eamon was true." He lifts his gaze to meet mine directly. "I trust no one else with your safety."

I seize a clump of ice from the forest floor, testing its weight in my hand before I hurl it at a tree. It explodes on impact. I can hear the pattering of fragments raining down. "I can take care of myself."

A slow, wistful smile curls Bastien's lips as he nods. "You always have."

"Then why come? Why you?" I can feel pressure beginning to form just behind my eyes. I hate the need to press him for an answer, yet I seem unable to stop myself.

Bastien's shoulders rise and fall with a sigh. He turns his face away so I can only see his profile, keeping me from reading the emotions hidden within the depths of his eyes. "Because I had to."

I lower my gaze and realize the pine needle I've been fiddling with between my fingers has nearly crumbled completely. I brush off the residue from my pants and lower my legs, crisscrossing them as I try to shift my weight into a less bumpy location.

On the horizon, I can see clouds brewing, dark and heavy laden. I frown and lower my gaze. I can feel the change in the air. A winter storm is on its way.

The silence that falls between us feels awkward. What is there to say that hasn't already been said? This is a job for him. Nothing more. It should be the same for me.

"Do you want to tell me what all of that was about back there?"

I blink, confused by the tension in his voice. His grip on his leg, drawn up into his chest, is tight enough that I can see the muscles flexed beneath the skin of his uniform. He doesn't look at me. Instead, he casts his gaze far out into the woods.

"Not much to tell." I shrug and feel my stomach begin to stir. Maybe I'm hungrier than I thought, but I'm not about to ask Bastien to pass the meat.

When he glances over at me, I am rocked by the depth of his open annoyance, and the familiarity of it. "Come on, Illyria. This is me you're talking to. I know something is terribly wrong and I want to know what it is."

I open my mouth to speak but instantly clamp it shut, biting down on my tongue. "I don't see how it is any of your concern," I finally respond coolly.

Bastien leans forward, releasing his leg so he can shift his entire body to face mine. He looks as if he's about to say something so I leap in to interrupt. "You chose to walk out of my life, remember? I don't owe you anything."

His fingers clench into fists atop his lap, but he slowly releases them. I watch as color slowly seeps back in, stealing away the white that painted his hands. "I knew this wasn't going to be easy—"

"Of course not." I grit my teeth and flip my hair over my shoulder. It needs a good brushing and I could use a long soak. For the first time ever, I find myself wishing I were back in my room instead of in the forest. "What were you thinking showing up like that? You knew you'd set Eamon off!"

"Of course I knew, but I never dreamed he would take his anger out of you!" His cheeks redden with anger. His eyes widen, slightly glossed as he leans back.

"He didn't—" I start but cut off at his livid gaze. I take a deep breath and hold it for several seconds before releasing it. "Eamon was upset. So were you. He didn't mean anything by it."

"You know, that's what my mom used to say when Dad had a bit too much to drink."

I raise my eyebrows in shock. I always assumed Bastien's parents had loved each other. He never mentioned problems. Bastien runs his hands through his hair absently, almost as if he still thought it was longer. "It only happened a couple of times, not long after the Caldonians moved in. Mom never knew he had a stash of alcohol. Dad claimed it was for emergencies."

He turns away, but not before I catch the distant look in his gaze. "The first time he hit her, I was seven. Took nearly a week for that bruise to disappear. Mom made excuses for him, especially after he assured her that he'd tossed out all of the alcohol, but there was more. There always was."

I draw my knees back up to my chest. I heard our parents talk about alcohol when I was younger. Several of them would express a longing for it just before they went on a raid, said it would calm their nerves. Mom said she caught a couple of the men dipping into our medical supplies once, said it made them act weird.

"What happened?" I whisper.

There is a bitter chill in his gaze when he looks back at me. "I stopped him."

He doesn't say anything more than that. A simple statement that seems to be weighted with a lifetime of anger. Bastien loved his parents; that much was obvious from the first time he spoke of them. They had died when he was younger, during a Caldonian raid that sent Bastien fleeing to the abandoned subway tunnels to survive. His mother was brutalized before his own eyes, his father gunned down. A terrible way to see your parents die.

"I'm sorry."

"Don't be." He rolls his head from one side to the

other, as if needing to release tension that has settled firmly on his shoulders. "Just don't make excuses for him."

That's not what I'm doing, I think as I lower my chin onto my hands, rocking slightly. *Is it?*

How many times have I excused away Eamon's neglect? Days, sometimes even weeks would go by before he would come visit me, and then it was always that widening hole between us that kept me from ever feeling truly loved. I knew it was there, maddeningly out of reach but still within sight. Eamon wanted to love me, needed to, but was too afraid to accept that he would someday lose it.

"Things change." I roll my head to the side and press my cheek against my hands. My skin feels flushed and clammy. "People change."

I can feel him watching me. I hate it when he does this. He always sees exactly what I don't want him to see, which is usually everything. "You're miserable," he whispers. His tone, although soft, is layered with disbelief.

I shrug, putting forth a brave face despite knowing it won't work. It's a reflex I've grown accustom to over the past few months. Especially any time Aminah was around. "It's not a big deal."

Bastien shakes his head as if he is disgusted by how blasé I am about it. "If I'd known—"

"You'd have what?" I cut him off, raising my head to look at him. "Come back for me?"

He flinches back from the venom in my voice. I grimace internally, knowing it's not fair to take out my bitterness on him.

When he finally turns to look at me, my breath catches at the sight of raw pain within his eyes. "I'd have wanted to."

As the sun is swallowed up in cloud, the frosty winds return, blustery and merciless. The forest changes around us, the shadows lengthening until they stretch into a wall of darkness. Bastien charges up his laser gun to light the way.

"How much farther?"

His hesitation surprises me. I pick up my pace to catch

up with him, only to find him staring intently at the cluster of stars still visible overhead, almost like fireflies appearing for the first time on a warm summer's night. The clouds will arrive sometime during the night. I shiver, rubbing my hands upon my arm.

From here I can still see the North Star, shining brightest in the sky. I follow Bastien's gaze as he lowers his head and peers into the woods. "You're lost."

"No." He holds up his hand and turns in a slow circle. "I am temporarily misplaced. That's all."

I lower myself to the ground, brushing aside a bed of needles to make sure this time I sit on soft ground. My tailbone has yet to forgive me for my earlier abuse. "You won't be able to find anything in the dark. Might as well bed down for the night and search in the morning."

Bastien's nostrils flare and he looks startled when I laugh. He looks down at me and I grin. "Must be hard for you."

"What?"

"To admit you're not perfect."

His lip curls into a smirk as he shrugs out of my pack. "Just don't tell anyone. I've got a reputation to uphold."

My smile wanes as I look away, realizing just how easy our banter came, like before. My lips turn downward into a frown as I lean my head back against a tree, closing my eyes.

"Do you have a tent in here?" I can hear him open my zipper, the clanging of pots, and the rustle of clothes as he searches. To be honest, I could sleep right here propped up against this tree, but I nod and point to the small pouch rolled and tucked into the bottom of the pack. Bastien insists on setting up the tent while I rise to hunt for firewood.

It is harder to find than I would've thought. The ample amounts of pine needles will work great as kindling, but the lack of dried twigs and broken off branches will make keeping a fire going a near impossibility.

I manage to scrounge a few small bits of limbs, but they are too pliable, still moist. Heading back to camp, I try not to wonder about the sleeping arrangements. I breathe a huge sigh of relief when I see he has set up a bedroll a little way from my tent. Although I hate to know he will be without shelter, I really couldn't imagine sleeping near him.

"There wasn't much to choose from," I say as I drop my pathetic load before him. Bastien turns to look at the small pile and nods.

"I can work with that." I nibble on my lower lip as he grabs his laser gun, drawing it near to see in the fading light. I hear a knob shift and the laser thrum to life. Squinting against the vivid crimson glow, I watch as Bastien runs the laser over the woodpile. It fans over the sticks in a long, narrow line. Steam begins to rise from the wood.

I kneel down beside him, mesmerized. "You're drying the wood?"

"Yes." He powers down the laser until it is nothing more than a dim glow to see by. He holds out a stick to me. "Break it."

It snaps between my fingers with hardly any pressure. "Amazing."

"Don't they teach you that stuff in the city?" He questions as he begins to stand the sticks in a pyramid, placing ample amounts of pine needles beneath for kindling.

"No need. We have electricity." His eyebrow rises at the sound of bitterness in my voice. "I prefer the old ways."

"I agree." With another knob adjustment a thin beam of light traces a circle around the small pile, igniting the kindling. The small burst of heat brings a smile to my face. No amount of flickering fluorescent lights or rattling overhead vents can replace the appeal of a real campfire. "Although these lasers do come in handy."

"You look like you've done that a time or two," I comment as he sets the gun aside and begins unpacking my bag. He sets out the cooking supplies and the meager rations we have left to make a meal.

I blush as he removes my clothes. I spy my cammo pants and familiar black top within the folds of clothes and smile. It's been too long since I was allowed to be comfortable.

Within twenty minutes, Bastien manages to concoct a rather impressive-smelling stew out of the leftover venison, some wrinkled root vegetables he found partially rotting at the bottom of my pack, and water from a nearby stream. He tips out some of the soup into a silver bowl and passes it to me while he dips his own portion into a drinking cup.

The first taste is bland but warm. It slides down my throat with ease. It doesn't take long for my stomach to gurgle in response. As I take another sip, pausing to grind a torn chunk of meat with my back teeth, I realize Bastien is watching me again. I'm tempted to keep my cup tilted so I don't have to look at him, but I know I can't hide all night.

"What?" I ask as I wipe the broth from my lips with my sleeve. Not the most ladylike thing to do, but we are roughing it.

"Nothing." He turns away, running his finger along the rim of his mug. I realize with a start that he hasn't taken a single sip yet. Something is on his mind.

I close my eyes for a moment, knowing I'm going to regret this. Setting aside my bowl, I rub my hands on my pants and turn to fully face him. "I have no intention of spending the next two days having you stare at me like that. You might as well spill it."

Bastien frowns, appearing to weigh out his words before he too sets aside his mug. He crosses his arms over his chest. "I want to know what happened between you and Eamon. I know I have no right to ask. Let's just chalk it up to wild curiosity."

I brush stray hairs back from my eyes. While Bastien chopped his long hair off, I let mine grow. It now drapes nearly to my waist. On most days, I wear it up in a messy bun or a ponytail when I'm in a hurry. I hardly ever let it fall free, but tonight I just don't care.

"It's really not about what Eamon did to me… It's more what he didn't that's the problem."

He doesn't move. In the flickering of the firelight, he almost looks like a statue, darkly beautiful. The light plays tricks in his eyes, dancing in the hollow of his neck. "Eamon's had a hard time accepting my future. After you left, he became obsessed with perfecting his control over seeing the future. He worked relentlessly with Kyan. At first we thought he was just trying to improve himself for the sake of aiding the rebellion, but we quickly realized he wasn't moving in that direction."

Bastien leans forward but says nothing. He doesn't pry or press me as I clear my throat. He waits patiently. "It didn't take long for him to begin to withdraw. At first it was small things. A wistful look, a missed sentence here or there. He hid it pretty well at first, but then he slipped."

"How?"

"He let me touch him." I stare into the flickering blues in the heart of the fire. It dances about, twining with the vivid oranges, spiraling and writhing in time together. "We were prepping for a battle in the fifth quadrant. The snow was falling in visible sheets, a freak late spring storm. The sleet pounding against the tent roof so hard I was sure it would pierce through it. The winds were howling so loudly I began to wonder if there was a pack of wolves just outside our door. Kyan was giving us our final instructions."

I look down at my fingers, realizing they have begun to tremble slightly, the tips red from the cold. "I was scared. I'll admit that. I knew it was going to be a hard fought battle. The intel was spotty and the storm came upon us so suddenly that I feared we would lose before the battle even began. That's why I touched him. I needed reassurance, but when our hands met, I was sucked into his vision."

"It was disconcerting at first. I'd only ever done that once or twice before and that was when I was expecting it. Everything was a swirl of gray, cold and confusing. I could hear voices, as if they were calling from a distance. I could hear my voice and…" I pause and dart a glance over at Bastien but quickly look away. "And yours."

"Mine?"

I continue on without stopping. "I could feel him searching, like he was wading through the ocean during a hurricane. I was tossed about, barely hanging on, but there was nothing tangible to grasp. That's when I heard the screaming."

Bastien's gaze is darkly intense. He looks as if he is holding his breath.

"I woke up on the floor with Kyan hovering over me. He was furious, not at me, but at Eamon. I realized as I looked up at him that there was snow in his hair, blotting his eyelashes. I remember looking past him to see that the tent had been torn away, the table and all of our maps lost to the winds. That is what I had tried to hold on to and when I lost my grasp, everything was gone except me."

I reaffirm my grasp about my legs, feeling a chill settle over me that I know has little to do with the night air. The fire rustles before me, warm and inviting. "I knew immediately what had happened. Kyan was furious with Eamon, not only for endangering my life, but for being so distracted before a battle. He made Eamon remain behind, trudging through the snows in search of our maps instead of leading the battle."

A hint of a smile crosses Bastien's lips. "That was your first mission."

I nod. "There was no one else to lead. Kyan gave me command and we sacked the base with only five men lost. It was a great victory."

"I know," he says. "The information you recovered in that base helped my men take out the base in the southern lands."

"That was you?" I whisper.

"Of course." he laughs. His smile slowly fades. "You didn't know?"

"No." I shake my head. "No one told me anything about you."

Bastien's jaw clenches. "I guess I should've known that would happen. A part of me thought it was a way for me to show you I was okay, still kicking and all that."

I grab my bowl once more, simply needing something to hold until the tremor in my fingers passes. "It was a good plan."

"Didn't help though, did it?" He tosses a handful of

needles into the fire and the flames surge into the air, igniting before burning out rapidly. He stares into the flames for several minutes. "No matter how bad things got, he should never have abandoned you."

"Why not? You did."

The instant the words cross my lips, I wish I could take them back. The color leeches from his face. "You know why I had to."

"Yes, but that doesn't mean I wasn't alone."

"Eamon was supposed to take care of you. To make you happy when I couldn't." Color rushes back in like a tidal wave, crashing over his face in splashes of scarlet. "I left so you could have a life, so you could be with him like you were supposed to be."

His words cut through me like a poison-tipped dagger, deep and visceral. A wound I wish was fatal. I drop my head to my hands, feeling the tremor rise from my fingers to encase my entire body. I feel nauseous, ill with regret.

"Why didn't you send word to me?" he says so softly I struggle to hear him over the crackling of the flames. "You know I'd have found a way to help you."

I lift my head. Despite how much it would've hurt him, I know, staring into the depths of his pain-filled eyes, that he would've done anything to protect me. Even if that meant protecting me from myself.

"I couldn't do that to you. The way things ended between us…" I trail off, shaking my head, knowing we shouldn't be speaking of such things. "I didn't want to hurt you again."

Bastien rises onto his knees, closing the gap between us before I can draw in a breath. He reaches out as if to touch my cheek but draws his hand back. It hangs awkwardly in the air between us as he searches my face.

Warm tears streak down the curve of my cheeks. My throat feels raw as I clear it and the moment passes. He sinks back down and looks away. "Nothing ever ended between us, Illyria. We just… we needed space."

"Did it help?" I wipe at my nose, wishing I had a cloth to use instead of my sleeve. This uniform is going to need a serious washing when we arrive at his base!

"No." He pushes himself upright, rising to his full height. I would have to crane my head to meet his gaze, but I don't even try. I can't bear to see the emotion that I would find if I did. "But you should have given me a choice."

Dipping low, he grabs his bowl of cooling soup and disappears into the shadows. I watch his silhouette in the moonlight until he disappears into a dense grove of trees. I clutch my arms tightly around myself as a chill that the fire can't touch settles into my bones.

Ten

I rise at dawn, my back and neck stiff from lying on the hard ground. The air within the tent is cold, much colder than it had been when I turned in last night.

I waited up for Bastien, stoking the fire and adding kindling when it burned low, but he never came back. At some point in the middle of the night, I heard him return, the covers of his makeshift bed rustling as he burrowed deep into its layers.

Rubbing my eyes and stretching my arms high overhead, grazing the canvas roof, I realize the material is damp to the touch and drooping low. It snowed last night and Bastien was stuck out in it.

Guilt cinches tightly around my gut as I grab my boots and shove my feet into them. *It's my fault, of course. I should have stuffed down my misgivings and invited him to sleep inside.*

The tent is more of a glorified tike-tent, as Eamon likes to call it. Big enough for one full-sized adult to crawl into or a couple of kids to mess around in. Considering most of the soldiers are used to roughing it, I'm sure they don't mind the cramped quarters, but when it comes to Bastien, his nearness is something I'm not sure I'm ready to handle.

When I emerge from the tent, I see the fire has long since died out. The embers are clumped together in balls of damp ash among the newly fallen layer of snow. It has drifted against the side of my tent and at the base of trees, making the two-inch snowfall seem more like half a foot. Bastien's bedroll has been lifted off the ground and slung over a crudely constructed lean-to, made of the remaining bits of firewood and our laser guns. Hardly ideal for sleeping in a winter storm.

As I turn in a slow circle, gazing deep into the woods, I

realize Bastien is gone. Did he leave sometime during the middle of the night?

I cast my gaze over the moist ground, peering at the blinding white of the snow, and spy a set of tracks moving off to the south. Did he leave me behind?

That's when I hear a whistle in the woods, faint and certainly far off but high enough in pitch to be heard over the rustling of the trees and the pattering of clumps of snow falling from heavy-laden tree boughs. The returning whistle is lower in pitch and staccato in rhythm.

I stand and listen as two more back and forth calls drift my way and then silence returns to the land. I work to busy myself around the camp, beating as much moisture as I can from Bastien's bedding before rolling it up.

I change into a new uniform, staring longingly at my cammo pants, but I know with the new chill on the air, I will need the insulation the uniform offers. Winding my hair into a bun, I draw the hood of my jacket up over my head to keep the small flakes falling from the sky from sliding down my neck.

I nearly have the tent packed away when Bastien returns with a handful of glossy, purplish berries. It looks like they had at one time been encased in ice. Judging by the bright-red patch on his palms, he used his own body heat to melt them. "Breakfast is served."

He dumps over half of the berries into my open palms and tosses the rest back. A small bubble of purple bursts between his lips, staining them momentarily. The corners of my lips twitch into a smile before I lower my gaze. "Friends of yours?"

"Scouts. We're closer than I thought. Must've taken a shortcut through the foothills and brought us out on the wrong side. No wonder I didn't find camp last night."

"Do we need to go back?" I ask. Supplies are in greater abundance than they were the year before, what with our supply lines better manned as more soldiers continue to mutiny against Drakon, but we never needlessly abandon resources if we can help it.

"No, a truck will be dispatched to collect it. We need

to get you back to base. The sooner we arrive, the sooner we can go after Drakon."

I wipe my hands clean on the sides of my pants, thankful that the purple stain won't show through the black material. I wish I could say the same for my hands, but at least breakfast wasn't wolf again.

If I'm not exhausted by the time we stop tonight, I'm going to go hunting. I could really go for roasted rabbit right about now.

"You ready?"

"Yeah." I reach for my pack, but Bastien is already there, snatching it away to sling over his back. His hair is lightly dusted with snow. Droplets drip from the spiked ends onto the bridge of his nose as we brush down the campsite to clear away any signs of our stay.

Even though this area is well within our territory, we can't be too careful. A rogue Sky Ship could easily spot a campsite from above if poorly attended.

The snows come and go throughout the day, falling in sprints of thick blankets and then fading away to nothing more than a faint trickle of flakes. The hike keeps us fairly warm and the slick terrain helps me remain focused, but when lunch rolls around and we stop to eat, I find myself longing to sit alone.

Thankfully, Bastien doesn't seem to be in a talking mood either. He spends his time fiddling with the zip of my pack, his gaze averted. I can tell he is lost in thought and wonder if he's thinking about our conversation last night.

The forest is quiet today, the birds nestled in their trees to weather the storm. The sound of our boots crunching becomes monotonous as we walk, heads bowed against the winds. I had hoped by heading south we would reach slightly warmer weather, but so far the tip of the southern borders have been less than welcoming.

From time to time, I hear the call of a hawk spiraling high overhead. I consider asking Bastien to stop to check out the newly killed animal to see if the meat is still usable, but I remain silent. I'll suffer through another meal of wolf meat if it allows me to keep the peace.

I envy the birds, swooping and gliding on the driving winds, viewing the world from an angle I haven't seen in a long time. I haven't flown since the day we attacked Drakon. A part of me wonders if I'm even capable of it anymore, but I still remember the feeling of the wind whipping through my hair. The feeling of freedom and weightlessness.

You aren't the only one that can fly, I think as I stare at the hard set of Bastien's shoulders as I walk behind him. I know he is angry. I just can't decide if that emotion is entirely pointed in my direction or if he has reserved a bit of it for himself.

The snows rise over my ankles, making our hike more arduous. With each step, I can feel myself wearing down, but Bastien never slows, although he seems more aware of my condition than Eamon was. Bastien may be driven to run from his own demons, but at least he is considerate along the way.

The only evidence of passing time is the slight darkening of the sky. I know it must be nearing late afternoon, but without the sun in sight, it is hard to pinpoint an exact time.

Bastien halts directly in front of me and I slam into his back, grunting as I break against him and slump to the ground.

"What'd you do that for?" I rub my chin, sore from where I hit.

He waves at me to be quiet and I'm instantly alert. I rise to my feet, crouching low as I hurry to his side.

His gaze sweeps the white landscape. I follow his lead but close my eyes, feeling my way instead. I'm about to tell him that whatever he heard must be an animal, but I hear a hiss pass through his lips. My eyes pop open and I nearly stumble backward.

A woman stands before us, less than fifteen feet ahead. She is elderly and hunched at the shoulders. Long white hair flows to her waist in a single braid, curled over her left shoulder. Small wisps stick out around her face. Her cheeks are thin and her face wrinkled with the passage of time.

Pale, translucent skin is pulled taut over arthritic hands, curled inward like claws.

I find myself completely lost in the woman's gaze. Her eyes are as blue as the deepest sea and filled with vibrant life, betraying a youth that is in sore contradiction to the state of her physical body. A silver cloak flows over her frail frame, the hood drawn back from her head to rest upon her back. Her sleeves are wide and billowy. Her feet concealed by the wide hem that rests upon the snow.

Bastien places a hand upon my wrist in warning. "Who are you?"

"I am Sariana, high prophetess of Calisted." Her eyes appear to twinkle from within. "At least I used to be until I was shipped off to this place."

"Are you a friend or foe?"

The woman laughs as she stretches her hands out on either side of her. "Do I look as if I can bring you any harm?" Bastien frowns but says nothing in response. The woman's smile broadens. "You are wise not to trust me, Bastien. Although, I think you may decide you need to hear what it is I have to say."

His grip on my wrist is almost painful. "How do you know my name?"

"Oh." She waves a hand noncommittally in the air. "I know a great many things. I wouldn't be a very good prophetess if I didn't, hmm?"

Casting a glance in my direction, I know Bastien is trying to gauge my reaction. I can sense nothing about this woman, no abilities, yet there is something different about her. Almost as if she weren't standing there at all. A void.

She turns her gaze upon me. "Although you may possess vast amounts of power, Illyria, you will not be able to search my memory. It is a gift given to seers at birth to protect our visions so none may be implanted or stolen."

"I can see her," I say to Bastien, never dropping the woman from my gaze, "but I can't feel her."

"Has that ever happened before?"

I shake my head. He draws me close to his side. "What is it that you want from us, prophetess?"

"You ask the wrong question, young man. What you should be asking yourself is what you want from me."

"I want nothing," he replies. I can hear his heart beating beside me, thrumming loudly. Or perhaps that is my own heart. I can't tell.

"On the contrary. You have one question that burns brighter than all the others." Lifting the hem of her cloak, she turns, glancing back at us over her shoulder. "You want to know why you are still in love with Illyria."

The small wooden building is hidden behind a grove of thickly overgrown spruce trees. I wouldn't have known it was even there if I hadn't been straining to see our destination. It blends perfectly with the woodland backdrop, the roof blanketed with snow and the walls hewn from trees of the same spruce family.

A small spiral of smoke rises from a chimney, the stone slightly wonky as it perches atop the slanted roof. Two small, square windows can be seen in the front of the home as we approach, smeared with years of grime.

When Sariana turns to smile back at us over her shoulder, pushing the door open, I realize with a start that her mouth is nearly toothless. *How did I not notice that before?*

Nervous tension wiggles down my spine as I cross the threshold into a dark room. It takes a moment for my eyes to adjust to the dim light of candles set about the room.

The elderly woman putters about the cluttered room, stepping lightly over stacks of books to lower herself into a rickety rocking chair nestled in the corner. I notice very little of my actual surroundings as I sink to the floor before her, careful not to knock over a stack of leather-bound books to my right. I feel lightheaded as I look at her, mesmerized by the glow within her eyes. It is a stunning trick of light, almost like the brilliant green glow in the eyes of a wild animal after the sun has gone down.

An unusual feeling passes over me. It feels like something gently massaging my brain. Not painful, just... odd. After a brief moment, the feeling passes.

The bent woman leans forward. "I have waited a long time to meet you, Illyria. Since long before you were even in your mother's womb."

She rubs her hands over the silken material of her cloak. "I am one of the three high prophetesses. The other two are my sisters, Liliana and Dinara. Sadly, Liliana passed some years back."

"And Dinara?" I ask.

Sariana's eyes take on a distant look, her voice soft. "She was taken from me, held prisoner by Aloysius before he became king. He feared our power yet was drawn to it at the same time. Together with my sisters, we were very powerful. After Liliana died, he chose to exile me here."

"I'm sorry. You don't care about my life." She blinks, as if waking from a dream. "I know what it is you seek. I have the answers."

Bastien leans forward, his expression one of caution yet edged with longing. "Can you tell us why Illyria is in such turmoil?"

I glance over at him, watching the shadows that play across his face. He draws back from my gaze, a flush rising in his cheeks.

Sariana says he seeks the answer to why he still loves me, but he hasn't said those words. Even now he can't seem to bring himself to say them. Is he hiding from himself or trying to protect me from more pain?

"Each of you has been given the DNA of your chosen mate. What Kyan told you is true. Illyria has been selected to be with Eamon."

I didn't realize I was holding my breath until it puffs out between my lips. Bastien's shoulders tense, but he says nothing, nor does he attempt to look at me. Sariana smiles. "But she possesses your genes as well, Bastien."

"So there was a mistake," I say.

"No. Not a mistake at all. The genes you received were the exact ones you were intended to have."

I scrunch up my nose, utterly confused. "I'm afraid I don't understand."

The crackling of the fire pit just behind Sariana seems

to brighten in intensity. I raise a hand to shield my eyes, but almost as soon as I glance away, the anomaly vanishes. I look to Bastien to see if he noticed, but he merely stares at the prophetess with rapt attention.

This is getting weird.

Grabbing a shawl from the arm of her chair, Sariana wraps it about her shoulders. I don't know how she can stand the added layers. Heat rolls out of the chimney grate in stifling waves. Already my clothes have begun to dry from the snows.

"You and Bastien share the same genes because you were *meant* to share them. Simple as that. The match you have with each of these men is both genuine yet complicated."

"That's one way to put it," I mutter under my breath.

The rocking chair creaks loudly as the prophetess rises unsteadily to her feet. She plods toward a darkened doorway, pushing aside the tattered brown cloth that acts as a door to separate the two rooms. I lean to the side to try to see through the slit that remains, but all I can make out is a wall of bowing shelves stacked haphazardly with books.

Large and small, square and rectangle. There seems to be no rhyme or reason to the stacks. Some boast golden lettering while others are scrolled in black ink. Upon the floor are scattered pages, filled from top to end with scribbled symbols and letters I don't recognize.

"Ah, here it is." She hobbles back into the sitting room with an oversize book in hand. Intricate scrawling letters are carved into the leather cover and binding, symbols that look foreign yet vaguely familiar.

"I've seen that book in my visions," I whisper, realizing only as the words tumble from my mouth that it is true.

"You have seen one similar to this. One belonging to my sister, Liliana." She drops the book onto the table beside her. A cloud of dust erupts into the air.

Bastien coughs as he moves to get a closer look. "I can't read the writing. What does it say?" he asks, brushing his fingers lightly across the worn, faded tawny cover.

"It is written in an ancient language, similar to your Latin. It is only spoken by the prophets of old… and only on Calisted."

I look at the woman, wondering just how old she really is. On Earth, I would guess her to be around eighty years old, although I've never seen a woman so old. The eldest among our group was in her late sixties when she passed of a fever some years back.

"I am among the first of men, those who lived before the war. By your calendar, I would have been born in the mid-1900s. Then the invasion came and I was whisked away with the survivors. Time slows to a near stop on Calisted, preserving not only our bodies, but our minds as well."

"And when you returned? Did you continue to age?"

"Yes." She nods. The loose skin under her chin jiggles. "I don't fear death, but I could have done without all of the body aches."

I realize with a start that she is laughing under her breath, as if her plight were actually funny. I suppose, being locked away in this tiny cabin in the woods, the tiniest thing might bring you humor… or a touch of insanity.

"What does this book contain?" I ask, drawing her back from her recollections

"Ah, yes." She opens the cover and flips through the pages. A faint musty aroma tickles my nose. The pages creak as she shifts them, yellowed and stiff. I wonder if it is as old as she is. "This is the *Book of Testimony*. It details all prophecies that've been handed down, both minor and large."

"And Illyria is in there?" Bastien shifts, drawing his legs in so he can move closer

"Of course, dear boy, but she isn't alone." She taps her chin as she continues her search through the pages. "Haven't you figured out yet that you are just as much a part of Illyria's destiny as Eamon is?

"I'm in there too?"

She lifts her gaze from the pages to shoot me an

amused glance. "Not too bright, though, huh?"

I struggle to hide my smirk. "Please, continue with your story."

"Very well." Sliding her finger along a page near the middle, she nods. "Here it is. What your friend Kyan told you was true. There are no mistakes with our genetic matching sequences. It is perfectly flawless. No one person has ever received two sets of genes before… until you." She stares pointedly at me.

"But why? What's so different about Illyria?"

"My dear boy." She gasps, placing a curled hand over her heart. "You assume it is she that is the special one here, but you are mistaken. Your circumstance, and Eamon's as well, is far more crucial." She pauses for effect, making sure Bastien and I are both giving her our full attention. "The reason Illyria has your DNA, as well as Eamon's, is because you two are fraternal twins."

Eleven

Eamon and Bastien… brothers? The idea is beyond ridiculous, yet Sariana hardly looks as if she is attempting to pull our leg. I glance over at Bastien. He looks stunned. His eyes are wide and unseeing, his face ashen, and his lips pressed together so tightly the color has fled from them.

"How is this possible?" I ask for him, knowing how desperately he must want to ask but is unable to do so.

Sariana's smile is kind as she stares down at Bastien. I'm surprised to see a warm glow of motherly affection in her eyes. "I know how hard this must be for you to accept, but I assure you it is the truth."

Bastien seems to find his voice. "You must be mistaken."

"I am not." She leans forward and clasps her hands together atop the pages. "I was your mother's midwife." His eyes clench shut as he shakes his head in denial. I watch, hurting for him as he struggles to accept her words. "Your mother and I have been close friends for many years. Even though she was far younger than I, she helped me through Liliana's death."

"Where is she?" Bastien begins to wring his hands in his lap. I can tell he needs to move, to release some of his energy, but there is hardly space to walk in this cramped room. "I have so many things I need to ask."

"Patience, Bastien. There will be time for that later, but I assure you that she is pining for your return. It broke her heart to give up her sons."

Bastien plunges his hands into his hair, beginning to rock slightly. "I have a brother," he whispers.

"I guess that explains why you two are always at each other's throats," I say, trying to lighten the mood.

He blinks and then a hint of a smile tugs at the corner

of his lips. "I never was too good at sharing."

Although I know he meant it to be a joke, I don't know what to say in response. He seems to realize the hidden depths to his statement and looks away. I turn back to Sariana. "Even if Bastien and Eamon are brothers, that still doesn't explain how I got their genes. Surely someone would have noticed when I got two pairs instead of one, twins or not."

The same strange massaging feeling I felt earlier passes over me. I stiffen. "Please don't do that. I'm right here. You can ask me anything you need to know."

The woman's eyes widen. "You can feel that?"

"Of course. I just think it's a bit rude," I reply curtly.

Bastien kicks out his leg and bumps me. "Be polite."

"I'm not the one rummaging through her brain." I meet her startled gaze and shove her out of my mind.

Sariana's lips tremble as she attempts a smile. It falters completely and falls away. "Impressive. No one has ever felt my touch before, not even Aloysius. Apparently you are more powerful that I first thought." She pauses to appraise me. "I wonder…"

"Wonder what?" Bastien snaps, his frustration showing through at the woman's silence.

"Perhaps she will be able to feel Aloysius's mental control. If that is the case, she might be able to fight back."

I surge forward, grasping the woman's hand, a thin layer of skin stretched over bony knuckles and twisted joints. "Is that even possible?"

She shrugs. "It has never been done before, but then there has never been anyone quite like you either, my dear." Her fingers curl in my hand and I suppress a shudder as her nails dig into my palm. It isn't painful, but it feels as if she is anchoring down as she draws me near. "If you cannot, all will be lost."

Her grip releases as she sinks back into her chair. She looks weary. Her head leans back against the chair, as if too tired to hold it upright any longer. She closes her eyes for a moment. Bastien looks to me, no doubt wondering if she has fallen asleep before us. She startles me as she sits upright. Her finger glides over the pages, searching for something.

I look beyond her and see small trinkets scattered about the room, items I assume hold great importance from her life on Calisted. There are no pictures on the walls, no albums on shelves, or family heirlooms proudly displayed.

This room is filled with knowledge. What a lonely life she must lead here. I find myself feeling sorry for the old woman.

"Here it is." Sariana pokes a finger at a page near to the back of the book. The binding creaks as she lifts it closer to her face. She squints against the dim light. "Kyan has told you that a destiny binds you, Illyria, but even he does not know all of its details. Very few people know more than what is shared as bedtime stories, but I know what is missing."

"How?" Bastien asks.

"I was the one who received the vision," she says in a hushed tone. The winds howl outside, making it difficult to make out the words. "My brother shared the same vision and afterward wrote it down in this very book."

"Your brother?" I frown. "You never spoke of him before."

"That is because he is the lesser of us, a mutation if you will. On Calisted, only women are born into the lineage of seers. He received the gift. When my parents discovered his abilities, they sent him away for fear that he would be killed. No man is supposed to possess the sight."

"Eamon does." I protest.

"No, he can see the future. That is different. We see all. Past, present, and the things to come. Kaladan is in seclusion on Murilian, one of the moons orbiting Calisted. It is an inhospitable place, one that Aloysius isn't about to search." She pauses to look at me. "Someday you will go to him. He will help you if you tell him that I sent you."

"And what about you? Were you exiled here?" Bastien asks.

"In a sense. I chose this fate once we realized Illyria had been sent here. We knew that someday she would seek answers, and I had to be here for this time."

I tuck my lower lip between my teeth as my stomach clenches. In her hands lie the answers to why Bastien and Eamon are tied to me. As desperately as I want to know, I am terrified at the same time.

As if sensing my turmoil, Bastien takes my hand in his, twining his fingers through mine. It is the first time we have really touched in a year, but the strength of his hands is exactly as I remembered. "You don't have to do this, you know? It doesn't matter what that prophecy says."

"On the contrary." Sariana breaks in before I can speak. "You of all people should want to know."

"Me?" Bastien's gaze hardens.

I squeeze his hand and take a deep breath. "I'm ready."

"So be it." The prophetess raises the book so high I can only see the ridgeline of her brow as she begins to read. "During our darkest hour, six teenagers will rise to lead us out of tribulation. Born of our time but returned to the past, they will suffer the fate of all humanity until the day comes for their birthright. The great tyrant will lash out against them. Some will falter, but only one will save our people. A girl will rise among them. She alone has the strength to harness the Ether." She hesitates before continuing. "You have heard this before?"

"Yes, apart from that Ether bit. What is that?" Bastien asks. His grip on my hand tightens.

"Ether is power. The power that controls the waves, hangs the stars in the sky, and keeps everything in motion. It is life in its more basic and wonderful form." She lifts her finger and continues. "A sacrifice will be given. A new leader rises to rule with a compassionate hand. All will seem lost when death takes the man she loves, but another will rise up to take his place. One shall live while the other passes on. A love debt paid by a single cry."

As her voice trails off, I feel numb, like I'm hovering above my body and looking down upon myself. Her words ring with resounding truth within my soul. Frightening and mind-blowing but real. I have no doubt this will come to pass.

I cry out as Bastien's arm falls over my shoulder, drawing me close. His grip is tight, his expression grave. "Is that all of it?"

"Yes. Illyria's destiny ends with the birth of her firstborn children, a twin boy and girl."

I suck in a breath. "I will have children?"

"Oh, yes." She smiles down at me. "Several actually. They will be a great blessing during the trials you will face."

A strange warmth spreads through my chest, chasing away the chill in the air. *Children.* I never really thought about having kids. Growing up in the rebellion with hardly any food, I knew the cost of bringing a child into the world, but now… the world is changing. Is it possible I could someday be happy?

I turn to smile at Bastien, to share in my joy, but I stop short. The pain in his eyes cuts me deeply. "What wrong?"

He shakes his head. I watch his Adam's apple bob as he struggles to control whatever hidden emotion he is feeling. "Are the prophecies ever wrong?"

"No. I'm afraid not. This will come to pass as has been foretold."

"I don't understand." I duck my head so I can look into Bastien's face, but he turns away. "The prophecy is good. It says we can win. We can save our people."

"Yes," he nods. "But at a great cost to you."

I look to Sariana for help, but she merely stares back. "I have already made my decision to marry Aloysius. The sacrifice has been made. This is what we planned. Now I know it will work."

When he finally lists his gaze to meet mine, I am rocked by the depths of the hollowness I see. "One shall live while the other passes on. A love debt paid…" He trails off.

"Oh." I clasp my hand over my mouth. How did I miss that part? "You mean… Eamon or Bastien?" I look to Sariana with pleading eyes, but she is no longer looking at me. Her eyes are closed and her head leans back against the chair.

I watch in wonder as the age lines begin to melt away from her face. The snowy white recedes from her hair. A rich mahogany replaces it, flowing over from the crown of her head like a waterfall. The curve of her back straightens. "I am free," she whispers.

Bastien scrambles to his feet. "How did you…?"

"I didn't," she replies, raising her hands before her eyes, twisting them back and forth to admire the long, graceful fingers. "My mission is complete. I can go home now."

"But Aloysius—" Bastien protests.

"Is no longer a threat. We can't help him. We are free from our burden."

I grab Bastien's hand, relying heavily on him to help me up. "Does that mean there won't be any more prophecies?"

"I suppose that will be up to you." She smiles. She rises to her feet with a long-forgotten grace.

"What about Illyria?" We watch as Sariana bounces on her toes, her hair floating about her face as she giggles with delight. She looks hardly a day over thirty, beautiful and full of life.

She sobers for just a moment, reaching out a hand to me. "May I speak with her alone for a moment before you go?"

I can feel Bastien's hesitation, but I nod at him. "I'll be all right."

He relents and grabs my pack, slinging it over his shoulder. He opens the door, swearing loudly as he is blasted with gust of icy air. The door slams shut behind him, but I doubt he had little control over it.

When I turn back, Sariana's face is downturned, painted with regret. "I am truly sorry for the trials that lie before you, my dear. I have carried your burden as my own for many years, knowing this day would come."

"Your prophecy has ruined my life," I mutter, feeling little warmth from her hand as she reaches out to grasp my arm. "You took Bastien from me, destroyed Eamon's life, and now you are going to kill one of them?" My voice shakes with rising anger.

"This is not my prophecy. I am just the messenger." She steps toward me and I have to fight the urge to retreat. "Fate chose you because of your heart, Illyria. Your love for your people proves that. You are willing to sacrifice everything. Not many people would do that, and *that* is what will make you a wise queen."

I shift my weight from one foot to the next, listening to the floorboards creak. "What if I can't do this? What if I'm not strong enough?"

She squeezes my arm gently. "You are already strong enough, Illyria. You just have to believe it."

I close my eyes, wishing I had never come here. "I won't let them die," I whisper.

"There is nothing you can do to stop it. You may be able to prolong it, but some day one of them will die to fulfill their role."

I step back from her grasp and shove my hands deep into my pockets. "You told me I have this power to control Ether, whatever that is. If there has never been anyone like me before, how do you know I can't change our fate?"

Sariana's smile is filled with tenderness as she clasps her hands before her. Against her silver robes, her skin no longer looks pale, but warm and filled with golden color. "If there is anyone who can defy the fates, it is you, but I urge you to be careful."

Her warning gives me reason to pause. I turn back from the door. "What haven't you told me?"

She looks toward the back room. "There is more to the prophecy. I did not think you would want Bastien to hear of it."

I walk back toward her. "Tell me."

She nods and disappears behind the cloth curtain. I can hear books tumbling off shelves, clattering carelessly to the floor by her feet. A cloud of dust puffs out of the room. She stumbles out, wafting her hand before her face as she coughs.

"Are you all right?"

"Yes." She chokes, shaking her head. "I hadn't

realized how disgusting it was back there. Poor eyesight and all that."

Tucked under her arm is a dark-blue leather-bound book, far smaller in size than the one she originally read from. Nearly small enough to fit within a pocket. A blanket of cold settles over me as she opens the book and I see pages of darkly scrawled jagged symbols. They look angry somehow.

"What is this?"

"My diary." She blows on the book and unsettles a thick layer of dust. She thumbs through, licking her finger each time before she turns the page. Her lips flutter with whispered words as her eyes scan rapidly across the page.

"Not long after I had the first vision, another hit me. I was afraid of what might happen if I added it to the *Book of Testimony*. If this were to fall into the wrong hands…" She trails off and casts a furtive glance toward the door. I can only faintly hear Bastien's pacing steps punching through the snow. He must be freezing out there. "I saw you, a power of unspeakable horror, capable of bringing entire worlds to their knees. A tyrant to replace Aloysius, beautiful and savage."

I don't have to close my eyes to remember the vision of blood and death that touched me a year ago. Bodies lay scattered at my feet. My friends' lifeless eyes staring at me from great funeral pyres. I blink away the image. "How does this happen?"

Sariana sets aside the book and approaches me. "There is a darkness within you that wants to be free. You have heard its voice, felt its need. You harnessed it when you attacked Thalar and battled Drakon, but it isn't gone. Your hair is a reminder of that. Do not forget how volatile you can be when you're upset. Anger and sorrow are when you are strongest. The death of a loved one could prove disastrous for us all."

"So both prophecies are true?"

"Yes. They are possible outcomes, but one thing is certain… One will happen. It is up to you which path you choose."

"No pressure, then," I mutter. I cross my arms over my chest, trying to hold myself together.

It is almost too much to take in. Eamon and Bastien are brothers. My love for both of them makes sense now, but knowing the truth doesn't make it any easier. Someday I will lose one of them. I can't bear the thought of that. "Will I ever see you again?"

"Who knows what fate has planned for us?" She walks me to the door. "Bastien needs you. Be there for him."

I can only imagine what Bastien must be feeling right now, to discover a long-lost brother and know he has lost everything because of him. And Eamon… he doesn't even know yet.

"I'm not sure I can," I whisper to myself as I open the door and step into the blizzard.

Twelve

The winds buffet against us, stealing my breath away as I stumble after Bastien. I can barely make out the shape of his back even though I'm only a couple feet from him. "We have to get out of this storm," he shouts back to me, cupping his hands about his face.

It is hard to walk. The snow is up to my calves, blowing into swells. I stumble, unable to see the uneven terrain below. My legs are nearly numb, my toes without feeling. I've tucked my hands into the sleeves of my coat, but they feel as if I've left them bare to the elements.

My hood whips about my face, offering little protection. We're not dressed for a storm such as this. If we don't find shelter soon, we'll be in serious danger.

We should have stayed at Sariana's. Even as this thought crosses my mind, I know that wasn't an option. Neither one of us wants to deal with the secrets we discovered within her home.

"I think I know where we can go." I stumble beside Bastien as he grasps my hand, trusting him to lead us to safety. The sky is a solid sheet of white, unleashing pellets of ice that sting as they strike against my cheeks.

My hand is slick in his, my fingers aching from the cold. I struggle to keep up with his fast pace as we weave through the forest, leaping out of harm's way seconds before a tree looms up before us. He raises an arm to shield his face as he plunges deeper into the storm. "There!"

I try to see where it is he is pointing, but only large, shapeless shadows rise before us in the wash of white. He doesn't wait for me to speak before he is yanking on my arm and I find myself tumbling after him, barely managing to stay upright.

At the first sight of a building, I tug back on Bastien's

arm. "Are you insane? You can't just go into a town and assume it's safe."

"I'm not. Besides, who else is crazy enough to be out in a storm like this?" He urges me forward. I can tell he's trying to be patient, but the blanket of ice settling over us is making that difficult.

I lurch forward through a cloud of breath and run on nearly frozen toes. Where did this freak storm come from? I had hoped moving south, we would avoid the early arrival of winter. Perhaps we didn't move fast enough.

We speed past several homes on the outskirts of the town. Many of them are missing their roofs, torn away by storms or laser fire. Entire walls and foundations have crumbled, leaving hollowed-out shells that we have to pick our way over. I slip as I try to crawl over a pile of bricks. Bastien helps me to my feet, wrapping his arm around my back as I slide down the other side.

Brushing the line of ice off the curve of my hood, swiping sleet from my face, I try to peer into the homes as we pass beside them. Sometimes I can make out an overturned table or pair of chair legs sticking up like a porcupine's quills.

I spy empty cupboards and rotting curtains dangling haphazardly from rusted curtain rods. Lifeless TVs with their screen smashed out and shredded couches seem to be a regular occurrence. Each home we pass saddens me, to be reminded yet again of how much was lost when the Caldonians arrived. Snow blankets everything, but at least within the narrow streets of the town, the wind has lessened and we can see farther ahead of us.

"Where are we going?"

"Just up there." I lift my gaze to look over his shoulder and realize where he is taking me.

"A church?"

He doesn't respond as our boots thump against the brick steps and he releases my hand. He quickly slips out of my pack and hands it to me. Turning sideways, he launches himself at the wooden door. It rattles and groans but doesn't give way.

"You're going to hurt yourself."

His lips purse with determination as he hits it again. On the third go, the door gives way and spills him into darkness. "Bastien!"

"I'm fine." He grunts and appears in the doorway, his dark hair lightened by a thick layer of dust. "It's filthy but dry. Come on."

I step over the threshold, feeling a bit out of sorts as I do. I've never been in a church before. My mother used to tell me about them. I've even seen a few remnants of churches within Thalar's city limits but have never entered one.

A part of me is still angry with God, if he even exists. Surely he played some role in creating the misery in my life. And if he did… what good is he anyways?

The sound of wind beating against the roof is loud as we close the door. In the far corner, I can hear sporadic splatter as clumps of snow drop through, a telltale sign of roof damage.

The light within is dim so Bastien charges up his laser. It splutters at first, no doubt affected by the barrage of ice that froze over its casing. Finally, it intensifies to a full glow and I'm able to look around.

This church feels old, dating far before the invasion. Its walls are peeling, revealing the wooden frame beneath. I can see deep grooves carved into the plank wood floor where the pews were shifted to be nearer to the remains of a fire in the center of the one-room building.

The floor around the fire has been permanently charred. A small hole above has been punctured through the roof to allow the smoke to escape.

There are signs of life in this room but nothing recent. Only used-up food cans, bedding that has been converted into a rat motel, and a small pair of black dress shoes for a little girl have been left behind. I stare at the shoes, praying this child made it out alive.

Bastien's rummaging draws my attention as I step farther into the room. I skirt around the hole that drips water and head toward a single-step platform near the front of the church. Tall, tarnished golden pipes line one wall. I peer up at them, confused.

"They were for an organ," Bastien says, stepping around me to check out a back room.

Beside the pipes is a square, hollowed-out space. I lift up onto my tiptoes to look over the edge. "Bathtub?"

I can hear his laughter through the holes in the wall. "It's a baptismal. For people who want to be saved."

"Saved from what?"

He reemerges with an armful of hideous purple clothes. He dumps them onto the floor and dusts his hands off on his shirt, leaving trails of fingerprints upon his chest. "It's really too complicated to explain."

I look back toward the baptismal, wondering if any of the villagers sat in the missing pews, praying to their God for salvation when the Caldonians arrived. A lot of good that did them.

"Did you ever do this? Come into a church?" I ask as I move back toward him.

He lifts the purple material and I realize they are something resembling a cloak. There are two armholes, but the material is so huge it would swallow you whole.

"There used to be one down from where I lived. Mom knew I was fascinated with some of the carvings and windows, so on my birthday, she would sneak me out so I could sit in the pews and watch the moon rise, casting a rainbow of colors on the floor. It was almost magical."

He holds out one of the cloaks to me. "Put on this choir robe. We gotta get these wet clothes off or we'll get sick."

I hesitate, not because of the overwhelming smell of age and disuse that clings to the fabric, but because I'm gripped by a memory: waking half naked in his arms after he pulled me from a lake. He saved my life that night, giving me his sweater to keep warm. I had thought he abandoned me in the city. I was wrong.

"I won't look," he says, and I realize he's staring at me with an odd expression.

I don't trust myself to speak. Instead, I turn my back on him and wait to hear him do the same.

My clothes don't want to go without a fight, clinging to my damp skin as if it were surgically attached. I wiggle and thrust out my hips, hopping on one foot and nearly tumbling right over until finally I am free. I toss the uniform to the side. It lands with a thick splat.

Holding my breath, I slide the purple robe over my head. It bunches at the floor, covering me from neck to foot. I can't even find my arms. Bastien turns and peeks over his shoulder, his grim expression shifting into one of mirth, shaking his head. "It suits you, I think."

"Very funny," I growl, doubling over to wring melting snow and ice from my hair. I realize I've just expelled enough moisture to form a small puddle at me feet and yank back on the fabric to keep from soaking the musty fabric.

I watch Bastien as he flattens out several more layers of cloth. "What are you doing?"

"Making a bed."

I glance toward the windows. Although they are covered by years of grime, I can still see light outside. "It's not dark yet. Shouldn't we wait to see if the storm passes?"

Bastien looks up to find me nibbling on my lower lip. "You really don't want to sleep near me, do you?" He sighs and points to a far corner. "I'll stay over there if that makes you more comfortable."

I'm about to respond with a cutting remark, but then I remember the snow last night and how Bastien remained outside to give me the space he knew I needed.

"No." I shake my head, wishing I hadn't lost my hair string in our mad dash for shelter so I could get my hair back out of my face. It hangs in thick, heavy locks over my shoulders, dampening the top layer of the robe. "It's fine. I just... It's weird, ya know. After what Sariana said."

"I know," he whispers.

"Do you want to talk about it?"

"No." He shakes his head as I sink down beside him. "Not tonight. Maybe not ever."

I wake sometime in the middle of the night to silence.

The pounding of the sleet has fallen away and the stillness that remains feels eerie.

Bastien breathes steadily behind me; his shoulder and leg presses against my back. I had forgotten that he likes to sleep on his back with a knife in hand. Just like me. I look down at the glint of steel in my hand. Old habits die hard.

"It stopped a little while ago." His voice rises from the dark.

I stiffen. "Did I wake you?"

I peer into the dark, wondering why he doesn't speak. *Is he as aware of how close we are as I am? The last time we lay like this was—* I cut off that thought before it takes me into dangerous areas.

"Can you not sleep?" I whisper.

A rustling outside the church makes me crane my neck. I can feel the tension coiling in my muscles as I wait for the sound to come again. When it does, I can hear the distinct ruffling of feathers and let my head fall back down onto my arm.

My right side is numb, but I'm too afraid to move, to shift closer to Bastien or farther away. I can feel his warmth against my back, and I close my eyes, wishing it didn't feel as good as it does.

"I've been thinking."

I stretch out my leg and nearly moan as the needles ripple along my calf. "About earlier?" Flexing my toes brings more jabs of pain, but they slowly begin to subside and feeling returns.

"No," he quickly says, leaving little doubt to just how far he wants to tread away from that subject. "About your mission. It doesn't make sense to me."

Now I do roll over. It takes some effort to toss my dead arm over, but I manage to shift onto my back. I stare up at the ceiling, noticing for the first time that I can see a small patch of cloud through the hole in the roof.

He continues on as if I asked him to. "I've been going over it again and again in my head, but I just don't get it."

Rising up onto his elbows, he looks down at me. His face is clothed in shadow, making it impossible to see his expression. "Why are we really going to this base?"

I frown. "You don't know?"

"Kyan sent word a week ago that we had discovered Drakon's location. I know about the downed Sky Ships and my scouts have evidence that he is moving forces away from the base. If that is the case, why not fly you directly to my base? By the time we reach there and then add on top the travel time, Drakon will have had the chance to escape again."

My hair feels dry against my forehead, slightly curled and frizzy. Staring at the patch of sky overhead, I wonder how long it will be until daylight returns and we can leave. Surely not soon enough for me to escape this conversation.

"I know something is missing." His voice is tight, controlled. "What haven't I been told, Illyria?"

I can't look at him. It doesn't matter that I can't really seem him in the near-pitch dark. I just can't face him, knowing that Kyan lied to him as well.

"We aren't going there for Drakon. We're stealing a ship."

To his credit, Bastien doesn't explode like I anticipated. Instead, he lies back down and crosses his hands over his chest. We lay in completely silence for several minutes before he speaks again.

"Why did you agree to this?"

I blink, confused by his question. "We need the ship. Of course I would do anything to help."

"No." He shakes his head, letting it roll to the side so he is watching me. "I don't buy that. Kyan would never risk your safety just for a Sky Ship. We have plenty of them."

I bite on my lower lip and realize just how tender it has become. I've been worrying a lot lately and it has seen its fair share of abuse. "We aren't stealing a Sky Ship, Bastien."

Even without light to see him by, I know his gaze is piercing and alert. "We're stealing a space transport."

His silence worries me. Bastien is nothing if not vocal about his thoughts. The fact that he has lapsed into a complete and utter calm is unsettling. He shouldn't be calm. He should be angry. Furious at Kyan for keeping this from him. Bastien isn't stupid. He knows what the ship is ultimately for.

"I'm sorry," I whisper into the dark.

I look up to see the rafters of the church building rising at a sharp peak. They are made from a dark wood and at one time were probably glossed and pretty. The wooden boarding between the beams was probably once white but is more of a dingy gray now, much like the walls.

Rolling my head to the side, I realize I can just make out the curve of his chin and the slant of his nose. His eyelashes look long as they rest just above his upper cheek. His eyes are closed and his breathing steady, but I can feel the turmoil brewing within him.

Bastien has always unknowingly given me exactly what I need, even when I don't know I need it. Even now he is giving me time to think, to ponder exactly what I feel about Kyan's plans and how they'll impact me.

It would be far too easy to lean on him now. To need him too much. Already I can feel myself longing for that connection we used to have, but I know I have to fight it or be lost all over again.

He stirs and I watch as his chest rises and falls, expelling a long, slow breath. "You have nothing to be sorry for. I knew this day would come."

There is profound sadness in his words, just as I had feared there would be, but there is something more, something Eamon could never quite manage—acceptance.

Bastien never tried to change who I was, even when I gave him a reason to fear me. He knows my struggles better than anyone, even Carleon. He also knows how terrified I'm of the thought of taking the next step toward my destiny.

Without saying a word, he holds out his arm and waits. I react before my brain has a chance to shout a warning, pressing into his side. He is warm and solid, safe. His arm closes around me and I lie there with tears brimming in my eyes as I feel the weight of the past year fall down upon me.

He lets me cry. Sometimes my tears are silent; other times they fall in wracking sobs that grip me so hard I struggle to breathe. Still, he holds me, giving me the support Eamon was never able to.

As my tears subside, I realize how dangerous this is, but I can't bring myself to care. He is here when I need him. For now, that is all that matters.

"Thank you." I wipe tears from my face, feeling the spreading dampness against his chest. He doesn't even seem to notice. I can feel his gaze upon me, searching. "What?"

"I want to come with you."

"You're my guide. Of course you're going with me." I laugh softly. I brush back my hair from my face, suddenly feeling overly warm.

"That's not what I meant."

I close my eyes, realizing my mistake. I walked right into that one. Shaking my head, I draw myself up to a sitting position. The covers fall away and the chill instantly returns. I shiver and wrap my arms around myself. "It's not going to happen so please don't push it."

Bastien thrusts upward, propping on his elbows. The planes of his face are hard set with fierce determination. Even his eyes look darker than normal against the pale light beginning to seep into the room. *When did the sun begin to rise?*

"I won't agree to take you to Drakon's base if you don't accept my terms. I go with you to Calisted, and there is zero wiggle room here."

I gasp, my hands trembling as I clench the covers. "You're threatening me?"

"Not because I want to." I can see the truth of his words in the way he lifts his chin and stares at me with an alert, expectant gaze. "I'll do whatever it takes to keep you safe.

"Why?" My voice cracks and I'm forced to clear my throat. I feel lightheaded, as if all the air has been sucked from the room through the small cracks in the windows.

"You know they will kill you."

"I don't care." He reaches out and places a hand against my cheek, cupping it with such gentleness my tears start anew. Every fiber in my being longs to press into his hand, to encourage him to hold me again, but I know how damaging it would be.

"You can't come."

He opens his mouth to protest, to fight for his right to be there to protect me, but then his gaze shifts beyond me. I can almost see the wheels turning over in his mind. I hate it when he does this. "You're hiding something."

"I just… I don't want you there."

He recoils as if he'd been gunned down with a stun laser from ten paces. His jaw goes slack and color leaches from his face. He swallows roughly and then returns his gaze to me. "I'm not buying it." He pulls the covers from his lap and shifts so our knees touch. "You've always been a terrible liar"

"Only with you," I mutter, absently curling a lock of hair around my finger, twisting it until individual hairs begin to tear from my scalp. The tip of my finger turns purple and numb, and still I twirl. I blink when Bastien places a hand over mine. "The truth, please."

Staring into his face, mere inches from mine as he unwinds my hair, I know it is time. "I had a vision about you a year ago," I whisper. "About your death."

I want to look away, to bury my face in my hands so he can't see the depth to which this has pained me, but I can't. He has consumed me. The last bit of color drains from his face, leaving behind a wash of white. "Was it—" He cuts off, shaking his head. "Never mind. I don't want to know."

There was so much blood… I think, shivering. I reach out and grasp his arm, startling him. "No matter what happens, please promise me you won't follow me to Calisted. If you do…" I don't have to finish that thought. We both know where it leads.

Bastien slowly nods, closing his eyes as he does so. I'm rocked by the raw pain I see when he opens his eyes once more. He claps his hand over mine, squeezing tightly. "If this is what it takes to keep you safe, then so be it."

"No!" I wrench back from his grasp, horrified at the resignation I see before me. How can he give up so easily? "I'm not worth it."

I can feel my nails digging into my palms, deep enough to reopen earlier wounds. Before all of this is over, I will most likely end up with permanent scars.

He doesn't shout or cry or rant as I need him to. Instead, he gently takes my hand in his, uncurling my fingers and pressing his lips to each one. The intimacy of this kiss triples as I hear him whisper my name over and over.

Oh, God! No!

The tears come fast and hard as I feel him drawing me into his arms. I need to resist, but I can't. I feel broken as I press my cheek against his neck and he envelops me with a love that should not be yet is. It always is.

"You're worth it to me," he whispers into my ear.

"Please don't say that," I plead breathlessly, feeling my resolve weaken. I know if he were to draw away now, it would shatter my heart. I need him, yet it is forbidden to me.

He left me. Not the other way around. I remember pleading with him to stay, knowing it would crush Eamon, but he was worth it to me. A year ago, I was willing to give everything up for him... and he is still willing to do the same for me.

"I can't bear to hear you say that, knowing we can't..." My voice quakes so badly that my words tumble into silence.

Bastien's arms tighten around me, so much that I fear I will not be able to draw my next breath, and I find I don't care. Not if it means living without him in my life again, being forced to say good-bye when all I want is to spend an eternity just like this.

"Kiss me," I whisper before I can stop myself.

He stiffens and his breathing halts. I wait for him to say something, to protest and remind me that this can't be, but he doesn't. I draw back to look into his eyes, knowing what I find there just might end me. Within the depths of sapphire, I see fear and longing mingled together, but there is something more… love.

He brushes his thumb across my cheek, slow and deliberate, as if testing the silkiness of my skin. I can smell the slightly minty scent on his breath and memories of a time when nothing stood in our way flood in. I close my eyes, savoring the moment.

And then his lips whisper across mine, so softly I hardly know he has kissed me until he presses harder on the second pass. His hands wind down my neck to clasp my back, drawing me near.

I can feel his restraint and his buried desire. It burns through him like a hot coal, but he holds back. Each of his touches is slow, gentle, and utterly beautiful.

His fingers trail over the curves of my face, as if attempting to memorize each detail. Did he dream of me as I did him? Did he lie awake at night yearning with such intensity that he would break out in a fever?

His touch tells me yes. His lips tell me yes.

Oh, God. My breath catches as I draw back to look at him. *Nothing has changed between us.*

Yet I know everything has. Sariana's earlier words encase my heart in ice. One of them will die. I can't let that happen.

I cry out as a vision grips me so suddenly I hardly have time to fling Bastien away. My hands curl inward and my body spasms and I flail onto the floor, lost within my mind.

A burst of color reflects in the mirror as I whip around to see a giant fireball spiraling toward the palace. "Duck!"

Bastien and Aloysius don't hear me. I throw out my hand and mentally shove them aside as flames erupt against the side of the building, spitting molten rock into the room. I cry out as one of the rock shards lands upon my leg, cauterizing my skin.

"Illyria!" Bastien drives his hand into Aloysius's side and a terrible snapping sound fills my ears. My husband howls and rolls to his side. Bastien scrambles to his feet

and throws himself to my side. "Oh, God, you're burning."

The scent of my flesh melting makes my head swim. I can feel his hands upon me as he digs the scalding rock out of my leg. Darkness edges my vision. The pain is localized but excruciating.

"We have to get you out of here!"

Another explosion rocks the palace. Over the cracking of stone and hiss of flames, I can hear shouting from below. "Eamon!"

Bastien rises to look out the window and nods. "They're coming. We have to—" His eyes widen and his mouth gapes open.

"No!" I shriek as a blood-tipped spike shoves through his stomach from his back. Aloysius's maniacal grin appears over his shoulder as he shoves Bastien aside. He shudders, blood bubbling from his lips. Pain pinches his features; his hands shake as he touches the spike protruding from his stomach. Gurgling moans rise from his throat as he locks his gaze on me, glazing over. "Illyria..." He stretches out his hand toward me.

I can hear the wet wheezing in his chest and feel numbness wash over me. Blood pools beneath him, thick and bright. I watch as it begins to seep toward me. When I look back at him, his eyes are unfocused and his chest is still.

"Bastien!" I shriek, reaching for him even as the vision fades. I fight against my husband's hold, clawing to be free.

"Illyria, stop! It's just me."

I fall still, in utter disbelief. "You're... you're here? But you..." I close my eyes as the room begins to spin. His arms tighten around me, drawing me into his lap. I let him cradle me, needing to be held.

"What did you see?" he asks softly.

My eyes widen as the fear returns with such swiftness it startles me. My first vision of Bastien's death was over a year ago. The sharp reality of it had faded over time, but this vision was longer, more detailed, yet utterly the same. "You can't go to Calisted. Please... promise me you won't go."

Bastien looks sick. His ashen face dulls the color of his eyes as he looks down at me with regret. "I can't."

I sob, nestling against his chest. "I can't lose you… not like that."

I tug at his cloak, hating the feel of it under my fingertips. It is rough and the fibers matted.

"What did you see?" He repeats his earlier question. This time his voice tenses with unspoken fear.

I shake my head. "Please don't make me tell."

My lower lip begins to quiver and I can feel hysteria simmering deep within my chest, taking root. "Shh." He soothes, running his hands across my back. "It's okay."

"No, it's not!" I pull away from him, pleading with him to understand. "What do I have to say to get you to believe me? I've seen your death. It's horrible and it's…" I hang my head. "It's my fault. Everything is my fault."

Bastien draws up my chin so he meets my gaze. "I won't go, okay? I'll stay behind if it really means that much to you."

I sniffle and dry my eyes. I can see how much this statement costs him and I love him all the more for it. "Really?"

He uses the hem of his cloak to dry the tears from my cheeks and smiles ruefully. "Don't I always give you what you want?"

His words have a sobering effect on me. "No." I shake my head. "Not always."

Thirteen

I didn't expect him to want to speak to me as we emerge from the church and catch our first real glimpse of the town in the rising dawn. A brilliant sheen glistens over the iced ground as we descend the church steps.

Up close, I can see this place took a bad beating, although it's hard to see if it was from the initial invasion or scavengers traipsing through since then. There is extensive damage to nearly every building within sight. Brick homes laid waste, nothing more than crumbled heaps. Wooden clapboard-sided buildings show extensive scorch marks. Roofs torn off or collapsed in. Mailboxes melted and disfigured. Play sets torn apart and rusted, rising from lawns filled with waist-high wild grasses.

There are signs still hanging over some of the buildings on what I would guess used to be the main street. The lettering is almost completely rubbed out. Everything is faded and broken, left to rot in the elements.

The sidewalks are cracked and pockmarked. Remnants of cars, smashed nearly flat, line the streets. "What could have done that?" I ask, staring in dismay as we pass.

"Tanks."

I turn to look at him. "Human weapons?"

He nods. "They rolled over this town and kept right on going by the looks of it. We aren't too far from an old military base. My guess would be that this place was evacuated before they bulldozed it to the ground."

A shudder worms its way through me as I spy a small foot sticking out from the tall grasses. Too small to be human. I wrap my arms about my waist, realizing some little girl left behind her toy.

"Illyria."

I turn at the sharp edge to his tone. When I do, I come

face to face with a woman and a charged laser gun. Bastien calls out a warning, but it's too late. I instantly drop to a crouch and knock her feet out from under her.

I'm rewarded with a cry of pain as she lands on her tailbone, her gun clattering away. My knife is in my hand and I'm dipped low by the time she leaps back to her feet. She is tall, shapely, and quick on her feet.

She moves with the grace and ease of a panther as she matches me step for step. I would think her olive skin and silky chestnut hair to be stunning if she weren't trying to take my head off.

The instant she glances toward her gun, I lunge and slam my shoulder into her torso. We sprawl to the ground and her legs wrap around me, tightening against my knife arm. I buck and land punches into her side, but she doesn't relent. The muscles along her neck cord as she fights to loosen my grip on my weapon.

"Enough."

Bastien's command startles me enough that I actually do let go of my knife. It clatters to the ground and I realize I'm free of her hold.

Pressing against the ground, I leap to my feet, cautious and confused. The girl shakes out her hair, adjusting the collar of her uniform. It is so tight that I'm convinced someone had to pour her into it. I can see a red line beginning to appear along her neck.

"I told you she's not so tough." The woman snorts, casting a withering glance in my direction.

My grin widens as I toss out my hand and snatch a board. Before she has a chance to duck, I whack her upside the back of her head. She cries out and falters forward, but Bastien is there to steady her.

He offers me a warning glare as he helps the girl stand. I frown, crossing my hands over my chest. "Want to tell me what this is all about, Bastien?"

I can almost feel the woman's anger rolling over her as she widens her stance and faces off with me. Her vivid green eyes flash with barely controlled anger at what she obviously considers a cheap shot. Bastien sighs and releases her arm.

The instant he does, the woman pounces. She leaps into his arms, crushing her lips against his with such fierce passion that I'm astounded. Bastien seems stunned at first but finally manages to untangle himself from her grip.

He steps back, placing physical space between him and the girl. His chest rises and falls as heat stains his neck. He clears his throat and refuses to make eye contact with me. "Illyria, this is Niyah... my girlfriend."

I don't remember too much of the remainder of my trip. The steady pounding of my heart matches evenly with the stomping of my feet as I walk up the dirt road that leads toward Bastien's base.

I know I'm going in the right direction because of how worn down the path looks. On the edges, I can see deep signs of tire tracks still left over from the ice storm that passed during the night. It looks like this area got a lighter version of our blizzard. I can tell a truck passed by here not too long ago.

Did it drop Niyah off earlier this morning for a secret rendezvous with Bastien? Was he supposed to sneak out and meet up with her? Was she the one he was whistling to yesterday?

Bastien's sidelong glances throughout the morning are enough to drive me mad. *Why didn't he tell me about her?* seems to be set on repeat in my mind.

I spend lunch by myself, adamantly trying to ignore Bastien's whispered conversation with Niyah. Although they speak in low tones, there is tension between them, and I can't help but feel happy about that. I don't really remember eating. Only that I did and it tasted like mud in my mouth.

Now I walk beneath a speckled pattern of sunlight that sneaks through the clouds above, unblinking and unwavering in my need to show him how much I don't care... but I do.

With each stomp, I can feel my anger mounting, wishing it was Niyah's head underfoot instead of muddy slush. I notice absently that my pants are splattered up to my knees, but I don't care.

Another voice needles its way through my anger. *Is this really so different than what I have done with Eamon?* I grit my teeth and send a spray of brown snow into the air with a stomp. *Shouldn't I be happy he has moved on?*

"You're acting childish." A voice calls from just over my shoulder.

I shoot a defiant glare at Bastien and continue walking. He easily keeps pace with me despite the extra weight of my pack on his back. I can hear Niyah walking behind us, feel her haughty gaze upon me. "I don't want to talk about it."

"At least let me explain."

I stop so suddenly he gets four paces ahead of me before he turns and comes back. I ignore Niyah as I get up into his face. "I'm here for one thing and one thing only. The mission. If you think any of this"—I stab a finger between him and Niyah—"matters, then you are wrong."

"Illyria—"

"No." I shake my head, feeling a spark of electricity skip down my arms. I'm starting to lose control. I need to get away. "Just back off, Bastien."

"I can't."

When I lift my gaze to meet his, he takes a step back. I watch as he pales and finally nods, raising his hands in surrender.

I turn and stomp on, knowing what he saw. I could feel the color of my eyes fading to black as easily as I felt the electricity on my arms. If there is one thing I've learned over the past year, it's knowing when I'm at my breaking point.

Bastien taught me that the day Drakon tried to kill him. I nearly tore down the entire city on top of my friends for him. I vowed after that I would learn control, or at least learn my trigger.

He has always been that for me, whether I like it or not.

I'm volatile when he is around. My emotions weigh

heavily on my powers, but I'm most lethal when I'm hurt. Bastien knows this better than anyone.

"What's with her?" I hear Niyah ask, and I speed up. I don't want to hear Bastien try to make some pathetic excuse for my temper. He could try to tell Niyah what I'm like when I lose control, but no one really knows until they see it firsthand.

I put a fair amount of distance between us as we round a large bend, lined with spruce trees and dotted with small knee-high bushes with bright-red berries. The clouds shift overhead, casting me in shadow.

At first I think it is this movement that catches the corner of my eye, but the hairs rising on the back of my neck say otherwise. I drop into a crouch, searching the woods. Someone is out there. I can feel it.

I hear Bastien approaching at a run and turn to warn him but see him waving his hands over his head. "He's one of mine!" I hear him shout.

Rising from a crouch, my grip loosens on my knife. I tap it against my leg, waiting for Bastien to arrive with Niyah right behind him, looking less than thrilled to have been forced to jog for my benefit. "He's one of mine," he says, sliding to a halt beside me.

"I heard you the first time." I glance at the man concealed in the woods. He is good. If it hadn't been for Bastien's warning, though, he would be a dead man.

He isn't alone. There are four more scouts up ahead. Two on the right, crouched within a tangle of thorns that mask their camouflaged uniforms. Two others are perched from above in perfect sniper position.

Niyah crosses her arms over her chest, looking perfectly comfortable with the scowl pinching her beautiful features. "So she saw one of them. Big deal. She didn't see the others."

"Yes," Bastien says without any hesitation. "She did."

His confidence in my abilities would've made me tingle with pride if I weren't so angry with him. Instead, I ignore him completely and look to Niyah instead. "I assume this was your idea."

Her eyes narrow into slits. Her fingers dig into her arm as she nods. "What of it?"

I toss my hair back over my shoulder and tuck my knife back into the sheath at my hip. "Bastien would never have made that mistake."

Without waiting to see the heat rise in her face, I walk on. Bastien sends out a long whistle followed by three short ones. His soldiers melt out of the woods, standing at attention on either side of me as I pass. I don't turn to look at them. Instead, I keep my gaze focused on the structure looming before me in the tangle of green.

Vines grow up a towering wall in a latticework pattern. The wood is dark, damp from the snow. The gates stand nearly ten feet overhead, crisscrossed with supporting beams on either side. I can't see the hinges at the rim of the doors as they begin to swing open. They disappear into the thick overgrowth, hiding the true length of the walls that spread out on either side of me.

This place speaks of age. It was not constructed a year ago, but was erected long before. Was this some sort of an outpost used by survivors?

We managed to endure the Caldonian regime by hiding out in caves. Was it possible that someone actually managed to live above ground and survive?

I crane my neck back to look at the towering doors as I pass through, marveling at the rope and pulley system that controls them. A wheel-like structure with eight wooden pegs thrust out in a circle is being manned by four men. I can hear the cranking sound of gears hidden within the walls as the doors begin to close behind us.

A guard tower is perched every hundred feet along the wall, the space wide enough for men to walk side by side along the top. Thick, pointed tree trunks line the front wall. Shielding my eyes from the sun, I realize there are large bowl-like structures set evenly between each guard house.

"What are those for?" My curiosity gets the better of me.

"They hold oil," a man beside me answers. "Just in case the Caldonians decide to scale our walls."

"Wouldn't the Sky Ships just blast through?"

He grins and I realize he is missing several teeth. "Perhaps, but I like to be prepared, just in case. Call me old-fashioned."

I take a closer look at him, surprised to see wrinkles etched deeply into his weathered face. It is unusual to see an older man among the Caldonians. Time moves differently on their home world. This man must be several hundred years old.

There are patches of age spots on his face and a definite sag to his cheeks. His eyes are a dull yellow, reminding me more of a finch than of the sun. His hands are leathered, with veins winding just beneath a thin layer of nearly translucent skin. His shoulders are hunched slightly, his back curved.

When he steps forward to offer me his hand, I accept it immediately. "I've heard much about you, young lady."

He winks at me and then casts an amused glance back at Bastien. From the corner of my eye, I can see the tension along Bastien's shoulders. "Illyria, I would like you to meet Otto. He is the keeper of the wall."

"A job to be proud of, I'm sure." I dip my head in greeting and offer him a smile. I like him and the crinkles of years of laughter that gather at the corners of his eyes.

"The pleasure is mine. I would be happy to give you a tour, if you like."

Bastien steps between us and claps the man on the arm. "Another time perhaps, Otto. We are tired from our journey."

"Of course." He leans around Bastien and gives me a wink. "I'm sure you'll drop by sometime."

There is a distinct skip in his step as he turns and walks back toward the wall as the doors shut with a resounding boom that echoes through my chest. When Bastien turns to look at me, I simply glare back. "He wasn't causing any harm."

"You don't know him like I do," he mutters and moves past me. I can see the sag of his shoulders and realize it wasn't my weariness he spoke of, but his own.

A tiny sliver of guilt settles into my stomach, but I ignore it as I turn to follow, not wanting to be left alone with Niyah as a companion.

"We house over a thousand soldiers here at any given time," Niyah says as she notices my wide-eyed gaze as we move away from the wall toward the heart of the base. Long two-story rows of wood and brick buildings span out on either side of me. Even rising onto my tiptoes, I can't see the far end of the base.

Everything is handmade but finely crafted all the same. Whoever originally built this place had skills I can easily appreciate. No concrete sidewalks, flickering electricity, or humming generators. I feel at home here.

As we walk between a row of buildings, their windows clothed in plastic, sheets, and other tacked materials to keep the winter winds out, we emerge into a wide-open courtyard. There is no grass here. It has been long since removed by the pounding of feet and movements of machinery. Snow drifts against the buildings, but farther out into the yard, it has begun to melt, leaving great puddles of mud and standing water.

In the distance, I can see large domed buildings that sit on a small rise. Great black openings within the front of the structures reveal trucks and two Sky Ships. Large blue barrels with evidence of a growing rust epidemic can be seen in a storage building leading to what I can only assume to be a landing area. Dirt roads lead to and from this location, winding through the base.

Everywhere I look, black-clad soldiers are busy at work—some doing minor repairs on buildings, others carrying heavy loads of linens from one squat concrete block structure and into one of the housing buildings.

The scent of food still lingers in the air as we pass by an outdoor lean-to. It has no walls, only steel beams holding aloft a wooden roof. Rows of benches and tables rest beneath. A large group of men still sits in this space, their empty bowls forgotten.

"This is where we train our new recruits, along with our special forces," Bastien says. I can hear the pride in his voice and I almost smile. It wouldn't surprise me if he trains personally with each of the groups. "These men are the best we have. Kyan knows I like a challenge."

And a reason to escape, I think absently as I look at the training field. Nearly five hundred men stand in square-like formations. It is a sea of black, each man bending, twisting, and shouting commands. They move with one fluid motion as they take to an obstacle course made of ropes, a climbing wall, weaving through barrels and sloshing through mud. I recognize Bastien in their movements.

Some men stand in a row nearest me, laser guns tucked into their waistbands as they aim for wooden targets. Others use small pistols, holding them with two hands to steady their aim.

I turn at the sound of clanging metal and see two men surrounded by a large group of soldiers, swords drawn and flashing in the sun. I move forward, enraptured by the sound. Their bodies glisten with sweat, naked apart from rolled pants that rise above their knees. Their muscles ripple and stretch as they dip and lunge, rolling to their feet to parry the next attack.

"They use real swords?" I've never seen one before, but now I want one.

"They aren't widely used, but some of the men prefer hand-to-hand combat as opposed to lasers." Bastien looks over at me as Niyah speaks. We both know I fall into that category as well.

I've always had a thing for knives, serrated and lethal. Guns are good at long range, but I prefer the heat of battle, up close and in my face. Reckless, as Eamon would say. I prefer to think of it as being personal.

Even I have to admit, as we continue to walk on the outskirts of the training field, that I'm impressed. Not even Kyan oversees a facility as tightly run as this, leaving it to Bastien to keep an entire battalion of men ready for war at a moment's notice.

"This way." I turn to follow Bastien as he leaves the field and heads toward one of the buildings that I assume to be lodging for the soldiers. There is nothing flashy about it.

No paint on the weathered walls. Only the base essentials. Back to the basics.

I pause at the door to look back and realize, if not for Niyah's presence, I would like it here.

"I'll show you to your room." I blink, surprised to realize it is Niyah who spoke instead of Bastien. "I'm sure a delicate thing like yourself would like to get some rest after such a long hike."

I bristle, ready with a comeback, but Bastien beats me to it. "Illyria has had plenty of time spent on the battlefield, Niyah. I would advise that you do not underestimate her abilities."

Cool green eyes drift over me as Niyah's lips peel back into a smile that is anything but genuine. "No. I don't think I will."

The sound of my boot steps along the floor echoes in the narrow hall. Doors line either side. Most of them are closed, but from time to time I peer through a doorway to find a room occupied. The space is small and square with hardly enough room to walk between two rows of beds, stacked on top of each other. I nearly stop and go back when I see the first set of beds, curious as to how such a construction is possible.

Near the middle of the dimly lit hall, we approach a set of stairs. I follow behind Niyah, trying not to notice how perfectly small her waist is or how her hips flare out. *You never used to care about your looks*, I think blandly as I keep my eyes fixed at my feet instead.

"So you're Eamon's girl, huh?"

I nearly trip over the last step as I look up to find her watching me from the doorway of the second floor. Her smile is smug, her eyes bright and knowing. I grit my teeth as I nod, knowing she wouldn't have been quite so brave if Bastien were still with us. Surely she knows this name is one he would rather never hear again.

"Yes." I nod, wishing I had one of those pretty swords from the training field to shove into her abdomen. "I'm with Eamon."

"I thought so. Everyone around here is so excited to

meet the prophecy girl. You'll be quite the celebrity. I hope Eamon has a lot of trust in you because I'm sure there are plenty of guys here that would like to get to know you on a more *personal* level."

I just bet she would enjoy that too. Distracting me while she sinks her claws into Bastien. I ache to challenge her out loud but know I'll regret it if I do. Not because of any guilt over angering her. I could care less about her. It's me. Saying the words aloud would make all of this real, and I much prefer to imagine I'm still tucked up in bed, back home, fuming over being locked away by Kyan. Why did I ever complain about that before?

"I've heard rumors about you," she says, seeming unfazed by the fact that I continue to teeter on the final step. She doesn't move away to give me space.

"Oh yeah? Anything I should know about?" I can hear the ice layering my words, and I grin. Two can play this game.

"Just that you seem to have a bit of a temper problem."

"Yeah." I nod as I shove past her, knocking her into the door. "That I do."

She lets the door swing closed behind her. I turn around when I realize she isn't following. "My room?"

Her flawless olive-toned skin darkens as she thrusts her hand toward the left-hand hallway. "All the way at the end. The door is unlocked."

"I'd say it's been a pleasure." I pause as I lean in close to her. "But I think we both know it hasn't."

Her eyes flash with anger, but she nods. "Likewise."

She turns on her heel and marches back toward the door.

"One more thing," I call.

Niyah flips her hair over her shoulder as she turns to look at me. I can see she is seething.

"If you ever hurt him, I promise your death will be slow and *very* painful."

She blanches for a second and then rapidly shifts into a deep crimson. I wiggle my fingers at her in a wave and then turn and walk away, grinning from ear to ear.

"I know all about you," she calls, and I stop mid-step.

I turn around slowly and force myself to lean casually against the wall. Might as well get this showdown over with now. "You know nothing about me."

Her smile returns, broad and haughty. "I know the only thing that matters. Bastien left you."

My mouth goes dry and my heart clenches painfully in my chest. I have to admit the girl knows how to throw some pretty good punches. "And you're just the rebound."

Niyah's eyes narrow and her hands curl into fists at her sides. She juts her chin toward the hall behind her. "Bastien forgot to tell you that if you need anything, our room is in the building next door. Top floor. This one is for men only."

Our room? I feel decidedly lightheaded and am grateful I'm already leaning against the wall as her words echo endlessly through my ears.

I can feel electricity spark along my wrists, vining up to my elbows, but I ignore it. "Your room?"

For a moment, Niyah looks like she's just popped a whole lemon into her mouth. "I haven't moved in yet, but it's just a matter of time. He's been dying to have me with him, but he insisted on renovating the room first. Isn't that thoughtful?"

"That sounds like Bastien. He always went above and beyond to make me happy."

Niyah's smile vanishes, only to be replaced by barely restrained anger. "You were the past. I'm his future. So hands off!"

I throw back my head, laughing. "Are you serious? Do you have any idea who you are threatening?"

A calculating smile returns to her glossed lips. "Of course. You're the girl who nearly destroyed him. I'm just here to pick up the pieces."

I see shadows before my eyes, feel the pulsating rhythm of energy coursing down my arms. I clamp my eyes closed and fight for control. "You need to leave now," I growl.

Niyah laughs. "Why should I?"

My toes curl in my boots as the invisible arcs of energy ripple down the length of my body. "Because if you don't, I'm going to throw you out… through that wall."

Strands of coal-black hair begin to rise off my shoulders, but Niyah seems oblivious, lost in her jealousy. "You think just because you're the prophecy girl that you can boss people around?" Her sneer alters her face enough to disguise her beauty. "You may have Kyan and Bastien wrapped around your finger, but I'm not fooled."

"Niyah, I'm warning you," I hiss as the floorboards beneath my feet begin to quake. The door beside me rattles in its frame, the handle jiggling as if someone were trying to turn it from within. I can hear beds stuttering across the floor behind closed doors as the ripples radiating out from me flood down the hallway.

I watch as her eyes widen, suddenly realizing her mistake. She begins to back away, her boots stuttering across the floor. I can hear shouting rising up from the first floor, winding around the stairwell. Doors slam and boots pound the floor as soldiers rush for the exits.

Almost from a distance, I can hear the winds howling as they beat against the building. At the end of the hall, the plastic covering the window tears free and sails off into the darkening sky. Hail begins to pelt the ground, but I hardly notice as I focus my gaze on the ceiling, fighting to pull back from my anger.

"You stupid girl!" I lower my gaze to see Bastien arrive at the top of the steps, his hair windblown and a trickle of blood dripping from his head. He must have been hit by one of the hailstones. "What have you done?"

He yanks on her arm, pulling her back from me. All I can do is stare and feel. From somewhere within the building, I can hear glass shattering, raining shards onto the wooden floor. I blink as fat drops of rain patter against my nose. I lift my gaze to see a hole being torn through the roof, as if a hand came down from heaven to peel back the layers.

"Her eyes…" Niyah gasps, raising a shaky finger to point at my face.

"Get out!" He yells and hurls her toward the stairs. "Evacuate the building."

Niyah looks terrified as she darts one last glance at me and then fumbles her way down the steps. I don't watch as she goes. Instead, I close my eyes and try to focus on the frantic thundering of my heart in my chest.

Deep cracks form in the walls as boards shift and mortar cracks. Bastien cries out as the floor bucks, nearly sending him to his knees. I can feel the paving stones that form the foundation of the building beginning to separate.

"Illyria, I need you to calm down. Just breathe and focus on my voice."

"You shouldn't be here." I open my eyes and realize how dark the hallway has become. I look beyond him and see that a near-pitch dark has fallen over the base. I can still hear the screams, but they sound farther away now.

The last time I lost control, I nearly destroyed everything I held dear. Now, the only thing I care about is standing right in front of me. This time it has nothing to do with revenge but everything to do with love and jealousy.

"I'll leave when you stop all of this." His voice is even and carefully controlled despite the winds that tear at him, driving him back. "You have to stop this before any more people get hurt!"

"I know!" I wave my hand to the side and shove Bastien back into the stairwell. With a twisting of my hand, I slam the door shut, sealing him out.

I slide down the wall, burying my head in my hands as the building shudders around me. It is hard to focus. All I can picture is Niyah's lithe body wrapped tightly around Bastien. An acrid burning churns in my stomach as I double over.

I never had a reason to feel jealous before. Now I understand what Bastien must have felt all of those months he watched me struggle to accept my relationship with Eamon. Why he had to leave me behind.

I did this to him, I realize as my power recoils, snapping back into me like an overstretched band. I slam backward into the wall, crying out as the wood splinters around me and I collapse inside an empty room, my head cracking against the floor.

Curling in upon myself, I feel the shift in the air. A dim light appears at the window and the howling winds fade to nothing. Warm, sticky blood coats my hand as I touch the back of my head. The room is spinning, but I know it has little to do with me.

"Illyria?" Bastien pounds against the stairwell door as I close my eyes, utterly drained.

Fourteen

I didn't speak to anyone after Bastien carried me out of the building, couldn't face the looks of awe and anger as he clutched me in his arms. This was all my fault. They know it just as well as I do.

Niyah may have provoked me, but I let her do it.

Looking back over his shoulder, I realize it's a miracle that the whole building didn't collapse on us. The walls are buckled, the boards warped and disfigured. A wide circle of crumbled stone and melting hail ring the building, but as I look ahead, I realize none of the other buildings were affected. Even the hailstorm was localized.

I guess I didn't completely lose control after all, I think wearily as Bastien storms directly past a pale-faced Niyah and into his building.

It looks hardly any different than the one I was to be housed in. The doors may be spaced slightly farther apart and the walls are a bit less dingy, but otherwise it feels like a mirror image until we reach the second floor.

There are only four doors spanning either side of this hall. I can see where doors were removed and framed, no doubt to enlarge the rooms. Bastien silently carries me to a door at the far end. His fingers tighten as he leans forward and sets me on my feet.

He doesn't meet my gaze, but I don't blame him. I deserve the silent treatment, a stern scolding, but this isn't in his nature. "This is my room."

That's all he says. I watch as he scratches the back of his neck, shuffling his feet from side to side before he abruptly turns and leaves me. The sound of the stairwell door slamming resonates through my chest.

I close my eyes and exhale a deep, long breath. *I shouldn't be here. Eamon was right. This wasn't a good idea.*

My knees begin to quiver as exhaustion grips me. I expended far too much energy with my little tantrum. My stomach growls ravenously, but I ignore it and grasp the handle.

I push open the door and feel my breath catch. The room is beautiful.

I step inside and close the door, pressing my forehead against the wood grain as I try not to think of how perfectly it was designed for me. Bastien must have spent days preparing for my arrival, even knowing Niyah would never allow him to give me the use of his room, yet here I stand. That knowledge makes this so much more painful.

The room is large and spacious but slim on furniture. An oval rug covers much of the floor. The furniture is handcrafted, planed smooth instead of glossed with a thick lacquer. A tall, two-door cabinet stands floor to ceiling opposite me. A delicate rose pattern has been etched into the top molding. It sits on wide, rounded legs so it is the perfect height for me.

A simple pot of winter mums stands upon a small rounded table. Two chairs sit beneath it, tucked tightly under the tabletop.

Candles, in various heights and colors, adorn the room. Most of the wicks have burned low, evidence of time spent in the room. Books stack high upon a three-legged table beside the bed and upon the floor.

I push away from the door and gently brush my fingers over the smooth book covers. The pages are slightly yellowed, the binding rippled with signs of water damage, but I can also see pages that have been turned down to mark where Bastien left off reading.

A smile curls my lips as I sink down onto the bed. *He still loves to read.*

The mattress is soft beneath me yet offers the firmness and warmth of a feathered bed. I reach down and unlace my boots, kicking them off onto the floor. I wriggle out of my pants and draw my shirt over my head, wincing at the muscles that scream in protest.

I've been on the move for too long. Casting a glance toward the bathroom I realize how disappointed I am that there is no bath. At least not one with running water.

Vaguely I remember seeing a well in the center of the base and have no desire to cart buckets of water up two flights of stairs just for a bath.

Tugging a few snarls from my hair, I sink into the softness of the bed, too tired to care to rise so I can slip between the covers. I am asleep almost as soon as my head touches the pillow.

A deep shadow has fallen over the room as I open my eyes, grimacing at the pounding in my head. No, not my head. The door.

An insistent hammering breaks through the peace and quiet of the room, forcing me to rise. There is a chill in the room that makes me shiver as I stretch my arm toward the floor in search of my clothes.

"Go away," I grunt as my fingertips brush against my pants.

"We need to talk. Open the door." Bastien's voice sounds off. I pause and look toward the door. *Has he been crying?* "Please let me in. I don't want to have to break down my own door, but I will."

"I don't want to talk to you, Bastien. I just want to be alone." I loop my finger around my shirt and shove it down over my head. It feels stiff to the touch, reminding me of how badly I need a shower.

I hear him shift on the other side of the door. "I know I have no right to ask it of you, but I need a chance to explain."

Pins and needles jab mercilessly at my feet as I plod toward the door. Even I know it wouldn't take much for him to burst through. The door squeaks on its hinges as I open it and leave it ajar and return to the bed.

Bastien looks awful when he enters. The skin beneath his eyes is puffed and rimmed with purple. His eyes are bloodshot. His hair lies plastered to his head; dried blood still curves his forehead from his wound. His fists are red and bruised from pounding against my door.

"It's your room," I say, sweeping my hand before me. "Come on in."

There is a definite measure of unease sitting in the pit of my stomach as he closes the door behind him, pausing to push the lock in place. I clasp my hands in my lap, determined not to let him get to me this time.

When he moves into the room, his steps are slow and stunted with a slight limp. I narrow in on his left leg and noticed a slash over his thigh that wasn't there before. "How does the other guy look?"

He looks confused for a moment, then glances down at his leg. "Better than me, unfortunately."

Crossing my arms over my chest, I wait for him to continue. When he doesn't, I grow restless and shift farther back on the bed. Bastien stands before me, looking broken and uneasy. He lingers, buying himself time to weigh out my mood. "You came to talk, so talk."

He clears his throat and moves toward a narrow, high-backed chair. It is wooden and without cushion, hardly suitable for comfort, but he doesn't seem to notice as he perches on the edge, leaned forward onto his knees. He starts to speak, but I interrupt him. "How could you not tell me about her?"

He purses his lips, clenching his hands so tightly they appear void of color. "I didn't know how to. Things between Niyah and me are... complicated."

"Complicated?" My eyebrow arches with surprise. "That kiss didn't seem all that complicated to me."

Wincing, Bastien hangs his head. "I didn't know she would be the one to meet us."

"Yeah, those kinds of surprises really suck, don't they?" I say pointedly, thinking back to the shock he gave me only three days before.

"I didn't know she would show up like that. She's never disobeyed my orders before."

I snort and thrust myself back onto the bed, propping myself up with his pillows. I hadn't noticed it so much before I fell asleep, but they smell just like him. "Oh, come on. She knows about our past, Bastien. Do you really think she wouldn't want to mark her territory?"

His gaze hardens as he sits up. "How does she know? I never said—"

"You didn't have to. She's a girl. She's not stupid. Besides, you of all people should know how rumors spread. Especially about the *prophecy girl*."

He presses back into the chair, looking torn between wanting to remain seated or begin pacing a rut into the floor. "They shouldn't call you that."

"And yet they do." I shrug indifferently. "It's true though, isn't it? I don't get a say in what I want. My life has already been decided for me."

"But Niyah..." He shakes his head. "I've never seen her act like this. If I had known..." He trails off as he scratches at his hair. He draws his hand back and sees caked blood under his nails and lets his hand drop back to his lap.

I watch him closely as a mixture of emotions plays across his face. Finally I understand his mistake. "You never truly let her in, did you? That's why you didn't return her kiss or let her move into your room. You weren't delaying her because of wanting to make this room perfect for her... You were avoiding her."

Even as I say it, I know it's true. One glance around this room and I know none of this was done for Niyah. She was too bold, too harsh to appreciate the craftsmanship that went into the design, but I see it. Whether Bastien meant to or not, he created a room for us, not them.

Bastien lowers his head in shame. "I had to find a way to put her off."

"Why?"

Bastien has a beautiful woman waiting with open arms to embrace him. Niyah may be abrupt and rude to me, but I have no doubt she is different around Bastien. She is a strong woman. He always loved that about me.

I can give him nothing but a life of regret and misery. Bastien isn't mine to fight for anymore. "You have a chance to be happy. You should take it."

Bastien's head jerks up. He throws himself out of the chair and kneels beside me at the head of the bed. "Surely you know I don't love her."

"It doesn't matter what I know or don't know, Bastien." My throat tightens as I'm forced to look away. I can't stand to look at him as tears rebelliously collect in the corners of my eyes. "She loves you. She wants you."

"But she's not..." He plunges his hands into his hair. He looks stricken as he spreads his arms to look back at me. "She's not who I want."

The coarse undertone running through his voice tears at me as I push up to my feet, needing space. I mutter something as I stumble away, clinging to a wall for balance. My legs quiver beneath me and I slide down the wall.

My stomach churns as I clench my teeth together, willing myself not to be ill. *Please, not again!* I sink back onto my heels, my hands clasped tightly over my thighs. I stare up at the sky, squinting up through the darkened window.

There is something soothing about the deep blue. I search for the moon and the stars, veiled from my sight by strips of low-hanging cloud. I know they are there, far beyond the reaches of my vision, but that makes them no less real.

Somewhere, floating among an infinite number of stars, is my home, the one I have no memory of, yet I know I have a family there. A mother who pines for my return. A father who never got to hold me in his arms.

Do they have other children? I never really thought to ask Kyan about that. Perhaps I'm not as alone in the world as I feel at this very moment.

A rustling behind me alerts me to his presence. I used to sense him just by a feeling, like a breath washing over my skin any time he was near. It was almost kinetic, like two magnets being drawn by an invisible force. Now it feels broken, awkward. I'm not the same girl I was a year ago. Too much has happened.

He is different too, yet when I look into his eyes, deep

down I know he's the same man I fell in love with.

"I need to be alone," I whisper.

"I know. I just don't want you to do it by yourself."

I laugh, wiping my nose with the back of my hand. When did I start to cry? I don't even remember doing it, yet my vision is blurred and my sleeve moist. "You always were stubborn."

"And you hated losing."

I nod, shaking my head at the memories. There are so many of them, tiny snippets of time spent alone with him. The look in his eyes when I took my first sip of soda and spat it out all over his subway car. The look on his face when he let me drop to safety when we were cornered in the factory and I knew he was sacrificing himself for me. The way he carried me tenderly through the moonlit woods after he pulled me from the lake, saving my life again. The haughty grin when he caught me bathing in the falls. The way the light faded from his eyes when I revealed my destiny to him. The fervor of his last kiss, as if the world was ours for the taking and nothing else mattered.

I close my eyes as tears flow freely. "I've spent a year trying to forget you, Bastien."

"I know." And I can tell by the tremor in this voice that he does. He knows all too well.

I swipe a finger under each eye to clear away the last few tears before looking at him. He looks awful. The transformation would be remarkable if I weren't the reason for it. "I wanted to hate you for leaving me…"

He nods and slowly sinks down the length of the wall until he is crouched less than a couple feet away. A moment ago, it would have felt he was encroaching on my personal space, but now it feels as if there is a huge trench between us. One that he willingly dug.

"Do you want to know the worst part of all of this?" I'm not sure I really do, but I can't say no. Not with him looking as if he is about to fall completely to pieces before me.

"It was knowing that you would blame yourself."

A bitter laugh escapes as I nod. "You always did know

me too well."

Bastien slips down onto the floor, kneeling beside me. "I don't expect you to say anything or even respond in any way. I just… You deserved to know nothing has changed."

He starts to leave, but I reach out and grasp his hand. He turns, surprised. "Tomorrow, we leave for battle…" I trail off, feeling heat stain my cheeks.

"Yes."

I know it isn't fair for me to ask, but I do all the same. "Will you stay with me? I just… I need to be held."

I know what this request costs him. I can see it in his eyes as he nods and helps me rise. He turns his back as I peel out of my jeans and slip under the covers. Crossing the room, he opens the cupboard and pulls down a spare blanket.

The mattress creaks as he sinks down on the bed beside me. He slowly unties his boots and sets them aside. He pauses with his hand over his zipper, and I hold my breath, wondering if I should turn away. Glancing over his shoulder at me, he meets my gaze, holding it for a moment before he twists and lies down beside me, covering his fully clothed form with the blanket.

I roll onto my side, my mind a mess of doubts and fears until he turns to cradle me. Stretching his arm around me, he cups my elbow in his hand and rests his cheek against my back. I breathe out a slow breath and close my eyes, comforted by his presence.

Fifteen

Warm sunlight streams down onto my face through the window, glowing beyond my eyelids. I don't want to move for fear of breaking the spell that sleep has woven over me, calm and peaceful.

I blink as I wipe away the last dregs of sleep. The snowbirds call forth the new day, and I must rise. As I stretch my arms overhead, bending them to accommodate the headboard, I instantly become aware of the fact that I'm alone in the bed.

Placing my hand on Bastien's pillow, I realize he has been gone some time. His warmth has fled, yet his scent still lingers. Rising up onto my elbows, I see that his blanket has been neatly folded and left on the chair.

I don't remember him leaving me during the night. He must have tiptoed out in the early hours before dawn.

A smile crosses my lips as I roll over to find a single flower laid across the pillow. I lift it and breathe deep its rich aroma. *Bastien*, I sigh inwardly. *If only you could be mine.*

A deep exhaustion still clings to my body as I push back the covers and double over into a full stretch. My muscles are sore and weary, unprepared for the battle that lies ahead. Today we'll begin our journey to Drakon's base. By nightfall, we'll be deep in enemy territory.

The ever-present reality that this might be my last day on Earth hits me as I run my hand over the space Bastien lay upon. My nails trail over the silky emerald blanket as I resist the urge to scoot to his side of the bed, just to feel close to him again.

Let me go while you still can, I think as I glance about the room, taking in all the small details that Bastien knew only I would appreciate. Pillows are piled high around the headboard, far more than any guy would ever need or want. It is only now that I realize there are white eyelet lace curtains framing the frosted windows and real glass in the frame, not plastic or worn spare material. The mums smell lovely as they stretch toward the light of the sun. The vivid yellows, oranges, and reds are brilliantly backlit. This is a room I could've fallen in love with under different circumstance.

Grasping a small jug perched upon a stool beside the sink, I pour clean water to wash up with, finally cleaning away the dirt, grime, and tears from my body. I take the time to wash out my hair, towel drying the excess moisture from my long strands before heading for the wooden closet where I dumped my bag yesterday.

I bend over to reach for my bag but realize the door is ajar. Drawing the door toward me, I'm inundated by the scent of Bastien. I close my eyes as I try to deny how easily it affects me, dredging up memories of being in his arms. I slam the door shut and turn away, my hands shaking slightly as I dig out my black uniform top and pair it with my cammo pants. I need a day of being me instead of who everyone else expects me to be.

I'll no doubt stand out when I walk through camp, but to be honest, after yesterday's meltdown, I don't think there are too many people who aren't going to stop and stare.

It takes me longer to lace up my boots than it should, the quiver in my fingers not having faded completely. I run my fingers through my hair and consider winding it into a bun but decide against it, letting my damp hair flow freely down to the middle of my back.

If Eamon were here, he would scold me for being so careless, reminding me that I would catch a cold in the blustery winter air. This is precisely why I don't dry my hair. Because there is no one to nag me.

I glance at myself in a small mirror that has been propped up on a rectangular table, its white pine top layered with uneven grains, yet to be sanded. As I grab the mirror, I wonder if Bastien overlooked this detail or if he found beauty in the flaw.

Pinching my cheeks to liven up my washed-out complexion, I set down the mirror and take a deep breath. *One night with Bastien is hardly enough, but it is all I can hope for.*

I don't look forward to seeing Niyah. Will she know Bastien stayed with me? Is she the reason he snuck out?

Sometime during the night, Bastien confessed to me the truth behind his relationship with the olive-skinned beauty. She is his genetic match, just like Eamon and he are mine. Another relationship torn apart by a destiny that none of us could control.

Bastien can no more love Niyah than I can swear him off. Kyan had hoped that when Bastien met Niyah, something within him would trigger, allowing him to move on, but Kyan's plan failed. Instead of bringing Bastien peace, he only made things worse.

To his credit, Bastien tried to warn Niyah, but he told me she wouldn't listen. For some reason, that bullheaded streak of hers doesn't surprise me. It certainly makes sense why she was so fiercely protective when I showed up. She knew she didn't hold Bastien's heart. I do, even if I can't accept it.

Closing my eyes now, I remember the moment he stole my heart for the second time.

"Were you ever tempted by her?"

He shrugged indifferently. "She isn't you. Even if she is the right one for me, I would never choose anyone over you."

"But you have Niyah..."

He took my hand in his and drew it up to his lips. "But she doesn't have me."

Those final words tore through my poorly constructed willpower and sent it tumbling to the ground. I knew from the first moment I laid eyes on Bastien that I was doomed, and he just sealed my fate... again.

The base is a barren wasteland today. No one is in the training yard. No one dares to brave the freezing temperatures. Except me.

The rope burns in my hand as I pull myself up the wall. My feet shuffle higher, slipping dangerously on patches of ice. Gritting my teeth, I release the rope and leap the final five feet. My numb fingers grip the top lip of the wall. I grunt as I slam into the wood, smacking my ribs against the wooden planks.

"That was a foolish thing to do," a voice calls from below.

I swing my weight back and forth, tossing my leg up so it catches on the ledge. With my arms trembling, I pull myself upright, perched with one leg on either side.

"Afraid I was going to fall?" I call down to Niyah.

"Hardly." She rolls her eyes. Her chestnut hair is drawn tightly back from her face into a severe bun. A few wisps fly away about her temples. Her cheeks are rosy from the wind. "We leave in less than an hour and you're here risking your life like an idiot."

I grin and swing my leg over the side. She cries out as I push off from the top of the wall and plummet. She hardly has time to raise a hand in warning as I land with a solid thud on the ground. The top layer of ice coating the mud-slicked yard spider-webs around me as I rise.

She looks between me and the thirty-foot wall. Her gaze hardens as she drops her hand. "You like to show off, don't you? Makes you feel special. Better than everyone else."

I grin as I walk past her, making sure to toss my hair into her face as I pass. "Nope. I'm just better than you."

I sense the attack a split second before she strikes. Ducking to the side, I narrowly miss a well-aimed kick to my head. I spin and crouch low, weaving side to side. She matches my movements, never dropping her gaze as she circles around me.

Her lips peel back into a sneer, her hands poised in front of her. "What are you waiting for?"

"For someone to stop this childish display," a voice calls from behind us. I don't have to look over my shoulder to know Bastien stands less than ten feet away. Judging by the sounds of scuffling feet, he isn't alone either. "I come out here to get you two so we can leave and I find you brawling."

"It's not exactly brawling," I say, rising from my crouch. "I haven't hit her yet."

She takes a swing at me and I step back. Niyah growls as she spins and leaps toward me. Her eyes widen in surprise as Bastien's arms close around her, yanking her back. "Enough. If you can't let this go, I will leave you here."

"But she—" She starts but cuts off at a fierce shake of his head.

"You are a soldier. Start acting like one." The temptation to stick out my tongue at her is nearly more than I can bear. "And you." He rounds on me, his neck stained red with anger. "What were you thinking to jump off that wall? You could've been hurt."

"I'm fine."

Bastien steps closer to me, blocking Niyah's view of us as he gently takes my hand in his. "You nearly gave me a heart attack," he whispers.

Painfully aware of Niyah's close proximity, I step back and offer him a rueful smile. "I thought you like a bit of danger."

A smirk cracks his stern exterior. He rushes to wipe it clear as he turns and addresses the men at his back. "Let's head out."

All are suited up and ready for battle. Their uniforms are black as night, their laser guns newly polished and charged. Thick woolen coats fall over their broad shoulders. Their faces are nearly completely concealed by facemasks to keep out the worst of the cold. Heavy black gloves protect their hands.

Small packs rest between their shoulder blades. There is no need for hiking packs. The trip to Drakon's base will be done by vehicle.

It is time.

Niyah makes sure to bump my shoulder as she passes. "Stay away from Bastien or you'll regret it."

The winds whip about my legs with cruel intensity. I tuck my hands deep into my armpits to keep them warm. Strands of hair whip about my face, lashing against my wind-burned cheeks, but I don't free my hands to tuck the strands back. There is no point. In only a few seconds, they'll be yanked free again.

The metal truck bed below me is frigid despite the blanket tossed over the floor. Six men huddle around me. The sound of teeth chattering can be heard over the crunching of ice beneath the tires.

I haven't spent much time in trucks. I can still remember the first time Kyan made me step foot into one. I clung to the dashboard with such force that I nearly ripped it clean from the windshield.

Gasoline is still a rare commodity. It is too volatile to be transported over open roads so it is smuggled in small barrels across enemy territory. Sky Ships are the best mode of swift transportation, but that won't help us today. I personally don't feel like being shot down from the sky.

The men around me are silent, each trapped within their own cocoon of misery. Mine has little to do with the elements, though. My internal battle is one that can't be won, knowing my failure will endanger the lives of the men beside me.

These are the same thoughts I ponder each time before I enter battle, but today is different. It is not just my life that I worry about. I have never truly fought beside Bastien. We ran for our lives a few times but never really fought. What if he makes me lose focus and someone gets hurt?

Surely Kyan knew this would be a struggle for me. Knowing him, he thought it would be a good training exercise. He does have a way of turning potentially deadly situations into a learning experience.

My unofficial bodyguard sits beside me, his shoulders nearly wide enough to span a third of the truck bed. His arms are mounded with muscle, his neck so thick I doubt Bastien could fit two hands around it. His hair beneath his hat is cropped short into a military cut. His eyes are wide and alert as the forest blurs past us.

Bastien is being overprotective. If this had been Eamon, I would've accepted the guard with a lot of sarcasm and no small amount of protests, but not with Bastien. I know his fear is stemmed from an emotion far deeper and far more frightening.

We both know how horribly wrong this mission might go. Bastien's only concern is getting me back out alive, mission accomplished or not. Gorgan will see to it. It wouldn't surprise me, should the battle take a turn for the worse, if he doesn't toss me over his shoulder and barrel straight through walls just to get me out.

Despite Gorgan's imposing height and breadth, he is actually a rather gentle giant. His voice is deep and velvety. His smile is broad and warm enough to melt the ice from the end of my nose. "Are you warm enough, miss?" he asks, leaning in closer.

I nod, biting against the near constant tremor in my lip. Without asking permission, Gorgan curls his arm about my shoulder and draws me into his side. Bastien casts a glance toward us but nods his approval before returning to his conversation with Olaf, a man who loves his knives even more than I do.

"How many times do I have to ask you to call me Illyria?" I smile up at my guard.

"At least one more time, miss."

I laugh and gratefully sink into his side. There is zero cushion to snuggle up to, but beneath his arm, I can feel the ice beginning to thaw from my bones.

Niyah leans forward to interrupt Bastien, placing a hand possessively high on his thigh. I try not to stare, but it's hard in such a confined space. I would've felt better if he'd shoved her hand away, but he is too busy arguing his point to notice.

"Don't worry about her, miss," Gorgan calls down to me softly. The man beside me emerges from the collar of his uniform to glare at us. I can't seem to recall his name, but the scent of smoke hangs thickly on his jacket. It sparks a memory—campfires and melting pots used to create new ammo. He yawns and returns to his dark hovel. "She's usually like this before battle. All fierce and blustery. It's just her way. Don't take it personally."

Oh, it's personal all right.

I stomp my feet against the truck bed as we whizz down the road. What started out as a mildly cracked concrete street has given way to a rutted dirt road slicked with ice and downed tree limbs. The driver seems particularly bent on hitting as many bumps as possible.

Dorian, son of Milorn, sits before me, his shoulder-length white hair flapping freely in the wind. If his white hair were not startling enough, his tiger eyes would be enough to make you pause. I long to ask how this could be. I've only ever seen vivid, solid colors. Never a design such as this, but Bastien warned me against speaking of such things to him.

This young man has a love of crossbows with poison-tipped arrows. He is currently in mid-argument with his companion Adonis, a stark opposite of Dorian. Where Dorian is white and fair, Adonis is ebony skinned with tight black curls upon his brow. Adonis carries four laser pistols. Two at his hip, one at his back, and one tucked into his boot. Gorgan warned me to watch out for him. He is as deadly with his charm as he is with his guns.

"All right, listen up, everyone." Bastien's voice cuts through the winds. I lean in close. Gorgan does the same, and I remain within the shelter of his arms. All hint of merriment vanishes, replaced with a grim tension that I know all too well. "The attack plan is simple. We get in and get out. No alarms. No firefights. We meet our transport soon for the next leg of our journey. Conserve your energy. Keep your weapons dry. Stay alert."

He smiles at each man in turn. "You are the best of the best. That's why I picked you."

I half expected some form of acknowledgement to Bastien's praise. A smile. A nod. Something. The men remain stone cold as statues. They've been trained well. Bastien should be proud.

"We ride through the night to read the edge of the southern province by dawn. From there we will gain access to a second transport and travel throughout the day. Our plan is to arrive at Drakon's base before sunup. We'll use the cover of night to hide our approach."

"Illyria's mission is to acquire a ship," Niyah says, assuming command from Bastien. He leans back, watching. I can't tell from the depths of his hood if his gaze is upon me, but I have a sneaking suspicion it is. "Our sole purpose is to assure her safety until that time. If we fail, she fails. That is not acceptable. Is that understood?"

The men dip their heads in unison. "Good. Prepare to disembark. We've got a long trek before us."

Sixteen

The next day is a blur of snow, ice, and darkness. We sleep when we can, alternating watch shifts. During the day, we huddle under blankets to keep from being seen from the air above. Our truck has been painted white to help conceal it on the snowy roads.

The shocks of the old truck are worn and in disrepair, making our ride even more excruciating than necessary. As I watch the moon drift across the sky on the final night, I vow that if I must, I will walk home.

My hips ache; my head pounds. I'm hardly in proper condition to fight. None of us are, but that doesn't matter. I can tell by the tense set of Bastien's shoulders that we're drawing near.

No one talks. The last of the untouched food was tossed over the side nearly ten minutes ago. I hardly remember chewing let alone what exactly it was that I ate.

Nervous tension ripples through my back, stiffening my already tight muscles. My legs are cramping. My only prayer is that I don't fall out of the back of the truck when we stop.

My stomach is queasy as the vehicle begins to slow, skidding slightly on the newly frozen ice. I grip the edge of the truck, willing myself not to be ill. I don't want to show any weakness, but I'm pretty sure vehicle travel doesn't suit me.

Bastien watches me from the corner of his eye. He has been attentive yet aloof during our trip. It doesn't surprise me with Niyah latched onto him every second of the day.

The snow radiates red as the driver applies the brakes. Gorgan pats my shoulder. "It is time, miss."

"I was afraid you were going to say that." I bite my lip as the truck slides to a halt. My head slams against

Gorgan's arm instead of the edge of the truck. I thank him with a smile as he eases me to my feet.

I feel guilty about my own weakness as Adonis and Dorian leap off the back of the truck, already in motion to set up a perimeter. Niyah leaps down without any help, landing lightly on her feet.

I scowl at her as she winks at me, then disappears into the night. "Where is she going?"

"On ahead to scout out the area. Normally Bastien sends Adonis, but she said she needed to stretch her legs." Gorgan shrugs. I must have missed that interaction sometime during the broken sleep I managed to snatch.

After two days mentally turned inward, it is a relief to be able to stand again, to stretch and feel my muscles pull taut. I tried to remember all of the lessons Kyan taught me. Close off my mind. Focus on my thoughts. Trust myself. And above all… don't lose control.

That last one is easier said than done.

Only one mile now separates us from the largest, most highly guarded enemy base known to us. If this doesn't go precisely to plan, none of us will survive the day. And even then, I'm not entirely sure we can pull this off.

Gorgan remains at my side as I fight to steady myself. Pins and needles jab viciously at my legs, making it hard to remain upright on the ice-crusted snow. I squint into the dark, barely able to make out Bastien's silhouette as Niyah runs back into view. They speak in hushed tones.

I grit my teeth as she attempts to give him a kiss, but he steps back out of her embrace. He says something curt to her and I can see her fists clench at her sides as she follows him toward us, hanging back a few steps. Adonis and Dorian approach from either side of me, weapons at the ready but lowered for safety. They nod toward Bastien, and I know no one has discovered our approach.

My breath puffs in the air before me in steady, fast pants. My heart hammers in my chest so loudly I'm surprised no one else can hear it. Normally I'm calm before a battle, but not tonight. Maybe that's because tonight we aren't trying to take prisoners. We're taking a really big ship.

Bastien slips past Niyah and comes to stand beside me. Although he doesn't turn to look at me, having him near helps calm my nerves. *I can do this. We can do this.*

I know he will not leave my side. He will protect me until death, if that is required of him, but I'll never let that happen.

"Alpha team take the southern route." He motions to Adonis and Dorian and two other men whom I've refrained from speaking to. They aren't like the others. I've never once seen them crack a smile or laugh. They are hard-core. "I will lead Illyria to the northern entrance. Gorgan and Niyah will follow along the eastern ridge and wait for our signal. All radios are to remain silent unless there is an emergency. Stick together and watch your back. We don't want to alert the entire base to our presence."

I nod along with the men, feeling nervous pressure billow in my stomach. This is it. The moment of truth. Either I'm about to pull off the biggest heist this world has ever seen or we're going to fail epically.

Niyah shoots me a vicious glare over her shoulder before she grabs Gorgan's arm and pulls him after her. Adonis and Dorian head up their team, leaving Bastien and me alone. Bastien pounds on the truck bed one time, the sound muffled by the blankets, and the motor turns over. With the headlights off, the truck pulls away, leaving us behind.

"I thought he was staying." I stare at the taillights as the truck slows to slide around a corner, disappearing into the forest.

"The extraction point for the men is a few miles south of here."

"A few miles." I gasp, turning to look toward the direction Gorgan went. "If Drakon's men discover us, they'll never make it."

"They know," he whispers. I turn back to see his shoulders slumped and his face lined with concern. "These men volunteered for the mission, Illyria. They knew the risks."

"But it's suicide." I protest, starting to go after Gorgan. I can't let him do this. Not for me. Not for anyone.

Bastien takes hold of my arm and pulls me back. "They have faith in you. So do I."

"But what if everyone is wrong? What if—"

He cuts me off with a kiss. My eyes widen in shock as he presses his hand against my back, holding me close. His eyes are closed, his hand firm against my spine. I sink into his embrace, placing my hands upon his arms as he shifts to envelop me in his embrace.

A moment later, he breaks off and steps back. "What was that for?" I ask, breathless.

"Seemed like a good way to shut you up."

I laugh, shaking my head. "And that's the Bastien I used to know."

He smiles, lighting up his laser so I can see him better. From the corner of my eye, I think I see movement in the trees, but when I look it is gone. "He's still in there, somewhere." Glancing to the sky, Bastien's smile wanes. "We've only got a thirty-minute window. We need to move."

I follow right on his heels as we burrow into the brush. The landscape is wild and untouched. A deer leaps out before me, startling me. Bastien reaches back and tugs on my arm to get me moving again, reminding me of how little time we have left.

Our boots punch through the ice as we dig into a slight incline. By the time we reach the top, my legs are on fire and my lungs feel as if they might burst. Bastien pauses to get his bearings while I suck in gulps of air. *When did I get to be so out of shape?*

"This way." He's on the move again, ducking low as we shift left, heading straight toward the lighted sky.

As we draw near, I spy floodlights perched atop a guard tower, scanning the woods in sweeping patterns. We flatten to the ground as the nearest beam casts our location in white brilliance. Bastien presses himself over my back, shielding me. The light slowly moves on and I breathe a sigh of relief. "You ready for this?" he whispers into my ear.

I nod, knowing that is a flat-out lie. I'm not ready. I want to run, to head straight back to that truck and get the heck out of here before the lasers start flying and blood taints the snow, but I can't.

Bastien grips my hand for a moment, squeezing tightly, and then he releases me and crawls forward on hands and knees. He drops flat as the light trails back toward us. Even at such a short distance, I struggle to see Bastien as he burrows into the snow, using the thick drifts to hide him.

I really need to talk to Kyan about designing some winter uniforms. I think as I rise and crawl to meet up with him.

Two guards are posted for the early morning shift at our entrance. We chose this gate because of its remote location near the back of the base. We'd hoped it would be lightly manned. For once, fate smiles on us.

My job is to slip up and take them out while remaining completely undetected. Too close to risk speaking, Bastien's fingers walk against the snow, signaling me to move. I close my eyes and wrap my powers tightly around me. I can feel the cold blanket of invisibility settle over me. When Bastien's gaze shifts, looking through me, I know I'm good to go. Rising to my feet, I leap in alternating directions to avoid the deepest sections of snow.

My random steps go unnoticed by the guards. I can hear their low murmur of conversation as they lean against the chain-link fence with their backs to me. A raucous burst of laughter masks my approach as my boots hit a firmer surface. I look down and realize I'm now on a gravel road layered with snow and ice. *Perfect.*

Crouching low, I feel the muscles in my legs coil and I spring into the air. I pull out of my somersault and grasp the top of the fence, hovering upside-down for a moment. I lock my knees together and swing down, both feet poised to strike, zeroing in on the stomach of the small guard.

The fence rattles as I send the guard careening back into it. A sickening crack of bones follows after. He emits a single groan before slumping.

His partner whirls around, braced for attack. The instant I'm on my feet, I lash out, shoving my fist straight up the man's nose. Blood spurts from his shattered nose as his eyes roll back into his head. He collapses over his partner's body, neither one ever having a chance to sound the alarm.

I reappear beside them and motion for Bastien to join me. He rushes forward, grinning from ear to ear. "That was brilliant. Don't think I could've done better myself."

"Thanks," I grunt, clutching my hand to my chest. "Think I broke my hand."

"Can you heal it?" he asks, dipping low to melt through the fence with his laser to join me on the other side.

"There's no time." We barely have a chance to snatch the two downed guards behind the guard shack before the floodlight swings back our way. Bastien drags the guards into the shadows and dumps them.

In a couple minutes, the Alpha team will be in position and cause a diversion at the southern end of the base, drawing attention away from the main hanger. With any luck, Bastien and I will be out of there before Drakon's men even realize they've been robbed.

"Grab on to me," Bastien hisses in my ear.

I thrust my good hand into his and run beside him, clinging to the shadows. We pause at the end of a squat metal building. "Can you give us some cover?" Bastien asks as he peers out at the landing field before us.

Gripping his hand tightly in mine, I throw up a cloak of invisibility over both of us. "That never gets old," he mutters as he leads me up a steep embankment. At the top, we find ourselves in the middle of a tarmac. The concrete is cracked and shifted, rising in some places and sunken in others. Kyan told me this used to be an old military base. Jets used to race down to the other end and soar up into the skies. I would've liked the chance to see that.

Several spider drones sit silently along the runway, dark and unmanned. Large, black orbs sit farther down.

"Sky Ships," I whisper.

I can feel Bastien nod beside me, but he pulls us away. Sky Ships weren't made for space travel. They're only short distance transports, meant for use only on Earth. What we need must bend through time and space.

Kyan had informed me that the ship we need will be held in a locked hangar. We'll know it by its sleek design, larger than a house and shaped like a bullet with two wings on either side.

Bastien leads us toward the main hangar. He peers in through the door and instantly ducks as a guard passes by. "You're invisible," I remind him as he tugs me toward a smaller building. This structure only has one hangar door. We press against the wall, struggling to regulate our breathing. Once the breath leaves our bodies, it can be seen. One of the few downsides to invisibility.

"How do we get inside?" I rise onto my toes to whisper in his ear.

"Through that door." Even though I can't see where his hand points, I spy a door halfway down the building that has been left slightly ajar.

I don't have time to point out this detail as Bastien yanks me forward and pauses only long enough to check for a guard inside before we're through and I feel warmth upon my cheeks. The hangar doesn't appear to be heated, but the lack of wind makes the air feel at least ten degrees warmer.

Bastien clamps his hand over my mouth as I cry out. An explosion from outside rattles the walls, surprising me. I turn and peer out the door and see a mushroom cloud rising into the air. "What was that?"

"Must have gone for a fuel truck."

Gunshots and the hum of laser fire piece the night air. I stiffen, silently counting the seconds between return fire. "That sounds too close—"

Bastien's radio bursts to life. Amid the white noise of static, I recognize Dorian's voice. "We are… ambush… abort…" The radio falls silent in Bastien's hand.

"Did he say ambush? How did they know we were

coming?"

"I don't know." Bastien looks grim. A scream breaks through the rapid fire and he closes his eyes, pinching the bridge of his nose.

"We have to go help them." I turn to head toward the door, but Bastien pulls me back.

"We stick with the plan."

"But—"

"No." He shakes his head. "Men die in war. You know this, Illyria. You would make the same call." Another explosion ricochets through the base. I duck instinctively, although we are well out of harm's way. "That's the oil field. There's nothing we can do."

Anger wells up in my chest. I know he is right. I've made this same call dozens of times. "Fine. Let's just get this stupid transport and get the heck out of here."

I remind myself that Gorgan wasn't with that group. Maybe he can still make it out alive.

As I turn to sweep my gaze across the room, sirens blare around the base. Engines roar to life, tires squealing as they speed away from us. The scent of burnt rubber hangs in the air as Bastien pulls away from the door. It's only a matter of time before someone finds us, invisible or not.

"This way," Bastien whispers, leading me through a maze of small aircraft. I spy planes with hulking engines, streamlined jets, and an oddly shaped machine with a propeller perched atop it instead of on the wings. "There it is."

I round the back end of an odd triangle-shaped aircraft to find a sleek black alien warship that, now that I'm up close, resembles an arrow instead of a bullet. It looks deadly, its design perfected to fly under enemy radar and spiral through the stars.

The nose is pointed, fanning out in a V before narrowing into a long shaft. It is the latest in a long line of lethal ships Aloysius has designed over the past year. "Can you really fly one of those?"

"Sure." Bastien doesn't look so sure as I release his

hand and he reappears. He reaches up and slowly trails his fingers over the hull. It ripples, almost as if he'd touched the surface of a pond instead of a metallic ship. "Can you really make this thing invisible?"

I eye the massive ship with apprehension. "Let's hope so."

Sliding my own hand across the hull, I realize it is cold as ice, yet the feel of the alien technology fuels are fire deep within my soul. As if some part of me has just awoken. "Can you feel that?" I whisper.

"Yeah." I turn to find him staring at the ship in awe.

I can sense its purpose through my fingertips, the sheer power and brutality this ship could unleash if given the chance. The urge to set the entire base on fire consumes me as I press my hand flat against the hull.

I cloak myself with anger, drawing on memories of our men's screams. The metal warms, glowing deep amber at first, and then it slowly begins to vanish. I can see the barrels of oil that stand behind it, the oil stains that seep out from a rusted hole in the bottom of the farthest canister.

My arms begin to tremble as I feel my powers pulsate. The entire nose of the ship is gone. The cloak of invisibility crawls across the surface, nearing the door. Like a creeping mist, the ship begins to vanish from sight.

My breath comes out ragged as I push with my mind, pressing myself beyond my limits. Nearly all of the ship has disappeared, but I am draining quickly. Sweat beads along my brow and the sound of laser fire fades into the background. I bite on my lower lip so hard I can taste blood on my tongue.

"Hold on to me." My voice is raspy and thin, but I feel Bastien surround my waist with one arm. The other rises to press my hand to the ship. My body quakes violently, nearly coming undone as he tightens his grip.

With one final push, the tail of the ship dissolves into nothingness. My knees give way and I collapse into Bastien's arms. Somehow he manages to keep me connected to the ship, knowing if I let go, I will lose my control.

"Very impressive." I raise my head at the sound of clapping behind us. "Too bad you wore yourself out for nothing."

The shock of Bastien's sudden movement makes me cry out as he spins around. The ship, along with myself and Bastien, materialize. The lone figure in the shadows steps forward, less than twenty feet away.

"Niyah!" Bastien growls.

Seventeen

I hardly recognize the girl standing in front of me. Her features are twisted with hatred, draining any hint of beauty that used to lie beneath.

"How could you betray our men?" Bastien roars, his neck blotchy with rising anger.

With her attention locked onto Bastien, I scan the walls around us in search of an exit but find none. I glance overhead and spy long metal beams running lengthwise across the room. *Maybe if I could gather some strength together I could pull one of those down*, I think but quickly realize I wouldn't have to energy left to keep us safe from the wreckage.

"Revenge is a fickle thing." A raspy voice draws my attention to the shadows. The hairs along my neck rise as Commander Drakon emerges. "It's so nice to see you again, Illyria. And Bastien… still alive I see. Saved by your first love and now scorned by your second. Oh, how that must sting."

Bastien's grip on me tightens. I can feel him shaking and pray he doesn't do anything stupid. I can't help him if he does. It's all I can do to keep my head upright. I fight to ignore Drakon's quip as he turns his scathing glare toward Niyah. "Why would you betray us to him?"

Meeting his gaze, Niyah winces.

"Isn't it obvious? She's jealous," I answer weakly.

Drakon nods in rapid agreement. "And jealousy can lead even the best person down a dark path." I slump against Bastien as my knees quake, giving way beneath me. "I do wish I could have seen your faces when she revealed herself. Did it hurt when you realized she is the one responsible for the brutal death of your men?"

Niyah's hands clench at her sides, but she remains

expressionless. "This is how you treat the man you love? By handing him over to a man who'll take pleasure in killing him slowly?" I spit at her, disgusted. "You're pathetic."

I can hear Bastien swallow beside me but don't have the energy to turn and look at him. I know what I would see if I did. The hollow man, broken and mortally wounded, but this time it wouldn't be me that lands the fatal blow.

"Sticks and stones, my dear." The wide sleeves of Drakon's robe waft side to side as he raises his hands. He looks almost feminine in his royal-blue attire. His face is still gaunt and bird-like, his nose severe, and his brow large and prominent with his receding hairline.

"Niyah has her own reasons for betraying you. She has done a great service to our king and will be greatly rewarded for her actions today." Drakon sweeps his arm back behind him, dismissing her. "You may go."

Niyah hesitates, her gaze shifting rapidly between Bastien and Drakon. "I played my part. Now give me what is mine."

Drakon's booming laughter echoes off the metal walls. "Stunning but naive. Surely you knew I would never keep that promise. Bastien is far too big a prize just to hand him over to the likes of you."

Her face blots with crimson. "You tricked me! You promised Bastien would be free."

"And he will be… eventually." Drakon's bloodshot eyes look crazed as he turns to appraise Bastien. "Did you think I would give up the chance to torture the man whose life is a constant reminder of my shame? No, my dear, I will have my revenge."

"I won't let you do this." She whips a laser pistol out from the back of her pants, lowering it to aim directly at Drakon's heart. "I'm taking him with me."

His smile wanes. "I grow tired of this. If you wish to live, leave now. I don't give second chances."

Black-clad soldiers slide out of the shadows, surrounding us. A dozen lasers glow a swirling crimson as they train on her. I watch as the fight dies from Niyah's eyes, enraged to see that she has resigned herself to Bastien's death. A veil of red falls over my vision. How can she turn her back on him so easily? Without a fight? What kind of love is that?

Niyah nods and glances back at Bastien one last time before walking away. "Coward!" I yell.

Bastien's arms tremble with rage. I can only imagine how deeply her betrayal cuts him. Not just of us, but of her men. It is unthinkable.

Drakon waits until the door closes behind her before ordering his men to lower their weapons. His smile is dripping with venom-laced honey as he approaches. "I had thought you would put up a bigger defense. How disappointing. And me with so many men aching for a good fight. A pity."

"Well." He shrugs. "I suppose we might as well get on with this. You don't want to keep the king waiting."

I can feel my anger slip away as cold dread washes over me. "And Bastien?"

"He is no longer any of your concern, my dear. I have plans for him." The crazed look returns to his eyes. He claps his hands in front of his chest, gleefully awaiting what is to come.

"He comes with me," I growl, fighting to keep my head upright.

"You are in no position to be making demands, I think. Unlike last time, I have the upper hand. Too bad. I would've liked to see you in action one last time."

One last time... His words spiral through my mind as darkness closes in on the edge of my vision. I can tell Bastien is struggling to keep me upright as I become dead weight in his arms.

Drakon motions for the soldiers to approach. "Escort her to my chambers. The boy goes in his cell."

Bastien reacts before I have a chance to process that I'm no longer being held upright. I stare in horror as a tawny-haired alien in front of me pulls the trigger of his gun, aiming his green stun laser directly at Bastien's chest.

"No!" I shout as I crumple to the floor.

Bastien cries out at the brunt of my mental push. He slams into the wall, his head connecting with a crack. He slumps to the ground, unconscious.

"Well." Drakon chuckles. "I suppose that couldn't have gone any better."

In a swirl of blue, he marches over to Bastien. I watch as he closes his eyes. Bastien's back arches; his mouth hangs open in a silent scream. A tear seeps from his unseeing eyes.

"Get away from him," I growl as I shove with my mind. It is a weak push but enough to knock Drakon off his feet. I collapse back to the floor, my arms too weak to hold me upright. I pant, watching as my breath appears and disappears against the slick floor.

Drakon brushes himself off as he rises, patting his hair back into place. He tosses a sickening grin at me before he slams his boot down onto Bastien's leg. With a nauseating snap, his lower leg rolls to the side.

Bile rises in my throat at the sight of his shattered leg. Drakon rears his leg back and slams it into Bastien's ribs repeatedly, grunting with exertion. Bastien's head lolls toward me and I can see his pain, but he can't seem to scream.

"Stop," I plead, pressing my face against the cold floor. I am helpless to aid him.

Drakon straightens his robe and steps back. Bastien curls inward, his leg twisted. "As much as I would love for you to watch me torture your lover, we are on a tight schedule." Drakon snaps his fingers and a soldier rushes forward. "Get that out of my sight. Make sure he is locked up tight. I don't want him tearing apart the ship in search of her."

Two guards rush forward, stooping low to loop their arms through Bastien's. "And, Amden, make sure you double the guards. This one has a few tricks up his sleeves. We'd hate for him to be harmed while trying to rescue the girl." His snicker lands like a punch to my gut. "That's my job."

Tears well in my eyes, streaming down my nose and

pattering onto the floor as I watch two guards drag Bastien away. His head hangs low to his chest and I pray he has passed out from the pain.

Shiny black boots pause beside my chin. Drakon crouches beside me. The hem of his robe falls about my face. "No cutting remarks today? I do so enjoy your fiery spirit."

I spit on his boot, enjoying the way the glob slowly slides down the side. Drakon growls, wiping the offensive fluid from his polished shoes. "You will be taken to my quarters. Don't bother trying to fight. I assure you, you won't win."

The soldier named Amden lowers his weapon and kneels beside me. He wraps his arm about my waist and hauls me to my feet. My knees buckle and he grunts as I nearly spill both of us to the ground. He hoists me into his arms, carrying me like a small child.

"What are you going to do with me?" I ask, my head resting upon the soldier's chest. His arms are long and lean, clothed in fine muscle, easily able to hold my weight.

"I'm going to collect my reward when I present you to my king."

The smug look on his face makes me wish I could summon enough energy to yank down the roof and kill us all. "I'm sure he won't be quite so pleased when he hears how you have treated me."

A knowing smile spreads along his sallow face. "You have nothing to fear. I know my place. No one shall lay a finger on you. You are safe… for now."

A deep sense of loathing seeps into my soul as Amden carries me past. "Wait," I say and he pauses, undecided. He turns to look back at Drakon, and I get my chance. "I will have you killed for this once I am queen."

I feel a thrill of triumph as Drakon's haughty smile falters as I am carried through the door.

The room is spinning. Not a gentle spin, but a horrendous, vomit-inducing spin. I clutch my head and pray for an end that comes slowly. The air smells odd, almost as if the room has been doused with smoke and pine. A deafening hum stabs at my eardrums, making me clutch my ears to try to block out the sound. A ticking, rhythmic and constant, makes me clench my eyes shut as it hammers into my head.

"What is that awful noise?" I groan and roll to my side.

Blinking several times to clear my vision, I see a tall wooden box standing before me. It has a glass front, a small square at the top, and a longer piece at the bottom. A pendulum swings to and fro in exact time with the ticking.

Pushing myself up from the bed, I realize this is the source of my pain. I stare up at the box, looking at the numbers fashioned in a circle. "It's a clock," I whisper, lowering my hands. I've never seen one of these that actually still works.

I turn to survey my surroundings. The overhead lights are dim, allowing my eyes to adjust with minimal pain. Spreading out my hands, I realize the bed I'm lying on is unusually firm, almost as if the thin layer of mattress has been laid over a slab of rock.

The air is cool against my skin. Panic seizes me as I realize I've been undressed. I cinch the bed sheet about my neck and peer into the corners of the room, searching for a guard, but see none.

The walls are curved near the ceiling, off-white and shiny, as if glossed. There are no windows in the room. The only light comes from a circular lamp that hangs above my head and small lamps scattered about the perimeter of the room.

There are no decorations to speak off. No pictures or mementos. The room is barren of all evidence of life.

I shiver, wishing I had more than a sheet to cover up with. Leaning to the side, I try to see if my clothes have been left by the bed, but they are gone. "Figures," I mutter as I rise, wrapping the sheet twice around me and tucking it in at the top to hold.

The floor is soft and warm against the pads of my feet. The sheet whispers across the plush carpet behind me as I walk toward a darkened room to my left. As I lean to peer inside, a brilliant light flares to life, startling me. Before me, I see a small yet efficient bathroom.

Dread sinks into my stomach as I press my hand to the wall, feeling the source of the hum ripple up through my hand. An engine. I'm on the ship and it has already left Earth.

I lean against the wall and press my palms against my eyes, fighting to shove down my fear. *Where is Bastien? Is he still alive?*

Pushing back my shoulders, I march back into the room, determined to find some clothes and then him. I'll tear this ship apart if I have to.

I press a small, nearly concealed button on the wall, and a closet door slides open. My lips press into a thin line at the sight of men's uniforms, neatly pressed and hanging in a row. All of them bear the red phoenix emblem over the chest, but they also bear the insignia that belongs to only one person: Commander Drakon.

I'm in his room.

Darting a glance around, I narrow my gaze on the walls, hunting for a secret compartment. If there is one thing I learned during our last encounter, it's that he likes to keep weapons close at hand. Hugging the wall, I trail my fingers over it in search of a seam.

I whip around and drop into a crouch when the door on the far wall hisses open. A young girl enters, carrying a washing basin and an armful of towels and linens. She seems startled by my defensive stance but offers me a wide smile and passes by. She moves into the bathroom and sets down the basin. I can see steam rising from the water.

"I thought you might like to have a wash before we arrive, my lady." She glances at my face and I wonder if I look as awful as I feel.

The girl can't be much younger than me. Perhaps sixteen or seventeen. Her skin is smooth and milky, her eyes a beautiful shade of violet. Her lips are pale rose and full, boasting tiny laugh lines at the corners. Her smile is sweet and genuine.

She holds out the towels to me expectantly. I rise

slowly but make no move to approach. "Who are you?"

"My name is Alesta. I've been chosen to have the honor of serving you, my lady." Her voice is high and pleasant, like the trilling of a songbird.

She stares at me with underserved awe. I shift uncomfortably. "There is no honor in serving a prisoner."

Her brow furrows with confusion. "I do not understand. Commander Drakon never said—"

"Of course he didn't." I sigh, sinking down onto the edge of the bed. I rub my temples, wishing the droning hum would cease. "He wants people to think I came willingly."

"You didn't?" she whispers.

When I look up, I'm surprised to see moisture in her eyes. *What is with these people?*

I bite back a cutting remark. "When will I be presented to the king?"

"Oh." A flush rises along her cheeks. "That will be within the hour."

"An hour?" I gasp. "How long have I been asleep?"

"Nearly three days, my lady. The commander ordered that you be left alone, so I have been waiting for you to wake."

"Three days," I whisper, closing my eyes as I press my hands against my stomach. *Bastien.*

I open my eyes and rise swiftly. "A friend came with me onto the ship. A boy. Dark hair. About a foot taller than me. Did you see him?"

She hesitates, shifting her gaze. I quickly close the gap between us and force myself to touch her hand. "Please. He means a lot to me."

Alesta scrunches up her mouth, debating. "I'm not supposed to say…"

I take a calming breath, forcing myself to stop and think instead of just react. I'm in Drakon's territory now. His ship. His rules. But that doesn't mean I can't bend them.

"Why do you call me my lady?" I ask.

Her eyes widen. "Because you are to be my queen."

"And does that mean you must serve me? Do as I

ask?"

She nods her head enthusiastically, eager to serve. I smile. "Good. Then I require to know the whereabouts of my friend."

"I..." Alesta pales and lowers her head. "He is down by the engine room. No one is allowed in apart from the commander. I know nothing else."

"Have you seen him?" I press.

Tiny ringlets of mahogany bounce about her face as she shakes her head. "No, but I have heard... screams."

My hand slips away from her as I clench my fingers into fists at my sides. Alesta raises her gaze to meet mine, and I realize she is a couple inches shorter than me, petite and beautiful. "Thank you, Alesta," I manage to say before turning my back on her.

"The commander spent little time with him, though," she says in a rush, almost as if she needs to please me. "He had to see to preparations for your arrival."

"Is my friend hurt?"

She hesitates. "Not as bad as he could've been."

I can feel my anger swirling with maddening speed. I twist my wrist, clenching my fingers. The sound of crumpling metal beside me startles Alesta. Her tiny hands cling to my arm as she steps away from the demolished closet door. "How did you—"

"It doesn't matter. What will happen to him when we arrive?" I glance back at her over my shoulder.

"He'll be taken before the king. His fate will be decided then."

I don't like the way that sounds. No doubt Drakon will plead for Bastien to be turned over to him. And I... Will I even remember who Bastien is to claim him for myself?

"I need clothes." I turn to look at her and see fright mingled with awe. It makes me sick. "Alesta. Focus."

Her hands tremble as she holds out the towel. "You need to wash first."

"I don't have time—" But this time she is the one who cuts me off. I'm not sure where the commanding voice comes from in such a small body, but she manages to make me pause. "I am here to assist you in preparations to be presented to the king. If I do not, I will lose my head."

I blink. "Literally?"

She nods solemnly. "The king does not like disappointment."

I blow out a weighted sigh, shaking my head. My heart yearns to go to Bastien, to free him from the chains Drakon has bound him in, but I can't just leave this girl to the king's mercy either. She is my people, one of the people I gave Bastien up for in the first place.

"Fine." I growl, not feeling overly hospitable, but I see no way around it. I need to bide my time. "Let's just get this over with."

Alesta's stern expression melts away as she scurries across the room in a rustle of silk. She presses a hand against a hidden wall panel and removes a small vial from the lower shelf. There are many vials within. Some glowing a bright flame-orange, others black and murky. The vial she selects is a calming aqua. "Here. This should help with the headache."

"I never said I have one." The small glass bottle has a black cork on top. I raise the vial and shake it. It bubbles slightly but settles back into its clear state.

"Human's don't travel well the first time." She watches expectantly as I remove the stopper. I glance at her, praying it is right to trust her. What reason would Drakon have to harm me now that he is about to get exactly what he wants? I down the medicine. It feels like ice upon my throat. "You will feel the effects rather quickly."

A strange fluid sensation flows over my body, reaching from toes to ears with amazing speed. Even as the pounding in my head begins to fade, I realize the stiffness in my neck and back begins to ease. The tender flesh about my waist, leftover from my initial hike with Eamon, heals over. I press my hand to my stomach and realize the pain is gone, as is the soreness in my calves and blisters upon my feet.

Alesta shoots me a knowing smile as she motions for me to follow her into the bathroom. "This stuff is amazing."

"It should be. It's my special recipe."

"You made this?" I glance back to the wall at all of the multi-colored vials. "And those too?"

"Yes. My mother was a healer. She taught me how to use nature to find the same essence in flowers and plants when I failed to inherit her gift. I may not be a normal healer, but I do all right on my own."

"So you're an herbalist?" My thoughts drift to my best friend Aminah and her skill for making salves and tinctures from the forest. She would probably have much to discuss with Alesta if she were here.

The girl frowns. "I don't think I know this word."

"It's pretty much the same… Oh, never mind. It doesn't really matter."

Alesta drops her head. "Yes, my lady."

"Okay." I place my hands on her arms and wait for her to look up at me. "We need to set some ground rules here. First off, as nice as you seem to be, I don't need a servant. I'm perfectly capable of caring for myself. And secondly, don't call me a lady. I'm not royalty."

Alesta looks stricken. "But you are to be our queen. Please don't send me away. The king handpicked me for you. If I fail…" She begins to tremble.

How did I get myself into this? I inwardly groan.

"If I ask something of you, will you do it?"

"Of course." She looks back at me with a hesitant smile, no doubt remembering how I tricked her before. "I can't do anything against my king's wishes, though," she quickly adds.

"Fair enough. I forbid you to call me by any name other than Illyria. No bowing. No rushing to get everything for me. Just be here when I do need you, okay?"

I watch as she struggles to hold back her shock. Her lips press into a colorless line, heat stains her cheeks into a pretty rose color, but she nods.

"Thank you. Now"—I look at the basin before me—"I would like to wash myself, if that is all right."

I can tell it isn't, but Alesta concedes. "I'll remain out

here to prepare your outfit."

"Fine." I press the button on the door and breathe a sigh of relief as it seals her out. I cling to the sink, my knuckles white as I tremble. *Bastien has been hurt and I'm stuck here playing dress-up with this girl. What is wrong with me?*

As I stare at myself in the mirror, noticing the circles beneath my eyes and the lifeless color within their depths, I realize I only have one option: to play along. Drakon will be suspicious, of course, and that is good. Let him worry.

Dipping a cloth into the steaming water, I rub a layer of grime from my brow. Slowly, I wash all of me, taking the time to inspect my newly healed injuries. No marks. No redness. It is if I had healed myself.

A small knock on the door reminds me that I'm running low on time. The door hisses as it opens. I snatch up the sheet from the floor to cover myself, but when she laughs, I realize how foolish I must look. "I'm not used to other people… you know, being here when I'm not dressed."

"It is perfectly understandable," she soothes as she motions for me to stand in the middle of the room with my arms stretched over my head. I hesitate, gritting my teeth as I hand her the sheet.

I don't know what I expected when I'm finally revealed. A weird look? A smirk? A look of horror? Alesta shows none of those. Instead, she hardly reacts as she slowly moves around me, her gaze sweeping over my curves with a critical, almost indifferent glance.

"This dress should fit you nicely. We might have to take it in a bit at the waist and flare it a bit at the hip, but the top should suit you well."

"Wait? What?" I turn to look at her as she moves away to the bed. "What dress?"

I stare in horror at a wispy bit of cloth that she lifts into the air for me to approve. Its color is rich as a field of lavender, yet I can easily see her fingers though the other side of the fabric. "Where is the underdress?"

Alesta laughs. "There is none."

I back away, arms outstretched. "No. No way. That thing is see-through."

She actually rolls her eyes at me. "Of course it is. Did you honestly think you would be allowed to wear that offensive uniform when you meet the king?"

"Well..." I had held out hope, but even I knew it wouldn't be allowed. But this... this goes way too far. "I'm not wearing that."

She turns and lifts a smaller triangle of fabric, darker and more solid-looking. "This goes with it. It will conceal you."

"And the top?" I peer over her shoulder at the flimsy bit of silk.

She winces and shakes her head. I grit my teeth and close my eyes. "This is beyond my worst nightmare."

I jerk when her hand falls lightly upon my arm. "I know this isn't my place, but I think you will look radiant in this."

"I don't want to look radiant," I mutter, crossing my arms over my chest. "I want to look fierce."

A tiny smirk tugs at the corners of my servant's lips. "Perhaps we can do both."

I stare at myself in the mirror, amazed at the transformation. The halter is low-cut, hugging perfectly to the curves of my chest. Delicate swatches of white fabric drape across my upper arm.

My neck looks long with my hair swept up into a mass of curls, adorning my head with beautiful multi-colored jewel clips that make my eyes sparkle. A single purple jewel nestles in the hollow of my neck. Its color is vivid, its surface veined with black.

Alesta worked her magic on my eyes, lining them with thick black around my eyelids. She used a charcoal-gray powder to highlight my eyelids. They shimmer with hidden silver flecks. My lips are a deep crimson, bold and fierce, just as I asked.

The skirt falls at my hip, dipping low into a V below my belly button. The gossamer fabric shows off the length and grace of my legs that I hadn't realized I possessed. My feet are encased in slippers of shimmering silver. The three-inch heels draw lines of definition on my calves. *Zahra would kill for a pair of heels like these*, I think absently as I turn to look at myself.

Alesta was right. The scrap of fabric she gave me does an adequate job concealing me, although it does nothing for my backside or my chest. I chew on my lip, dreading stepping outside that door. "People will stare," I mutter under my breath.

"Of course they will," Alesta says as she pinches my cheeks to revive some color. Not that I'm going to need it. The moment the first person lays eyes on me, I will be red as a beet. "You are the future queen. You demand attention."

"Please tell me I don't have to wear this long." I turn to look at her, hearing the pleading in my voice.

Her eyes widen in surprise. "If you don't like the color, I can select another one. There are plenty to choose from."

My heart rises in my throat. "More?"

"Of course." She laughs, teasing my hair. She has primped for nearly half an hour. "King Aloysius had an entire wardrobe made for you."

"Of course he did," I grumble and wave her off. "What now? Do I just wait here?"

Alesta grins. "We'll be arriving shortly. I thought you might like to view our landing from the main deck. The view from there is spectacular."

She doesn't wait for me to protest or ask just how many other people will be taking in the view as she tugs on my hand and keys in a code at the door. The door hisses open and I'm blasted with a cool breeze that makes me shiver. Space is cold.

Two guards turn from their posts at the door and stand shoulder to shoulder before us, blocking our path. I watch as heat stains the neck of the one on the right and feel my own blush rushing over my body as he dips his gaze toward my chest, lingering. Alesta clears her throat. "I am taking her to the main deck for the viewing."

The soldier who remained coolly indifferent to my painful state of undress shakes his head, his laser gun lowered. "Drakon's orders are that she remains here until we land."

Alesta's smile melts away as she steps forward. "This is your future queen. Who do you think should be giving orders? The commander or her?"

He casts a glance toward me and then meets Alesta's gaze head-on. "She's not my queen yet."

I glare at the soldier before me who openly caresses my chest with his gaze. Feeling electricity spark against my wrist, vining around my fingers, I strike out, smacking him across the cheek. His cries out as he stumbles back, the flesh of his cheek red. The hum of a laser and the warmth of its swirling core attracts my attention.

I turn to look down the barrel of the other guard's gun. I smile, feeling the sparks rise along my forearm. My next punch will send him through the wall into the next room.

"I said return the prisoner to her room."

Alesta's eyes narrow and she reminds me of a cat with sharply pointed claws about to swat at a dog. "How dare you—"

I reach out and place a hand on her arm, oddly touched by her defense. The man's gaze never leaves mine as I step forward, nearly pressing the barrel of his gun against my chest. I know it would burn should I touch it so I stay just far enough back.

"Do you know who I am?" He nods once. "And you know what I am capable of?"

He hesitates this time. I smile. "If you don't move out of our way, I will break you over my knee like a twig. Is that understood?"

The man's gaze darkens as he fingers the trigger. My chest is awash with green as he prepares to stun me.

"No!" Alesta shouts.

I thrust out my hand and send the guard toppling backward. His shot goes wide and leaves a scorch mark along the wall and ceiling, and he lands on his back. He gasps, the wind knocked from his chest. I walk forward and kick away his gun. With the tip of my heel, I slam my foot down on his neck, pressing it into his skin. His lip curls into a snarl as I knick his flesh. Blood trickles down into his collar. That is when I hear screams of agony stabbing at my mind. My gaze narrows as I listen, shuddering at the shrieks of this man's past victims.

With a twist of my heel, I snap his neck. Alesta cries out, her hands fluttering over her mouth as she stumbles forward. I ignore her as I turn to find the first guard pressed up against the wall in a seated position, his gun trained on me. "I wouldn't do that if I were you."

I can see his indecision, but he powers down his gun and tosses it aside. Alesta reaches me and tugs on my arm, staring in horror at the man below me. "You killed him."

Grasping the wall, I twist my ankle and wipe his blood off my heel on his chest. His head rolls to the side, eyes wide and staring. "You would have too if you could read his mind."

Eighteen

I follow Alesta down a long and winding corridor, through arched doorways and glass-paned elevators. I clench tightly to the railing as the small cube rises with heart-dropping speed. Although I realize it is irrational to be worried about an elevator crashing when I am stuck zipping through space in a ship, the fear is still present.

When the doors hiss open, I unlatch myself from the elevator and stumble out, inelegantly tripping on my heels. I glance around to see if anyone noticed, but all eyes are turned toward a large glass-like dome. Releasing the hem of my dress, I straighten and my mouth gapes in wonder.

Streaks of white light flash past too quickly for me to really glimpse the stars. If I focus too long, I begin to feel dizzy and am forced to lower my gaze. "This ship is too big," I whisper to Alesta, clutching to the silver railing that separates us from the lower deck. The loft area we stand upon hangs over what I assume to be the command center of the ship.

At least two dozen men and women man stations, brightly lit with flashing green lights and vivid blue consoles. Strange symbols scroll over large screens before me, but I can't figure out what they mean. "Too big for what?" I hear her questions beside me.

"This isn't the same ship I tried to steal, is it?"

She laughs, her curls bouncing as she shakes her head. "Of course not. The commander would never let you arrive in such a small craft. "This is the *Pegasus*, the largest transport in our fleet. You should feel honored. It is the king's personal transport."

That is hardly the emotion I would choose as I watch a man below me raise his hand and tap the air. I gasp as light illuminates beneath his finger and realize there is some sort of a screen hanging in the air before him. I crane my neck to see if I can spy the edge of it, but at an odd glance from Alesta, I lean back and resume my cool, disinterested gaze.

I take it all in, feeling my heart thrum wildly in my chest. Everything feels so cold and foreign to me. *I want to go home. I want to see Bastien*

The sound of boots upon the metal floor alerts me to a presence. I turn to find Drakon approaching, having just stepped from the elevator. His eyes trail slowly and pointedly over my dress. I resist the urge to cover myself. Instead, I press my shoulders back and stare him down.

A smile curls his lips but doesn't reach the cold calculation I see in his eyes. "You are a vision. Our clothing suits you rather well."

Saliva begins to pool in my mouth and I have to grit my teeth to keep from spitting at him. The only thing that holds me back is knowing that Bastien would pay for my actions. I turn away from him and look to the stars once more, focusing beyond instead of directly at them. "Alesta informed me that we'll be arriving soon."

He appears at my side. I shift my hand away so it is out of reach as he curls his fingers around the rail. "Yes. You are obviously excited to see your new home, I'm sure"

Ignoring his snide remark, I notice the flashes have begun to slow. The hum of the engines has changed. "How long?"

"A minute. Perhaps less. We use spatial anomalies to travel, a wormhole as you may have heard it called, to make the jump between worlds. Without it, it would take years to reach Calisted." He pauses, leaning forward as the ship slows. The stars seem to crawl past now. "You will want to see this."

A burst of blue erupts before my eyes. I gasp, taken aback by the giant sphere that hangs before me. It is perfectly round against the black sky. Swirling aqua mists seem to hang over the planet. "It's beautiful," I whisper, mesmerized by the sight of my home world.

All this time I judged Calisted with thoughts tainted from my visions, but in reality, standing here with this breathtaking view, I know Aloysius can't ruin the beauty of an entire planet for me.

"Welcome home, Illyria." Alesta smiles as she clasps my hand in hers.

I grip the metal railing before me as the mists swirl around the ship as we descend straight down through the cloud cover. The sunlight below is blinding. I raise a hand to shield my eyes, grateful when I feel the ship touch down and I am able to turn away.

A strange longing floods through me, almost as if coming home isn't truly a terrible thing. Kyan said I have family here. Will I be able to meet them? Ask them why I'm so different from everyone else?

Although Sariana cleared up the mystery surrounding my relationship with Bastien and Eamon, I have yet to hear what makes me unique. Perhaps no one really knows.

"This way, my dear." Drakon holds out his hand, motioning for me to walk toward a door that sits beyond the elevator. Below me, men and women rise from their seats. I can hear the engines power down and real terror begins to seep into my bones.

I am here. There is no turning back now.

The seal on the door breaks and sunlight streams in. I feel warmth upon my skin as I approach the door, marveling at the prism of light upon the floor, broken and molded into multifaceted spheres, although I can't see anything that would create this phenomenon.

I take a deep breath and follow Drakon into the light.

What I see beyond the doors steals away my breath. Rainbows dance across my skin, hovering in the air before me. Everything seems draped with a warm, hazy glow, like clouds ringing a full moon. "How is this possible?"

Alesta answers. "Calisted has three moons. When the sun reflects off of them, it creates a fascinating display."

I follow Alesta's finger as she points to the sky. Hovering above us are three spheres of different sizes, all revolving a brilliant white sun. The smallest moon is ruby in color, the medium glows as brilliantly as a newly mined emerald, and the third reminds me far too much of

Bastien's sapphire eyes.

I take a deep breath and realize the air feels lighter here and has almost a sweet taste. I look to Alesta and she simply smiles back.

"The gravity is different than on Earth," Drakon says as he ushers me forward. "You will get used to it after a while."

It is difficult to maneuver the stairs in my high-heel shoes, but somehow I manage to reach the bottom without breaking my neck. As I step onto the ground, I realize we have landed on a wide bluish patch of grass. I stare at it, confused.

"It is the mists," Alesta informs, like my own personal guide to Calisted. "The planet is draped in the aqua color you saw from space so it alters the colors you see here on the ground. What might be green on Earth appears darker blue here." She lifts her hand toward the town. "Welcome to Calahorra, City of the King."

As I look at the city stretched out before me, I realize the light sparkles with the same wondrous glow off of buildings, cobblestone streets, and a gushing stream that winds through the town, carving the road in half.

It is the most enchanting thing I have ever glimpsed. No words could truly describe the sense of peace and beauty this place possesses. I stand, staring all around me in awe, until Drakon snatches my hand and yanks me forward. "There will be plenty of time for you to look around later. Someone is waiting for you."

I work hard to smother my fear as I smile sweetly back at him. "Let us hope he is in a forgiving mood. After all, it did take you over a year to finally bring me to him. I've heard he isn't the most patient man."

With a flick of my wrist, I shake him off and walk ahead with my head held high. *Let him chew on that for a bit.*

Dozens of men and women flow out of the ship behind us. I can hear shouts of welcome as several break off from our landing party to hug a loved one. Craning my neck back around, I search over the group for Bastien, but he has yet to be brought from the ship. No doubt Drakon wants to keep us separated for as long as possible.

It is hard to appear aloof and disinterested as we walk through town. The streets are bendy and the homes built in endless rows. The roofs are thatched and droop over the edge. Everywhere I look, flowers grow. Some drape from low-hanging trees that bend so low their fronds grace the ground. Yards, neatly spaced and contained within metal fences, are bursting at the seams with wide blue petals, vivid purple sprouting vines that weave a pattern across the stone house face. I can see heart-shaped flowers, starbursts, and shaggy black balls that I'm not entirely sure what they are.

Orange moss hangs from the trees, tickling my cheeks as I pass under. Footpaths run on either side of the stream banks, littered with pastel-colored stones rubbed smooth over time. I cry out in delight as a small orange-and-blue fish leaps from the stream and dives back under its cool, lavender surface. I hear the gushing of greater waters up ahead but am unable to spy a river before Drakon pushes us off down a different road.

The streets are made of stone. Sand weaves between the rocks, and as I take a closer look, I notice white glass pressed into the handmade pavers, glinting in the sunlight. Birds swoop from above, looping and cawing as they spiral through the sky.

Up ahead I can hear laughter. It spurs me on. I can't help but grin back at the children who stand along a fencerow, waving wildly as we approach. They are each beautiful. Tiny noses. Small hands. Eyes with every color of the rainbow and some with a swirling mixture, like paint splattered on a canvas.

There is an overwhelming sense of wonder here. "Where are the transports? I don't see any vehicles." Dozens of people mill about. Some lean against tree trunks and chat with neighbors. Others walk with packages under their arm, whistling and dipping their head in greeting as they pass. They act as if they have all the time in the world.

"We don't use them here. There's no need." Alesta

waves as a young girl steps out from a small wooden bungalow-style home. This roof is woven with what looks like palm leaves. The door is wide open. There are no coverings on the windows.

I realize as I look all around me that this is a tropical climate. I stare at sun-kissed faces and browned arms. Their clothing, although far less flimsy than my own, is made of lightweight material in whites, yellows, and soft blues. A warm breeze unsettles my hair about my neck as I turn my face up to the sun. "Is it always warm here?"

"Yes," Alesta says. "Earth is one of the few planets that has a winter. You have seasons because of how your planet revolves around your yellow sun. Our sun is white and we are closer to its surface, providing us with year-round warmth."

"But how is that possible? Surely when you are on the back side of the sun, this city would be farthest away."

"Yes, but we have those." She points to the moons again. I look closer and notice how the sunlight seems to reflect off their glossy surface.

Our party winds through the city, soldiers lining up on either side to clear away the crowd that grows with each street we pass. Shouts ring out as kids grab hold of their parents to bring them near. I stare down at the little children and realize that no matter how terrible this past year has been, it was all worth it for this moment.

These are my people, resonates loudly within my soul as I wave back.

Lines of people now edge the streets as we begin to climb a small hill. My shoes have hardly any traction as I attack the stones, praying I don't fall flat on my face in front of all these people.

From somewhere behind me, a song begins to emerge from the crowd. I pause and look back over my shoulder, trying to make out the words. "What are they singing?"

"Hail to the queen, a savior born," Drakon growls. He motions his hand toward a soldier and the man surges back through the crowd, commanding loudly in a tongue that I'm unfamiliar with. Soon the song cuts off and I feel saddened by the silence that follows.

"It was a beautiful song," I say.

Drakon's cheeks are flushed as he turns back to glare at me. "It's forbidden to sing it. Treason by penalty of death."

"For a song?"

"No." He shakes his head and raises his hand out before him, pointing ahead of us. "For what it stands for."

I follow the length of his arm and come to a halt. Before me, a giant palace looms behind a towering stone wall. A massive gate resides at the end of this street, blocking our path. Drakon calls out and the gates begin to swing open. A group of men dressed in cloaks of royal purple rush forward and form a line directly behind me. Large, curved swords of gold, silver, and bronze are drawn, their backs toward us to face off with the crowd.

More guards line up on the other side of the gate. Towering spiked spears rise beside them, clutched in gloved hands. On their other side, I see shields of hammered metal held aloft by leather-like straps. I can't imagine what Drakon thinks I need protection from, but I remain silent and we walk beneath the gates.

Although no less beautiful than the city below, a chill seems to lie over this land. Sweeping grounds lie before me, rising ever so steadily toward the palace. "Why are the walls so high?" I ask. "Is there some beast that roams your lands that would seek to harm your king?"

Drakon appraises me before speaking. "There are always enemies seeking to gain access to the palace. If you think this is impressive, just wait until you see the palace."

"I can't wait. Oh, never mind," I reply sourly. "I can."

He smirks and shoves me forward. There is a guard on either side of each step as we rise toward the palace. Each bows low as I pass. This sign of undeserved reverence grates on my nerves. *Do these people actually think I came here of my own free will?*

As my foot touches the top step, I gasp, taken aback by the strange animals roaming about the perfectly manicured lawn. Bird-like creatures with four wings, two heads, and feathers of the purest silver flap about. Water fountains glisten with crimson waters. Beyond the edges of the palace, I can see great purple mountain peaks. Streams of water flow down toward the palace, entering through small grated holes into a pond that ripples peacefully in the sunlight.

A multitude of flowers are in full bloom, their aroma enticing and heady. Trees of green and blue shade the grounds, their star-like leaves dancing in the breeze.

"These Eltalik are rather tame animals." Drakon points to a black feline that looks dangerously similar to a panther.

"Rather tame?" I question as one rolls onto its back and yawns, bearing sharp white teeth.

"Well… they have been known to take a hand or two from time to time. It is rather rare, though." Drakon grins down at me. His threat delivered with silky poison.

I smirk and stretch out my hand to brush the soft fur of the nearest cat. "My kind of animal."

I can feel it purring beneath my hand, rumbling through its chest. Drakon scowls and yanks me away. His fingers dig into my arm, but I do not protest. If he is fool enough to leave a mark on my arm when I'm presented to Aloysius, the better it will be for me.

My heels seem to echo upon the stone steps as we begin our final climb up to the stone palace. Its walls are veined like marble, appearing to have been mined from pure gold. The palace shimmers as the sun shifts from behind a cloud, snatching away my breath.

Drakon was right. This is beautiful. From the towering stone archways, with their intricate architecture, to the two-story gossamer fabric that drapes from the ceiling, billowing beautifully in the wind. Everything shines; everything glistens.

How can such a vile man live in a place of such exquisite beauty?

With each step I take, I turn inward, wishing I'd a chance to say good-bye to Eamon. I can't bear the thought of him living a life without ever knowing he is not alone in the world, or that I do truly love him.

And Bastien… I can't even bear to think about him as I pause before two enormous doors. They appear to be made of bone, although I can't imagine how that would be possible. An intricate scrolled pattern weaves across the surface, making it hard to see the crack of the door until it swings inward, admitting us to the inner foyer.

I stare in amazement as two men, as tall and well-built as Gorgan, strain to open the doors, pushing them back until they nearly disappear against the whites of the wall. As I glimpse the interior of the palace for the first time, I wonder if I will ever stop gasping in wonder at new sights.

Large stone archways break off in either direction, forming hallways and vaulted entries to rooms beyond. A large sweeping balcony before me hangs over the foyer, where people can stand and look down upon new arrivals. The ceiling is draped with curtains of deep purple, attached every few feet to create the illusion of a flowing wave. The walls are papered in gold. Chandeliers, crafted with white stones the size of my fist and smaller opaque stones, hang overhead.

Sunlight streams naturally through the floor-to-ceiling windows, casting dappled colors across the polished floor. Huge paintings hang in thick wooden frames, lining the walls as far as I can see down either hall. I can't help but wonder what the rest of the palace looks like if the foyer is as grand as this.

A door to my right opens, appearing seamlessly from the decorated wall. A squat man with a rotund belly and pointy shoes shuffles toward me, his face glowing with happiness. "Ah, you have finally arrived." He grabs for my hand, but I draw away. He looks only slightly flustered by my dismissal as he laughs. "I'm sure all of this is slightly overwhelming. It just takes time to adjust, dear."

"Who are you?" I ask, staring at the balding patch near the crown of his head. It looks unusually slick, as if he actually buffed it to look shiny.

"I am the royal steward." He bows low in greeting. "The king is anxious to meet with you. Please, follow me." He waves a hand and totters off. "He's waiting in the throne room."

I fear the stability of my voice so I simply nod and walk forward, but Drakon snatches my arm. He releases me instantly as the steward turns back and bows low. "I look forward to serving my new queen. After you meet King Aloysius, you will feel like a brand new person."

My gaze narrows at his pointed statement. "Don't think I will forget your treachery or how you've tortured Bastien. You pose a threat to the king. That is not something I'm likely to forget even when I'm under his control. I would tread carefully if I were you."

Drakon scowls and seizes my arm. "Right this way, my queen."

He yanks me down the hall, leaving Alesta to stand with her mouth gaped open with confusion. I glance back at her. She tries to smile but doesn't quite pull it off. I look forward, lifting my chin high. *I will not show fear.*

The hall we pass through is lined with paintings that look oddly familiar to me. "What are these?" I ask without meaning to.

Drakon casts a severe glance at me. "You don't know?" I shake my head, staring in wonder. I can tell these are of Earth. The colors are bold and vivid, normal. "These were once landmarks from your planet. The pyramids of Egypt, the Great Wall in China, the Eiffel Tower, and the Statue of Liberty." He points at each in turn. An ache forms in my chest as the images go on and on, depicting a world I never had a chance to know.

My mind screams at me to turn and run, but there is nowhere to go. Even if I could escape the palace, it would be pointless. I stand little chance of escaping this planet and zero chance of outrunning my destiny. Drakon would hunt me down and return me to this very spot, and I would be forced to let him.

"Come, come. It's this way," the pudgy steward calls. His coat flaps whip about him as he faces forward once more.

A single tear falls down my cheek as I arrive at the door. The last heartbroken cry of my heart is for Bastien, and then… all falls silent as an odd sensation washes over me.

The doors open to reveal a man standing at the bottom of a set of steps that rise behind him, leading to a golden throne. The man appears both noble and kind. His shoulders are broad, his arms and chest well defined from years of labor, although I can't quite figure what sort of labor would be required of a king. His hair is dark and cut short, lying across his head in such a way it complements his angular face. Flecks of gray are interspersed with his neatly trimmed beard.

Although he appears to be nearly thirty years my senior, I find him pleasing to the eye. A man sure to catch any girl's attention.

He stares at me from across the vast room, his expression anxious. As I step forward to go to him, I realize his eyes are dark, like the bark of a maple tree back home. A royal blue and golden cloak billows about him as he raises his hands in welcome.

"How long I have waited to finally meet you, Illyria." My steps seem almost wooden as I approach. He closes the gap between us and takes my hands in his. They are soft yet boasting of strength with his firm grip. "You are far more lovely than I had imagined."

Oh, how disgusting. Don't touch me!

He raises my hands and places a kiss on each of my fingers. My smile falters. This feels familiar yet foreign at the same time. The king's crown glints in the lights above, capturing my attention. My heart hammers in my chest. I'm fearful it will give me away.

A blush rises up from my neck as he steps back to admire me. His gaze lingers long over my curves, his smile growing broad as he finally sweeps back up to meet my nervous gaze. "You are perfect."

"Thank you, my king." I dip my head and bow as Alesta had shown me. Drakon reaches out to grab me before I tumble completely.

Smooth one, Illyria.

"She is still a work in progress, my king," Drakon

says, shoving me back upright.

I turn to glare at him. The king follows my gaze and clears his throat, drawing me back. He offers me his hand, and I step out of Drakon's grasp. "Don't mind him. He won't be around long."

"Yes, my king," I say softly. I feel… odd. Mingled with pleasure to finally be standing with my future husband, yet I can hear myself screaming to be free, as if trapped within my own mind. It is so confusing.

"Please." He pauses, ready to step upon the first stair leading up to two thrones, one only slightly larger than the other. "You mustn't be so formal with me. Call me Aloysius."

I smile and lower my gaze as I draw up the hem of my dress to follow his lead.

"My king?"

Aloysius's smile freezes as he pats my hand and turns. "Your interruption had better be important, Drakon."

"Yes, my king." He dips into a low bow. "I wanted to inform you that we have a prisoner to deal with. He is just arriving."

"A prisoner?" His face brightens as he clasps his hands together. "Bring him in."

A guard rushes to the door and reappears a moment later with a young man. His head is bowed, his shoulders slumped. I can tell by the blood that clings to his neck, hands, and arms that he has been badly mistreated. I feel sorry for him.

Drakon shoves him from behind and the man grunts as he falls to his knees. A swift kick to his back sends him sprawling. I close my eyes, sickened by the sound of his moist, wheezing breath. What has this man done to deserve such a punishment?

Grabbing a chunk of his hair, Drakon yanks his head back. I gasp at the patchwork of blood and bruises that conceals his face. A deep gash seeps from his hairline and into his purplish right eye, swollen nearly completely shut. His skin is sickly pale, nearly translucent. I can see his veins prominently through his skin.

But it isn't his physical condition that startles me. It is the way his one good eye searches the room, frantically seeking something. When his gaze falls upon me, I can hear an audible sigh of relief and he ceases his search. Blood seeps from a deep tear in his lip as he tries to smile at me. The sentiment is unnerving but also oddly touching. Doesn't he know that by looking at me he is putting his life in further danger?

Bastien! You know him. Remember! I blink, confused by the voice screaming in my mind.

"So this is your prisoner? I see he has already undergone a round of torture at your hand, Drakon." Aloysius's gaze narrows. "Bring him closer."

I watch as the young man is heaved to his feet. He cries out and seems to favor his right side. Despite the pain, he never stops looking at me. I shift uncomfortably, wishing he would turn his gaze away.

Please, the voice whispers, raw and throaty in my mind. *Don't let him die.*

His gaze is piercing, almost as if he can see right through me. "Illyria?" His voice is low and raspy, edged with pain. "It's me, Bast—"

"Silence!" Aloysius's face blots with anger. "You will not speak in my presence unless spoken to. Nor will you address my future wife in such an informal manner."

There is something oddly familiar about him, like a dream just out of reach. "So"—Aloysius's voice draws me back—"what are we to do with you? You look strong enough. Perhaps we could make a soldier out of you."

I turn to look at my future husband. His words seem wrong to me. This man is obviously more than a normal soldier. Not many men could go through such a horrific beating and still be able to think, let alone speak, yet he stares back, not in fear, but in defiance. There is great strength within him and he seems to think he knows me.

"My king?" I call softly. Aloysius turns, his expression softening as I step toward him, my hand outstretched. He grasps it lightly and draws me near. I look down upon the wounded man and know this is right. "May I have him?"

Aloysius sucks in a breath, his hand clenching around mine. I smile up at him, showing him the pleasure I take in knowing I am marrying a man of mercy. "What an odd request. What would you possibly want him for?"

I turn my gaze away and look down upon the man. "He is strong. You need only to look at him to see this is no normal man. He is a warrior. Look at the way he holds himself. He doesn't cower in fear." I take a step and draw Aloysius nearer. "I would like him as a personal bodyguard."

From the corner of my eye, I can see Drakon shaking his head. "But I have already selected Malek as your guard, darling." He points to the man standing against the wall. He seems nearly as wide as he is tall, and although I'm afraid to ask, I almost wonder if there are real giants living on this planet.

"A fine choice, my king, but I stand by my request. This prisoner will be my slave and that binds him to me until death. A soldier, no matter how great he might be, will never have that sort of bond with me."

Aloysius strokes his beard, tugging it into a point as he deliberates. "Yes, you do make a solid argument."

"Sire!" Drakon splutters a few feet away. "I highly protest this idea. Don't you know who this boy is?"

His protest cuts off into a gargled cry as Aloysius bears down upon him. "You dare question my judgment? Do you think me a fool not to know the longings of her heart and mind?"

I frown, wondering what my heart has to do with this.

Don't give in. You've got him convinced. You can save his life.

I press back my shoulders as Drakon flings himself to the ground in an act of humiliation. "No, my king. Never!"

"Malek." The seven-foot-tall guard jogs forward, his body armor clanking together. "Remove Drakon from my sight. See to it that he learns how to mind his tongue."

Drakon's pleas for mercy turn to wailing cries as Malek grabs Drakon by the scruff of his neck and drags him from the room, kicking and shouting. Aloysius turns his back on the scene and clasps my hands in his. "Are you sure you want him?"

I nod, feeling my curls bounce about my cheeks. "His eyes look honest," I say, turning to search the young man for any sign of deceit. "I believe we can trust him with my life. He is the one I choose, if you are willing."

A kind smile spreads across Aloysius's face as he leans in and places a kiss upon my cheek. "Then let this prisoner be my first gift to you."

I grin as I tuck my arm into his, pleased with how proud he looks. Placing his hand over mine, he addresses the man. "What is your name?"

The wounded man hesitates, casting a wary glance between us. He pushes up to his feet, wincing as he holds his side. He wavers slightly on his feet but stands up tall. "Bastien, my... king." His gaze shifts toward me and I feel heat rise from the bodice of my dress.

Bastien... I'm here!

"I promise I will give my life to protect my future queen," the man announces boldly.

Aloysius dips his head. "And so you may, someday. For now, leave us. Alesta will see to it that you are cleaned up properly."

He struggles to offer a bow. Aloysius waves him off and ignores him as he returns his attention to me. He raises a hand and slowly trails a finger across my cheek, staring intently into my eyes. "You are even more beautiful than I imagined."

His eyes dip low, lingering upon my chest. I can feel a blush rising into my cheeks.

What I wouldn't give to knee him in the groin.

My smile wavers as he suddenly steps back. "How rude of me to keep you so long. I'm sure you are exhausted from your journey. Alesta will see to it that you have time to rest and freshen up. I would be honored if you would join me for a tour of the palace this evening."

"Of course." I smile, pleased that he is so attentive. I had hoped he would be.

"One last thing before you leave." He tugs back on my

hand as I start toward the door. I frown, sure that I have somehow displeased him, but when he dips his head and presses his lips against mine, I realize his intent. I slip my arms around his neck, drawing him close as I sink into his embrace. His arms tighten around me, unwilling to leave an inch of space between us.

Oh, gross! Get him off me!

"You taste like the sweetest honey," he murmurs against my lips. His hands rise along my spine, pulling me closer as his lips explore my cheekbones and dip to my jaw

"I'm glad you find me pleasing."

His hands splay across my back, his fingers digging into my flesh. I can feel a sense of urgency within him and laugh, pulling back from him. He frowns. "So much that I fear I may compromise our wedding night if you remain."

I laugh and lean in to him. "It has been very nice meeting you," I whisper and kiss him once more. "But I really would like a bath."

"Of course." He finally releases me and watches as I walk toward the exit. A guard pushes open the door for me. I turn back in the doorway and wave. Aloysius seems pleased as he waves back.

The instant the doors close behind me, I double over, feeling as if I've been punched in the gut. I gasp, frantically wiping at my lips.

"My lady? Are you ill?" The guard rushes forward.

"No." I shake my head, rising up as I fight to compose myself. I offer him what I hope to be a convincing smile. "I'm just tired from my journey. Could you please take me to my room?"

"I'll take her," a familiar voice calls out.

My knees nearly give way as Alesta appears, her hand sweeping gracefully over the curved staircase bannister as she descends from the floor above. "Let's get you to bed, shall we?"

I nod, allowing Alesta to guide me down winding halls and past countless doors. This place seems to have no end. Just as I begin to fear I will never be alone, Alesta stops in front of a pair of hand-carved cherry-colored wooden doors. The engraving is exquisite, but I hardly have the heart to care as I pass through the archway.

Alesta releases me the moment I'm inside and turns to lock the doors. "Are you all right? I was so worried about you. When I heard all of the shouting, I feared the worst."

My hands tremble at my sides as they hang limply. Tears stream freely down my cheeks as I sink to the floor.

I feel dirty, used. If I close my eyes, I can still feel Aloysius's hands upon my body, hear myself screaming in protest, locked within my own mind.

"It was horrible," I whimper. Drawing my legs up into my chest, I wrap my arms about them, rocking ever so slightly. "I could hear myself talking, could feel everything, but I was helpless to stop it."

Alesta eyes me warily. "Are you… you again?"

"Yes." I nod. "I think so."

"There's only one way to be sure." She steps past me and opens another set of double doors. Inside, the room is darker, the lights dimmer, but I can still make out a shape upon the bed. I can smell the metallic scent of blood.

"Bastien!"

Nineteen

I sink down beside Bastien, my hands quaking as I grip his hand. He groans but does not wake.

"He was like this when they brought him in. All they told me was to take care of him for you, but I didn't understand what they meant." Alesta chews on her lower lip, hovering just behind me. "Is this your friend?"

"Yes," I whisper as I brush my fingertips across his swollen eye. "Drakon did this."

Alesta stands silently beside me. I can feel her concern, but she doesn't speak as I lean forward and place a kiss upon his forehead. His skin is clammy. "He needs medicine. I don't have any here, but I can return to my home and get something for him."

"No need." Lifting Bastien's hand to my lips, I close my eyes and concentrate. I can feel warmth beginning to spread along my limbs, rising to meet up with my heart. Behind closed eyelids, I can see the healing glow, hear Alesta's gasp, but none of it matters. I focus on the beating of his heart, pushing the healing fires from my body into his.

I saved his life in much the same way a year ago, the day before we faced off with Drakon. In a surprise attack on our base, Bastien had been gravely wounded. I arrived in time to save him, but his healing came with a cost.

"Illyria?"

A hand reaches out to cup my face. I press my cheek into the palm of his hand, not caring that he can feel my tears. "I thought I lost you," I whisper.

He blinks several times, obviously confused about his surroundings. He rolls his head to the side and smiles. "You look good."

I laugh and wipe at my eyes. "It figures you would like

the outfit."

"Nah." He grunts as he lifts himself into a sitting position. "I like what's in it."

Blushing furiously, I avert my gaze and realize Alesta stands behind me. "Oh, I'm sorry. Bastien, this is Alesta, my…" I pause, unsure of what exactly I should call her.

Alesta smiles and steps forward, her hand outstretched. "I'm her maid."

He casts a wary glance at me. "Do you trust her?"

She stiffens and lowers her gaze. I reach out and take her hand, squeezing it once. "I do."

Her cheeks flush with a pleasant rose color. "What will you do with him?" Alesta asks. Her gaze sweeps slowly over Bastien and I can feel my ire rising as she blushes.

"He's my bodyguard. Is there somewhere he can stay?" I look around the room. The walls are lined with freshly picked flowers; an array of beautiful petals of different shapes and sizes adorn the shelves.

"Over here." Alesta places her hand on a hidden panel. It opens to reveal a very masculine bedroom beyond. It holds a double bed with black covers, a writing desk, a wardrobe on the far wall, and a small functional bathroom. Certainly nothing like my own room, but it will do.

"It's perfect. Do you mind if we have some privacy?"

Alesta smiles and motions that she is going to wait outside. The door closes behind her and I am instantly swept into Bastien's arms. He presses his face into my neck, holding me tightly. "I thought I'd never see you again," he breathes.

The memory of seeing him so badly beaten, lying helplessly on the floor, makes my stomach turn sour. I cling to him, trembling. "I saved you. I don't know how, but I did."

He leans back, staring deep into my eyes. "When you looked at me, I knew you didn't really know me."

"I know." He reaches up to wipe away my tears. "It was like being trapped in a cell with no walls, no doors. I screamed and screamed, but I couldn't stop what was happening. It was like a fog had fallen over my mind. I was confused, especially when I saw you. I knew you felt familiar. Oh, God!" I clasp my hand over my mouth as I sink down onto the bed.

"What's wrong?"

"What if I hadn't stopped Drakon? You might be in a prison somewhere right now, or worse. Oh, Bastien." I cling to him, tugging at his torn shirt, needing his strength. "I don't know if I can do this."

His breath unsettles my hair as he presses his cheeks against my head. "You can. I've always had faith in you." Placing his hand over my heart, he smiles. "Aloysius may have control over your mind, but he can't touch this. Not your soul, not who you really are. Kyan said once you were near Aloysius, you would be his for good. And yet here we sit, normal and of free mind. Doesn't that prove something?"

I listen to his words, wishing I could turn back time, or at least wipe away my memories. "You aren't supposed to be here. My vision…"

"Can't be changed," he says, drawing back. "I had a lot of time to think after Drakon got done pounding on me, and do you want to know what I realized?" He pushes me back gently so he can look into my eyes. "I was right. You are worth dying for."

"No." I drop my head, feeling as if all is lost. "I won't let this happen."

He gently lifts my chin. His smile is sad but content. "I'm a tough guy to kill. Haven't you figure that out by now?"

I laugh and nod. "You do seem to get lucky a lot."

"Luck." He scoffs. "When are you going to learn that I'm awesome?"

I glance away, feeling my throat constrict. "I never forgot."

I stare down at the crimson dress that Alesta has laid out for me and sigh. Same design. Same painfully sheer top. "What is it with guys and breasts?" I mutter.

"I heard that," Bastien calls from the other side of the

door. We haven't spoken all afternoon, not after my little reminder of topics that neither of us are comfortable discussing at the moment. Despite Bastien revealing that he's still in love with me, neither of us have spoken about it since then. I simply don't know what I can say that will make any of this less painful. Having him here with me is the complete opposite of what I wanted, yet I couldn't imagine going through this without him. "And to answer your question, breasts are beautiful."

"What?"

"I'm not strictly speaking about yours... not that there is anything wrong with yours," he rushes to add. I can hear him pacing in his room. "Yours are, wow, totally perfect, but... I just... aw, crap..." He finally trails off. "Never mind. I'm an idiot."

"No." I smile at myself in the mirror. Red actually suits me rather well. "It's kinda sweet."

"Sweet?" He stops pacing. "Sweet as in brotherly affection sort of sweet or sweet as in you want to rip my clothes off and thank me for the compliment?"

I laugh and slip the top over my shoulders. The black lace that trims the bottom falls just over my ribs, making the curve of my waist look more slender than normal. Alesta has a good eye for fashion. "Which would you prefer?"

"Honestly." He blows out a breath. I peek around the door to see him sink onto the bed and run his hand through his hair. He falls back and stares up at the ceiling. "I don't know."

I hide my smile as I push open the door, standing timidly in the doorway. I clear my throat. He rolls his head to the side, his eyes widening. "Definitely the clothes-ripping one."

I cross my arms over my chest and lean against the door. "I feel so exposed in this."

"Well..." He clears his throat and averts his gaze. "There's, uh... there's not a whole lot left for the imagination."

I grab a pillow off the side chair and hurl it at him.

"Hey! What was that for?"

"For stating the obvious." I turn and exit his room. He quickly follows after and I can't help but wonder if he is staring at my backside as I flee.

"What did you want me to say? It's the truth."

"I know." I close my eyes, sighing. "I'm sorry. It's not your fault I have to wear this stupid dress."

He steps closer, hesitantly resting his hand upon my shoulder. "Would it help if I stripped down to just my pants? It would be a bit more fair."

"I'm not sure that would be a good idea," I say, looking at him from over my shoulder.

"Why is that?" he asks, clearing his throat. I watch as his gaze dips to my mouth and then jerks back up to focus on my eyes. It's hard not to notice how stunning he looks in his new uniform. It stretches tightly over his well-defined stomach and arms. His hair is still damp from his shower, his face cleanly shaven. I ache to touch his chin now that the stubble has been removed, but I resist.

"Because I think Alesta might enjoy it a bit too much."

His brows dip in confusion. "Alesta..." He smirks as I crack a smile. He shakes his head, snorting. "Yeah. Wouldn't want to get the help all hot and bothered. Good point."

I turn around, lowering my arms. There is no sense in hiding from him. I step toward him and take hold of his hand, watching as his gaze flickers but remains fixed on my face. "Look at me," I whisper.

"Illyria, I don't think—" I pull him toward me, cutting him off.

"Please. It's bad enough I have to worry about what everyone else is thinking. I don't want to wonder about you too."

Bastien's gaze is guarded as he stares at me, giving me the chance to change my mind. "You're sure?"

I nod and step back. Although the lights overhead are dimmed, I know there is plenty of light to see every detail of my body. As Bastien slowly lowers his gaze, I know there will be little hidden from his eyes.

His gaze flits over my body, not pausing long on any one area. He doesn't ogle me or make me feel dirty. Instead, he makes me feel appreciated. Finally, he tugs on my hand, drawing me back to him. Lifting my chin, he smiles. "You are just as beautiful as I imagined you would be."

A blush warms my cheeks and his smile broadens. "I think you might need to figure out how to use that lock, though."

"Why?" I look toward his door, confused.

He leans down and whispers into my ear, "I have a tendency to sleepwalk."

Walking beside Alesta through the great halls of the palace, I can't help but wonder where everyone is. Surely we're not the only ones who live in this massive building, yet the only people I see are guards standing watch over doors sporadically placed throughout the palace. There seems to be no rhyme or reason to where they're located.

I'm painfully aware of Bastien walking behind me, three steps back as Alesta informed him is required. My stomach is balled with nerves. *Will he stay with me while I'm on the tour with Aloysius? Will he be forced to endure silently alongside me?*

I cast a glance back over my shoulder and he gives me a curt yet expressionless nod. A nod that any common stranger would offer.

There is a tension between us that we all sense. Me most of all. Alesta likes Bastien. It's as obvious to me as the sun sinking below the distant tree line. What I find to be even more frustrating is the fact that Bastien noticed as well and did not turn away. Instead, he smiled back.

Bastien reaches out and touches my hand, and I motion for Alesta to lead the way. He draws up beside me, chin lifted high, eyes focused forward. "It's not what you think," he whispers, barely moving his lips.

"No, I get it." I shrug. "She's gorgeous. Why wouldn't you check her out?"

A growl rumbles in his chest and I can see him fighting

to conceal his frustrating. "When are you going to stop treating me like every other guy? I didn't check you out when you stood before me in that… dress. Why would you think I would do that with her?"

"I saw you smirk."

"Yeah." He tugs on my arm and I slow my pace. Alesta frowns over her shoulder at us but moves on. "That's because she reminded me of you. Of the way you used to look at me when we first met."

"Oh." I release a breath. "I see. Well, you don't have to encourage her."

Bastien places a hand upon my arm and increases our speed. To a normal outsider, this might look completely innocent, but I know it isn't. "If I didn't know any better, I'd say you're jealous."

"Of course I am," I hiss.

"Well, I won't hold it against you." He releases my arms as we draw closer to Alesta. "It's impossible with you looking so hot."

Rolling my eyes, I grit my teeth at the blush that I can feel rising to my cheeks. "Stop that. You know I hate it when you make me blush."

"But you look so sexy when you do." He hides a smile behind his hand as he pretends to cough. "I just can't help myself."

Alesta waits for us near the turn in the hall. I look beyond her for any sign of an exit but see none. I inwardly groan, wishing someone would let me walk barefoot instead of tottering on these ridiculous heels. She casts a glance over my shoulder at Bastien and draws me away. He falls back to allow us room to speak in private.

"I have heard rumors this afternoon," she whispers. She reaches out and teases my hair almost as an afterthought. "The palace servants seem abuzz about wedding plans."

My mouth suddenly seems very dry. "Wedding… wedding plans? So soon?"

Alesta's hand tightens upon my arm. "King Aloysius is nothing if not motivated. Knowing him, you will be married within the week, if not sooner."

I can tell by her gaze that she is saddened by this thought. Her illusions of a happy bride were burst the first moment she walked into my room. Bastien doesn't trust her, but I choose to. It may be foolish of me, but I need to believe there are some good people here.

Staring down at my hand, I wonder how long my ring finger will remain barren. I suppose they exchange rings here. I realize with a start that I know nothing of their customs. Kyan always steered us away from that topic and now, when I need the information the most, I'm left clueless.

Alesta resumes her rapid pace. The sun has begun to set and I know the king must be waiting. "I feel like I'm losing myself," I whisper conspiratorially to her, but I know Bastien heard too.

"I'll be with you." Glancing back over her shoulder, she smiles at Bastien. He simply nods. "We'll be with you."

"Thank you." My throat tightens as Alesta brings me to a halt before two sweeping glass doors, covered in beautiful white gossamer. I can see the palace grounds beyond, glowing with a nearly iridescent hue in the fading light.

Opening the doors, Alesta steps aside. "I'll be here when you are done."

I step through the doors, grateful that Bastien is right on my heels. He walks closer than he needs to, but I don't tell him to back off. I feel more confident with him near me.

"You have a tear in the back of your dress," he mutters under his breath.

I stiffen, horrified at the thought, but then I realize there is hardly any need. It's not as if people can't see everything already. "Why didn't you tell me before we stepped outside?"

"I was going to… but then I started to enjoy the view."

If there'd been a way to swat him without gaining the attention of peering eyes, I would have gladly done it.

Instead, I force a smile onto my face and walk ahead. I put a little sway into my walk, enjoying the slight hitch in his breath. *I can play this game just as well as you can*, I inwardly gloat.

I spy Aloysius standing with his hands clasped behind his back and feel panic grip me. "Stay with me," I whisper just before he turns and I feel myself fade away.

"My darling." Aloysius hurries to my side, leaning in to place a kiss on both of my cheeks. "I was getting worried. You were delayed."

Of course I was. Did you really think I would want to be near you?

"There is a tear in my dress." Aloysius glances beside me at Bastien. He stands rigid several feet back, staring blankly at the water fountain. The image of a perfectly obedient servant. "I do apologize for keeping you waiting. I only wanted to look my best."

I wish I could knock myself out!

"Of course." He offers his arm and I take it. "My thanks to you, slave, but you may leave us. She will be perfectly safe in my company."

Bastien bows low and spins on his heel, leaving me without a single glance back. His steps are wooden, forced.

No! Wait! Come back! Don't leave me with him!

I smile up at Aloysius as he leads me from the stone garden and down a path leading away from the veranda. "It's beautiful here," I whisper, peering across the darkened lawn. Small pots of flame line the pathway, flickering in brilliant reds and purples. I stare at them in wonder, but Aloysius draws me past. "I feel as if I'm in a dream."

"A good dream, I hope."

"Oh yes," I say breathlessly as he leads me toward a bench. It is low and smooth, made of the same veined stone as the palace walls. He allows me to sit before releasing my arm. He sinks down beside me, his hand resting against my back, his thumb brushing against my spine.

A shiver ripples through me and I laugh, leaning into his shoulder. "How can you live among such beauty and not be awestruck by it?"

"Perhaps"—he leans in close, brushing his lips against my cheekbone—"because I have seen something of far greater beauty."

I flush and lean into his touch.

I'm going to be sick.

His lips are soft as they explore my neck. I laugh and pull away, rubbing at the spot where he touched the sensitive skin near my ear. "I thought we were taking a tour of your home."

"There is time for that later." His voice has deepened, growing hoarse. I can feel the pressure against my back increase as he leans in closer.

I hear a whinny from nearby and rise up. "Is that a horse? Do you have those here?"

Aloysius offers me a tight smile along with his hand. "I suppose a tour is what I promised. Let me show you."

He leads me down a winding path through a dense patch of weeping trees. Nestled inside is a large white wooden building, filled with row after row of stalls. The animals within the stalls remind me of the horses I've seen back on Earth, but these animals look more like a fairytale creature.

Large, flowing wings unfold by their sides as they stomp their black hoofs into the ground. The shiny silver animal nearest to me has a mane as dark as night, braided with sparkling silver and purple threads. Its back is adorned with a beautiful hand-woven blanket. The rest of the animal is a match to a horse in every way.

"What are these animals called?" It nuzzles against my hand, sniffing in search of a treat.

Aloysius reaches into a bag that hangs from the stall door and hands me a bright-purple fruit, its skin glossy and cool to the touch. "This is an Inara. They are found only on Calisted and our surrounding moons. We have searched the stars and never come across another creature like these. I named my ship after them." I turn to look at him, confused. "Pegasus, from Greek mythology."

I glance back at the animal. "I never heard of that before."

"Really?" He reaches out and pets the animal as I feed it the fruit. Warm juices run over my fingers as it bites through half of it and the returns for the rest. "I suppose there is much I could tell you about Earth."

I smile and twirl my fingers through the Inara's hair. "I would like that."

"Would you like to take a ride with me tomorrow? I know a perfect place that we could go." His gaze shifts down the long row of stalls and he smiles as he takes my hand in his, ignoring the sticky residue of the fruit. "Pick any one and it is yours."

"Really?" My eyes widen with wonder. "May I have this one, then?"

Boy, he sure knows how to lay it on thick.

My future husband laughs, nodding in consent. "I had thought she might be your first choice. Her name is Edana, which means fire. I think the two of you will get along just fine."

"Hello, Edana," I coo, pressing my hand to her nose. "I know we will be the best of friends."

"Tomorrow we will meet after breakfast. You will love the beach. The oceans are quite spectacular and the view… Well, you'll have to see it to understand."

I arrive at the stables early, hoping to surprise Aloysius. Secretly, I want to spend some time by myself with Edana. She is beautiful in the sunlight, her coat sparkling like a multi-faceted precious stone.

She is soft as silk and warm beneath the dappled sunlight. The sound of hooves catches my attention, and I glance up to see Aloysius approaching, already in his saddle. His mount is strong and nearly a hand taller than Edana. Muscle ripples beneath a sheen of black. "He is beautiful, my king," I gush, forgetting to use his name as I rush forward to stroke him.

Aloysius fondly pats his mount's flank. "This is Eron. His name means mountain of strength."

"I can see why," I laugh, stepping away. "He suits you well, my king."

"Darling, please call me Aloysius."

I grimace, realizing my mistake. "I'm sorry. It just seems so informal and I barely know you."

He reaches down and brushes his hand along my cheek. "You will know me better than any woman has before. Come. Let's ride."

I whoop with glee as I swing up into Edana's saddle, amazed at how natural it feels. I gallop behind Aloysius, using what little instruction he gave me the night before to steer. In all fairness, Edana does all of the work. I'm merely along for the ride.

After ten minutes at a hard gallop, we reach the far wall. At the sound of our approach, the gate begins to swing open and we race through without slowing. Trees line the dirt path, blurring past as I feel the strength and agility of Edana between my legs. My dress billows around me, flapping wildly in the wind.

Edana moves with smooth, flawless strides. Her hooves dig into the ground, easily keeping pace with Eron.

I bet he'd throw a fit if he came in last. Do it! Let's see if he does.

I urge Edana forward, grinning as she begins to take the lead. My hair escapes out of its clips, rippling behind me like a sail. I feel alive. I feel powerful.

My soul connects with this land, the wind, sun, and moons beyond. I can feel a stirring deep within me. Strange currents of electricity flow over my arms, lassoing about my waist. I feel invincible upon Edana's back.

An opening in the trees up ahead reveals our destination, and I pull back on the reins as the beach comes into full view. It is breathtaking. Never in my wildest dreams could I have imagined such beauty.

A cover sits below us, the sand white and perfect. The ocean stretches out before us, appearing to fall off the horizon. Beyond that, a million twinkling lights hang in the sky.

"Why can I see stars?" I ask breathlessly as I slip down from Edana's back. She dips her head and begins to hunt for food nearby. Aloysius dismounts and comes to my side.

"The atmosphere here is different. It doesn't reflect light in the same way." He lifts his hand to point to the sky. "All of those pinpricks of light are worlds waiting to be discovered. We can do it, you and I. Together we can conquer."

Conquer? Is that supposed to be romantic? Please!

"And the planet?"

In the distance, I can see two of Calisted's moons, but looming in the sky before me is a planet nearly three times the size of ours. It fills my vision, stretching from the sky and dipping low into the ocean. I can see spirals of clouds upon its surface.

"That is Andromesus. A sister planet."

"Can we go there?" I ask eagerly.

Aloysius laughs, nodding. "Someday I'll take you there. It is not nearly as populated as our planet but is just as beautiful."

I lean forward to stare at the ocean. "Can we go down there?"

He grins and clasps my hand. We run with the wind in our hair and the horses happily grazing on the hill above us. The sand feels hot upon my feet, and Aloysius sweeps me up into his arms until we reach the water's edge.

The lavender waves lap over my toes, warm as bathwater and just as relaxing. The surface of the water is surprisingly calm, breaking farther offshore. In the distance, I can spot flashes of color as fish dart back and forth. I laugh as a wave crashes against a rock outcropping and sprays high into the air. I feel as if I have been here before.

"It is almost magical," I whisper as I sink to the sand, spreading out my dress so I'm not burned, and then pull him down too. "Thank you for bringing me here."

"I'm glad you like it." He reaches out to tuck stray hairs behind my ear. "This is your beach. You're welcome to come here whenever you like."

"My beach?" I glance back at the ocean spread wide before me. "You own all of this?"

His laugh is deep and throaty. "I am the king, you

know?"

I slap my forehead, feeling foolish. "Of course you are. It's just hard to imagine sometimes."

His arm slips around my shoulders as he draws me into his side. "Everything that is mine will soon be yours. This used to be my private beach, but now I want you to have it. It seems to please you." He trails his finger down my nose.

"Thank you." I hug him tightly to me, amazed at how lucky I am.

Really? Lucky? What is wrong with you? Wake up!

Aloysius draws back, his gaze soaking me in. "You look radiant in this light. It's a shame we can't have a beach wedding, but I'm afraid we'll never fit all of our guests out here."

I lower my gaze, flushing with pleasure. "You flatter me."

He leans in and whispers in my ear, "I only speak the truth. You are even lovelier when you blush."

Note to self: stop blushing!

Clasping his hand over mine, he looks at out the sea. "We need to speak of our wedding plans. If it's all right with you, I don't want to wait. Two days is all I need to throw the best wedding this planet has ever seen."

"Two day?" I say breathlessly.

Two days? Is that all I have left?

"Does that bother you?"

I can see how important my answer is and smile warmly. "It is perfect."

"And will you grant me one wish?" I sit up, waiting expectantly. "I know on Earth it is a tradition for the bride to wear white, but here on Calisted the royal color is purple. It would please me to have a dress made of the finest lavender fabric available. It will look lovely with your coloring."

"The color doesn't matter as long as it pleases you." I smile, nearly bouncing with excitement. "I'm getting married," I whisper with a smile.

I'm getting married, the voice in my mind echoes sorrowfully.

Twenty

Bastien is pacing in my room when I return. He looks at me expectantly, but his face falls with regret as I walk into his arms and bury my face in his neck, wrapping my arms under his to clasp his shoulders.

It is the same every time I return from being with Aloysius. Bastien holds me, not having to say a word. His presence is enough to wash away the feeling of being in Aloysius's arms. That and a scalding shower.

I pull back and step away, unable to look at him as I speak. "We have two days."

"'Til what?"

"'Til the wedding."

"So soon." He hisses as he sucks in a breath. I can tell even without turning around that he is gritting his teeth. "You okay?"

"No," I whisper, wrapping my arms about my waist.

Strong arms encircle me and I lean back into his grasp. He presses his lips against my neck, holding me. I can feel his anger and his helplessness. Being by my side, waiting for me to return, has meant more to me than he will ever know, but there is nothing he can do to stop this. My destiny is unfolding before my eyes and I'm powerless to stop it.

"I asked Alesta to have your food sent here tonight. She agreed that you need to rest. She muttered something about bags under your eyes when she left."

He ushers me out of the sitting room and into my own, locking the door behind us. He waits as I go into the bathroom to tame my hair and clean the sand from my feet. When I return, I find him sitting on the edge of my bed, lacing and unlacing his fingers together. I sink down beside him, leaning into his shoulder. "Why the rush to get married? It's not as if you're fighting him?"

I sigh and lie back on the bed. "He is getting more anxious around me. I think he's worried he won't be able to restrain himself much longer."

I dig my nails into the bed covers as he turns to look down at me. His face is shadowed in the dim light. I didn't turn on any of the lights when I returned, but there is some sunlight filtering around the curtains. "I promise I won't let him touch you."

"He already has." I bite on my lower lip to stop its tremble. No matter how many times I wash out my mouth, I can still taste him on my lips, feel his hands sliding under my dress.

"Not like that. I would rather die than let him be with you on your wedding night."

I close my eyes to the tears that come. He knows of my vision, knows that as my time draws near, so does his.

"I won't let that happen," I whisper, renewing my vow. I don't know how I will save him, but I know I will. Even within the grip of Aloysius's power, I still feel protective of him. I can only hope when the time comes I can break his spell once and for all. Sariana said that if anyone could do it, it would be me. I hope she is right.

"There's something about this place, Bastien." He lies down beside me, rolling his head to look at me. "I can't explain it. It's a connection. Have you felt it too?"

"No, but maybe it's different for me." He smiles at me as I yawn. Leaning forward, he presses a kiss against my forehead. "Get some rest. I'll make sure no one bothers you for a few hours."

The mattress shifts as he rises and moves to the door. "Bastien?" He turns back. "I'm really glad you're here with me."

He smiles. "There's nowhere else I'd rather be."

I can't place the exact reason why I wake with a start. Glancing toward the window, I realize night has fallen. An untouched tray of food sits on a side table. The door to Bastien's room is closed and his light is off.

My room is dark, eerily so. I know I have no reason to fear with Bastien nearby, yet something feels off. I cling to my sheet as I slowly rise up in bed, peering into the shadows. I am not alone.

"Who is there?" I call out, my voice barely above a whisper. Bastien would never scare me like this. I glance toward my door and see the key lock is in place, so Alesta couldn't have gotten in either. Bastien was adamant about not giving her the code, even when I protested on her behalf.

Over the past couple of days, I've grown fond of the young girl and that worries Bastien. He sees spies around every corner.

I wait in silence for my eyes to adjust to the darkness. The only light in the room is the moonlight streaming through the large window to the left of my bed. A warm breeze ruffles the edge of my sheet. A cold dread washes over me as I stare at the partially open window. I didn't open that.

Just as I open my mouth to scream for Bastien, a hand clamps over my mouth. I thrust back my elbow, aiming for anything solid. He groans and I manage to wiggle free from his grasp. Leaping from the bed, I turn and crouch low in the bath of moonlight.

I watch as the intruder rises from the bed, his outline barely seen. I can tell he is a man by his height and the breadth of his shoulders. He raises a hand to stop me and I leap, throwing out my leg. He dives to the side, narrowly missing my attack. The instant he is on the floor, he turns and strikes out at me, knocking me off balance. An arm winds around my waist and I grunt as the full weight of my attacker settles onto me.

"Nice to see you too, Illyria.

My mouth gapes open and I stop fighting. I hardly recognize the sound of a door opening before the man above me is tackled and two shadows roll end over end, grunting. "Bastien, no!"

I hear the sound of punches being landed and rush forward, yanking on whoever is on top. "Stop," I cry. "It's

Eamon!"

Bastien falls slack beneath my hand. "You're sure?"

"Of course she's sure, you idiot. Get off me!" Eamon grunts from below. "Wait a second... You know me? Why do you remember who I am, and what the heck is he doing in your bedroom at this time of the night?"

"Yep, that's Eamon all right." I watch as Bastien rolls off and rises swiftly to his feet. Eamon doesn't move quite as fast. The instant he's on his feet, I race into his arms, nearly knocking him over.

"Easy." He laughs, wrapping his arms around me. I bury my face into his chest and breathe in deep. He smells like home.

"What are you doing here?" Bastien asks. Realizing how awkward this must be for him, I step back a few paces and move to turn on the light. "No! Someone will see."

Of course they will. Get it together, Illyria.

Bastien hurries toward the window and locks it, pushing a button beside it. A privacy screen lowers into place, casting the room into complete darkness.

"How did you get here?" Bastien asks, moving back toward his room. He switches on the light in the bathroom and closes the door partway.

Eamon shifts, crossing his arms over his chest. I call tell he is still ticked at finding Bastien here with me, but he leaps into his tale. "After Illyria went off with you, we received word that Drakon was on the move. Kyan knew we were in the area, so instead of heading straight back, we took a detour to a base about ten miles north. When we arrived, we found nothing. Even the buildings had been demolished. There was only one thing found in the rubble... a note."

"What did it say?" I ask.

Eamon wipes a hand across his face. "I win."

A shiver races down my spine as he continues. "I radioed back to Kyan and we headed home, only to arrive back to find a message from some girl named Niyah."

Bastien stiffens. I shoot him a warning glance and he remains silent. "Kyan was agitated. He paced for nearly an hour straight. I'd never seen him so intense before. When he finally spoke, he ordered all of the Sky Ships to head to that base."

"All of them?" I can't believe he would risk our entire fleet for me.

"Yeah. It caused quite an uproar, but Kyan was adamant that we had to get there as fast as we could." He pauses, scratching the back of his neck. "We arrived to find the base burning to the ground. The weird thing was that we couldn't find many bodies. It was almost as if they set the fires themselves."

"They did," Bastien says, sinking down onto the edge of my bed. "It was an ambush and we walked right into it."

"Yeah, we figured that out when we picked up that Niyah girl. Kyan was furious. He screamed at her for over an hour before he finally calmed down. She took it, though. No tears. Just nodded in agreement."

"'Course she did," I mutter bitterly. Eamon casts a glance in my direction, but I wave him off.

"She smuggled one of the space transports before the whole place went up in flames. We all hopped aboard and came after you. Turns out Kyan knows this planet really well. He had some connections that helped us fly in under the radar. We've only just arrived a short while ago."

"And you came straight here, of course," Bastien mutters.

"Of course." His response feels like a challenge, and I have no doubt it will be perceived as such by Bastien.

"What about Niyah?" I ask to divert their attention. Bastien stiffens, his hands clenching into fists upon his thighs.

"She came with us. Said she needed to make amends, whatever that means. She was pretty tightlipped on the way here. Refused to talk to anyone besides Kyan, and he wasn't too forthcoming with information either."

I look to Bastien, knowing I should get his permission before revealing anything to Eamon. He shrugs indifferently, but I'm not fooled. He is seething inside. Niyah had better stay far out of his way.

"Niyah is the reason we were captured. Her betrayal wasn't because she was in league with Drakon," I say, treading lightly. Bastien turns away. "She was jealous... of me. She thought if she handed me over to Drakon, he would let Bastien go."

Eamon frowns. He tilts his head for a moment, thinking. I see the light of understanding brighten as he looks between us. A scowl settles onto his face. "Breaking hearts wherever you go, huh, Bastien?"

He is on his feet and in Eamon's face before I can even react. I dive between them, pressing my hands on both of their chests but make little effect. "This isn't the time, guys." I push, my arms trembling as they lean in toward each other, going toe to toe. "Don't make me force you," I grunt, sending tiny shocks through my hands to get their attention.

Bastien backs away first, but not because he wants to. I shove him back toward his room. Finally, he breaks off his staring match with Eamon to look down at me. "I need to talk to him... alone."

His jaw clenches and for a moment I think he might protest. Instead, he dips his head in agreement, but not before tossing out a final threat. "If anything happens to her while I'm gone, I'll hold you personally responsible."

He leans forward and presses a kiss to my temple. "I'll see if I can track down some food for you. I'm sure you're hungry."

"Thanks," I reply awkwardly as he squeezes my shoulder and lets himself out. I wait to hear the security code keyed in from the opposite side of the door before I turn on Eamon. "Why do you two always have to be at each other's throats?"

Eamon shrugs and sinks down into a chair. He looks tired. No, he looks exhausted. "He gets under my skin."

I step into the light to close the door to Bastien's room a bit more, and I hear Eamon gasp. "What are you wearing?"

I look down and groan, realizing I'm still wearing my darn dress. Crossing my arms over my chest, I turn and face him. "Don't ask. This was *not* my idea."

"You, uh... you do know that dress is see-through, right?"

"Oh my gosh! Really? You think I haven't noticed that already?"

"Sorry." He rises slowly from his chair and approaches. His steps are slow, measured. "I guess this has been really uncomfortable for you."

"Uncomfortable?" I can hear the pitch of my voice rising as he stops before me. My back is to the light so I know he can only see the outline of my body, but I feel so exposed before him. First Bastien and now Eamon. Is there no ounce of privacy left for me? "I've had complete strangers eyeing me up since I got here, and Aloysius..." I shudder, not wanting to go there.

Eamon reaches out and grabs hold of my arms. "Has he hurt you?"

"No," I mutter. "He's been... kind."

"Kind?" He draws me near. "How kind?"

"Don't worry. So far he's focused all of his attention above the waist."

Eamon's hands grip me so hard I cry out, not from pain, but from surprise. "Bastien let him do that to you?"

I pull out of his grasp. "He didn't *let* anything happen. He's just as much a victim here as I am. Even if he were there watching, he wouldn't be able to do anything to stop it." I shudder at the thought, thankful that any private moments I've shared with Aloysius have been just that: private. I couldn't bear for Bastien to be forced to watch.

Eamon begins to pace before me, no doubt angered by the fact that Bastien is the one here with me instead of him. Almost as if on cue, he turns and I see that his scowl has returned as I shift away from the light. "I bet Bastien's been loving this outfit."

A smack rings out in the silence of the room. My palm stings as I draw my hand back from his face. "Bastien has been a gentleman. I expect you to be the same."

He looks hurt as he stumbles back. A myriad of emotions play across his face, finally settling on guilt. "I'm sorry." He backs away, burying his head in his hands. "That was uncalled for. I know that he... that you would never do that. It's just been a really long few days."

A slew of snide remarks flit through my mind, but I bite my tongue down on every one of them, remembering how just yesterday I'd wished for one more chance to speak to him and here I am picking a fight.

"We need to talk." As Eamon sinks back into his chair and I return to the bed, I lay out all of the details of the events leading up to now, being sure to edit a few of the details for my time spent with Aloysius. I don't want to dwell on that any more than I have to.

By the time I've brought him up to the events of this afternoon, Eamon has leaned forward, his elbows against his knees and fingers steeple before him. "So you're only under the king's control when you're with him, right?"

"Yes, but so far Bastien has remained relatively normal. I think Aloysius's pride believes me so tightly wound around his finger that Bastien no longer matters. We act like complete strangers when anyone is around, apart from Alesta, of course."

"And you trust her?"

I nod. "Bastien still keeps an eye on her, but she has given me no reason to doubt her yet."

"Only one slip could be fatal, Illyria," he warns.

I smirk. "Now you sound exactly like Bastien."

"Well, in this case, I'll take that as a compliment. You can't be too careful." He leans back in the chair, closing his eyes. "I've seen this played out over and over in my mind. Spent the past year watching you fall in love with Aloysius again and again. He's the reason I lost you."

"You know that isn't true. You pushed us apart long ago." I speak softly but know the sting of my words will still hurt.

Staring across the room at him now, I regret the way we parted ways. Him broken and me confused and tormented. None of this ever should have happened. He should have been the one giving me a shoulder to cry on, not Bastien. "I know how hard it must've been for you to look into my future, to know that someday I would be sitting right here, but you should have trusted me."

Eamon twitches as he sits up. "You think I didn't trust you?"

"What else could I think?"

He blows out a breath, shaking his head. "It was never about my lack of trust in you. It was a lack of faith in my own abilities."

I curl my finger around a strand of hair, contemplating what he has just revealed. Then it hits me. I jerk upright in bed. "You saw something else, didn't you?"

The sound of the keypad unlocking and the door opening sounds distant to me. I don't realize Bastien has returned until I feel his hand upon my arm. "Illyria? What's wrong?"

I don't look away from Eamon. "He was just about to tell me what little detail he forget to mention about my future."

Bastien's grip tightens on my arm. He swivels his head to stare at Eamon, but he doesn't notice either of our gazes. His eyes are downturned, focused on the floor. "Eamon?"

His shoulders rise and fall as he takes a deep breath. "I didn't see any point in telling you…"

"Well, there is now," Bastien growls as he raises his arm to grip my shoulder. "So start talking."

Eamon clears his throat before he speaks. "For the past year I've been monitoring Illyria's future, trying to find some way of altering it. I know it's impossible, but the thought of losing her to that monster… It was more than I could bear."

Surprisingly, Bastien nods in agreement. "So what haven't you told her?"

"There's nothing to see past her wedding night. It's all blank."

Bastien stiffens beside me, but I don't react. This isn't a surprise to me. "I've already seen that, Eamon. I know what happens."

"You never said…" Eamon trails off, lifting his head to look at me.

I shrug. "What was the point in hurting you even more? I get married to an evil monster. End of story."

Bastien and Eamon both cry out.

"How can you be so apathetic about this?" Bastien asks.

I release the breath I feel like I've been holding for over a year. "Because it haunts my dreams every night."

"You've known all this time," Eamon whispers, plunging his hands into his unruly curls. "I was trying to save you from this. To protect you from the pain."

"And all you did was alienate her and force her to deal with this on her own. Smooth move," Bastien growls beside me. I can feel his anger in the strength of his grip upon my arm.

"I didn't know." Eamon protests, beginning to rise from his chair. Bastien's grip on my arm slackens and I know he is going to rise up to meet him.

"Stop it!" I cry, surging to my feet. "I am sick and tired of you two bickering. You're family, for goodness sake!"

Eamon comes to a complete halt, blinking rapidly. "I'm sorry, what did you just say?"

Bastien groans. "Great. This is exactly how I wanted him to hear the news."

I could kick myself for letting Bastien's secret slip out, but in the heat of the moment, I used what ammo I had available. "I'm sorry, Eamon. That wasn't... I shouldn't have said it like that."

Bastien shifts uncomfortably beside me. I look to him for help, and he shoves his hands deep into his pockets. "Turns out you and I are brothers. Funny that, huh?"

Eamon stares at him with open disbelief. He looks between Bastien and me, waiting for one of us to start laughing. When neither of us crack, he sinks back into his chair. "You're my brother?" he repeats, as if needing to hear it out loud for it to be true.

"Yeah. I pretty much reacted the same way. Sucks, huh?" Bastien says, blowing out a breath.

"Yeah." Eamon snorts. "Little bit."

I close my eyes and think over how completely

opposite these two guys are. Night and day. Fire and ice. Summer and winter. And yet, under Eamon's overprotective nature and Bastien's sarcastic swagger, both men love deeply and fully. Perhaps, in the ways the matter most, they aren't so different after all.

Twenty-One

It feels weird watching Bastien and Eamon try to figure out how to be civil with each other, if for no other reason than to give this brother thing a shot. I know it won't last, but it's kind of nice for a change.

"Where are the others? Are they close by?" I ask, interrupting their hushed conversation. I know they were talking about me.

Eamon lifts his head and glances back at me. I sit propped up in bed, fighting against a yawn. The pillows are far too comfortable and the blanket warming and inviting.

"Kyan and the girls are here now, but more will be arriving soon. Carleon has gone into the villages to collect soldiers loyal to our cause. We'll be ready to fight."

"There isn't enough time," I whisper, fiddling with the edge of the sheet. "I'm to be married in two days."

I half expect Eamon to rise in anger or throw something, but instead he simply lowers his head, as if he already knew. And then I realize he did.

"And until then? Where will you go?" Bastien questions Eamon, staring past him to the night sky. Already, the distant horizon has begun to lighten.

"We won't be far. There's an old series of mines under the woods that lead to the ocean. Kyan knows them well. We'll use that as our base for now while we gather support." Eamon slowly rises, obviously reluctant to leave, but he must with the coming dawn.

"Wait!" I stretch out a hand toward him. "Please, don't go yet."

I look to Bastien, pleading silently to understand my need to say good-bye. No one really knows what'll happen during the next two days. The one thing I do know is that I need all the support and love I can get to face it.

Bastien's lips press thin, but he nods and closes the door to his room behind him. Eamon rubs the back of his neck nervously as I rise from the bed and move toward him. I watch as his gaze flits down over my dress in the moonlight before he looks away. "I should get back. I've been gone longer than planned. Kyan will be worried." His voice is raw with emotion. "I just needed to know that you're safe."

I reach for his hand and draw him near. I can feel his hesitation even as I wrap his arms about me and place my head upon his chest. Months of pain and loneliness rise up as tears gather in the corners of my eyes. This is what I needed. To simply be held.

"I'm sorry about before," I whisper as my fingers trail across the black material of his shirt. I can feel muscle beneath it, tensing and releasing as he breathes.

He presses his cheek against my head, finally sealing me into his embrace. "I never meant to hurt you. I just… I didn't know how to say good-bye."

His hands splay across my back, warm and comforting. I press my face against his neck, smiling at the rapid pulse I find thrumming there. "I've missed you," I whisper.

Eamon pulls back. His ice-blue eyes are tender as he smiles down at me. "Not as much as I've missed you."

And I know that he means every word of it. Gone are the worry lines in his forehead and about his eyes. There is still reason to fear, but in this moment, he lets it all wash away. It's sad that it took us coming to this point for him to finally realize there was nothing he could've done to prevent this. The gift of a seer is a curse and a blessing, depending on what you do with it.

I close my eyes as he reaches up to cup the back of my neck. He leans in and gently brushes his lips against mine, so softly I hardly know he is there. I lean up into him, unwilling to let him leave. Wrapping my arms around his neck, I crush my lips against his, rising onto my tiptoes to close the height distance.

Eamon's hand upon my back flinches as I press into him, pushing him against the wall, molding to his lean frame. When I draw back, I can see a change in him. My Eamon is back. He smiles and clears his throat as I step back. "Wow." He chuckles. "We should fight more often."

The distant sky is painted with vivid greens and yellows, chasing the night away. He reaches out for me one last time, squeezing my hand. "I have to go, but I'll be back."

As he turns to slip back through the window, I feel the pain of his leaving. He pauses, crouching low. "Be careful. Stay close to Bastien. I know he'll keep you safe."

I nod as he slips from the window, disappearing into the shadows of the hedgerow that lines the foundation of the palace. Leaning forward, I strain to see his dark figure darting across the grounds. I gasp as he leaps behind a tree a mere second before a guard appears, swinging a light as he walks up the stone path leading away from the stables.

I release a breath as Eamon waits for him to pass and then darts for the woods. Being able to see the future does have its rewards from time to time.

Once I know he is safely hidden by the tree line, I sink to the floor, watching as the sun begins to rise. It feels weird to me, knowing it should be rising in the east like back home, but here the sun trails north to south. There are still so many things about this place that feel odd to me. Will I ever truly be able to call this planet home?

"You okay?" I turn and look up at Bastien. I never heard his footsteps but I could feel his approach. His handsome features are pinched, his emotions under tight reign. I sigh, knowing how hard it must've been for him to wait in his room for Eamon to leave. We have done this before and it didn't end well for anyone. His eyes look dull as I shrug. "I guess you two talked?"

I wrap my arms about myself as I rise, feeling a chill that contradicts the warm morning breeze flowing in through my open window. "Please don't do this."

"Do what? Care?" The bite in his tone makes me grimace. I know this look, this body language all too well. I was forced to watch it while in Kyan's camp a year ago. The steady progression of his withdrawal had nearly destroyed me then. I can't go through this again.

"We both knew this would happen. Sariana said we can't change fate."

"Fate?" He snorts, shaking his head. "This is you I'm talking about, Illyria. I don't care what some old lady saw in a vision. I don't live my life based on what-ifs. I believe in what I can see and feel." He takes a step forward and my breath hitches at his nearness. "I believe in you. That's all that matters right now."

"And Eamon?" I press.

His gaze narrows, but he doesn't show any other reaction. "He's a distraction that you don't need right now. We need to get you through the next two days, and whatever happens after… well, it just happens."

I hate the resignation I hear in his voice, as if I have already begun to slip between his fingers and he's just waiting for the final separation. "You know," I say, looking up at him, "the only thing I ever truly wanted was for you to fight for me."

His jaw clenches as he turns and walks back to his room in silence. I almost think he's going to shut the door on me, but he turns back with his hand upon the knob. "I did, every night in my dreams."

The rest of the day passes in an absolute blur as I am whisked from one decorator to the next. Flowers are thrust before my nose, tiny squares of sweet-tasting sponge are shoved into my mouth, and my hair is yanked in so many directions I fear I'll be forced to wear a wig to cover up the bald spots on my wedding day.

Alesta is a lifesaver. While I spent the day before sleeping restlessly in bed, she was bustling about, making preparations. Sometime around noon, Aloysius came in to find me waist deep in bolts of material, my hair frazzled and my stomach churning from too many sweets, but he looked pleased, and in his presence, it all felt worth it.

The instant he left, I wanted to die.

Despite the enthusiasm Alesta has shown in the royal wedding preparations, I can sense sadness in her. She knows how desperately I don't want this wedding. As she sits me down before a table of endless meal selections, she squeezes my hand, offering me a smile.

I suppose she thinks if she keeps me busy enough, I won't really feel the terror rising up within me. Perhaps she would be right if I weren't dealing with my own inner turmoil.

Bastien and Eamon, together again. There is no part of this situation that will end well.

Both will be heartbroken. One may not survive.

The stress of this wedding pushes me to the brink. "Enough!" I shout as I toss down my napkin. I feel ill, not just from the rich foods I've consumed, but from how quickly the room has begun to spin about me.

Alesta looks up in surprise. I smile weakly at her and motion for her to approach. She whispers her apologies to the servants who've been underfoot to the point that I'm constantly tripping over them.

"Illyria?" she whispers as she kneels beside me. "Are you okay?"

I sink back in my chair, pressing my hand to my forehead. "I can't keep this ruse up any longer," I mutter. "I need air. I need to get away."

She smiles as she pats my hand and rises. "I believe the final decisions have been made. Our lady is weary from the day and would like to rest. Please see to it that all of the food selections are prepared for tomorrow's festivities."

The group of men and women, all dressed in fine purple dresses and suits trimmed with golden tassels and buttons, bow and hurry from the room. Alesta waits for the doors to close before she lowers down beside me once more. "I'm sorry that took so long. It was important that we blended your tastes with the king's."

"But I don't care," I whisper, feeling how dry my mouth has become. "I don't care what he likes, what he wants, what he thinks will make me happy."

Alesta's gaze shifts about the room. "You shouldn't say such things. People will hear."

"Maybe I don't really care." I slump in my chair.

"You must!" She clasps my arm so suddenly I cry out in surprise, but she doesn't let go. "If the king knew you were not under his control at all times, he would seek to change that. Who knows the damage he could do if he dug deeper into your brain."

I watch as she shudders. "You really care, don't you?"

She smiles. "Of course I care. You are to be my queen."

I place a hand over hers, grateful to have a friend within the palace. "I need you to swear something for me." She waits expectantly as I lean in to whisper in her ear. "Don't let Bastien out of your sight after the wedding."

"Bastien?" She draws back. "Why would you care—" She breaks off with a sigh. "I knew there was something between you two."

I wave her off. "It was a thing that could never be, but I know him far too well. When the fighting starts, he will head straight for me. I need you to promise that you'll do everything you can to stop him. I can't bear for him to get hurt."

She lowers her gaze. "I've warned my family not to attend the wedding. If their absence doesn't go unnoticed, they could be punished."

Grasping her arm, I wait for her to look up at me. "I promise I won't let that happen. No one else will die under the hand of the king."

I pace beside my window, wringing my hands as I watch the moon rise. Eamon should've been here by now. What if something went wrong? What if he was captured trying to see me again?

"Psst." A whisper slips past the curtains. I whirl around, searching the darkness.

"Eamon?" I push aside the privacy screen to look out over my window but can't see anything.

"Step back." I hardly have a chance to get out of his way as he swings down from above and lands lightly in my room, the screen clattering as it swings back into place. As he straightens, I throw myself in his arms, relieved to see him safe.

"I was so worried. I thought you'd be here at sunset, but it's been hours."

Eamon cups my face with both hands and gently brushes his lips across mine. He pulls back and smiles. "Hi."

I laugh and sink into his embrace. "Hi back."

"What's going on out—" Bastien cuts off as the light spilling from his room illuminates us. He goes rigid. "Never mind. I'll leave you two alone."

"No," I call as he turns. "You don't have to go."

"He doesn't?" Eamon arches an eyebrow.

I ignore him and step out of his arms. "Please, Bastien. You need to hear this too."

He hesitates, obviously not wanting to be anywhere near Eamon at the moment, but he turns and leans back against the wall, in the room but with some definite distance between us. That will have to do.

I turn back to Eamon. "Why were you late?"

"There was a skirmish over in Merolina, a city about fifty miles south of here. Carleon ran into some trouble and we had to bail him out."

"Is he okay?" I can't bear the thought of something happening to Carleon.

"Yeah. Kyan managed to wipe the guard's memories with the help of Balan and Delyth."

I remember the first time I met Balan. I was mesmerized by his ability to transport people from one place to another in the blink of an eye. He'd been one of the reasons we managed to survive Drakon's attack when he discovered Kyan's base in the mountains. Balan fought bravely then and ever since. I'm grateful to have him here.

"What about the girls?" Bastien asks, giving me a knowing glance. Of course he knows I'm terrified that Aminah and Zahra are here. They were never cut out for this life. They are peaceful... Well, at least Aminah is. Zahra can be a fighter when provoked.

"They're fine. Kyan and Toren are keeping them close to base. They won't be coming out to play until the wedding."

"After the wedding," I amend. Eamon glances toward me, obviously not the least bit happy with my correction. "If you bust in before I'm married, then I lose my title to the throne if… when Aloysius dies. You can't attack until after the ceremony."

"But that doesn't give us enough time to rescue you," Eamon protests.

"I've tried telling her that. You know Illyria. Stubborn as an old mule," Bastien growls, his arms tightly crossed over his chest.

Eamon glances at him and then back at me. "If we don't make it to you in time, he could—"

I hold up my hand. "I know the risks. It still has to be this way. You know that better than anyone, Eamon."

He grits his teeth and looks to Bastien for help, but he merely shrugs. "When have you ever been able to talk her out of anything?"

Eamon's lip curls into a scowl. "Good point. Fine, we do it your way, but… I want you to be the one to tell Kyan."

Dipping low into the closet, I uncover my bag, ripping into it to pull out my cammo pants and black tank top. "Heaven," I whisper as I run my hands over the material.

In less than a minute, I have tossed my see-through dress aside and don my familiar clothes. It feels wonderful to be concealed for the first time since I arrived. Standing before the mirror, I pull the clips from my hair, watching as black waves fall over my shoulders, loosely tousled and curled at the ends.

"You look stunning," Bastien whispers from behind as he emerges from his room.

I knew he wouldn't sleep, not while Eamon remained in my room. We talked for over an hour, lying side by side in my bed. It felt oddly comforting, almost like it used to be between us.

I glance down at my tank top and grin. "At least it leaves a bit to the imagination."

Bastien nods. "I like this better."

"Me too." I sink down onto my bed and begin lacing up my boots.

"And Eamon?"

I wince, knowing this was bound to happen. "Don't worry. Nothing happened. We just talked."

He lowers his gaze, turning so I can only see his profile. "I wasn't trying to pry…"

I laugh. "Of course you were. I'll bet you stayed propped up right next to the door, trying to listen."

"A tempting thought," he says dryly, "but it's not my place to monitor you. Your relationship with him is none of my business."

The heaviness in his voice hurts. "I'm sorry," I whisper.

"For what?" He moves closer in the dark. "You did nothing wrong."

I stand and face him, unsure of what do with my arms. They feel awkward at my sides yet oddly placed if I cross them. I settle for stuffing my hands in my pockets, grateful to have them once more. "Then why does it feel like I did? I hate that I keep hurting you, that no matter what I do or say it's never enough. It's not fair."

Bastien closes the gap between us and gently lifts my chin up toward him. "I'm here because I want to be. Don't worry about the rest. I can handle it."

My hands clench into fists within my pockets. "You always do this for me. Having you and Eamon so close isn't a good idea."

To this Bastien nods. "I agree. Things get… complicated, but that's not something I want you to worry about. I'm fine. You need to focus on finding a way to break Aloysius's mind control."

I remove one hand from my pocket and brush my hair back from my face. "Will things ever be easy again?"

His gaze shifts beyond me, unseeing. "Someday it will."

"But not today," I mutter.

"No." He looks back at me. I can see the hidden depths

of his pain. "Not today."

Staring at him now, I can't imagine my life without him. He has always known my thoughts and emotions, been the backbone I needed when I was too weak. He roots me in reality, but that ability reminds me that I'm not free to love him.

"You'd best pretend to be sleeping when Alesta arrives. Otherwise, she'll think you were in on my escape plan. You know she'll be furious about messing with her wedding day schedule." I move toward the window, turning back with one leg up on the sill. "Oh, and try not to look too gorgeous when you first wake. It's really not fair to her."

Bastien cracks a smile. "It'll be tough, but I'll see what I can manage."

I grin and leap from the window and out into the night.

As I hurry along the path leading to the stables, glancing back over my shoulder from time to time, I can't help but think of one thought: today I'm getting married. I had hoped that when this day came, it would be filled with joyful nerves and butterflies of excitement, not dread and fear.

Dawn isn't far off as I hurry down the steps and toward the stables. I can hear the whinnies of the Inara and grin. Bastien's plan was brilliant. Of course the guards would allow me to breach the palace walls to go for a ride, even one so close to my wedding. My beach is private, secluded. No harm would come to me there.

We decided it best to leave Bastien behind or risk raising unnecessary warning flags should we be seen together. To this point we have given Aloysius no reason to doubt either of us and now is not the time to give him the chance.

Edana waits for me in her stall, her head bucking as I reach out to smooth my hand over her nose. She nuzzles against me and I laugh, stepping aside to grab a fruit for her. "You don't want to eat too much or you'll spoil your breakfast."

It takes me a few moments to figure out how to attach the saddle. Watching one of the stable boys do it is hardly a good enough lesson to learn by. As the first droplets of color dot the sky, I steer Edana out of the stable and break into a run.

My hair whips behind me and I laugh as I leave the palace behind, feeling free for the first time in days. Edana eats away the distance in only a few scant minutes. Nervous tension roils in my belly at the thought of seeing my friends again.

Aminah is sure to crush me in a hug if she comes. Zahra might even be happy to see me. Although, if she tries to go for a hug, I'll be shocked. And Kyan... I need him more than I realized. He'll know what to do. He always does.

The gates loom before and I lean low over Edana's back, waiting for the gates to open. As we draw near, I realize that two guards stand before them, hands outstretched. I pull back on the reins, my teeth rattling as Edana digs in her feet.

"What is the meaning of this?" I growl as we slide to a halt only a few feet back from the towering metal gate. "I order you to stand aside."

The guards look at each other before answering. "I'm afraid I can't allow that, my lady."

"By whose authority?"

"Mine," a raspy voice calls from my right side.

Edana paws at the dirt as I shift uneasily in my saddle. Drakon emerges, his hands clasped behind his back. His face is battered and bruised, his upper lip split and laced with stitching. Apparently Malek had a good time teach Drakon his lesson.

His gaze sweeps over my attire and I can feel his smug grin hit like a punch to my ribs. "I should have known you would try to escape to your rebel friends." He steps forward and grabs my reins, yanking them from my hand.

The guards rush forward and I scream as their hands clap upon me, unseating me. Drakon smiles as I buck in their arms. I can feel his touch as he prods at my mind and snarl as I mentally shove him back. "Don't touch me."

"I wouldn't dream of it." His eyes glint black in the rising dawn. "However, I think the king will be *very* interested to hear where it is you were heading, don't you?"

Twenty-Two

I strain against Drakon's grasp, clawing my nails against his arms as he drags me across the slick palace floor. I grunt, digging in the soles of my boots, giving myself only a small amount of traction to resist. "Let go of me."

"And miss the chance to see Aloysius turn his rage on you? Not a chance. I've been waiting far too long for this moment."

I lash out at him, raking my nails across his face. He howls as thin red gashes appear and rears his hand back to strike.

"Let her go," a deep voice growls behind me.

"Bastien!" I strain to see over my shoulder, but Drakon yanks me around, crossing his arm over my chest, pinning me tightly against him.

"I tried to warn Aloysius about you two." Drakon sneers. I feel something sharp jabbing into my side and realize he has pulled a knife on me, positioning it between my ribs. "The fool's arrogance and lust has blinded him to the truth."

Bastien's gaze narrows dangerously. "Illyria?"

"She can't do anything," Drakon laughs. I gasp as the knife pierces through my shirt. A tiny droplet of blood seeps down my side. "If she does, Aloysius will know that she isn't under his control and she doesn't want that, now does she!"

His hand tightens over my chest as he reads Bastien's reaction. "Oh, yes. I know all about you two. Alesta may be a cunning girl but I've been playing this game far longer than she has."

"What have you done with her?" I jerk in his grasp, ignoring the stab of pain as the knife digs in deeper.

"Nothing...yet." He shifts to look at the hall behind him, inching us backwards. Despite the vast size of this building I am familiar with this part of the palace. He is taking us to the throne room.

My gaze flickers to my right as I try to send a silent message to Bastien. He doesn't nod, doesn't show any reaction. I can't tell if he understands.

"So what now?" Bastien asks, following after us, his body positioned to attack when given the slightest chance.

"Aloysius will decide what to do with her." His breath smells off. There is a sickening, overwhelming aroma to it, as if he has been drinking something foul.

I can see the double doors up ahead and begin to panic. The guard manning the door looks up. I can see his surprise and confusion. "Sir?"

"Get the King!" Drakon grunts as I slam my heel into his shin, running it down to his foot. "Get him now!"

"Bastien," I call, but he is already on the move. We both know what will happen the instant Aloysius is within sight of me. We have to take Drakon down now.

In a blur of black, Bastien leaps. I slam my head back into Drakon's face, shattering his nose. His arm releases me and I fall to the floor just as Bastion lands beside me, his punch driving Drakon into the ground.

A loud crack echoes around the hall. I turn and see Drakon's eyes roll back. Blood begins to pool around his head as it rolls to the side. Bastien snatches the front of Drakon's uniform and draws his arm back to strike again.

"What's the meaning of this?" a voice booms.

I feel the cold sensation slip over my mind as I slump to the floor. I gasp as I clutch my side, feeling the reverberations of approaching footsteps. When I look up, I see Aloysius' livid face hovering over Bastien. "You've killed him!"

"Aloysius," I call, reaching out to him. He pales as he rushes to my side, taking my hand in his. He turns it over and stares at the blood on my palm.

"Darling, you're hurt." A growl rumbles in his chest as he pulls me into his arms and turns on Bastien. "Did you do this?"

"No," I whisper as I rest my head over his pounding heart. "Bastien saved me."

The afternoon has grown unseasonably cool. I wrap my arms about myself as I stare out over the palace grounds. The main gates opened nearly an hour ago. Streams of people arrive from the city below, each dressed in their best clothes. I can see children running and playing, their laughter like music on the air.

I have lost count of their numbers as they pass out of sight and through the main doors of the palace. I sink down onto my bed, fighting back the tears that threaten to fall. *I'm trying to be strong.* I swipe at my eyes before I ruin my makeup.

Alesta has done a wonderful job making me beautiful. As I look at myself in the mirror I almost smile. She made me look perfectly fierce.

A knock sounds at my door. "I want to be alone."

There is a pause and then another knock. "Alesta, please."

"I am not Alesta."

I turn to look at the door, struggling to place the gentle voice. It sounds familiar somehow and yet I know that I have not heard it while staying in the palace. Lifting my skirts, I turn to face the door. "Come in."

When the woman enters I am struck by her beauty. Her skin is fair and flawless. Her golden hair is coiled about her face, trailing down her back. Slender shoulders dip into the curve of a beautiful scarlet dress that cinches at the waist and flares back out at the hip. Her delicate hands clasp before her. Violet eyes search my face after she closes the door behind her.

"I'm afraid I'm not in the mood for visitors," I say, rising slowly from the bed. My skirts are ridiculously large and heavy. The bust of my dress is tight, crushing my ribs together. I feel as if I will come popping out of it at any moment. My purple dress sparkles like diamonds woven into each strand. The rich color deepens as your eye trails from my chest to the floor.

The woman takes a step forward. "I have Alesta to thank for allowing me to see you. I know you must be very busy so I won't stay long."

I glance around my empty room and laugh. "Not really. I'm just waiting for the music to start."

Her responding laughter sounds like wind chimes, soothing and pleasant. "Your friend came to see my yesterday. They thought you might like to see me before…" she trails off as she lowers her gaze.

I realize with a start that she is fumbling nervously with the beading along her skirts. "Alesta?"

"No," she smiles and looks up at me. I watch as she takes a deep breath and presses her shoulders back. "Kyan thought it only right that you have your…your mother with you on your wedding day."

My mouth gapes open as I take a step back. I swiftly appraise her again, searching for any sign of myself in her. Her nose is similar to mine and her lips are full, boasting a tiny dip in the middle that is identical to my own. I press my hand to my stomach as I realize our eyes are the exact same shade of violet.

"Mother?" I whisper, needing to hear the word spoken aloud. "How did Kyan find you?"

"Sariana actually found me. She has a way of knowing exactly what needs to be done." Her smile is pure radiance as I stare at her, too numb to know exactly what I'm feeling. She looks expectantly at me and I realize how awkward this must be for her too.

"I, uh…" I smooth my hair, needing something to do with my free hand, "I don't even know your name."

"It's Laeydria. Most people just call me Dria."

"Dria." I roll her name over my tongue several times before I smile. "I think I prefer Laeydria."

She grins and I watch as her skirts sway from side to side, brushing along her calves. "So do I."

"And my father? Is he alive?"

"Oh, yes." She shuffles forward a few steps. I can tell she is wary of upsetting me, no doubt thinking that I would prefer my space for now. "Locan is here and waiting to meet you. Alesta was only able to sneak me in. You'll be able to meet him after…" My smiles fades as she trails off. "I'm sorry. I know this isn't easy for you."

I snort and wrap my hands about my waist. "There is little that I know about you and I have so many questions. Who am I? Why am I different? Do I have any brothers and sisters?"

Laeydria laughs, holding up her hand. "That's a lot of questions and I wish I had more time to answer them for you, but I can at least answer the first one."

I hold my breath as she steps forward and reaches for my hand. Her hands are soft as I allow her to pull my hand into her own. I don't know what I was expecting when she touched me. A spark? A sense of familiarity?

I feel nothing.

She squeezes my hand as she smiles down at me. I realize even with my heels on she is still a couple of inches taller than me. "You are exactly who you are meant to be. I don't know why you are special, only that you are. Your father and I are commoners. I'm a Healer and he is a Kinein. He can move matter with his mind."

"I can too," I whisper. "Both actually."

Her smile grows fond. "I hear you have far more talents than that."

I nod, biting my lip. *Is this how all of us will feel when we meet our real parents? Misplaced and yet mingled with an odd sense of longing? I can only hope all of us have parents as Laeydria seems to be.*

"I wish that we could have-" her head jerks around as the door opens and Alesta enters. She is a vision in a pale pink dress that shimmers with each step. Her hair flows down her back in silken waves. Her cheeks are nearly the same color as her lovely dress.

"I'm afraid this will have to wait," she says, looking at me with sympathy. "It's time."

I have never been to a wedding before. Where I come from a simple vow is spoken before friends and family to bind you together. My parents spoke their vows when I was six. I don't know why they waited so long. Everyone in our group knew they were meant for each other, both likeminded and of strong personality. They chose me as their daughter after the invasion, but sometimes I like to think that I helped bind them together.

I can hear the din of murmurs on the other side of the doors leading into the throne room. A thousand or more people wait to catch their first glimpse of me. I feel as if I can't breathe as I pace back and forth.

Alesta watches silently beside me. From time to time she sends glares at the guards who stand outside the doors and they avert their gaze again.

I'm lost to my own world as I pace. Time seems to slow as my hands begin to tremble. *I don't know if I can do this.*

The sound of approaching footsteps grasps my attention and I look up to see Bastien striding toward me. My breath catches at the sight of him in a fine coat of purple and silver. His pants are black and trimmed with silver, trailing down the outsides of both pant legs.

"Wow," Alesta whispers behind me, blushing as I turn to look at her. "Sorry, but wow."

I nod in silent agreement. "Can you give us a moment?"

She hesitates, glancing back at the closed doors. "Be quick. Use the side room."

I grab Bastien by the arm and drag him through the open door. The curtains are drawn across the windows, dimming the sunlight that fights to stream in. I push on the door, my heels slipping on the slick floor.

"What are you thinking?" He hisses over my shoulder as he reaches to help me push the heavy door closed. "This is hardly the proper behavior of a woman madly in love with her soon-to-be-husband."

"I don't care." I turn under his arm and rise to crush my lips against his, my hands tugging urgently on his coat.

His eyes widen in surprise and for a moment seems unsure of what to do. "Kiss me, you idiot."

With a groan, he gives in, pressing the length of his body against mine. The doorknob jabs into my spine. My hands are everywhere and nowhere at the same time. The feel of the velvety coat under my fingers is wrong but as his lips trail down my neck, pausing at the hollow to place a fiery kiss, I can't bring myself to care. I arch up into him as he grips my waist, needing to be closer.

My breath comes out in pants as I weave my hands through his short hair, realizing he has spiked it with some sort of gel that crunches when touched. He groans as I press up into him. His lips dance dangerously close to the plunging neckline of my dress.

I feel flushed, my heart pounding wildly in my chest. "Don't stop," I whisper, urging him on. He smiles against my sensitive skin as he places soft kisses just along the top of my chest. My leg curls around the back of his, forcing him to lean into me.

A loud knock at the door startles me. I cry out as Bastien lurches back and I lose my balance. "Illyria, the music is starting," Alesta calls through the door.

"Crap." Bastien reaches out to steady me against the wall before wrenching open the door and nearly sends Alesta tumbling into the room. "I have to go."

I watch in disbelief as Bastien rushes away, smoothing his hair and straightening his jacket. He quickly disappears around the corner. "Are you alright?" Alesta asks, reaching out to grab onto me before I falter.

I press my hand against my lips, feeling how swollen they are from his touch. "He didn't even say goodbye."

"Perhaps he couldn't." Alesta's smile is soft with compassion. "I'm sorry, but you must take your place or the King will suspect."

Nodding absently, I allow her to walk me out of the room and toward the set of double doors that lead into the throne room. She does her best to straighten the hairs that have fallen free from my clips, but I hardly notice as the doors swing inward and I am struck with the overwhelming scent of flowers.

The high ceilinged room is draped in flowers of all

colors. Some bold with wide petals and large drooping leaves, others are smaller but softer in hue. I stare in wonder at the cascade of color all around.

Alesta did an amazing job.

I reach back and take her hand. "At least it's stunning."

She grins as she places an all-white bouquet in my hands. Aloysius felt it only fitting since I had so graciously agreed to the purple wedding dress.

I am drawn forward by the sound of music. The aisle before me seems to flow in endless rows of smiling faces. I can see beautiful hats with feathered plumes that stretch nearly two feet overhead and men dressed in fine silk suits who dip low as I pass.

The sounds of my shoes against the marble floor echoes in my ears, although I vaguely realize that it would be impossible to hear over the music. I keep my chin high and my shoulders back as I walk down the aisle.

Nearly halfway I realize that my knees have begun to quake and I'm dangerously close to collapsing. My stomach roils and a sheen of sweat beads along my brow.

A man steps into the aisle, tall and thin and bearing a kind smile. "May I?"

I blink, surprised by his offered arm. Movement behind him captures my attention as I see my mother in the pew, wiping tears from her eyes.

"Illyria," the man whispers as I allow him to take my arm. That one word, my name spoken on his lips tells me all I need to know. My father is walking me down the aisle.

I grip his arm tightly in gratitude. He leads me with grace and poise, never faltering in his steps. Looking forward I can see a deep purple runner has been placed over the steps leading up to the altar.

As we reach the final row of spectators, I get a wide-angle view. Aloysius stands regally beside an elderly man, whose graying beard stretches nearly to his knees. He is draped all in white and a great jeweled necklace-like ornament dangles from shoulder to shoulder.

I feel the cold wash over me, but just before it takes over completely my gaze shifts onto the person standing just behind my future husband. My steps falter.

He has chosen Bastien to be his best man.

Twenty-Three

I stare out of the window, feeling alone as mists crawl down from the mountains, highlighted by the setting of the sun. The ring on my finger and the crown upon my head feel like a heavy burden.

I'm married.

For a year, I have feared this moment. It is identical to my dreams, even to the last detail. I've never been in Aloysius's room before, but I recognize it as if it were my own.

My wedding dress drapes across the chair that sits before a tall, ornate-looking mirror. It wouldn't surprise me if Aloysius spends a lot of time primping in front of it as his servants dress him each morning.

I turn to look at myself in its reflective surface. My hair is still beautifully woven into a long braid, the strands glittering with jewels that can hardly compare to those nestled in the crown that perches atop my head. It was handcrafted for me, made of the finest metals mined from this land.

My lips are pale rose, glossed and full. The black shadow spread across my eyelids makes my violet eyes seem to glow. My skin is flushed, whether from heat or turmoil I can't tell. The dress that was chosen as my wedding nightgown is hardly more than a slip of sheer fabric. It falls across the top of my bared thigh and laces down the front. Tiny straps are the only thing giving me a hint of modesty.

Thank God I didn't have to walk around the castle in this!

I lift my gaze to stare about the room, curling my lip with disgust at its lavish decor. The walls are carpeted in fine silks, draping from ceiling to floor. A plush plum carpet cushions my bare feet as I step back from the mirror.

The windows stretch up to the vaulted ceilings, their glass set in crisscrossing sections, each piece a different color. In the dimming light, they create a path before me of blues, reds, yellows, and oranges.

The air is cool against my skin. Goose bumps rise along my arms as I pace. It won't be long until he comes. I can still remember my internal screams as I heard myself speak the vows that bound me to him. Just beyond him I could see the effort that it took Bastien not to leap forward and strike Aloysius down right then and there, but somehow I managed to shake my head.

I remember his eyes widening in surprise and I knew I'd somehow broke through Aloysius's control. It was only for a moment, but it was something. Something I've only dreamed was possible. Maybe I really can learn to shut Aloysius from my mind.

A door opens and closes behind me and I take a breath, preparing myself for what I know will come after. The instant Aloysius steps into sight, I feel the haze fall over my mind and a smile curves my lips.

"My king." I dip low in greeting as he approaches. I notice he has already removed his shoes as I lower my gaze.

He places a hand upon my arm and lifts me up. His smile is broad as he pulls me to him. "You're my wife now, dearest. There will be no more bowing."

I smile hesitantly as he slides his arm around me and pulls me so close I can feel the buttons of his suit jacket digging into my stomach. "Our guests?"

"Are leaving." He grins, leaning in to press his lips against my temple. He draws back and does the same with the other. His free hand settles upon my waist, his fingers kneading my side. I can feel his growing urgency. "There'll be no one bothering us tonight."

That's what you think.

My smile falters. I can see it in the mirror. Confusion pinches the corners of my eyes as I stiffen in his arms. "Illyria?" I blink and realize he's looking down at me. "Is everything all right?"

I start to answer, but I feel a feather-light touch in my mind and gasp. Aloysius's gaze narrows and the touch increases. *I can feel him.*

"Yes," I manage a rather convincing smile and press my hand against his chest. "I'm just... I'm nervous, I suppose."

His gaze grows tender with understanding as he shifts his hand to hold my chin. He places a soft kiss upon the tip of my nose, like a father would for a child with a cut on her knee. "I promise I'll be gentle."

A deep flush rises along my cheeks as the odd touch in my mind fades away. Apprehension ripples through me as he lowers his hand to grasp mine, pulling me toward the bed.

It stands nearly as high as my waist and is circular in shape. A mountain of pillows leans against the curved headboard, each one white but with different patterns. Some with fury patches, some soft as leather, and others shiny. The blanket looks soft and fluid, like water rippling on a moonlit pond. It is made of a black material that I'm unfamiliar with.

Aloysius pauses by the table that stands beside the bed and removes the crown from his head. It glints of yellow gold and clanks softly as he sets it down. He motions for me to come closer and raises his hands to remove mine as well.

The weight of it is freeing as he unwinds it from my hair. Jewels shimmer as they fall from my hair and onto the ground. I gasp and sink down to retrieve them, but Aloysius laughs and tugs me back up. "Leave them. You're far more precious than those rocks."

He lightly brushes the back of his hand down my arm. "You have made me the happiest man today, Illyria."

"And I'm the luckiest woman in the world to have been chosen to be at your side, my king."

I'm gonna throw up!

He leans back and appraises me again. I smile nervously. "Are you sure everything is okay?"

"I..." I look down, my cheeks flooded with heat of embarrassment. "I'm afraid I won't please you."

Really? How lame! Kick him in the groin!

"How could you not?" He sounds surprised. His hands grip my arms as he lightly pushes me down onto the bed. I sink onto the edge of the soft mattress. "You have nothing to worry about, darling. I will guide you."

I raise a hand and gently run the sheer white curtains that drape over the bed through my fingers. They drift lightly in the breeze, pulling away from my grasp. I turn to look at the window, frowning. "Did you open—"

A terrible crash sends me shooting to my feet. Aloysius pushes me back behind him, facing off with the man who now crouches in a sea of glass. Fear strikes me as I grip my husband's arm.

My vision.

A strange sensation rolls over me as the man looks up. His gaze sweeps past Aloysius and fixates on me. There is a tugging in my stomach, as if I need to be standing at his side instead of my husband's. His face is grim, but his gaze is gentle, almost loving.

I feel a sharp stab in my mind and I blink, dazed. I try to clear the haze from my mind as the man rises slowly, rolling his shoulders back. Shards of glass rain down from his spiked black hair.

"You?" Aloysius growls. "I should've killed you when I had the chance."

I turn and stare at the man, confused. "Do we know him?"

Sapphire eyes stare back, and I can see something flicker in his gaze... pain. "She doesn't know you," Aloysius gloats, placing himself firmly between us. "Though, it would appear that somehow you two managed to screw with my mind control. I had my suspicions when I saw you take down Drakon in the hall, but I knew the moment I saw the pain on her face when she saw you standing next to me at the wedding."

Cruel bastard.

Aloysius laughs, openly gloating. "It was one of my

better ideas. I could feel your anguish behind me. It made our first kiss as husband and wife that much sweeter, and I have you to thank for that."

The young man's back teeth grind. He doesn't look at me again, and I'm glad. The darkness sweeping over his face makes the hairs on the back of my neck rise. "Who is he, my king?"

"A prisoner who needs to learn his place."

"Illyria..." I feel an odd stirring in the air just before the man's face wipes clean of emotion. He stands upright woodenly, as if he were a puppet being controlled by a master.

"What have you done to him?" I ask, stepping back from my husband. This feels wrong.

Aloysius walks toward the man and pokes him in the chest. No reaction. A malicious smile crosses his lips as my husband turns back toward me. "He is no longer a threat to you, my dear. I'll have him removed."

He starts to walk away but stops and turns back. "On second thought, perhaps it would be better to just remove him altogether."

No! Wake up! Please, wake up!

My hands tremble at my sides as I watch my husband march across the room. He presses a panel on the wall and a door slides back to reveal a secret stash of weapons. I spy daggers, spear-tipped lances that expand out, a circular blade with a metal bar running through the center, and a laser pistol.

Aloysius's hand hovers over the weapons, skimming back and forth. "My king?"

He glances back over his shoulder at me. "Yes?"

"You won't hurt him, will you?" I cast a worried look at the man. It bothers me that he is so lifeless. I can barely see him blink.

My husband selects a serrated dagger and closes the door behind him. A trickle of unease flows over me.

You've seen this. Wake up! He's going to kill Bastien.

I blink rapidly, confused.

"It will all be over soon." My husband's voice is low

and dangerous as he stalks forward. I feel paralyzed as Aloysius lowers his dagger, poised to strike.

"No!" I thrust out my hands. An invisible energy surges from them, knocking Aloysius off his feet. He cries out as his shoulder slams into a bedpost and he crumples to the floor.

My chest rises and falls as I suck in huge breaths, shocked at what I've just done. Aloysius is shaking as he rises, his skin blotched with red. I can feel him searching my mind, his touch no longer soft but stabbing. His eyes narrow as he jabs again.

The air ripples before me as I lower my hands and I feel the haze lift. I tap my temple and grin as I bat aside his mental touch. "I feel you."

"That's impossible," he growls, stepping closer. "No one can do that."

"And yet... I can." I stretch out my hand and push the boundary of my shield to encompass Bastien. He blinks, coming out of a daze. "You okay?"

"You know me now?"

"Yes." I smile, wiggling my fingers. He lifts his gaze and notices the shimmer around him. "Huh. Why didn't we think about that before?"

"Didn't know I could do it. It's a new trick." I train my eyes over the shield, amazed. "I wouldn't advise stepping out of my—" I cut off as Aloysius drives his shoulder into Bastien's waist and sends them tumbling to the ground. Bastien hits hard, grunting as he beats against Aloysius's grasp. I struggle to keep him within my shield, shifting it constantly as they wrestle upon the floor.

"You will not take her from me!" I see the glint of silver a split second before it carves through the air. Bastien cries out as the knife slashes across his arm, leaving his sleeve sliced and dangling from his arm.

His blood seems unnaturally bright as it splatters against the floor. Pain mars his features as he clasps his arm, twisting and turning to try to buck Aloysius off. My husband raises his hand for another swing, and I dive, raking my nails down the backs of his arms. He howls and releases his hold on the knife.

I spin and grab for the knife, but Aloysius snatches a handful of my hair and yanks. My scalp is in agony as I grapple to reach for the knife. My fingertips brush over the blood-slicked handle, but I can't quite get it. "Bastien."

He bucks hard and sends Aloysius sprawling to the floor. Several black strands remain between his fingers. I grab the knife and dash to Bastien's side. He cradles his arms to his chest, his face pale. "You need to get out of here."

"No." he shakes his head. I can see his fierce determination. "I'm not leaving until—"

He slams his good hand into my shoulder, knocking me out of the way as Aloysius attacks. They roll end and over, landing punches. The sound of flesh pounding flesh and the shattering of bones makes me sick. I try to find a way to dive in to help, but they're tangled together too tightly.

A burst of color reflects in the mirror as I whip around to see a giant fireball spiraling toward the palace. "Duck!"

Bastien and Aloysius don't hear me. I throw out my hand and mentally shove them aside as flames erupt against the side of the building, spitting molten rock into the room. I cry out as one of the rock shards lands upon my leg, cauterizing my skin.

"Illyria!" Bastien drives his hand into Aloysius's side and a terrible snapping sound fills my ears. My husband howls and rolls to his side. Bastien scrambles to his feet and throws himself to my side, stomping out the flames igniting on the carpet around me. "Oh, God, you're burning."

The scent of my flesh melting makes my head swim. I can feel his hands upon me as he digs the scalding rock out of my leg. Darkness edges my vision. The pain is localized but excruciating.

"We have to get you out of here!"

Another explosion rocks the palace. Over the cracking of stone and hiss of flames, I can hear shouting from below. "Eamon!"

Bastien rises to look out the window and nods. "They're coming. We have to—" His eyes widen and his mouth gapes open.

"No!" I shriek as a blood-tipped spike shoves through his stomach from his back, nearly three inches in diameter, punching a hole through his intestines. Aloysius's maniacal grin appears over his shoulder as he shoves Bastien aside.

Bastien shudders, blood bubbling from his lips. Pain pinches his features. His hands shake as he touches the spike protruding from his stomach. Gurgling moans rise from his throat as he locks his gaze on me, beginning to glaze over. "Illyria…" He stretches out his hand toward me.

I can hear the wet wheezing in his chest and feel numbness wash over me. Blood pools beneath him, thick and bright. I watch as it begins to seep toward me. When I look back at Bastien, his eyes are unfocused and his chest lies still.

"Bastien!" I start forward, but Aloysius steps between us, blocking my path. Tears burn in my eyes and I grit my teeth, fighting to comprehend that he is really gone. Rage burrows into my chest as invisible sparks vine around my hands. I glare at my husband. "You will pay for this."

Twenty-Four

I rise slowly from the floor, ignoring the pain in my lower leg as I stand. The air sparks around me. The glass shards on the floor begin to clatter against the tile. The hair atop Aloysius's head lifts, flapping in the rising winds.

The sound of the gale drowns out the screams below, though the flash of laser fire can be seen against the walls. I ignore it all. Aloysius is all that matters—my anger… my revenge.

His eyes are wide and glazed as he looks back at me. His face ashen and drawn with fear. I can feel my powers rippling across my skin. Aloysius backs away. I follow, stalking after him as he stumbles on the edge of the rug and knocks over the bedside table. He skirts the wall, nearing his weapons cache.

His fingers fumble over the keypad and the door hisses open. He grabs the first thing he can find and turns to face me with the laser pistol pointed at my chest. I roll my eyes. "Why did I ever fear you?"

With the flick of my wrist, I bat aside the first shot. It ricochets off the wall, searing a hole through the white gossamer curtains draping from the ceiling. The second and third leave scorch marks across the bedding and walls. The blanket catches fire. I can see the flames flickering in Aloysius's eyes.

I step toward him and he cowers back. His needling jabs at my mind are laughable now. "What are you?" He gasps as my hair begins to rise from my shoulders.

"You know…" I tilt my head. "I don't really know."

I clap my hands together in front of me and the windows shatter in a rain of glistening glass. My husband is thrown back off his feet. He slams into the wall and slumps to the floor. Small cuts line his forehead, making his eyes look as if they are weeping blood as I leap forward and snatch a jagged shard of glass and press it to his throat.

His eyes widen as his hands claw at my arms. I press my weight against him, watching as a seam of blood appears along his neck. His mewling sounds turn moist as I dig in deeper, feeling the layers of his skin peel away. Warm blood flows over my hands, but still I press, ignoring the splatters against my cheeks and neck.

His throat gurgles as his grip on my arm slackens. His eyes glaze over, unseeing. With a cry, I slice the glass straight across his neck and toss the shard away. A sheet of blood pours from his neck as his head collapses against his shoulder.

I rise to my feet and back away, my hands quaking. I can feel his blood on my face, clinging to my hands, and frantically wipe it away. I've never killed a man in cold blood like that before.

"Illyria!"

Slowly I turn, blinking to clear my vision as two men burst through the door. One has crimson staining his tousled blond curls. The other stands tall and strong, like a beacon of hope. I sink to my knees, tears streaking from my eyes as Eamon and Kyan rush forward.

Eamon takes me into his arms, cradling me as I cry. I can hear him calling my name, but it sounds distant. Kyan kneels beside me, but his gaze is focused on Aloysius.

"It's okay." Eamon soothes, brushing his hand down over my hair. "Everything is going to be okay."

I shake my head, pushing away from him. The sight of my bloody handprints on his chest makes my lips begin to tremble. *I failed.*

"Bastien," I whisper and point toward the bed.

Kyan rises fluidly and rushes around us. He goes absolutely still, his expression filled with remorse as he turns back to look at me. "I'm so sorry."

"Sorry?" Eamon says, looking between us. "Sorry for what?"

Kyan closes his eyes. "He's gone."

My shriek is long and mournful as I collapse into

Eamon's arms, knowing I'll never see Bastien's smile again, never hear him call my name or hold me in his arms. He is gone… and it's all my fault.

I feel as if my heart is on the brink of imploding within my chest, but it doesn't. It refuses to die, leeching poison into my body, chilling but nonlethal. As my body begins to quake, I pray I could join Bastien in death.

"I can't believe he's really gone," Eamon says, stunned. I can see him staring at Bastien's feet and feel rage swell in my chest. Rage at Aloysius and at the fates.

"No." I grunt as I push out of Eamon's arms. I swipe my arm across my cheeks. "I won't let him die."

Kyan grabs my arm as I go to past him. "He has already passed over. It's impossible to bring him back."

"Not for me." I shove him away, sending him toppling over Eamon.

I stand before Bastien, my hands clenched into fists at my sides. I can feel my power crashing around me like waves in a torrent. The wind whistles through the shattered windows, whipping my hair into my face, lashing against my eyes. The lights begin to flicker overhead, the pillars in the four corners of the room cracking.

"Kyan, her eyes!" Eamon calls out.

"I know!"

I'm barely aware of Kyan as he circles around to stand in front of me. I don't look at him. I stare at Bastien's lifeless body, at the pool of blood he lies in. So much blood.

"Illyria, think about what you're doing. You have to pull back."

"No," I shout into the wind. "That's exactly what I can't do!"

I lift my hands out to the sides, my toes rising off the ground. A warmth begins to rise up from my extremities, drawing lines of gold along my veins, glowing beneath my clothes as they converge on my heart.

"What is she doing?" Eamon shouts, but Kyan doesn't answer as he begins to back away. The instant the lights connect, my entire body jerks and the winds stop. A brilliant light fills the room, so bright it feels like I've harnessed the sun. I'm vaguely aware of the air rippling in front of me, a protective shield I subconsciously threw up before the blast. Glancing down I see Eamon and Kyan cowering on the floor but safe within my protective bubble.

I can no longer hear the screams or the sounds of laser fire in the palace yard. All I hear is pure, unadulterated silence.

"What have I done?" I stare down at Kyan.

He rises slowly, his hands visibly shaking. "I don't know. I think... I think you've somehow stopped time."

I look around me in amazement and realize he is right. I can see glass hovering in the air just beyond my shield. The flames mounting the curved headboard of the bed stand still. I look up to see the white curtains that drape from the ceiling have been blown sideways and hang motionless in the air.

Stepping lightly over the glass-strewn floor, I peer out the window and gasp. "It's not just in this room. The men below are frozen too!"

"How is this possible?" Eamon asks, rising shakily to his feet. He brushes his hair back from his face, revealing a deep cut along his right cheek.

"I have no idea," Kyan mutters, sounding out of breath. "I've never heard of such a thing before."

"Why are we the only ones not affected by this?" Eamon rises onto his toes to look out the window nearest him.

Kyan glances around and then rises to meet my gaze. "Because she's shielding us from it."

I turn and walk toward him, showing no sign of pain as the glass slices into my feet. "If I stopped time, does that mean I can reverse it as well?"

Kyan blows out a breath, shrugging. "I honestly don't know. It would appear at the moment that you can do anything you want."

I glance down at Bastien. *I will save you.*

"Hold on tight," I whisper aloud.

"To what?" Eamon says, but I ignore him.

Closing my eyes, I wrap my powers about me, feeling them cocoon me, fluid and deadly. This time, the darkness is different. There is a light, vivid in its intensity. I open my eyes and realize I can still see it.

I gasp, stretching out my hand. Like specs of dust floating in the wind, my hand passes through the bronze-colored particles. They feel gritty against my fingers, and I laugh.

"What's going on?" Kyan asks.

"It really is like sand." I grin as I turn to look at Kyan. "Time. I can see time."

The line fluctuates, weaving among itself like a curtain being held together by an infinite darkness, illuminating each tiny grain. Kyan moves forward and I gasp as he steps right through the curtain. I realize by the way his brow furrows that he is confused. "You can't see it, can you?"

"No, but that doesn't mean it's not real. Try pushing back on it and see what happens, but for goodness sakes, be careful, Illyria. You have no idea what you're doing. One wrong move and you could kill us all."

I bite on my lip and refocus. I stretch out my hands, taking a step forward until I can feel the glistening particles and gently push back. The curtain recedes ever so slightly.

"Oh my gosh. She's doing it!" Eamon cries a moment later. "Keep going!"

I take another step and push again, this time with a bit more pressure. All around me things begin to shift, slowly at first, but there is definite movement. I can see a ghost of Eamon and Kyan as they burst through the door. I watch the crimson glass shard fly back into my hand, watch as my muscles uncoil and the line across Aloysius's neck diminishes until it is completely gone.

Eamon and Kyan turn in amazement as the blood rises from Aloysius's clothes, watching as the glass knits back together in its frame.

I grit my teeth and close my eyes, feeling my arms begin to quiver with effort. Time may be reversing, but it is going much too slowly. I push with all of my might, feeling sweat cling to my brow as my knees begin to feel weak.

"I'm losing it!"

"Just a little more," Kyan says, rushing to Bastien's side. "I only need you to get to him to the moment his heart last beat to save him. If you can give me that, I think I can save him."

I nod and a scream rises from deep within me as I push, leaning into the rippling curtain. It feels cold to the touch, like the burn of ice. My hands are numb, my legs muscles screaming in agony as I brace myself for another push.

"Tell me when, Kyan. I don't know how much longer I can hold this."

"I only need a few more seconds…" he says in a distant voice.

A great rumbling roar fills my ears, drowning out my screams, like standing at the base of a giant waterfall. I can feel Eamon's presence beside me, but I can't hear or see him. I am lost to the temporal abyss.

Just as I feel my knees buckle, I feel strong arms wrap about my waist. "I've got you," Eamon shouts. He leans over my back, pushing for me. "Just keep your hands out. I'll do the rest."

"You'll have to time this perfectly." I grunt at Kyan. "I have to release you from my shield so you can be in sync with Bastien. You'll be trapped in time for a second, and then I will conceal you again."

"If you lose control, he won't make it," Kyan warns.

Colors burst before my eyes as I nod, feeling Eamon's arms tighten about my waist as he pushes forward. "Illyria, now!"

It all happens in the blink of an eye. Amazing when you think about it, considering I have time within my grasp. I draw the shield back just as Kyan's glowing hands press down upon Bastien's chest. A second later, I wrap the shield around both of them.

"I've got him, Illyria. You can let go now," Kyan calls to me.

My arms shake so badly that my teeth are chattering. Eamon tugs on me. "Illyria, let go. It's time."

"I... I can't!" Terror rises up in me as I begin to feel the gravitational pull of a vortex before me, unseen but very real. "Kyan, help!" Eamon roars beside me.

"I can't. I'll lose Bastien if I let go!"

I can feel myself being drawn forward, out of Eamon's arms. He grabs at my waist, fighting to lock his arms in place to anchor me down. "I can't lose you," he cries. "I'm sorry!"

Blinding pain rips through my head and I cry out as we're thrown backward. Eamon grunts as I land atop him, rolling end over end. My head strikes the far wall and darkness closes in on me.

"Illyria? Kyan, she's hurt!"

His face swims before my eyes in the fading iridescent glow. The curtain billows and crests behind him and then vanishes from sight. I groan and close my eyes, praying I held on long enough. My head lolls to the side as a cool void envelops me.

Twenty-Five

A blanket of warmth covers my body, calling me forth from the darkness. I don't want to go back. I'm at peace here. There's no pain. No sorrow or misery. Only infinite serenity.

A voice calls to me. *Illyria.*

I become aware of my eyelids and attempt to open them. They slowly flutter, and as my vision begins to clear, I see a man kneeling over me. "Are you okay?"

"Yeah," I grunt, raising a hand to touch the bump rising on the back of my head. I grimace and lower my hand. "Never better. What happened?"

Kyan reaches down and presses his hands to my head and a blissful warmth steals away the pain drilling through my eye. "What happened?"

"You passed out… for nearly an hour. I wasn't sure I'd be able to wake you. You seemed lost somewhere else."

"I was," I say, remembering the void. *Time… I was lost in time*, I think silently.

"I worked on you for quite a while. Apart from your head, you had nothing physically wrong with you. I was worried you sapped your powers again." He places a hand beneath my head and slowly eases me to a sitting position. I raise my knees and hang my head, willing the room to stop spinning.

"How do you feel now?" His gaze sweeps across my face.

"Fuzzy. I…" I scrunch up my nose as I try to remember what happened. "I don't really remember much."

He nods, as if he expected this. "When you lost control, your shield slipped. Somehow you managed to conceal us, but you were left unprotected." He fixes me with a grim stare. "I won't pretend to understand how you controlled time. Your powers are stronger than I even imagined, so I can't predict what effect this may have on you."

"I'll be fine. Just a little woozy is all."

"Too woozy to see a friend?" I look up at him, confused. As I turn to look where he points, I gasp. Eamon kneels beside Bastien, his hand pressed against the rise and fall of his chest.

"Oh!" I crawl to his side, my hands trembling as I reach for him, but Eamon pulls me back.

"He's sleeping now. We shouldn't wake him." Eamon's voice is low and soft, but I can hear the hesitation in it.

"But he'll be fine now, right?" I turn to look back up at Kyan. He smiles and nods. "Thank you."

He kneels down beside me, placing his hand upon my shoulder. "I didn't think it was possible." I tilt my head to the side, confused. "You changed fate." He looks past me to Bastien. "Maybe it is possible to write our own destinies."

With a pat on my arm, he rises and slips silently from the room, leaving Eamon and me alone with Bastien.

"He's right, you know?" Eamon whispers beside me. "You changed everything."

I nod, shifting my hand to grip his. "And I nearly lost everything in the process."

"But we won." He turns to look at me with a hint of a smile, pained but no less a smile. "You're the queen now."

"But..." I look around me in confusion. I see Aloysius's body slumped against the wall. "Why isn't he alive? I turned back time."

Eamon nods. "You did, but you didn't protect him when you released it. Everything sort of snapped back into place. We were saved only because you protected us. Bastien too." He glances down and pulls his hand back from his brother's chest.

"So I'm... I'm the queen?"

Eamon smiles. "Seems that way. A newly widowed queen to be exact."

Laughter bubbles up in my throat. Once I start, I can't seem to stop. A year of pain, misery, and fear could've been avoided if I had only seen this outcome. My breath catches. "I understand now."

I grip Eamon's hand, grinning like a fool. "I know why we couldn't see past this room. It's because I altered time. The path we saw no longer exists. We are forever slightly off schedule."

He nods, running his thumb across the back of my hand. "I thought that too."

"Do you know what this means?" I hold my breath. "It means they were wrong. The prophets don't know everything. We *can* change our fate."

Eamon lowers his gaze. "Yeah, I thought about that too."

My happiness wanes as I see the droop of his shoulders. "What? What's wrong?"

He sighs and pushes up to his feet. He casts a glance back at Bastien before he looks at me. "Now you're free to love him. There's nothing binding you to me anymore."

"That's not true." I scramble to my feet, desperate to reassure him. "I'm still bound to you. I can feel it."

He nods. "Yeah, but it's not as strong as what you have with him."

I bite my lip as tears well up in my eyes. I reach for him, but he steps away. "It's okay. You should be here when he wakes up."

My heart breaks as he turns and leaves, closing the door silently behind him. I sink to my knees, wrapping my arms about myself as I cry. It starts as a whimper before rising into shoulder-shaking sobs. Strong arms wrap around me and I sink back into Bastien's embrace, somehow knowing he would be there exactly when I needed him the most.

"I'm sorry," he whispers in my ear. "I heard everything."

"I don't... I don't know what to do." My voice cracks as I cling to him, feeling shattered and irrevocably broken.

"I know." And I know he does.

News of Aloysius's death spreads through Calahorra like wildfire. Torches light the streets. Music and dancing can be heard all the way into the palace. The gates are open wide, allowing all people to enter as they please.

Standing on a large, sweeping balcony, peering down at the joy in the streets, I smile. Aminah squeezes my hand as she clasps hands with Toren on her other side. Kyan and Zahra embrace on my other side, silent and strong. Eamon stands beside Toren and Bastien beside Kyan, polar opposites to the very end.

The crown sitting upon my head is heavy, weighted with the hopes and dreams of an entire race. Kyan said I was born to lead. I'm not so sure I believe him, but I'll do my best to make him proud.

I know somewhere out there, my parents are waiting for me. A tiny smile crosses my lips at the thought of getting to know them. To know all of our lost parents.

I spot Carleon on the yard below, waving obnoxiously at me, his arm slung over Alesta's shoulders. I frown, glancing at Kyan. "He sure moves quick. What about Anwen?"

Kyan smiles. "I suppose she never thought to tell you. Alesta is Carleon's sister."

"Oh!" Somehow I know I should've sensed that connection from the first moment I met her. I wave back and then shoo them away to join in with the party.

"So what now?" I ask, sweeping my gaze over Calahorra, newly dubbed the City of the Queen.

"Now"—Kyan reaches over and grips my hand—"you lead."

I will do my duty to bring peace and harmony to my people. I will work relentlessly to help our two races work side by side to bring healing to our lands, to stop the earth's destruction that still looms ahead. With my friends at my side, we will create a new world together.

We will be free.

Epilogue

A man stands with his hands clenched upon the railing, overlooking the palace grounds, still moist with newly fallen rains. His face is grim, his heart burdened, as dark as the regal uniform he wears. The fire in his eyes has gone out as he waits.

Footsteps approach from behind. He turns and waits for the man to stop before him. "Thank you for coming, Kyan."

"Of course." *Kyan stands rigidly before the man, his hands placed awkwardly at his sides.* "I hear you have decided to leave again."

He nods. "It's the right thing to do."

"But things have changed. Illyria is no longer bound to the prophecy. She can choose a new path for her life."

The man swallows, unable to look up. "She still loves him."

"No more so than she loves you."

He raises his head. Light glints off his sapphire eyes. "I can't ask her to give him up for me. This was her destiny." *He swallows as his voice cracks.* "I won't stand in the way of that."

"Don't do this." *Kyan protests, grabbing onto his arm.* "It will destroy her."

"No." *He shakes his head.* "It won't. That's why I need you."

Kyan steps back. "What do you mean?"

Strain lines his face as he sighs. "Wipe away her memory of me. All of their memories. Leave no trace of my presence in any of their minds."

Kyan inhales sharply. "You can't ask that of me. It's cruel."

The man slowly nods. "And yet it is far more kind than

what life would be like if I remained." He steps forward and grips Kyan's arm. *"Please, do this one thing for me."*

"I... I don't know if I can."

The young man smiles and releases his grip. "I have faith in you. You have only ever done what is best for her."

He steps around Kyan and heads toward the door but pauses as Kyan calls out. "Are you sure this is what you really want, Bastien?"

The man turns back, his face a mask of grief. Moisture clings to his eyes as he shakes his head. "No, but it is what is best for her. I love her too much to stay."

The sound of retreating footsteps echoes in my mind as I jerk upright. I hear a rustling beside me and smile, realizing I'm not alone. A warm glow of a reading lamp perches atop a side table, glowing warmly beside me. Arms wind around me, holding me close.

"Hey," a sleepy voice murmurs in my ear. "It's okay. I'm right here."

I sink into Eamon's embrace, closing my eyes to the dream. I stiffen, raising a hand to my cheek, realizing it is damp with newly fallen tears. Eamon shifts on the couch, turning me so he can look upon me fully.

"You're crying," he whispers.

I nod. "I had the same dream again. This time it was longer."

Eamon takes my hands in his, raising them up to press his lips against them. "It's just wedding jitters. Kyan says it's normal to have weird dreams, and with the wedding only a few weeks away, this is bound to happen."

I smile, knowing he is probably right. "It just... It felt so real."

"I know." He draws me toward him, setting his book aside to cradle me to his chest like he has done so many times before. "Want to tell me about it?"

I hesitate for a moment, feeling oddly protective of my dream. It is silly, of course. I share everything with him. "I dreamed about Bastien," I whisper.

He presses his lips against my forehead and murmurs, "Never heard of him."

COMING 2014

VENGEANCE
Book Three

~ A RISING Novel ~

ABOUT THE AUTHOR

Amy Miles was born and raised in a military family but now lives with her husband and son in South Carolina. She is also the author of Forbidden, Reckoning, Redemption and Captivate. To learn more about her and her books, visit www.amymilesbooks.com/

SNEAK PEEK

COMING March 2014

DESOLATE

Book I of the Immortal Rose Trilogy
~ An Arotas Prequel ~

ONE

1690, Transylvania

Caro de carne mea. Os ex ossibus meis. Lorem nocte in saecula saeculorum.

The words whisper through my mind like a long forgotten song as my eyes flutter open. Light and dark battle around me, seeking purchase on the room. Flames lick the wooden walls, trailing overhead to embrace the knotted timbers that hold the inflamed roof aloft.

Ash pelts down upon me like a livid rain, singeing flesh and hair. I cry out as I roll away from the gaping hole above, beating at the embers that set the hem of my dress alight.

I pause as my fingers glide across the rich fabric of my voluminous skirts, seizing it between my fingers to draw it up so that I can see it in the dim light. The material was once white and adorned with lace, accustomed for a wedding. It is now a dingy gray, soiled and charred into fraying bits. The ruffled hem of my dress crumbles into ash as I run my finger along it, fluttering down to land upon my bare feet.

I had slippers, I think as I turn to look about me, confused and dazed by my odd surroundings.

Heat from the flames strokes my cheek with mounting intensity. I can feel my eyelashes beginning to mat together with a sweat that drips from my brow. I swipe the beads away with the back of my hand and realize a fever has captured me in its grasp.

The air hangs thick before me, weighted with smoke and the scent of something repulsive, as if the grave itself spewed forth its inhabitants.

I blink to see through the haze, startled to discover that when I focus, I can see each particle of ash that drifts to the floorboards, leaving a thick dusting on everything within sight.

"Hello?" I call, my throat croaking with lack of moisture.

My hands tremble as I push against the floor, attempting to rise. My leg muscles coil and I am sent careening backward. The wind is knocked from my chest as I slide down the inflamed wall. The scent of my burning hair stings in my nose as I crawl forward to escape the sweltering heat.

How did I jump like that? I stare down at my fingers, noting the definition of my skin stretched taut over pale flesh.

I was never one for hiding from the sun, as some ladies were accustomed to. I lived for the moment when I could escape the confines of my father's home and be free. My mother loved to scold me about my freckles and sun kissed skin, but as I turn my hands over, I realize the golden hue of my flesh has been sucked away.

My gaze trails up from my hands, pausing over the corded muscles that now lie just beneath the nearly translucent flesh of my forearms. I poke at the muscle, bewildered by its presence, but I have only a scant second to wonder at the changes in my body before I become aware of the blood that coats my upper arm, vining down to my wrist. I draw my hands up to my face and see drying blood caked within the half crescent circle of my fingernails.

"Hello?" I whisper as I lower my hands and stare in horror at the billowing smoke before me. The fire has begun to spread to all corners of the room. I hear movement in the darkened shadows but cannot spy what causes it. "Is anyone there?"

A low, guttural chuckle rises from somewhere within the depths of the thick cloud. My stomach clenches painfully as the laughter rolls over me like a glacial downpour.

A memory seizes me: My family, perched resolutely in long wooden pews. My brother Petru sat beside my mother, stiff backed and vexed to silence. Storm clouds brewed along his handsome features, darkening his eyes. His hair was combed and slicked with mother's cooking oil, a look that would have brought tears to my eyes had I not been so preoccupied with my own ordeal.

My sister, Adela sat beside him, prim and proper in her beautiful dress and ribbons. Her hair shone like waves of summer wheat in the candlelight and her heart shaped face lit with excitement. This was her first wedding.

Ahead of me had been an altar of glossed wood and gold, achingly familiar from my mornings spent in this very room for weekly service. A large crucifix stood atop the altar and an aged, cracking leather bible rested atop its polished surface. I fixed my gaze on the likeness of Christ, praying for deliverance, but none came.

I can remember hearing my feet whisper across the wooden plank floor as I slowly made my way down the aisle. My father's rotund stomach jiggled as he nodded at each of the guests seated nearest the aisle.

My cousins arrived just this morning for the wedding, all the way from the southern province of Wallachia. I had not seen them since their youngest, a wee pig-faced runt of a boy, was added to their rather excessive litter. My entire family had gathered from near and far for the occasion, nearly fifty people in all. My father had seen to that.

It is not every day that a Dragomir married into such a highborn family.

I remember the feel of my intended's hand as he clasped mine in his. His flesh was supple with youth and oddly warm to the touch. If I had reason to care I would have questioned him as to his health, but I dare not. Not after I met his eye.

Hunger...that is what I saw when I looked at him for the first time, not one moon past. It was as obvious as it was appalling. His dark gaze made my skin crawl and my fingers tremble from within the confines of my skirts when my father presented me to him.

There was something indescribably evil about my betrothed. Why was I the only one to see it?

I suspect that Petru knew, but he was too busy chasing skirts to think much of it until Father announced a deal had been struck. I was sold like cattle in a market. My pleas did little good. Nor did my tears.

I believe my mother knew of my distress but she had learned long ago that no one defied my father's wishes. His word was law in the Dragomir household, and to many without. My sister, dear sweet Adela, knew of my fears. She would cradle me in the night, just as I used to do for her when nightmares plagued her as a child. She would whisper to me, plotting our escape. We would head to Wallachia and marry farmers and be blissfully happy. Childish dreams, but I prayed for them none the less.

When Vladimir Enescue seized my hand before the altar, I wanted to pull back, to run and hide in the woods so that I could not be found, but his grip was far too tight and my father's reproval fierce.

I was trapped.

I do so pledge. My own damning words echo endlessly through my mind as I crawl forward, my hands flailing about before me in search of the pews my family sat upon. Heated splinters easily burrow into the flesh of my palms as I hunt, drawn inexplicably toward a sweet, yet oddly tinny scent.

My hand touches something damp and sticky and I rear back. My knees ache from kneeling upon the hard floor, but I dare not move. "No," I moan as I stare down at my mother's corpse. The flesh of her throat has been shredded, as if a rabid animal tore at her repeatedly. The front of her gown is a blanket of crimson. It clings to her like a vile sludge.

I turn away as my stomach contracts. I know that I am about to be ill, but my convulsion stutters to a halt as I spy my father's hand just beyond my mother, sticking out from behind the second pew. Only his hand. I cannot see where the remainder of his body has gone.

Beyond him I see piles of my fair-haired relations strewn about the room, some dangling over the backs of pews while others have been carelessly tossed aside in the aisle. Their clothes are alight from the embers that flitter down from the crumbling ceiling.

The scent of death rises in my nostrils and I gag. Bile burns in my throat as I peer through the smoke that now escapes through the charred hole in the roof to see my brother's body hung from the double doors leading into the church. A rusty nail impales through Petru's shoulder so that he slumps to one side, his chin propped against his sunken chest. Blood coats his wedding clothes, dripping from the tips of his shoes. The sheath at his hip is barren, his sword lost among the carnage.

I remember everything. I turn about in place, searching for my new husband. I know he is here, somewhere.

Vladimir Enescue did this. He and his horrid brother.

Threads from the woven tapestries along the walls drift to the floor in charred piles of irreplaceable ash. The plank walls groan as the foundation of the church begins to deteriorate.

The fire appears to leap from body to body before me as I lurch to my feet and weave among the blue flames, desperately trying to fight against the pain swelling in my chest. It is not the dull ache of remorse but a sharp, jagged pain that steals my breath away. Warm blood clings to my throat and chest like a second skin, sticky and maddening. My bronze ringlets feel heavy laden as they slap against my face, matted with congealing blood.

The scent of boiling flesh needles at my eyes and turns my stomach rancid. The flames chase after me as I frantically scour the pews in search of my sister.

I cannot see my husband but I know he is here. I can hear his laughter around me, caged within the shadows. I can feel his taunting eyes upon me as he watches and waits.

Blood rains down from my hair, splattering against the bodice of my wedding dress. I do not know to whom the blood belongs. Myself? My husband? My sister?

"Adela!" My voice is hoarse as I grip a pew to pull myself over a slain cousin, Remus and his young wife, Valeria beside him. I try not to think of the unborn child within her womb that will never see the light of day.

My nails dig deep into the flesh of the pine seatback. I cry out as the pew tears free from the floor and crashes atop Remus. I stare in disbelief at the flames that crawl up through the new cavity I opened in the floor. *How did I manage that? Surely it is because the floor is severely compromised by the fire.*

But as I move to step around Remus, I spy deep indentations where my fingers laid buried within the wood. I step forward to brush my fingers across the markings but a sickening squelch from below my foot makes me feel faint. *Oh, my Lord! Who did I tread upon?*

I dare not look for fear of losing my nerve as I pick my way through the carnage. Dismembered body parts lie scattered before me like a gruesome puzzle. Is this Lucien Enescue's doing? My husband's brother was the one who butchered my family and stole the life of my brother as I watched in stunted horror. I have never a more vile man.

My hands tremble as I clutch my stomach and lurch to the side, expelling the acid as it burns in my throat. I wipe my mouth clean but the taste of guilt lingers. My chest rises and falls as the sound of crackling flames consume my mind. The smoke is growing thicker, hanging heavily in the air before me. Though much of it rises from the blistered slant of the church gable, the smoke pouring from the walls around me is suffocating.

The room begins to spin as I fight back the terror that

grips me. "Adela!"

My voice is gravelly as I push back to my feet, ignoring the flames that seize the hem of my dress. The floor is unbearably hot on the soles of my feet but I press on, gritting my feet against the blisters that form.

Nothing seems as it should, almost as if I have awoken into a terrific nightmare. If only I could pinch myself and wake.

My sister's golden hair should be easy to spot in the firelight but she is nowhere to be seen. "Adela, answer me!"

I slip on the blood slicked floor and crash to my knees before the altar, jarring my jaw so that I nearly bite my tongue in half. Blood seeps between my teeth, but I ignore it as the copious amounts of fabric from my dress shield my knees from the brunt of the impact.

A terrible crash from behind sends me scrambling to my feet. I glance back over my shoulder to find the timbers nearest the door have collapsed, sealing me inside. I can no longer see my brother upon the far wall.

"Help!" I stagger up the steps toward the altar, terrified. Flames eat away at the wooden crucifix before me. Already half of the Lord's body has been destroyed, the other portrays a gruesome reminder of the eternal torment my mother so loved to preach to me about when I was headstrong as a child.

Am I dead? Is this my damnation?

My gaze lands upon a glint of silver and I lurch forward to retrieve a bloodied dagger, clutching it tightly to my chest as another memory envelopes me: *Adela's wide eyes latch onto mine. Mewling sounds rise from her throat as she thrashes against Lucien's grasp. The muscles along her forearms pull taut as she fights to touch my outstretched hands.*

"It is time, brother," Lucien growls as his gaze focuses on the moonlight streaming in through the windows.

"Time for what?" I whimper as I turn to face my new husband.

Vladimir smiles down at me, curling his finger along

my cheekbone. "Do not fret. It will all be over soon."

Adela's piercing screams tear at me as Lucien waves the silver blade before my sister's eyes. She bucks wildly as his arms snakes about her chest and her cries give way to wailing pleas.

"No, please!" I beg as stinging tears blur my vision. "Take me instead."

Vladimir's hauntingly handsome face shows no emotion. "The pain will only be for a moment."

"Roseli-" Adela's cry gurgles in her throat as the blade slices clean through her flesh. A thin red line appears first, and then a shower of blood cascades down from her neck, staining her pale pink dress. Her eyes bulge as she fights from breath. Delicate fingers attempt to staunch the outpouring.

I fall to my knees and the dagger clatters from my hands. My hair falls in a heavy veil over my face as I bow my head. Salty tears stream down the curve of my cheeks, pattering against the heated floor. Small puffs of steam rise from where they fall. My shriek of agony weaves among the rafters of this desecrated church and up into the night.

That is when I smell it. The heady bouquet that clings to my skin is sweet, delicious. My throat clenches as the scent rolls over me and I fight the urge to lick my lips. I lower my gaze and notice fresh sheets of blood staining my corset for the first time. It trails down from my throat and oozes into a deep, cleanly edged wound just over my heart. The hole has already begun to mend, sealing over with a new layer of pale flesh.

Reaching up with quivering fingers, I touch the sticky warmth that adheres to my chest. "No, no, no!"

I shake my head at the memory of Vladimir plunging the dagger deep into my chest, tearing flesh and scoring bone. The pain had been excruciating, but it paled instantly as a new pain surged through my veins. The fires burned hotter than any mortal flame, charring everything in its path. The darkness had come...but not fast enough.

It was all real! I cannot breathe as mocking laughter draws my gaze upward and I meet the dark, maniacal eyes of Lucien Enescue perched among the charred rafters. His long hair drapes about his shoulders, thickly matted with blood. The flesh of his right cheek is scored deeply with claw marks. His chin is layered red with fresh blood. As he peels his lips back into a grotesque smile, I feel faint at the crimson that paints his teeth.

The scent of death permeates the air around him as he leaps down to the floor before me in a billow of black silk. There is no sound as his feet connect with the ground. Only the whisper of air shifting.

"She remembers." His words feel like a thousand snakes writhing across my skin. Goosebumps rise as I flail backward, scuttling away from his slow, purposeful approach.

My fingers snag in something moist and stringy as I frantically try to flee. I turn slowly toward my hand, terrified of what I might discover. Tears roll unhindered down my grimy cheeks. Lifeless blue eyes stare back at me as I untangle my fingers from my sister's golden strands.

"Adela!" I wail as the room begins to darken around me. My head grows unusually light as I blink against my shock.

The wooden floor trembles beneath my hands as something lands beside me, but I can only see my sister. A clean gash is carved into her throat, cut deep to her spine. I can see bone protruding from the wound and realize her head is only partially attached by a thin layer of stretched skin. The blood that spilled from her wound has already begun to congeal against her ashen chest.

It is not this wound that consumes my attention, but the semi-circle of teeth marks on the tender flesh nestled in the hollow of her neck. A tremor rises through my body at the taste of Adela's blood on my lips. *I bit her!*

"Guard the door, Lucien." A husky voice seems to call from the distance. "I do not want to be disturbed."

"But the fire-" Lucien's protest cuts off and I hear him move away.

My vision blurs as a dark face appears before me. I try to focus as strong hands press me roughly to the floor. I know that I must fight back, to scream for help but my thoughts splinter.

I can feel my skirts being lifted and a weight pressed down upon me.

"Congratulations, my dear." Cold fingers slide down my inner thigh as the hard voice of my husband whispers in my ear. "Your first kill."

Tears spill down my cheeks as my head rolls to the side. I stare into the unseeing eyes of my sister as my husband takes me for the first time.

Printed in Great Britain
by Amazon.co.uk, Ltd.,
Marston Gate.